Bloods
REVOLUTION

Angus Donald was born in China in 1965 and educated at Marlborough College and Edinburgh University. For over twenty years he was a journalist in Hong Kong, India, Afghanistan and London. He now works and lives in Kent with his wife and two children.

www.angusdonaldbooks.com

Also by Angus Donald

Blood's Game

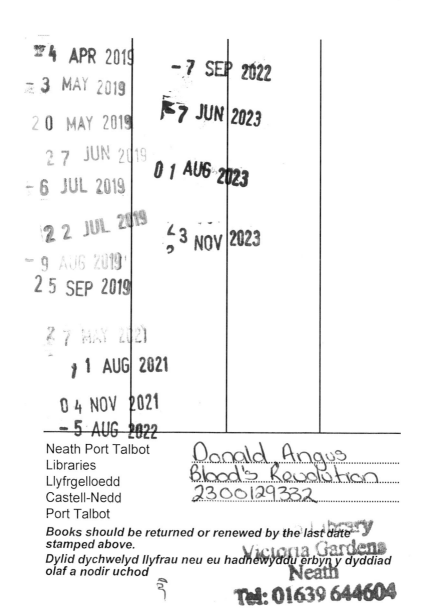

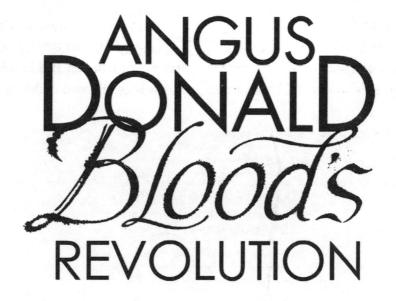

ANGUS DONALD
Blood's
REVOLUTION

ZAFFRE

First published in Great Britain in 2018 by

ZAFFRE

80–81 Wimpole St, London W1G 9RE
www.zaffrebooks.co.uk

A CIP catalogue record for this book is
available from the British Library.

ISBN: 978-1-78576-404-2

Also available as an ebook

1 3 5 7 9 10 8 6 4 2

Typeset by IDSUK (Data Connection) Ltd
Printed and bound in Great Britain by Clays Ltd, Elcograf S.p.A.

Zaffre Publishing is an imprint of Bonnier Zaffre,
part of Bonnier Books UK
www.bonnierzaffre.co.uk
www.bonnierbooks.co.uk

Prologue

28 June 1685: The English Channel

The Frenchman who called himself Narrey stood in the waist of the *Saint-Denis*, his leather-gloved hands clutching the frigate's gunwale, and looked out at the black, greasy swell of the Channel. Somewhere in the mist-shrouded darkness, somewhere ahead, were the famous white cliffs of his destination.

He wore a heavy black woollen cloak with a turned-up collar against the spitting rain, and a wide-brimmed black felt hat pulled low over his eyes, so that his lean body was rendered shapeless and his face almost completely hidden. He was tired, deep down into his marrow: the interrogation had been long and the prisoner recalcitrant but, after many hours of labour, almost the whole sea journey from Calais, the fellow had finally confessed. They all did in the end. Even the most stubborn. In the master's cabin underneath the quarterdeck, which had been put at his disposal for the crossing, the broken clerk was now being put to a last few follow-up questions by Guillaume, his loyal lieutenant, bodyguard and most efficient factotum.

Narrey, made a little queasy by the suffering he had ordered to be inflicted, had left the cabin to take a breath of sea air before the last act. This barbarousness was necessary, he told himself, for the security of the mission. Nothing else mattered. The mission was everything. One life was nothing against what they hoped to achieve.

The clerk, Jean Petit, had been caught red-handed by Guillaume going through his master's always-locked portable writing desk, riffling through his secret correspondence, just as the ship was weighing anchor in Calais harbour. Petit had pleaded that he was merely searching for a spare stick of sealing wax for a private letter but Narrey had looked deep into his eyes and seen the lies and the terror there.

Petit had stuck to his story for two whole hours, while Guillaume piled the instruments. The clerk had wept and pleaded, screamed too, until the gag had been fitted. There was no need to disturb the sailors of the *Saint-Denis* unduly. Indeed, Narrey had struggled to mask his own revulsion at the age-old intercourse between a prisoner and his torturer. He had told himself that this was a test from God. A test he had passed, and for which the Almighty had amply rewarded him. For in the end, of course, Jean Petit, the faithless servant, the forsworn spy, had told them everything.

The clerk had been approached a month ago by a fellow called Jupon, an English merchant living in Paris with a reputation for unscrupulous dealing. Petit had been promised gold and a comfortable retirement in England if he would play Judas and report on Narrey's every move to Jupon. His ultimate paymaster was the Earl of Danby – a disgraced English minister, once known as Sir Thomas Osborne – who had soared in the English court under the second, the restored King Charles – now four months in his grave. The new English king, James, was Charles's younger brother.

James Stuart was a very different man to his brother. He had revealed himself to be a true Christian, even before coming to the throne, acknowledging the one Holy Catholic and Apostolic Church, and pledging his allegiance to the Holy Father in Rome. He diligently sought more tolerance for his Catholic countrymen, who were now fewer than a tenth of the whole population and dwindling every year, but many Protestant noblemen such as Lord Danby plotted to thwart the King's will and expel the last remaining faithful from their heretic nation, to extirpate Catholicism entirely.

The traitorous clerk had comprehended nothing of Narrey's mission – praise be to God. The mission was *not* betrayed, Narrey was certain of that. Even *in extremis*, Petit had denied that he knew anything of the true reason for their night-time voyage to England. That had been what he was trying to find out for his English paymasters when Guillaume had discovered him with his hands deep in Narrey's private papers.

Jean Petit must die, of course – and not just as a punishment for his disloyalty. Much more importantly, Narrey could not allow anyone to learn of this embarrassing penetration of his defences. His position in Versailles was already dangerously weak.

Narrey looked down at his gloved hands on the gunwale and saw spots of gleaming blood in the moonlight. Disgusted, he reached inside his cloak and pulled out a handkerchief, wiped the gore from the black leather and looked for a moment at the red streaks on the delicate lace. The blood of a sacrifice, he told himself, as he opened his fingers and let the breeze whisk the fine cloth away and into the darkness.

We must all be prepared to make sacrifices. Just as Our Lord Jesus Christ did. Jean Petit must make his sacrifice too. And soon. They would be in Dover within the hour. There was no room for weakness in his mind, nor mercy. *This is God's holy work*, he told himself. He shivered a little, not just from the cold wind coming off the dark sea, not just from the grubby death he must accomplish this night; but from the knowledge of the sheer magnitude of the task on which he was now embarked.

The Sun King had briefed him, practically alone, in the vast, exquisite ornamental gardens of Versailles. Louis XIV and Narrey had spoken for nearly an hour, sitting on an iron bench almost like two old friends. And when the King had put the commission papers into his hands, their fingers had briefly touched. This was a sacred task, the King had said. Narrey wholeheartedly agreed with him. And with the sacred task and the blessing of royal touch had come a warning. The plan must succeed, Louis le Grand had said, looking into his eyes. Furthermore, it must remain a deadly secret, buried for ever. Narrey swore on his soul that he would ensure that it could never be revealed. The Bourbon monarch had repeated this simple message several times in several different ways. An embarrassing failure, the Sun King had stressed, the exposure of this grand design to the public eye would be catastrophic.

Louis le Grand did not have to say that it would mean the end of Narrey's career, and also quite possibly his life, if this enterprise were to be discovered, but that was very clearly implied. Narrey knew that his many rivals in the deadly *milieu* of French intelligence were circling like crows on a battlefield, envious of Narrey's position in the King's favour; he also knew that, after the embarrassing debacle of the Holcroft Blood affair – another God-cursed spy – he could not afford another error.

From behind him, the Frenchman heard the sound of the brass bell on the quarterdeck ring out mournfully, telling the naval hour. It would be two of the clock on land. He'd absented himself from the cabin long enough. Jean Petit had had ample time to reveal the last of what he knew. It was time to silence him. He must put away his compassion and summon the strength to do what must be done. He shoved himself off the gunwale, sighed heavily and made his way back to the master cabin.

Narrey pushed up his hat brim and looked over at the prisoner, who was still lashed to his wooden sea-chair in the corner of the small cabin. Jean Petit's face was so swollen that it was difficult to see if his eyes were open or not, but Narrey thought he saw a gleam of life. His mouth was gagged with a thick wad of lambs' wool tied in place with a strip of rag. His bare chest was covered with a hatching of deep lacerations, scorch marks, and areas of oozing lymph where wide patches of skin had been removed. Both nipples had been excised, leaving twin gore-crusted pits. The man's hands, dangling from forearms strapped to the chair rests, were huge balls, the gross sausage-like digits purply red, the skin stretched almost shiny where the bones inside had been expertly shattered.

Guillaume, a brawny, balding man, was carefully cleaning his instruments with an oiled rag. The tools were laid out on a cloth-covered table by the bulkhead.

'Is there anything more?' said Narrey, riding another wave of nausea as he observed the clerk, and his lieutenant looked up from his work and shook his head.

'No, Monsieur le Comte, and I am perfectly sure this wretch knows nothing of the true nature of our mission. I have garnered a few more minor details of their craft. Codes, in lemon juice, written between the lines of love letters and left behind broken masonry in several churches. He and Jupon also used identical copies of Molière's play *Tartuffe* for their cyphers. Chalk mark signals, too. White: all clear. Red: danger. Nothing very new or interesting – I'll write it all up in my report. But, Monsieur, I do suggest it is high time that we settled our accounts in full with this Jupon creature.'

Narrey nodded. 'I will attend to it directly when I return to France.' But he was not thinking about Jupon, he was thinking of Lord Danby, the clerk's paymaster. And, on the edge of his mind, Holcroft Blood. Had that elusive English spy also been one of Lord Danby's hired men like this doomed little wretch before him?

'How much does our friend weigh, do you think?' he said.

Guillaume looked up. It was not a question he had anticipated.

'I . . . I don't know, monsieur. Two hundred *livres*, perhaps.'

Narrey looked closely at the prisoner; it was difficult to tell with him sitting down but he suspected that the bruised and bloodied fellow was a little lighter.

'Ask him.'

Guillaume selected a pair of heavy pliers from the table in front of him, turned to the prisoner and rapped the iron instrument once sharply on Petit's grossly swollen right hand. The prisoner jerked and gave a muffled scream behind his gag.

'No more noise now, Jean,' he said, roughly pulling away the lamb's wool gag. 'Just tell the Monsieur how much you weigh, as near as you can estimate.'

Jean Petit was whimpering, weeping, writhing in his bonds, eyes jerking from side to side in their fleshy slits.

'Tell him,' said the torturer. He raised the iron pliers once more.

'I don't know, monsieur, truly I do not know. A hundred and eighty *livres*, perhaps a little less. I beg you, highness, mercy, have mercy on me, I shall never betray you again. I cannot say what made me do it. I was weak. It was wrong, so wrong, but I swear by all the saints that I will serve you well from now on . . .'

Narrey closed his ears, hardened his heart. He walked over to the side table where a jug of wine was laid out with several fine crystal glasses. He reached inside his cloak and brought out a leather wallet. Opening it, he selected a small paper packet from inside. With his back to the prisoner, he emptied a quantity of grey powder into a delicate, long-stemmed glass then filled the vessel with deep red wine. At only one hundred and eighty *livres*, he judged, three quarters of the dose would be more appropriate. He stirred the wine with his gloved finger, wiped it dry on his cloak and brought the glass up to his nose. He could smell nothing. The crone he had visited in the Paris suburb, in the faubourg Saint-Germain, had sworn by her 'inheritance powder': it was undetectable in food or wine, she said, and very swift acting. It also had the advantage of giving death the appearance of nothing more sinister than an attack of apoplexy. The victim, she said, died with a minimal amount of paroxysm.

He walked over to Jean Petit and held the glass to his puffed out lips. 'You will be of service to me if you drink this wine,' he said gently.

Petit twisted his head away from the proffered wine. 'Monsieur, I beg you, let me atone for my sins, I swear I shall be the perfect servant . . .'

'Drink it, Jean,' said Narrey, smiling down at his clerk, and pressing the glass to his bruised mouth. 'It will swiftly end your sufferings. Think of it as a mercy.'

Jean Petit looked up at his master's face. There was no forgiveness in his black soul, there never had been. Indeed this mercy – if it was such – was unexpected.

'Monsieur,' he said, 'I can still be of service to you, I could go to Lord Danby and tell him whatever you wanted . . .'

'I could never trust you again,' said Narrey. 'Never. Drink it, Jean,' he pushed the glass forward again, 'and you shall indeed be of some small use to me. It will be very quick, I swear it. And I will have a Mass said for your soul. The alternative, which I'm certain neither of us would prefer, is to make your death a long, slow one.'

Jean Petit opened his lips and drank the poisoned wine, gulping fast as if he were thirsty, swallowing hard, red trickles spilling down over his chin in his haste.

Narrey looked at the empty glass. There was no residue. Perhaps the old witch had spoken the truth. He pulled out a heavy round watch from his waistcoat pocket, flicking open the gold cover to note the time. It was seven minutes past two.

He dropped the poisoned glass and crushed it under his boot. Then he returned to the table and poured himself a large portion of the red in a fresh goblet. He sipped wine, wanting to gulp, wanting the alcohol to wash away his guilt – but knowing it would not. He must bear it, for the cause, for the mission, as he bore the weight of so many other terrible crimes. It was his lot. This was his personal sacrifice. Just as Jean Petit's sacrifice was to suffer torture and death. He could feel the exhaustion pressing down on his shoulders, an almost physical weight about his neck. In London, in a few hours, he could sleep a little. If his conscience would allow him to rest.

'Monsieur le Comte,' said an urgent voice behind him. He turned to look at Guillaume and saw that his lieutenant was pointing at Jean Petit.

'Mary, Mother of God, that is indeed surpassingly quick,' said Narrey.

Jean Petit was squirming in his chair, jerking against his ropes. His face had a grey pallor behind the bruises, he was coughing weakly, spitting out a bloody soup of phlegm and wine over his chest. Guillaume hurriedly crossed himself.

Petit was moaning now, a low clogged sound, his face screwed up in pain; his neck was rolling on his shoulders, he hiccupped madly, spat out another gobbet of spew, and then his bowels emptied in a horrible fluttering sound. A noxious stench quickly filled the cabin. The clerk gave one last violent heave against his bonds, then sagged. His body loose as an abandoned child's doll, his spirit gone.

'Less than two minutes,' said Narrey, looking at the timepiece in his hand. 'It's almost unbelievable. That faubourg Saint-Germain crone truly is a sorceress.'

Part One

Chapter One

5 July 1685: Somerset

A cone of orange flame, speckled with black fragments of burning wad, erupted from the cannon's muzzle. The gun's report crashed over the tranquil landscape of the Somerset Levels and startled a flock of roosting starlings from a hawthorn beside the road from Taunton to Bridgwater. The sound seemed different when the Falcon was fired without its three-pound ball, or so thought the tall English officer who stood beside the smoking gun. It was a higher, more childish tone, far less ferocious.

Lieutenant Holcroft Blood, a big, broad-shouldered fellow of about thirty years in the blue coat with yellow turn-backs of the Ordnance, squinted against the dying sun, following an imaginary flight path of the absent ball. In his right hand he gripped a linstock, a long wooden pole that held a burning length of match cord at the end, which he had used to fire the cannon. The iron round shot would have struck the base of a clump of alder bushes, he reckoned, about three hundred yards away in the middle of a sheep-cropped field, striking the ground there and bouncing on at about the height of an enemy's chest, maybe a little lower. He might be wrong, of course, but he doubted it. He was gifted in this small way, being able to accurately predict the fall of shot – real and imaginary – within a margin of error of only a handful of yards.

However, there had been no shot in the Falcon and no enemy in sight. The rebel forces – some six thousand men under James Scott, Duke of Monmouth, the late King Charles's eldest illegitimate son – were snug inside the newly dug earthworks of the market town of Bridgwater three miles away across the marshy fields of Sedgemoor.

Tomorrow, perhaps, the heavy guns of the Royal Train of Artillery would be hauled by their horse teams to within half a mile of the earthwork fortifications of Bridgwater and fired in earnest, pounding the rebels into submission. But that was tomorrow. On this warm evening in early July, Holcroft Blood turned to the small, wiry, sharp-faced redcoat hovering beside him and, handing him the linstock with the burning match cord, said: 'Sergeant Miller, you may set the watch for the Train.'

'Sir,' said Miller briskly, and bustled away trailing a thread of smoke from the match and barking commands to the soldiers leaning against cannon barrels, sitting on boxes of equipment or barrels of powder, or just lounging idly on the grass.

Holcroft put a hand on the Falcon's bronze barrel. It was pleasantly warm. He noticed a smudge of dust on the gleaming metal, twitched out a snowy kerchief from his coat sleeve, and wiped it away – giving the barrel a few extra swipes of the lace-edged linen cloth for the peace and satisfaction of his own tidy mind.

Then he turned and contentedly watched Miller, in his usual energetic fashion, detail off the guard soldiers of the Train – the red-coated men of the newly formed Royal Fusiliers – setting sentries at intervals along the front of the line of cannon and dismissing scores of others back to their tents and cook fires next to the baggage park a hundred yards behind the line of guns. These men belonged to a specialist regiment, which had begun life as the Tower Guards, had briefly been the Ordnance Regiment, and this year had been renamed the Royal Fusiliers. Its task was to protect the Train – the mile-long column of cannon and gun carriages, ammunition wagons, ox-drawn fodder wains, equipment-loaded mules and other assorted beasts of burden – on the march and the pieces of artillery in battle from attacks by enemy infantry and cavalry.

Each fusilier was armed with the new flintlock musket or 'fusil' – rather than the old matchlock – as it was considered safer to arm soldiers who were frequently around open kegs of gunpowder with a weapon that was discharged by the single striking of flint on steel, rather than with a musket that required a constantly burning match. And while the Royal Fusiliers could be used as regular infantry, if necessity demanded it, and they trained like any other regiment in these tactics, they also took great pride in their special role and in the big killing machines under their protection.

There were twenty-six of these heavy bronze cannon in Holcroft's charge that fine evening, lined up neatly north to south along the line of the Bussex Rhine – a deep muddy ditch that marked the forward defensive line of King James's encamped army. The guns ranged from the heaviest pieces in the Train, the twelve-pounder Demi-Culverins, to the six-pounder Sakers and down to a pair of light three-pounder Falcons – one of which Blood had just fired to signal the end of the military day.

The guns had been hastily positioned that afternoon by the Comptroller of the Royal Train of Artillery, Holcroft's commanding officer, Colonel Henry Sheres – a surveyor and fortifications expert, even an intrepid traveller in his youth, but now a man who was more interested in wine than in winning battles. The guns had been placed to dominate the dusty, unpaved road to Bridgwater with their fire. This was the most direct, and therefore most likely route that the enemy would take to attack the small royal force, if they chose to come out of their earthworks and fight. There were two other smaller crossings of the Bussex Rhine in this section, crude narrow fords known as plungeons, which were used to drive sheep from one pasture to another. The lower plungeon was a hundred yards north, to Holcroft's right as he looked out over the fields towards Bridgwater; the other one, the upper plungeon, was half a mile beyond that where the Rhine curved round to the east.

Holcroft turned to his right and watched the men of Colonel Percy Kirke's foot regiment responding to the signal gun and setting their own watch on their stretch of the line. A company of flint-lock musketeers formed up beside the lower plungeon, saluting and stamping with precision. These fifty or so redcoats would provide the picquets for the first four hours of the night. All four hundred men of Kirke's Lambs – as the regiment was known for their badge depicting a Paschal lamb – were drilled to a peak of perfection and it gave Holcroft a deep sense of rightness and pleasure to observe their clockwork-like drill motions.

Holcroft, shading his eyes with his left hand against the sun's dying glare, looked beyond the Lambs to their neighbouring regiment – Trelawny's – which was comprised half of pikemen, and half of flint-lock musketeers. Beyond Trelawny's came three battalions of crack Guards regiments under Colonel Edward Sackville and the Duke of Grafton – another of the late King Charles's many bastards, but this one loyal to the legitimate Stuart lineage; and, finally, at the extreme right of the line, the Earl of Dumbarton's contingent of five hundred matchlock bearing Scotsmen. All in all, nearly two thousand royal infantrymen. A formidable military force.

Holcroft began to walk slowly down the line of his guns, their brilliant polished metal catching the last gleams of sunlight. He stopped halfway down behind 'Roaring Meg', one of the six-pounder Sakers, an elderly piece but one of his favourites, and bent to look along its nine-foot barrel towards the darkening fields to the front. The barrels of the other guns were parallel with each other but Meg was out of alignment, only a little, a matter of a few inches, yet it made him feel uneasy.

'Sergeant Miller,' he shouted. 'Two men to shift old Meg. On the double.'

When the wiry non-commissioned officer came running up with two fusiliers in tow, Holcroft directed them as they lifted the heavy wooden trail of the gun carriage and shifted it three inches to the right. He looked along Meg's barrel once more, and then walked to the next gun, a bruiser of a twelve-pounder, to see that it was perfect. He nodded with satisfaction.

'Lieutenant Blood – what the Devil do you think you are about, sir!'

Holcroft whirled and saw Quartermaster William Glanville striding briskly towards him from the direction of the baggage park. His
superior's face, under the huge black periwig he always wore, was
flushed a purplish red with rage.

'You are moving the guns, sir. Moving the guns! How dare you!
Against the explicit orders of the Comptroller himself!' Glanville
nominally held the rank of captain but, as the quartermaster – in
charge of rations, uniforms, munitions, fodder, and all manner of
kit from horseshoes to gunpowder scoops – he was the *de facto* second-in-command to the Comptroller of the Train, Colonel Henry
Sheres.

'Sir, I was merely . . .'

'Do not answer back, Lieutenant. I saw you with my own eyes.
The Colonel was gracious enough to place the Ordnance exactly as
he wished it to be placed and now I see you taking it on yourself to
redeploy His Majesty's guns. Do not deny it.'

Holcroft said nothing. He saw that Sergeant Miller and the two
fusiliers were standing stiffly to attention, shoulders back, feet
together, faces artfully blank.

Glanville was a bully, as Holcroft knew well. A short, fat, florid,
military tyrant. He was well-born – he came from an aristocratic
French family who had transplanted to England two generations
ago – but ill-educated; cunning but rather stupid, and suspicious
of anyone more gifted than he. Glanville was famous in the lower
reaches of the Ordnance for his incompetence, dishonesty and
almost total lack of morality.

Early in their acquaintance, Glanville had conceived a deep and
abiding loathing of his most senior lieutenant, loading him with extra
duties whenever he could and complaining on occasion, sometimes
within Holcroft's hearing, that he was too clever by half, an odd fish,
not a proper gentleman, and unfit to bear the King's commission.

Holcroft had been tempted on more than one occasion to challenge the fat little bastard, or strike him in the face to provoke a

meeting, and then skewer him. But he had refrained from making the challenge. He desperately wanted to stay with the Ordnance, he wanted to stay with his beloved guns. And a duel, even a discreet one, if he survived it, could mean expulsion, disgrace and an end to his career.

After returning to England after many tumultuous, violent and dangerous years abroad – mostly spent in clandestine activity in France – Holcroft wanted nothing more than peace and stability. No upsets, no alarms, no more chaos. He had resolutely turned his back on intelligence work, vowing never again to have anything to do with that murderous world of deceit and lies. He had found himself a nice quiet berth in England with the Board of Ordnance – a home – and he fully intended to keep his new position. Even if it meant swallowing Glanville's ridiculous insults.

'I won't have it, do you hear me!' William Glanville was still ranting. 'You are not to move the guns about willy-nilly, putting them here, putting them there, without express permission either from me or from the good Colonel, do you hear me, Mister Blood. Disobey me and I'll have you cashiered. Am I being clear?'

'Yes, sir.'

Captain Glanville turned on his heel and strode off muttering under his breath.

Holcroft heard the other three soldiers breathe out.

'As you were, Sergeant,' he said.

Miller dismissed the two redcoats with a jerk of his chin.

Holcroft, with Miller bobbing along at his shoulder, resumed his walk down the line of the guns. Holcroft, as was his habit, remained silent. To his surprise, Miller spoke up. 'Don't let him trouble you, sir. He's a pig, that man, just an angry swine who hates the world and everyone in it.'

Holcroft stopped and stared at the smaller man in astonishment.

'None of the men have any respect for him, sir. Not one of them. He's no true gentleman, not at all. Just a fat furious pig—'

'That's enough, Miller.'

'Battle's coming, sir, you know that. We could always arrange a little accident. Quiet, like. All that confusion. A wild shot. A gallant officer tragically cut down.'

'I have no idea what you mean. You cannot arrange an accident. If you do that it's not an accident.' Holcroft frowned at the diminutive sergeant.

'Well, if you change your mind, sir, just tip me the wink. I'll be most discreet.'

Holcroft shook his head. John Miller was babbling again. He was a good solider, an excellent sergeant but sometimes he did come out with the strangest utterances.

The two of them walked on in silence. They stopped at the last but one twelve-pounder and gazed down at a monkey-faced veteran who was seated cross-legged beside the carriage next to a small pyramid of iron twelve-pound balls in a wooden frame. The man had one ball between his knees and with a small hammer and chisel he was carefully chipping away at a patch of rust, turning it in his hand between taps, feeling for roughness with his broad fingertips in the dying daylight.

'Still at your labours, Jackson?' said Holcroft. 'The soup is up in the lines, you know. A cider vat will have been broached too, I should imagine.'

The master gunner, whose perfectly bald sun-brown head was as smooth as one of his heavy round shot, glanced up at the officer and jumped to his feet.

'"There is no peace, saith my God, to the wicked",' he said and grinned, displaying a mouth full of broken, blackened teeth.

'Isaiah 57:21,' said Holcroft immediately. 'But, consider this, even the most wicked of men – and you certainly must count among their number, Enoch Jackson – needs to eat. I would therefore urge you to consider the wisdom of Ecclesiastes 9:7.'

They often played this game, although Jackson, who had been a fiery dissident preacher in his youth, was far more proficient at it. As a speaker, he had commanded a large following in his native Lincolnshire, and was famed for his excoriating sermons on the supreme virtues of chastity until, almost inevitably, he was discovered *in flagrante* with the nubile daughter of one of his congregation.

The young preacher was tarred and feathered and run out of Skellingthorpe and like so many other young men of the time he was swept up in the long, brutal wars between the first King Charles and Parliament. He had learnt his new trade on the bloody battle-fields of Marston Moor, Naseby and Edgehill and though he had never risen above the rank of master gunner he was one of the most respected and well-liked men in the Ordnance and certainly one of the most experienced.

' "Go thy way, eat thy bread with joy, and drink thy wine with a merry heart; for God now accepteth thy works",' Jackson intoned. 'Aye, right enough, sir. I'll be along presently to the mess lines when I've finished this little lot.' He nodded at the pile of iron balls at his feet.

Holcroft was about to move on when the old gunner said: 'Do you think they will come at us tomorrow, sir?' He nodded in the direction of Bridgwater and the unseen rebel army. 'It's just that I was wondering, if there's going to be a dust-up, whether we shouldn't perhaps bring up a few more Number Five powder kegs . . .'

Holcroft shrugged. 'They have the greater numbers. And they know we are here.' He paused to think. 'They would be wise to attack sooner rather than later. Their men are drifting away, or so our intelligencers tell us, returning to their farms and homes. While we, of course, grow stronger every day. The King has summoned more of his regiments back from the Low Countries and Ireland. If they do not fight us soon they will surely be overwhelmed. So, yes, Enoch, yes, maybe they will come tomorrow – maybe they'll all come marching up that road yonder with the dawn.'

'If they come, sir, we'll be ready for them.' The master gunner put his hand on the long cannon beside him. 'I'll pass the word for some more of the Number Fives to be broken out and made readily to hand. If they do come, we'll give them a warm reception, never fear, sir. You will remember Deuteronomy 3:22, of course.'

Holcroft nodded: 'Of course.' In idle moments during his service in France, Holcroft had read the whole Bible in English from cover to cover and his near-perfect memory allowed him to recall most of it in detail. But his mind was no longer on their game. He was thinking of a possible rebel attack in the morning. Were they truly ready? He thought so: there was enough powder, wadding and shot with each of his guns for an hour or two's engagement – and that gave them ample time to bring up more. The two hundred men of the Royal Train of Artillery – the red-coated fusiliers, the master gunners, the engineers, the pioneers, the matrosses who did the heavy lifting work with shot and powder, the civilian drivers of the horse teams, the carpenters, collar-makers, wheelwrights and far-riers, all the diverse men who made up the huge artillery cavalcade – were almost all in the tent lines now, sampling the powerful local cider, supping up their turnip soup and barley bread, preparing for bed. But they could all be briskly summoned to their duty in the morning, if it were necessary. They *were* ready if they came in the morning, Holcroft decided.

His fountain of thoughts was broken by Sergeant Miller, who nudged him hard with his elbow and jerked his head in the direction of the lines. Holcroft whirled around half expecting to see Captain Glanville returned to berate him further for some footling misdemeanour. Instead he saw a white-haired gentleman in a long black cloak, black skullcap and white collar not three yards away who said loudly and clearly: 'Ye shall not fear them: for the Lord your God he shall fight for you.'

'Beg pardon, sir?' said Holcroft.

'Deuteronomy 3:22,' said the old fellow. 'It was a favourite of my old sergeant major. Always quoting it. Every soldier in the world knows that old chestnut.'

Holcroft looked at the man: he must have been in his mid-sixties, yet he had the muscularity of a man half his age. His long pointed nose and mean mouth, coupled with a large patch of black cloth fixed to his left cheek, which seemed to cover a long-healed wound, might have made him appear sinister had it not been for the pair of cheery blue eyes that fixed on Holcroft's own.

'This is a splendid display, Lieutenant, quite splendid,' said the newcomer. 'I count twenty-six pieces. A noble array of metal if ever I saw one. I congratulate you on it, sir!' Then he jerked in surprise. 'Bless my soul, can it be? Can it really be? How splendid! Tell me, young man, is that not Roaring Meg herself over there?'

Holcroft saw this odd fellow was pointing a bony finger at the Saker halfway up the line of guns. 'Don't tell me old Meg's still in service. After all these years!'

'That she is, Captain, sir,' said Jackson, shouldering his way past Holcroft and extending his right hand. 'And she fires as sweet and true as the day she was cast.'

'Jackson, Enoch Jackson, you dissenting old rascal, God bless my soul!' The old gentleman was heartily shaking the master gunner's hand. 'This is indeed a day of miracles and wonders. How are you coming along, Enoch? Well enough, I would say. Still managing to amuse yourself with the King's Ordnance, I see. Splendid!'

'Yes, sir, I'm a difficult man to get rid of, or so I'm told. But how are you, sir? I haven't set eyes on you since Naseby. Sorry to hear you was wounded . . .'

'Who *are* you?' interrupted Holcroft, a little more brusquely than was polite. He was bewildered by this oldster who dressed like a prelate and looked like a pirate, and who seemed familiar not only with his cannon but also with his master gunner.

'Beg pardon, sir,' said Jackson. 'Might I introduce the captain, Captain Peter Mews, as was. My old commander during the late wars. A fine officer, sir, brave as a lion, lays a six-pounder most elegant, too – a staunch man of God, who's been raised to the rank of Bishop of Bath and Wells.'

'It's Winchester, these days, Enoch. Bishop of Winchester, for my sins. And I haven't laid a Saker in forty years. But you're kind to remember my modest skills.'

'And this is Lieutenant Blood, sir,' Jackson continued, 'an officer who might have the makings of a half-decent gunner one day, if he applies himself.'

Holcroft said, 'My lord,' and made his bow. He could hardly believe a prince of the Church of England was standing there discussing the pointing of a cannon.

'Splendid, splendid! Just the man to accompany me while I inspect the guns!' said this bishop. 'Lead on, Lieutenant Blood, I wish to see them all. Don't hurry, I've plenty of time 'fore supper with Lord Feversham. I particularly want to see old Meg, pay my respects. I'm sure you understand. Do you remember, Enoch, that time when old Hoppy Featherstone-Haugh – he was killed at Maidstone, you know, poor fellow – but d'you remember when he made me that wager for fifty pounds that I couldn't hit a haystack with Roaring Meg at five hundred yards. Of course, I said to him . . .'

So Holcroft found himself leading a bishop and a master gunner, chattering like fishwives, back up the line of guns as the last light dissolved into inky black.

Chapter Two

6 July 1685: Somerset

Holcroft wiped the rim and passed the nearly empty flask of brandy to his friend Jack Churchill, his saddle creaking loudly as he leant across. The two men were slowly walking their mounts northwards along the line of the Bussex Rhine. On their left was the black line of the ditch, and a few scattered individual redcoats keeping watch. A hundred yards to their right was the sprawl of tents and cooking fires where the various infantry regiments were encamped. Somewhere in the darkness Holcroft could hear a man singing an old country love song quite beautifully, against background rumble of soldierly snoring. But apart from that the night was quiet.

He pulled out his brass pocket watch and flipped it open. It was half past one in the morning, a good three hours before dawn and four and a half before he might expect any breakfast. He wished he had taken the time to visit the officers' mess in the past few hours. Even if there had been no food on offer, he might have managed to refill his brandy flask from the decanter on the sideboard. Jack, God love him, had a way of hogging the spirits; he'd no sense of frugality on a chill, misty night when it came to other folks' flasks. It was the result of him being so disgustingly rich, of course. There was never shortage of fine French bingo for Major-General John, Lord Churchill, and he seemed naturally to assume it was the same for everyone else.

Holcroft could not complain, in truth. Jack Churchill, despite his swift rise, elevated rank and recent ennoblement, treated the lieutenant the same way as he always had since they were young men trying to make their way in the jungle of White Hall in the reign of the second King Charles nearly fifteen years ago. That is to say with a mixture of exasperation, good-natured teasing, generosity and affection.

'Tell me more about your mad gunner-bishop, Hol,' Jack said, tossing the now empty brandy flask back to his friend.

'I spent above two hours showing him the pieces – never met a man of the cloth more enthusiastic about ordnance – and he wanted to know everything. Range of each gun, weight of charge, reliability in action . . . He's not a bad old stick, to be honest. Very knowledgeable about the art. But in the end I had to leave him alone with Enoch Jackson to go off and make my rounds of the rest of the Train camp.'

'And what is he doing here?'

'Apparently he heard a rumour three days ago that we had Monmouth's whole army trapped and so came down in his carriage from Winchester immediately. He wants to see a great victory, he told me. He was something of a hero in the last wars, or so I collect, and he misses the excitement of combat, the smell of burnt powder smoke and mass slaughter. Quite mad, you see. Not right in the head. Though I judge him to be a fairly harmless sort of lunatic.'

Jack Churchill gave a meaningless grunt. He knew that Holcroft hated the gore and stench and waste of life that a battlefield entailed – his joy lay in the cool, bloodless calculation of a cannon-ball's flight. The mathematics of mayhem – not its messy actuality. But Jack knew the grip the raw excitement of battle could take on a man. He'd proved his own courage in combat more than once as a young officer and, sometimes, just sometimes, he missed the hot, breathless roaring of bloodlust in his veins. But it was not seemly for an officer of general rank – or indeed for the second in command of the Royal Army, subordinate only to Lieutenant-General Louis Duras, Earl of Feversham – to speak of the joy of slaughter, even to an old friend.

'There's no guarantee your mad bishop will even get his battle, let alone a victory. It's no good counting your chickens before they hatch,' said Jack.

Holcroft frowned at his friend. 'Why are you talking about chickens?'

Jack stifled a smile. Holcroft Blood possessed a most unusual brain: strikingly brilliant in some areas, such as with numbers or cards or mathematical problems, but also, strangely narrow, even blinkered, in many others. He knew that it was a waste of breath to use even quite common figures of speech or metaphors with his old friend.

'I mean that if Monmouth has any sense he will slip away north to Bristol and beyond tonight. But if he does stay here, Lord Fever-sham means to close and assault Bridgwater – perhaps as early as tomorrow noon. You'd best make sure the guns are ready to move up in good time.'

'They're ready.'

The two men lapsed into silence. They were approaching the upper plungeon and a picquet of the Earl of Oxford's red-and-blue-coated cavalry, which marked the farthest end of the line. Major-General Churchill received a crisp challenge, and salute, from the captain of the cavalry guard, then Jack and Holcroft turned their horses around and, walking the beasts slowly, they began the three-quarters of a mile journey back along the line of the Rhine towards the cannon at the far southern end.

Jack broke the silence. 'It is not right, Hol, you know. You being a mere lieutenant. I could help you rise, if you would let me. Are you sure that you won't allow me to put you into one of the line regi-ments? I'm sure I could manage a captaincy at the least. You could be a major in a year, given a bloody battle or two, maybe a lieutenant-colonel with your own battalion by the time you're thirty-five.'

'I'm content with serving the Board of Ordnance, Jack. You know I'd miss my guns if were to leave them. I'm happy to remain a lieutenant for the time being . . .'

They rode on in silence for a few more yards.

'And have you heard from your lovely widow, Elizabeth Fowler?'

'I've had one letter from her—'

Holcroft's words were interrupted by the distinct sound of a shot. It came from somewhere out on the moor, out in the mist-wreathed darkness.

Jack and Holcroft looked at each other.

'A dropped musket?' said Jack. 'A poacher out in the marshes?'

'That was a pistol shot, Jack.' Holcroft knew his ordnance. 'Horse-pistol. Half-ounce ball. One and half drams of powder. Standard side-arm for Oxford's Blues.'

For a moment they both stared out across the Bussex Rhine into the black night. And then came the sound of hooves drumming on the turf.

Out of the curtain of mist, like a mythical monster of yore, came a lone trooper on a rearing horse, the beast snorting twin plumes of white breath from its flaring nostrils. The rider, in the red coat with blue facings of the Earl of Oxford's cavalry, saw Jack in his general's froth of lace and finery and called: 'Beat your drums, my lord, sound the alarm. The enemy is come! Call out the men, sir, for Christ's sake. The enemy's upon us . . .'

'How many? From what direction?'

'Looks like the whole pack of 'em, sir. We glimpsed many hundreds, maybe thousands of the rebel bastards. And coming in from the north. That's all I know, sir. The enemy are on the move this night.'

From the north, Holcroft thought, *while our whole line faces west! They are coming out of the darkness on our right flank. They could roll us up like a carpet.*

'Well done, man,' Jack shouted across the ditch. 'Well ridden! We are forewarned. Now be a good fellow and spread the word down the line. Off you go!'

The trooper galloped off south calling out his message to the picquets he passed.

Jack turned to Holcroft. 'To your guns, Hol! Quickly now.'

'Yes, sir!'

As Holcroft turned his horse, Jack called: 'Your mad bishop will see his battle, Hol, if I'm not mistaken. But tell him to start praying for all he is worth for, if he wants to see victory tonight, we're going to require a lot of help from the Almighty.'

'Hold your fire, damn your black souls. You will not fire, I say. I repeat you will not fire your weapons. A bloody back for any man who discharges his musket without my personal permission. You hear me, you scoundrels? Stand firm. Do not give fire.'

The Scots-inflected bawling of Lieutenant-Colonel Lord Archibald Douglas, commanding officer of five musket companies of Dumbarton's Regiment at the extreme end of the Royal line, could easily be heard above the ragged crash of the enemy muskets. And the dogged soldiers of that unit obeyed his command to a man. The Scotsmen stood in their perfect ranks in the foggy darkness on the field of Sedgemoor, their lit matches smoking and glowing, and calmly received the incoming musket balls of the rebel regiments on the far side of the Bussex Rhine.

The enemy had first emerged out of the mist a quarter of an hour ago – hundreds of wild horsemen in long buff-leather coats and huge plumed hats who charged with a great drumming of hooves out of the darkness, hallooing madly, waving their swords. It had been an undisciplined, unfocussed and largely useless gesture. The leading mounts had balked at the obstacle of the Rhine, shying, whinnying and skidding to a halt, their riders cursing foully – although in daylight and under proper control they might well have jumped it. The King's infantry on the far side of the ditch watched them impassively, almost contemptuously, as several hundred rebel riders regained control of their excited mounts and turned their horses' heads to their right and – still making enough noise to raise the dead, and discharging their horse pistols to little effect at their enemy – galloped off down the far side of the ditch, heading south, evidently seeking a crossing point, one of the plungeons, perhaps, or even the old stone bridge at the extreme south of the line.

The King's infantry watched them disappear again into the darkness. It was clear that they had lost their way in the crossing of the moor and had attacked the wrong part of the line. Or maybe they had been merely unaware of the existence of the Bussex Rhine. As the last horseman galloped away, one wag from the ranks of Dumbarton's Regiment shouted out: 'A pleasure tae make your acquaintances, gentlemen, do call again soon!' before he was silenced by a snarling sergeant-major.

The mass of rebel infantry, which arrived shortly after the cavalry, presented far more of a threat. A single regiment approached first, visible only in the darkness as an amorphous mass of tiny glowing coals on their matchlock muskets. The rebels had halted on the other side of the ditch about a hundred and twenty yards away from Lord Douglas's men. They seemed to be waiting for something, perhaps for the officers to order their ranks. Or for the rest of the army to catch up with them. But a quarter of an hour after the comic departure of the cavalry, several hundred enemy troops, seven or eight hundred at least, were soon in position opposite the royal line, and that was only a small part of the rebel force. The men of Dumbarton's eyed the mass of enemy troops on the far side of the Rhine. They were easily outnumbered, perhaps two to one. There were no smart quips now.

And now there was another whole regiment coming up on the enemy's left flank, another cloud of red dots, a shuffling horde of hundreds of men now forming up beside the first regiment. Two great blocks of rebel troops now stood against Dumbarton's – perhaps fifteen hundred men. After a short pause, broken by the shouting of the rebel sergeants, a lone musket cracked out, and a moment later the whole enemy front opened fire. There were no regular disciplined volleys, no firing by platoons or files of men, the fire was made up of hundreds of single shots, as each rebel fired his matchlock and then went through the elaborate process of reloading, shoving down the bullet and wadding, priming the pan, aiming and firing again. They might not have been disciplined, but to the Scotsmen facing it, it was deadly enough. And, in ones and twos, Dumbarton's men were falling, bleeding, dying in their ranks.

'Hold your fire. You will not fire, I say. You can take this battering, lads. You can bear it. I know you can. Show them the kind of men you are.'

The Scotsmen heeded their colonel. They stood firm and received the fire.

The rebel regiments were, in fact, too far away for a decisive effect. A range of fifty yards was the usual distance for a first exchange of musket fire, followed by a howling charge with bayonets and swords. The rebels – West Country farmhands and craftsmen mostly, and good plain Protestants all – were showing their inexperience and lack of training. But to the men receiving it, this was a lethal fire, nonetheless.

Major-General Lord Churchill walked his horse slowly along the front of the assembled ranks of Dumbarton's, affecting not to notice the sporadic musket shots from the rebel ranks and pretending to be equally oblivious that some of the brave Scotsmen, hauled as they were from their slumbers, were improperly dressed – a coatless man here, a hatless one there, and one or two who were only clad in their linen drawers. All of them, every single man, had his matchlock musket, shot pouch, spare match and powder flask and bandolier of twelve pre-measured charges in stoppered wooden cylinders. All the men were capable of answering the enemy. But obedient to the orders of their red-faced colonel, they stood in silent ranks and took their punishment like the professionals they were. Jack Churchill nodded his approval at Douglas, who was standing, legs spread, chin out-thrust, half-pike in hand, two paces ahead of the front line of his men. The position of maximum danger.

Jack pondered his options. He could not move Douglas's men into safety. If he pulled them back, the royal line would be broken and the enemy would gleefully advance into the gap they left and could swing in behind the rest of the army and cause utter panic. The battle would be lost almost before it began. So the Scotsmen must stand and receive the enemy's fire until it was clear what his plan of attack was. At least there seemed to be no rebel cannon, Jack told himself.

It would also be fruitless for Dumbarton's men to return fire. At this distance, they would blaze away, waste their ammunition and achieve little – just as the enemy was doing. But good men *were* dying. Occasionally a bullet would crack by Jack's head, and he felt the chilling wind of its passing, and every few minutes one of the redcoats would give a muffled cry and fall to his knees, before being hauled away by the ever-present sergeants who called for the other men to close up, close up.

A dozen or so of Dumbarton's five hundred men were dead and two dozen more were wounded. But, for the moment, the regiment was solid. It would stand firm.

As Jack reached the left-most file of Dumbarton's men, he looked further down the line of the Bussex Rhine, due south, he could see that the rest of his infantry force – some fifteen hundred men, and all the musket men armed with the new flintlock – had been called to arms and was lined up neatly between the tents and the ditch in their companies and battalions. The enemy cavalry had long disappeared, swallowed by the night. But the alarm had been raised in good time, and the army was ready. The next regiment along from Dumbarton's was the crack First Foot Guards, his old regiment. No glowing cloud of red dots for these men. In the darkness, the battalions of his flintlock-armed foot were just indistinct masses, here and there illuminated by a pine-resin torch held by a junior officer or sergeant. He saw one of his aides, Captain Sedley, cantering towards him, and another rider coming up fast behind that.

Where is Lord Feversham? he asked himself. He had sent Captain Sedley to rouse the commander-in-chief in his quarters in Weston-zoyland a good half hour ago and yet there had been no sign of the General. Was he to take full command? Should he begin the counter attack? Dumbarton's poor men should not be made to endure much more of this. Should he march a regiment or two over the Bussex Rhine – a difficult manoeuvre in darkness and under fire – and take the rebels in the flank, push them back? He could do it, if necessary. Or should he delay, out of courtesy, stand firm, take the punishment and wait patiently for the more senior officer to show himself? He could not afford to prevaricate much longer. The Scotsmen were dying.

Captain Jonathan Sedley cantered up pink-faced and breathless. 'My compliments, sir, but Lord Feversham cannot be awoken from his slumbers.'

'What the Devil do you mean, sir?' said Jack. 'We are under attack here, in case it has escaped your notice; why cannot he be woken? Is he sick? Is he dead?'

'Begging your pardon, sir, but we knocked and knocked at the door of his chamber with no response. In the end I gave orders for two men to break it down. And they did so, most noisily, I might add. And still Lord Feversham did not awaken. He had taken a good deal of wine at supper with his guest, the jolly old Bishop of Winchester, a very great deal of wine, in truth, and well, my lord, I am ashamed to say he is still abed, even now, and snoring like an ogre.'

'Good God! How extraordinary! Well, I must act then, there is not a minute to waste. You will ride immediately to—'

The rest of Jack's words were drowned out by a gigantic crash. On the far side of the Rhine, to the left of the nearest rebel regiment, a cannon spoke, a three-foot tongue of golden flame illuminating the misty night. The three-pounder ball struck the centre left of the mass of Dumbarton's men, carving a bloody furrow in the battalion ranks and leaving half a dozen men maimed or dead. Jack stared into the night. He saw movement on the extreme left of the enemy line, on the other side from the cannon, yet another cloud of red dots like a plague of infernal fireflies, another force, six or seven hundred men at least, coming out of the mist to join their fire with the two rebel regiments already engaged with Dumbarton's.

Understanding came to Jack in a single moment, all of a piece.

'Jonathan, listen very carefully to me, you must take this word to Kirke's and Trelawney's. The enemy are all coming here. All of them. The whole rebel force is concentrated here on our right flank. They believe this is the centre of our line. Not our right. They cannot see the formation of the rest of our men because of the flintlocks.'

Captain Sedley goggled at him – had General Churchill gone mad?

'Listen to me, Captain, flintlocks do not require burning matches and so those formations of our men cannot be seen in the darkness. We can see them' – Jack pointed at the clouds of red dots in the dark – 'and they see Dumbarton's. And they think this is the centre of the line because they do not see our men with flintlocks . . .'

He looked at the blank face of his aide-de-camp and promised himself that the man's military career was over after this fight. Behind Sedley, he saw Holcroft Blood riding up, his old friend's face white with anxiety.

'Never mind all that. Captain Sedley: you will take this command to the colonels of Trewlaney's and Kirke's regiments. They are to march their battalions north, to me, without delay, and position them on the far side of Dumbarton's, to extend our right flank.' Sedley looked confused. 'Over there.' Jack pointed to the black space to the north beyond the companies of Scotsmen, between the end of the line of infantry and the northern plungeon somewhere out in the darkness, which was guarded by Oxford's cavalry. 'Just bring them up here to me, all right?'

'All right, sir,' Captain Sedley turned his horse and spurred away.

Another cannon fired, on the far side of the ditch at the extreme left of the rebel line, and Jack saw a shadowy ball skipping along the black turf away off to his right, mercifully missing the end of the last file of Dumbarton's stoic men.

Jack turned to Holcroft: 'This is the centre, Hol,' he said. 'This is the focus of their whole attack. I need all your guns up here right now. Bring them up with all possible speed and position them on either side of Dumbarton's. Here and here.' He made two chopping motion with his hand, indicating the placement of the batteries.

'Jack, I cannot.'

'What d'you mean? That is an order. Do it now, Holcroft, and don't argue with me. I don't have time for your quibbling.'

The crack of a musket ball split the air between them. Neither man moved a hair nor commented on its passing

'It's the horses and the drivers, Jack – they've gone!'

'What?'

'It was the rebel cavalry. They rode all along the front, firing off their pistols, yelling their slogans like silly children. And, even though they were in no real danger, the civilian drivers, they're not used to battle, and they saw the enemy horse and panicked. They began shouting that Monmouth had come in all his might and they were to be murdered in their beds.'

'They ran?'

'They cut the horse lines, jumped on their beasts and galloped off into the night. The horses followed them. They're all gone. I have no horses to move the guns.'

General Churchill's face was as grim as an ice-bound January. The rebel cannon fired again and an entire file of Dumbarton's men was ripped into bloody ruin.

'I don't care if you have to drag the bloody pieces up here by hand, Lieutenant Blood. But do it. I must have the cannon here.'

Jack leant in closer to Holcroft, and spoke softly so that no other ear could catch his words. 'Without cannon to match theirs, Hol, and very soon, Dumbarton's will break. They cannot endure this fire for ever. And if they break, the whole rebel army will be through our lines and into the baggage park and beyond. And I cannot hold the line without your guns, Hol. Bring them up, any way you can. And quickly.'

'Sir,' said the lieutenant, saluting, and he turned his horse and galloped south.

'Colonel Douglas,' said Jack, loud enough so that every man within fifty yards could hear him. 'I believe we have shown these rebel rascals that good Scotsmen can take any punishment they care to dish out. Now it's time to deal out some punishment in return. Dumbarton's Regiment will advance thirty paces, up to the very lip of the Rhine, and give fire by files, if you please. And as briskly as you like, Colonel.'

Chapter Three

Holcroft racked his brains as he galloped south again. Without horses he could not move the guns – well, that was not strictly true. He could not move the heaviest guns, the twelve-pounder Demi-Culverins. It might just be possible to shift the smaller pieces, the Sakers and the Falcons. It normally took six horses to draw a Saker such as Roaring Meg, but he had seen similar guns on campaign in France drawn by two dozen soldiers after all the horses had been killed in action. It depended on how many men of the Train had resisted the urge to run.

He was certain that the half company of men of the Royal Fusiliers under Ensign Pittman and Sergeant Miller would not have deserted their posts. But that was only thirty men – they could move one Saker and perhaps a single light wagon of shot and powder. Would one piece make much of a difference to the fight? And it would take time for the men and ropes to be assembled and to haul the cannon north.

Holcroft arrived at the line of guns, saw that Sergeant Miller had paraded his tiny force of fusiliers in a double line, and slid off his horse. He walked up to Ensign Rupert Pittman, a blond angelic youth, who was standing underneath a guttering torch twenty paces behind the line of guns. The young gentleman saluted smartly.

'We must drag some of the guns north, Rupert. You will lend me your men? My horses and drivers have all run. All I have left is a handful of gunners.'

'Perhaps I might be of assistance, Lieutenant,' said a voice at Holcroft's side.

He turned and saw that the Bishop of Winchester was standing there in a white linen nightshirt, night cap on head, accompanied by two servants bearing lanterns.

'You are very good to offer, sir,' said Holcroft. 'And I should be glad to have the help of your servants. A few extra strong men on the drag-ropes will make this operation go very much faster. We could use you too, sir, if you are willing.'

The bishop threw back his head and laughed, a startling, almost shocking noise. *Mad, quite mad.* Holcroft thought to himself, involuntarily taking a step backwards.

'I had not intended to pull the guns myself,' the bishop said. 'I meant to say that I have a coach and six in Westonzoyland and I thought we might use my horses.'

Before the half hour was up, Holcroft and Bishop Mews – assisted by the bishop's coachman, two of his ostlers, two of his footmen and with help from half a dozen assorted gunners, matrosses and pioneers that Holcroft had rounded up from the horse-trampled camp – had managed to haul Roaring Meg and a wagon-load of munitions up the line and into position to the left of Dumbarton's Regiment of Foot.

What remained of Dumbarton's Regiment. In the half hour that had passed the five companies had taken a brutal mauling. With the massed fire of three rebel regiments concentrated upon them – even at such a distance that made the majority of the shot inaccurate – and the ire of three small cannon aimed in their direction, the Scotsmen were now in a sad state. Bullets cracked and whistled through their depleted ranks, and every few minutes a cannon ball would bounce lethally among their broken and bleeding numbers. Almost half of the men were dead or wounded, and while they had been allowed to return fire, simply to improve their morale, there was a decided shakiness about their decimated lines that made Holcroft realise that what Jack had said to him was true. They were about to break. And if they broke, the rebels would immediately pour over the Rhine and all would be lost.

But, while Holcroft and Bishop Mews and his servants had been hitching the heavy wooden carriage of Roaring Meg to three matched pairs of black geldings and whipping them up to battle, Major-General Churchill had not been idle. Jack had brought three companies of First Foot Guards up on to the left flank of Dumbarton's to add their weight to the Scotsmen's fire. More practically, he had ordered two full squadrons of mounted infantry, the King's Own Royal Dragoons, the elite regiment of which he was colonel, to dismount and form up with their flintlocks at the ready directly behind Dumbarton's men. If the Scotsmen broke and ran, they could swiftly move in and plug the gap. On the far side of Dumbarton's, the northern side, Kirke's Lambs were lining up in three impeccable ranks and beyond them Trelawney's pike and musket men were moving into their places on the extreme right flank.

'I knew I could rely on you, Hol,' said a breathless Jack, as he galloped to where his friend was shoving a bagged five-pound charge of black powder deep into Roaring Meg's barrel with a rammer. 'Even the one cannon will be most useful.'

'More on the way, Jack. I've got a half company of fusiliers man-handling a Falcon up here. And the good bishop's carriage horses' – here Holcroft nodded over at a figure in a long flapping nightgown who was approaching with a six-pound iron shot in his hands – 'are bringing up another Saker into position over on the right between Dumbarton's and Kirke's men. We will bring up as many guns as we can but I thought it best that we should get old Meg into action as soon as possible.'

'General Churchill,' cried the bishop, raising the iron ball in both hands as some sort of salute. 'What a splendid battle you have arranged for me! I've no doubt 'twill be a thumping victory. I con-gratulate you – and Lord Feversham, of course.'

'You are more than kind, my lord,' said Jack, touching two fingers to his lace-trimmed hat. 'Alas, Lord Feversham is still peacefully snug in his bed. However, I shall surely pass on your warm congratula-tions when – or if – he sees fit to join us.'

From across the Bussex Rhine the cannon roared and a shot came skipping through the darkness. It smashed into a redcoat on the far left of Dumbarton's second line who was in the act of reloading his matchlock. The man was instantly mashed into pulp, one of his legs, spraying blood, spun away end over end like a thrown log.

Holcroft looked on in awestruck horror. His stomach lurched and for a moment he thought he might vomit. He mastered his rebellious belly, and turned and glared out into the black night at the spot from where the enemy cannon had fired.

'Do not concern yourself with that enemy gun, Lieutenant Blood,' said Jack formally. He knew what his friend was thinking. 'There is no chance of locating that cannon, let alone silencing it, until first light. Your battery would do better to play on the nearest enemy regiment. We can see where they are. If those foot can be discouraged, even sent packing, it will take the pressure off Dumbarton's. You hear me, Holcroft, forget that lone cannon and concentrate your fire on the infantry.'

And with an elegant wave, he turned his horse and cantered away.

Holcroft ignored his departure and remained stock still, staring out into the darkness, marking in his mind the place where the flash of the enemy cannon's muzzle had been. *A three-pounder*, Holcroft thought, *probably a Falcon*. Two hundred yards, he judged it, maybe a shade more, although it was impossible to be sure with no visible feature to use as a reference. Manned by four men, probably.

A very small target, he concluded, *an almost impossible target. But it might be done. Yes, with luck, it might just be done.* He decided to disobey his general.

'I believe we shall put the first three rounds into their infantry, my lord,' Holcroft said over his shoulder to the bishop, as he accepted a thick round wad of felted wool from a waiting matrosse and pushed it into the cannon's mouth, shoving it all the rest of the way down to the end with the wooden rammer. 'Just till Meg gets herself warmed up. Then we'll see if we can't put that Falcon yonder out of action.'

'An inch to the right, and another half inch. Stop!' said Holcroft fifteen minutes later. He was looking down the barrel of Roaring Meg staring into the mist-shrouded blackness where he believed the enemy Falcon was placed. The enemy would be manning their gun, as Holcroft and his men were, by the meagre light of a single horn-windowed dark-lantern, emitting just enough light from the candle inside to see the touchhole. They could not afford the risk of the naked flame and sparks of a pine-pitch torch so close to barrels of loose black powder. But with the thick mist Holcroft could see nothing of his opponents. He was working by guesswork. Behind him Enoch Jackson and a pair of matrosses were using hand-spikes to move the trail of the gun carriage.

'You'll never hit it, Mister Blood,' said Jackson, 'Not in a hundred years. You're shooting blind. It's just a sad waste of good powder and shot.'

'Don't nag me, Enoch,' snapped Holcroft. 'Just tend the match!'

Jackson said no more. He stepped forward with the linstock. The four other men around the Saker took a cautious step back; Bishop Mews cupped hands protectively over his large ears.

'Give fire!' said Holcroft, and Jackson brought the linstock down and put the burning match tip to the touchhole. With a roaring cough, Meg spat fire and the six-pound ball rocketed away into the night. Holcroft tried to follow its flight but it was almost instantly swallowed by the black mists.

'Where are you? Where are you hiding?' Holcroft muttered.

As if in reply to his question, the enemy Falcon fired. A blossom of flame two hundred yards away, the high crack of the report and, an instant later, the three-pound ball bounded past, bounced once and ripped a head-sized hole in the canvas covering of the munitions wagon ten yards behind the Saker.

'They're firing direct at us now, Mister Blood,' said Sergeant Miller, 'and they have marked us well, that's for sure.' His men had laboured hard to bring up the Train's only two Falcons, which were now in operation on the far side of Dumbarton's Regiment, under the command of Captain Glanville. Then they had brought up another Saker, with the bishop's carriage horses, and positioned it beside Roaring Meg. And there were two more six-pounders being brought up, which should arrive on the field in the next quarter of an hour. Sergeant Miller had even positioned a file of fusiliers a dozen yards behind Holcroft's battery, flintlocks at port, ready to protect the two Sakers and their crews if the enemy swarmed over the Rhine.

'A duel, by God,' said Bishop Mews happily, rubbing his hands with glee. 'A proper battery duel. What could be more splendid!' One of his servants had fetched him a pair of linen breeches by this time, and some stockings, and a black broad-brimmed hat to replace his nightcap. But, with the black patch on his cheek and voluminous linen nightshirt nipped in at the waist by a belt from which hung an ornate-handled rapier, he still cut a disturbingly piratical figure for a man of God.

Holcroft was too busy to comment. He was already issuing the familiar orders to his gun crew in a quiet, methodical voice, the litany of the artillery man, which caused the barrel to be cleared of debris, sponged out and reloaded with a five-pound charge of powder, felt wadding, a six-pound iron shot and more wadding to keep the ball in place: 'Advance the sponge . . . tend the vent . . . sponge the piece . . .'

The second Saker, under the command of Master Gunner William Rodgers, was sending a regular barrage of round shot in to the ranks of the enemy infantry. But Holcroft, ignoring Jack's orders, was embarking on his private and probably fruitless battle with the single Falcon on the other side of the ditch. As Jackson had pointed out several times, the chances of him hitting the enemy gun were slim to nothing. Yet, as he mechanically spoke the commands that would cause Roaring Meg to be reloaded as speedily as possible, he kept his eyes fixed on the spot where he had last seen the blossom of fire.

'. . . Prime the piece . . . tend the match . . . have a care . . . Wait!' Holcroft abruptly stopped the ritual chanting. He thought he saw a glimmer of red through the curtains of black mist – the glow of the enemy Falcon's match, perhaps, blown on by a rebel gunner to keep it burning bright. Or was he imagining it?

'Rose and Fisher, help me shift the carriage. Now!' With the help of his two burly matrosses, he shifted the carriage a fraction to the left, less than half an inch.

'Where were we? Yes. Tend the match, Enoch Jackson, and look lively about it. Everybody clear? Right, give fire!'

Meg boomed. The six-pound shot sailed away into the darkness. Nothing.

Holcroft automatically began the litany again – 'Advance the worm . . . Search the piece . . . Advance the sponge . . .' – but his mind was elsewhere. He was sure that he had the right line, absolutely sure of it. He checked again anyway, peering down the length of the barrel into the black wall of night.

Out in the darkness the Falcon fired. Holcroft felt the wind of it. By God, whoever was out there, the enemy gunner, he was a good man, a master for sure. Holcroft heard screams behind him. He turned and saw that two of the fusiliers were down: one had been cut in half by the Falcon's ball and another man, standing behind him, had lost an arm. Holcroft felt his gorge rise: *Stupid, stupid, stupid*, he thought, *I am missing something. I am definitely missing something. And my stupidity is killing the men.* Roaring Meg was firing at point blank range. Zero elevation. And this was perfectly correct for a target only two hundred yards away. The ball would be flying in a flat trajectory, about chest height, no arc to it, and he was sure that he had the right line. He should be hitting his target, black of night or not. And all the while he was furiously thinking this, he was also chanting out the familiar litany: 'Ram down the charge . . . Pierce the charge . . . Prime the piece . . .'

The ground was flat, was it not? It looked flat, like this whole damned Somerset countryside. But was it? He kicked at the turf. Seemed flat. But in the mad scramble to get Meg up to the battle and into action, he had not prepared the ground, measured it, smoothed it, tamped it. There simply had not been time.

'Tend the match . . .' he intoned. Then: 'Wait a moment, Jackson!'

Holcroft reached into the inside pocket of his big blue coat and pulled out a brass contraption the shape and size of a slice of apple pie, a gunner's quadrant, a plumb line on a pivot and curved rule measuring degrees of angle underneath. He sat the little machine on the top of the hot bronze of the Saker's barrel and squinted at the plumb. At first glance it appeared to be hanging vertically. He beckoned for the lantern to be brought close and peered again. It was not quite vertical. The brass needle pointed to just a hair past the zero. The ground was not flat. It was almost imperceptibly sloping upwards. Not by much, just seven tenths of one degree, according to Holcroft's quadrant. But the gun barrel *was* slanted up at a sliver of an angle and, at two hundred yards, that meant the ball was travelling – Holcroft did the calculation effortlessly in his head – three foot and one and a half inches higher than he had imagined. The Saker ball was not travelling flat at chest height, as he'd believed, it was rising. And at the target it would pass through the air three feet higher. Unless the rebel gunners opposing them were giants, the Saker's balls were flying harmlessly over their heads!

'John Rose, fetch me the Number One quoin and the mallet,' Holcroft tried to quell the rising tide of excitement inside his chest. He listened to the anguished screams of the wounded fusilier, quenching his high spirits with pity and horror. When the matrosse brought him the implements, he fitted the slimmest wooden wedge of the set under the breech end of the Saker, tapping it gently to drive it a few inches in, under the barrel, and depressing the muzzle a fraction. He bent quickly with his little brass device and confirmed that the barrel was now perfectly straight.

'You ready there, Enoch Jackson,' said Holcroft. And hearing a disapproving grunt from the master gunner, said: 'Have a care . . . Give fire!'

The old man brought his linstock down, touched the burning coal to the vent and the Saker discharged in a great bellow. And a moment later every man could hear the clang of an iron ball hitting bronze and crash of breaking wood and a man's voice out there in the darkness began to scream like a half-butchered hog.

'You got him. By God, you got him,' Bishop Mews was pounding Holcroft's shoulder with his powerful right hand. He noticed that the lower half of the bishop's left nightgown sleeve was now red with blood.

'You are hurt, my lord?'

'Just a scratch, man. Musket ball clipped me. Nothing really. But you, sir, you have performed a miracle, a splendid miracle. Well done, my boy. To strike a lone piece, in pitch darkness at a range of better than two hundred yards. It's a *bona fide* miracle. The Lord is with us! Even in my prime, I couldn't have done better myself. You never spoke a truer word, Enoch Jackson, your man Blood is a *gunner*!'

Holcroft felt an almost shameful glow of pride. He did not know of any gunner who had achieved a similar feat. Yet he also knew that he had been slow off the mark. By not realising that he was firing high, he had caused the death of one and probably two of his men. But he did not have long to savour his triumph – or his guilt. To his right he could hear Colonel Douglas, a bloodied, soot-grimed, exhausted figure bellowing at his last few men. 'Stand your ground, men. Stand and fight, Dumbarton's, like the heroes you've shown yourselves to be. Now is the time to find that last ounce of your courage. The enemy are advancing! The bastards are coming on. Stand. Fight. Let them come and take your bloody revenge on these rebel scum.'

And it was true. Across the ditch, the cloud of red dots was moving, dancing in the darkness, steadily advancing. The enemy, at last, were making their attack.

'Load partridge!' roared Holcroft. 'You hear me over there, William Rodgers! Let them come a little closer and we'll give them a taste of our best case shot.'

The rebel regiments advanced slowly, at first, walking the hundred yards to the Bussex Rhine with a measured pace. They had ceased firing their muskets and most of those were unloaded, some clogged with burnt powder residue. But they were certainly not useless. Reversed, the long lump of heavy wood made a formidable club for crushing skulls. Other men had ancient swords, or pikes, pistols and daggers, but a good many had only modified scythes, rakes and other potentially lethal farm implements. No one, however, could doubt their courage and, after the long, bloody firefight, and having endured the cannon blasts that lanced out of the night, blowing away scores of men, they were ready for a proper set-to, hand to hand, face to face, to punish these idolatrous dogs, these soldiers of the Pope-loving King James.

Fifty yards from the Rhine, and the rebels could now see the nearest enemy clearly. A ragged block of men, under flaming torches and huge limp flags. Many gaps in the line, men lying bloody on the grass. A battered, shrunken force. Half beaten already. But there were blocks of formed men on either side of Dumbarton's bloodied Scots, untouched, ready, and the evil glint of bronze cannon between the lines of men.

The order came: 'Charge! For Monmouth. For the Protestant Duke! Charge!'

The West Countrymen leapt forward, pelting towards the Rhine over the damp turf, the night erupting with their war cries.

The first blast of 'partridge' smashed into the running men, hurling back dozens with its murderous fury. Thin tubular metal canisters had been loaded into the cannon, instead of the usual round shot, each canister filled with hundreds of musket balls. The canister disintegrated when the cannon were fired, spraying the musket balls in a lethal cone of death directly into the ranks of the enemy, like the blast from a giant's fowling piece. The first killing charge from Roaring Meg scythed into the rebel regiments, snapping limbs, ripping flesh, stripping the skin from their bodies. A second blast, from Master Gunner Rodgers, knocked a deep hole in the centre of the running men. From the far side of Dumbarton's Regiment, Quartermaster Glanvilles's two Falcons added their lesser weight to the misery of the charging foe. But the rebels were nearly at the Rhine now, men stopping to peer down into the muddy darkness, feeling their way over the lip. Holcroft's men worked like maniacs – sponging, loading charge and canister, ramming, priming the vent, firing. And Roaring Meg crashed out once more, wiping rebels from their feet and hurling them into writhing piles of flesh. Moments later the second Saker crashed out again, too.

The King's regiments on either side of Dumbarton's, the First Foot Guards on the right, and Kirke's Lambs on the left, opened up. The musket volleys crashed into the fear-crazed mob of rebels milling about on the far side of the ditch, knocking men down, punching them clear off their feet. The battered Scotsmen were firing too, loading, aiming, discharging, reloading. Taking their revenge for the long mauling they had received. And, at Jack's command, the King's Own Royal Dragoons from behind their position were coming forward, threading through the Scotsmen's ranks to add their weight of fire to the battle. A gale of musket shot lashed the milling West Countrymen on the lip of the Rhine, the storm punctuated by the regular thunderous booming of the six cannon now opposing them. Each flash and blast of partridge claiming the lives of a dozen men, sweeping them higgledy-piggledy into the next world like a gigantic bloody broom. By now, a few of the luckier rebels had got down into the slime of the Rhine bed – and there they stayed, ducked low, if they wished to live, while the holocaust of lead crashed and whined over their heads, the balls cracking and whistling through the air, ripping it apart. By now the agonised screams of hundreds of wounded men on the bank above were as loud as the gunfire. Louder.

And Monmouth's men broke.

The farm hands and cloth weavers, the leather workers and shepherds, the simple men who devoutly wished to see the new Catholic King deposed and a proper God-fearing Protestant set on the throne, hurled away their heavy, empty matchlocks, dropped their scythes and rusty swords and ran back into the blackness of the moor, leaving the western bank of the Bussex Rhine thick with the corpses of their comrades and the broken, blood-slick, mewling forms of wounded men.

Chapter Four

8 July 1685: London

The man who called himself Narrey stood at the back of the classroom and watched as seventy children aged between eight and nine seated on rows of long benches, guided by a small lean priest in a black habit, chanted out the letters of the alphabet in unison and the name of an object that began with the letter. '. . . H is for House; I is for Ink-pot; J is for Jug . . .' The noise had a strangely calming, mind-soothing effect, it was almost soporific and reminded him, oddly, of ancient monks softly singing Matins in the middle of the night in some remote mountain monastery.

He was aware that Guillaume, standing beside him, was agitated, nervous even. He knew that his lieutenant was waiting for a word of praise. In the past six months, Guillaume had been back and forth from Paris three – or was it four? – times to arrange the set-up here in this ramshackle corner of London. He had recruited the three teacher-priests, and the gang of ruffians who protected them, and had arranged suitable permissions from the powers that be for this humble school to be formed.

Guillaume had led Narrey on a tour of the whole facility, the courtyards, the dining hall, kitchen, the other classrooms and spaces where many people could be accommodated in reasonable comfort for a considerable length of time. The location was perfect, too, close to Narrey's lavish accommodation in the French Embassy in White Hall, and very convenient for that and other much more important reasons. Narrey inhaled deeply: the sharp smell of chalk powder filled the air from the priest's work on the blackboard. But he could also detect the sweet grassy scent of healthy boys' sweat and a whiff of spicy incense from the little chapel off the courtyard.

'It's all good, Guillaume,' he said, and watched the younger man relax, his shoulders dropping with relief. 'You have done very well to secure this place.'

'Thank you, Monsieur le Comte. Would you care to meet the head teacher – Father Palmer? I believe he is anxious to personally thank his most generous patron.'

'Not on this visit, Guillaume. But you may tell him I am pleased with his work.'

Narrey was wrapped in his customary black cloak, his body shape disguised, his face shadowed by his broad-brimmed hat. He always preferred that as few people as possible ever saw his face, even if they knew nothing of his professional activities.

A younger priest came into the classroom from the door leading to the courtyard, and for a moment, Narrey felt a shock of unpleasant surprise. The man was tall, broad-shouldered, long-limbed with a mop of brown hair. For an instant, Narrey thought that he was looking at Holcroft Blood – the English spy who had humiliated him in Paris not six months ago. But the priest was not him. Narrey could see it now. This fellow was thinner, sharper featured than Holcroft Blood, and he was younger, too, by a good ten years. The young priest conferred briefly with the head teacher and then turned and disappeared again into the courtyard, the door banging behind him.

The shock at apparently seeing his former enemy – even though he was not the same man at all – changed Narrey's mood from deep calm to something akin to rage.

Blood. Holcroft Blood. Narrey had read his secret file more than a dozen times; he had even ventured out with one of the Paris surveillance teams and spent an uncomfortable night on a tiled rooftop opposite Blood's cheap apartment on the Right Bank watching through the open shutters as the man peacefully snored. If only he had sent in Guillaume that night and had him cut his throat while he slept . . .

But regrets were of no practical use. Blood had made him look foolish. That fact must be faced up to. It must be borne.

According to Narrey's much pored-over file, the Englishman had been accepted into the elite Cadets of the *Gendarmes de la Garde* a dozen years ago. He had served the Sun King, first as a trainee officer in the Household Guards then, after completing his military apprenticeship, as a *Sous-lieutenant* in the *Corps Royal de l'Artillerie*. He had been posted to the artillery school in Douai, Flanders, and apparently had greatly distinguished himself there. His commander's final report had been glowing – he had been described as a future master of the noble art of gunnery. Then, as a full lieutenant, Holcroft Blood had been posted to Paris, based for most of the time at the Arsenal next to the Bastille prison. He had remained there for more than seven years.

And in all those years of apparently loyal service to the Sun King there had never been a single black mark against his name. He had been a model soldier, a perfectly behaved, perfectly disciplined if somewhat unambitous junior officer. But all the while, it seemed, he was sending his secret little coded reports back to the Court of St James, telling his paymasters in King Charles's White Hall everything he could discover about Louis XIV's ever expanding military machine.

His reports on the state of the big guns of the royal artillery, and on the Sun King's multitudinous regiments of infantry and cavalry – no doubt gathered during jolly dinners with fellow officers in Paris and wherever else his superiors in the *Corps Royal de l'Artillerie* might send him – had found their way to the generals and ministers of the enemy states that ringed France, from Spain in the south to the Holy Roman Empire in the east to the Protestant Dutch in the north.

Narrey had for the longest time been completely unaware of Holcroft Blood's clandestine activities – how should he know? There were many hundreds of foreign officers, perhaps even thousands, in the Sun King's service. And for the most part they were hardworking, professional soldiers who were grateful to serve with the crack French forces and utterly loyal to their commander, Louis le Grand. And though there were always rumours of spies in Versailles and in the salons of Paris and the garrison towns across the land, and though Narrey had successfully hunted down and interrogated a handful of traitors of all nationalities, he had never so much had a sniff of Holcroft Blood's secret work. He had underestimated Blood – that was the truth – he had appeared to be a simple-minded English soldier. A stolid, uninteresting fellow who diligently did his duty day-in day-out and never caused any trouble at all.

Narrey clearly remembered the expression on the Sun King's face at the High Council meeting a little over two years ago, when Francois Michel Le Tellier de Louvois, the brilliant and ambitious Minister of War, had announced that he had reliable information that there was a long-time spy deep in the army. Louis had looked at Narrey across the polished tabletop with a blank, enquiring face, as if to say, 'So, Monsieur, you made this your territory, what have you to say about this?'

And Narrey, who had indeed carved out a fiefdom as guardian of *le Sécurité de l'Intérieur*, had floundered. He made the mistake of pretending that he had the same suspicions. And Louvois, that snake, had given no details of his own knowledge but had merely blandly asked Narrey what information he had. After blustering for a minute or two, Narrey finally got off the hook by suggesting that this was a subject that would be best dealt with in private – with just the King, Louvois and himself in conclave. The rest of the High Council – some half dozen of the highest ranking officials, including two dukes, were either mystified at this extreme secrecy or deeply offended that they were to be excluded from such an important meeting.

Word spread that there was an important spy in the heart of the army – disseminated no doubt by disaffected High Council members – and that Narrey was on his trail and would have him in irons shortly. The spy was reckoned to be someone capable of doing extreme damage to the King's armed forces – someone high up, it was rumoured, perhaps a general, perhaps even a Marshal of France. Every military setback in the past ten years was laid at the spy's door. But that cunning fox Narrey would catch him, or so the gossip-mongers said. He had sworn on his honour to do so.

Narrey's first mistake was to admit that Louvois was right and there *was* a spy deep in the Sun King's military machine, when he had no idea if this was, in fact, true. At a vulnerable moment, the lure of appearing omniscient had proved too strong. His second mistake was to claim that, after a thorough investigation by his men over several months, there was no such a spy after all. That Louvois's secret information, garnered from one of the old man's own agents in the English court, was quite wrong.

The Minister of War had responded by furnishing the King with a copy of a recent report written by this very spy. It was in code – which one of Louvois's many clever young men had broken – and, after a few simple deductions based on the timing of the message and the specific intelligence it contained, it became clear that the report's author could only be a junior officer in the *Corps Royal de l'Artillerie*.

Narrey had his men place a watch on Blood, and three other artillery officers, who fitted the bill. But there appeared to be no evidence of any wrongdoing, none.

The King was growing impatient, a year had passed since the first revelation – Louvois was now suggesting silkily that perhaps his own people ought to take over this grave responsibility, if it proved too much for one poor, overworked spymaster – and Narrey still had no one in custody and no chief suspect. He overheard whispered jokes made about him, and satirical songs being sung in the disreputable wine shops of Paris about his incompetence, and he was about to pull in all four of the suspect artillery officers and torture the truth out of them – regardless of the consequences – when Holcroft Blood suddenly disappeared from the Arsenal, not even bothering to clear out his desk in the barracks, vacated his apartment with two months rent paid in advance, and slipped away to safety almost before Narrey knew he was gone.

The King was furious. People now openly sniggered when the spymaster's back was turned. He was even mocked on stage in Paris in a play by Racine. He had been humiliated, made to look an incompetent fool, and one man was entirely to blame – Holcroft Blood, lately a traitorous lieutenant of the elite *Corps Royal de l'Artillerie*.

But all that was in the past. Narrey had confessed his failings in the High Council and survived the embarrassment. His position was weakened but the King had forgiven him and given him this task. His hatred for Blood, however, endured.

Narrey saw that the old priest had dismissed the schoolchildren and was making his way through the crowds of little boys towards him. Narrey clapped Guillaume on the shoulder. 'Tell him I shall be delighted to dine with him next time I am in London,' he said. 'But at the moment I am indisposed. Meet me outside.'

He turned his back on the advancing priest and slipped out of the schoolroom door, pulling his broad hat even further down over his brow as he left the building.

As he waited outside the school, covertly watching the English faces of the men and women who passed him, his thoughts turned once again to Holcroft Blood.

How would he react if he encountered him here in England? There was a reasonable likelihood of it happening, particularly if Blood was now residing in London. Blood might or might not know who Narrey was – but he thought probably not. He always took great pains to keep his identity secret, and their paths had not crossed in the court of Versailles or in the military salons of Paris. For a moment or two he entertained the delightful idea of eliminating Holcroft Blood from the world. Guillaume would do it, with knife or gun or his bare hands, if necessary. And would not even question the order. Narrey himself had no moral qualms – the man had taken Louis XIV's *livres* and sworn an oath of service to the Sun King. Then he had betrayed his commander-in-chief. He deserved death. But that was not the question: the true question was one of risk. How dangerous would it be to have Blood killed?

Moderately so, Narrey judged. He might have friends who would investigate, magistrates might call for witnesses. There might be a hue and cry. And that could draw attention to Narrey – and to his mission. Which must not be allowed to happen.

Reluctantly, Narrey concluded that he could not justify to himself the pleasure of having Blood murdered. He could not afford to endanger the mission even in the smallest way just to fulfil a whim. Blood must be allowed to live, for now. Unless, for some reason, he proved to be a threat, either to Narrey or to the sacred task itself. In that case, Guillaume would have his orders – and Holcroft Blood would be dead.

Chapter Five

13 July 1685: Tower of London

'The charge is gross insubordination, Lieutenant Blood. Which under the military code carries with it a sentence of death. What have you to say for yourself?'

Holcroft remained silent: he was coldly furious at this preposterous threat. He stared expressionlessly at George Legge, Lord Dartmouth, Master-General of the Ordnance, Colonel of the Royal Fusiliers, Constable of the Tower of London, Admiral of the Fleet, etc, etc – a man who, as far as the Ordnance lieutenant was concerned, was the ultimate figure of authority in his life, second in power only to His Majesty King James II and the Lord God Almighty, maker of Heaven and Earth.

The silence lengthened and became painful.

'Well, sir, what have you to say for yourself?' Lord Dartmouth's tone was testy.

Holcroft was standing rigidly to attention before his master's long oak desk in his office in the headquarters of the Royal Fusiliers on the eastern side of the Inner Ward of the Tower of London. It was seven days after the slaughter of Sedgemoor. They were the only two people in the large wood-panelled room. And, since the day was a little grey and wet for mid-July, a cheerful fire was burning in the iron grate.

'Speak up, Mister Blood! I haven't got all day.'

The lieutenant let the question hang in the air a little while longer, then gave a shrug and said, with more than a touch of anger: 'I did what I thought was right, sir. You have, I believe, been fully informed of the events at Sedgemoor – I have submitted a lengthy report; you have heard Quartermaster Glanville's version; you have the statement of the Comptroller of the Train, Colonel Henry Shere – although I saw nothing of him that night. Major-General Lord Churchill has also written to you as, I understand, has the Bishop of Winchester. And I know that you have spoken at length to several of the gunners who fought, including Enoch Jackson, who was with me for most of the engagement. If, after all that information, sir, you have somehow bizarrely come to the conclusion that I deserve to be put to death for my actions that night, I will not contradict you. Nor will I beg you for my life. I will say only that I did what I thought was right at Sedgemoor. And, sir, I believe I did my duty.'

Half an hour earlier, he had listened in silence while Captain Glanville had made an impassioned complaint about his deliberate disregarding of the orders not to move the guns of the Royal Train of Artillery. Glanville had then been dismissed from the Master-General's office. Next Holcroft had heard Henry Shere give a stumbling, stuttering, rambling and incoherent account of his absence from the battle – the Comptroller had taken possession of a comfortable farmhouse in Middlezoy, a hamlet a little over two miles away, and after placing the guns along the Bussex Rhine, guarding the road to Bridgwater, he had gone back to Middlezoy and proceeded to drink himself into a stupor. By the time that the news of the rebel attack had reached him, and his servants had managed to wake him and get him reasonably sober, mounted and fit to join his command, the night's fighting was all but over.

Lord Feversham, who was also much embarrassed about sleeping through the encounter – although an old injury to his skull, he claimed, not common drunkenness, was the reason *he* could not be awoken – had emerged with the dawn in time to order out the cavalry to pursue and slaughter any of the fleeing rebels they could catch.

Monmouth himself had been captured two days later hiding in a field of peas, deserted by his men, who were scattered halfway across the West Country. The Protestant Duke was now in chains in the White Tower not a hundred yards from where Lord Dartmouth was attempting to berate Holcroft for his dereliction of duty.

'A man who did not know you as well as I, might say you were too arrogant, Mister Blood. He might even call you insolent,' said Lord Dartmouth. 'But I can see things from your point of view. Frankly, I can't decide whether to punish you or not.'

Holcroft let out an exasperated breath. He was fond of Lord Dartmouth, and believed the Master-General of the Ordnance to be a good and honest man, but his bouts of paralysing indecision were intensely frustrating for those under his command. He held his tongue and waited for the man to come to his conclusion.

'You might at least pretend to be contrite, for the look of the thing. Captain Glanville, your superior officer in the Ordnance, gave you a direct order not to move the guns and yet you did exactly that. You moved them! Tell me you did not.'

'It was a ridiculous order, sir. Not to move the guns in the middle of a battle? Guns should be moved according to necessity. They came at us from the north, not from the west. You know as well as I do, sir, that no battle ever goes exactly to plan. The officer on the spot has to take the decision. Besides, I was given a direct order by General Churchill to move the guns up to Dumbarton's as quickly as possible.'

Dartmouth sighed. 'You make a good point, Mister Blood. And I am moved to decide in your favour. But this squabbling between you and Glanville must stop. That is an order. Any more of this discord and I shall be extremely angry. D'you hear me?'

Holcroft said nothing.

'Very well,' said Dartmouth, smiling at last. 'It seems clear to me, upon reflection, that you have behaved rather well in this affair – I'm told you silenced an enemy battery in pitch darkness with a single shot. And I may tell you that it is Lord Churchill's opinion that your performance went a long way towards bringing the engagement to a

successful conclusion. So, lieutenant, here is my decision: privately
I congratulate you on your conduct. Publicly I shall be forced to
punish you—'

'Sir, this is unjust—'

'Be quiet, Mister Blood. I have made my decision. You have done
well but you *did* disobey orders, therefore you must be punished.
This is my judgment. So ... as your punishment, you will command the detachment of Royal Fusiliers that is to accompany His
Grace the Duke of Monmouth to the scaffold on Wednesday morning. It's a nasty job, none of the fusilier officers want to do it, nor
do any of the gentlemen of the Ordnance. So it is yours. You may
ponder the wages of rebellion against rightful authority as you take
the rebel Duke to his well-earned execution in two days' time.'

Holcroft's stomach felt cold and empty. He genuinely hated to
witness bloodshed and now he must watch this nobleman meet the
axe on Tower Hill. Still, at least it wasn't his own execution, and
it should be swift, one good blow and it would all be over for the
man who had tried to seize the crown. And Holcroft knew that for
disobeying orders in time of war, this unpleasant duty was a light
punishment indeed.

'Yes, sir,' he said and saluted crisply. Just as he was turning to
leave the office, Dartmouth said: 'There is one more thing, Mister
Blood. Another matter entirely.'

'Yes, sir?'

'Come, sit by me.' Dartmouth gestured to a chair beside the desk.
His air had changed completely, the formal disciplinary tone was
gone, replaced by a kindlier, almost paternal demeanour. He wasn't
a bad old soul really, Holcroft told himself, setting himself down on
the chair and looking into his commanding officer's pouchy ageing
face beneath the cascading curls of his huge blond periwig.

'What is it, sir?'

'I want you to oblige me in a small matter. You are aware of that
young fellow, John Matthews, the one that we caught in the powder
magazine three days ago?'

'Yes, sir.'

The incident had been the talk of the officers' mess when he had returned to the Tower of London with the Train the day before. One of the locally employed civilian clerks, just a young fellow, had been discovered trying to steal a keg of Number Three gunpowder from the massive Ordnance magazine. The powder stores, usually guarded by two fusiliers under a corporal, had been carelessly left unlocked and untended with so many of the officers absent on campaign in the West Country.

It looked as if the young clerk had taken this opportunity to purloin a small keg of valuable black powder. He had only been caught in there by sheer chance as he had accidentally kicked an empty metal can inside the dark store, creating a loud, suspicious rattling noise, which alerted a passing sergeant of pioneers.

'We have the fellow in the White Tower awaiting trial,' said Lord Dartmouth. 'I have full jurisdiction in these royal precincts, of course, even though he is not a soldier, and I was thinking a quiet court martial and a quick execution – a hanging, not a firing squad, as he's a civilian – possibly next week or earlier, if I can find the time. I am so damnably busy. What do you think, Holcroft: is that the thing to do?'

'If you say so, sir.'

'It's just that there is something fishy about this Matthews. His fellow clerks say that he does not attend Anglican services with the rest of them and, well, they suspect him of adhering to the old Romish faith. You can see why that might be a problem.'

'I see, sir. A Catholic caught in a powder store has unfortunate associations.'

'Quite. I think it most unlikely that he is another Guido Fawkes. But I can't decide if I should turn him over to the Earl of Sunderland's people for interrogation – or deal with it myself. Plots seem to be on everyone's mind these days. But then perhaps this is all a fuss about nothing – and I should not like to cry wolf and be made to look a fool. I was hoping you would help me get to the truth in this matter.'

'Would you like me to question him, sir?'

'Yes, yes, I think that would be best. I would like to be able to tell the King, or indeed Lord Sunderland, that I have had one of my best officers investigate the matter and there is nothing to be alarmed about. So, you will speak to Matthews? Yes? Make the inquiries? You're a man who knows how to ferret out secrets . . .'

Holcroft's face closed. He stopped smiling at his commander and leant back in his chair, recoiling instinctively. He disliked any mention at all of his covert activities for the English government in France. It had been this sort of loose talk in London, he suspected, that had allowed the French to unmask him as an agent of the Crown. It had nearly cost him his life.

'I understand, sir,' he said rather coldly. 'I will make suitable inquiries of this fellow and question him myself. May I promise him anything if he co-operates?'

'Promise him anything?'

'Yes, sir. He faces death at the moment. May I promise him life – transportation to the plantations rather than the noose – if he is honest with me? An incentive, sir.'

'Ah . . . Oh . . . I don't know. I don't want to be too soft on him. How about this: you may plead for clemency on his behalf at the tribunal, if he is co-operative.'

Holcroft decided not to press his request. If the prisoner proved to be worth saving, he was sure he could persuade the Master-General to show mercy.

Lord Dartmouth was a decent, reasonable man, kindly even. Holcroft felt a deep sense of obligation to him. When he had returned to England six months ago, largely friendless and very, very frightened, Dartmouth had given him a home in the Tower and accepted him into the Ordnance as a junior officer. So Holcroft was perfectly happy to oblige his patron in this small matter of the Catholic gunpowder-thief.

'Very good, sir. Will there be anything else?'

'Yes, Holcroft, there is. I want you to try, to really try, to rub along cordially with Captain Glanville. I do not like discord among my officers. We are one family. Be emollient, be respectful, win him over. Make William Glanville your friend.'

'Sir,' said Holcroft, his eyes sliding away from his superior's concerned face.

'I mean it, Lieutenant Blood. You will make a friend of Captain Glanville.'

'As you command, sir,' said Holcroft, standing and making a deep bow.

Chapter Six

13 July 1685: Drury Lane

'It's bloody unfair, Aphra,' Holcroft was drinking brandy. He was helping himself to the flask of good cognac that he had brought with him to his friend's shabby little house in Drury Lane, west London. 'I'm being punished for saving the army at Sedgemoor. Jack told me – he told Dartmouth too – that my actions went a long way towards winning the battle. Yet I'm being punished. I have to escort His Grace the Duke of Monmouth to the scaffold the day after tomorrow, watch them hack off his head.'

Aphra Behn, a fine-looking lady in her forties in a low-cut emerald gown that was much too young for her, was sitting by the window at a desk piled high with papers. She was an old friend of Holcroft's, like him a former spy in Charles II's service, and now an actress, poet and playwright. She had a quill in her hand and was annotating a manuscript before her, only occasionally looking up sympathetically and making the appropriate noises. She knew Holcroft, and men in general, very well and she was wise enough to allow him to rant uninterrupted. She had accepted a glass of brandy from Holcroft when he had come bursting into her rooms a half hour past but had not yet touched the liquor.

'Could be worse,' she muttered.

'Worse? I don't deserve to be punished at all.'

'He's just given you an unpleasant chore. The Duke richly deserves to die and someone has to take him to Tower Hill. There's no point whining about it.'

'I'm not whining, I'm just . . .'

Holcroft stopped talking. 'It's all that fat turd Glanville's fault. Reporting me for disobedience. I should call the bastard out. Kill him.'

'And what would that achieve?'

'William Glanville would be dead. That would be the main achievement.'

'And you would be drummed out of the Ordnance, defrocked, stripped all of your brass buttons or whatever they do, homeless, without gainful employment . . .'

'That bastard Glanville would still be cold in his grave.'

'Well, that would make disgrace and destitution completely worthwhile, then.'

Holcroft said nothing. He knew she was right. In truth, he couldn't do anything about Glanville except endure him. But he always felt better after speaking candidly to Aphra – she was one of the few people in the world with whom he could open his mind. He took a sip of his brandy. He could hear through the thin walls of the house the sounds from the next room of a woman in the throes of ecstasy, yelping rhythmically, wailing, calling on the Almighty as she approached her climax.

'Is that Sarie, the little blonde one?' he asked eventually.

'Yes, I believe she's got the new Earl of Westbury in there. One of her regulars. Listen to her! Quite ridiculous. She's the most talentless actress I have ever had the misfortune to cast in one of my plays. No wonder she had to change her profession.'

Holcroft listened to the noises, which increased dramatically in volume and frequency before suddenly stopping. He sipped his brandy, calmer now.

'Why do you live in this . . . this awful house?'

'You know why. It's near the Theatre Royal. And it's very cheap. Since they merged the Duke's Company and the King's three years ago they say they don't want my plays any more, they tell me the novelty of a woman playwright has worn off. It's all Shakespeare, Shakespeare, Shakespeare these days. That's what the people want.'

'So what is that you are writing?'

'It's a romance in three parts, a story about a lord who is in love with his sister.'

'Indeed?' Holcroft had no interest in romances, even titillating ones about incestuous noblemen. He'd nothing to say about Aphra's plays either, which he hated.

Aphra set down her pen. She shook sand over her manuscript from the octagonal pewter shaker and looked up, sensing Holcroft's storm had blown itself out.

'How was the battle? Apart from winning it with your famous disobedience.'

Holcroft considered her question for a few moments.

'It was disgusting, to be honest. Ill-trained working men, peasants mostly, some armed only with farm tools against the King's finest troops: scythes against Sakers, muck-rakes against flintlock muskets. We slaughtered them. We destroyed them. It was no more than a massacre. And the worst of it was they were our own people: Englishmen, almost all of them. You should have seen that moorland in the dawn the next day. After the cavalry had had their fun chopping up the fleeing, broken rebels. The dead piled in mounds. Parts of human bodies. Blood and bits everywhere.'

'I heard that it was very bad in the days after the battle, too; hundreds upon hundreds of prisoners just hanged out of hand, young men and beardless boys strung up without trial; women, too, hanged on suspicion of harbouring rebel fugitives.'

'Yes, all that, and they're transporting hundreds more to the West Indies where they'll be treated little better than slaves. They are calling it the King's Vengeance.'

They looked at each other gloomily.

'He's sowing dragon's teeth,' said Aphra. 'Every man or woman hanged or transported has brothers, sisters, wives, cousins who must now hate the King with even more passion. God knows I despised Monmouth, and his pathetic little rebellion. And I firmly do believe James to be our rightful sovereign – but what bloody whirlwind will he reap with this barbarous treatment of his own subjects?'

Holcroft shrugged. 'He's the King. He can act as he likes. Hang the whole population of Somerset and Dorset, if he chooses to. He is God's anointed on Earth.'

'And God has anointed a Catholic to rule over us.'

'So it would seem. But you know, Aphra, that I care nothing for these things – Catholic or Protestant, the King's soul is his own business. As long as he gives his kingdoms peace and order, I don't care if he chooses to become a Mussulman.'

'You're not particular about faith, Holly? You don't fear for his soul, or yours?'

Holcroft stared at her. Then he noted the smile on her face, and realised she was teasing him again. He knew that she herself had little time for religious wrangling.

'Religion, when made public, seems to be just another thing to divide us. It should be a private matter. Anyway, my soul belongs to the Ordnance, as well you know. And I'd best get back to it. I've to interrogate a thief tomorrow morning. A Catholic, as it happens, who stole a keg of powder. Dartmouth fears it may be a plot.'

'You don't believe so?'

'I don't know. It seems very unlikely. But I said I'd look into it anyway.'

He got up and went over to her table and placed a kiss on her cheek. *She looks tired,* he thought, as he came close to her. *Tired and poor. The failure is ageing her, dimming her lovely eyes.* He fished in his big Ordnance coat pocket and pulled out a slim leather purse. He laid it on the desk with a very slight chinking sound.

'Oh Holly, no need for that.' But she put her hand on the purse, a slim, almost scrawny hand, and gripped it tightly.

'Something towards the rent,' he said awkwardly. 'You know I can afford it.'

Holcroft was, indeed, reasonably well off. He had bought an annuity many years ago which paid him several hundred pounds a year, enough for a frugal gentleman to live on; and the late King Charles had been generous enough to grant him a sinecure in Ireland for his secret services in France. He was still nominally the Clerk of the Crown and Peace in County Clare, and he received a stipend quarterly, although he had never yet set foot in County Clare. There was also his lieutenant's pay from the Ordnance, of which he spent little as he ate at the officers' mess in the Tower most days and paid no rent. Then there were his winnings at the tables.

Holcroft was acknowledged to be one of the finest card players in London and perhaps even the whole of England. Indeed, his reputation was such that many gentlemen refused point blank to play cards with him at all, preferring to be thought lacking in sporting spirit than almost certainly losing a small fortune to him across the green baize table. And this skill had made him moderately rich.

'Let me at least give you something for it in exchange,' she said. Their faces were only a few inches apart. She leant in closer. He could smell her sweet perfume over her ordinary womanly smell. In the next room, Sarie the blonde began wailing and yelping again, there was the sound of a brass bedstead rattling against the wall.

Holcroft looked at her in surprise, eyebrows raised.

'Not that, you lustful devil. Men! Always thinking with their members. Besides, aren't you supposed to be in love with Elizabeth Fowler, the widowed English rose?'

Holcroft backed away, embarrassed that even the thought of engaging in such a bout with Aphra had crossed his mind. They were friends of long standing. They had never been lovers. They never would be. Their unusual relationship resembled the bond between a brother and his elder sister: and was just as strong and enduring.

'I haven't seen Elizabeth in a month or so,' he mumbled.

'Well, you should hurry up and grab her. She won't wait for ever with her fine looks, widow or no. And it would put an end to your doggish lusts. Go and see her, woo her, marry her, bed her – that's my advice. It might well be the making of you.'

Holcroft had hurriedly swallowed the last of his brandy and was doing up the brass buttons of his big blue coat. His face was still burning with embarrassment.

'Wait a moment, Holcroft,' said Aphra, in quite a different voice. 'Don't go just yet. I have something to tell you. This is my gift. You know that I am still in touch with some of my old *friends* in Paris, and at Versailles. Yes? Well, from time to time I get snippets of news from them. Nothing earth-shattering, my days as an agent are well behind me. But I do get some items of note, on occassion. Little gifts from old colleagues. And I think one of these snippets might interest you. Are you listening?'

Holcroft looked at her attentively.

'Narrey is in London. That's what I heard. He has been given a special mission to accomplish here by Louis. I was told the Sun King commissioned him personally.'

Holcroft felt the floor shift beneath his feet. *Narrey here!*

'Who is your informant?'

Aphra shook her head, smiled a little archly.

'What is Narrey doing in London? He can't still be after me.'

'I don't know what he is up to – neither does my informant. But he is still as dangerous as ever. My informant says he lost one of his people trying to find out. The poor man disappeared at sea but it is obvious that Narrey or his men murdered him.'

Holcroft looked at his friend steadily, fixing her gaze, his mind working fast. He stifled the fear that the mere mention of Narrey conjured up and tried to be rational.

'I don't think he can be looking me,' he said slowly. 'He has a great many more weighty matters to deal with – that commission from King Louis, you mentioned – I was a small embarrassment to him. But I can't believe he would come here, interrupt all his other schemes and designs, just to seek petty revenge. What do you think?'

'I think you are right. Whatever he is doing here, his primary aim cannot be to settle a score with one little spy who escaped his clutches. But that doesn't mean that he would not gladly try to kill you, if the chance arose. You must be on your guard.'

'I shall be. But it would help if I had even the slightest idea what he looked like. In France, he was always just a name – not even a name, a code name. He was a bogeyman that our people only whispered about fearfully with the shutters closed and all the doors locked. Does your informant actually *know* Narrey?'

Aphra shook her head again.

'Does he know his true name? Or can he describe his appearance? Even a distinguishing mark, a mole, a scar, would be a help. Anything about him at all?'

'He says he knows nothing more. You know as well as I do, Holly, that Narrey rarely allows anyone who can identify him to live. If I find out anything else, I will tell you straight away. But you must be alert to danger at all times. I'm sure that murderous bastard would seize the slightest opportunity to put you down while he's here.'

Chapter Seven

14 July 1685: Tower of London

The next morning, immediately after breakfast, Holcroft walked to the entrance of the White Tower and was admitted to the prison by an ancient dwarf-like gaoler named Jeremiah Widdicombe, who had had charge of the building for decades. Holcroft was thinking, not on the task at hand, but about what Aphra had told him the night before. It had been a shock, no question about it, to hear Narrey's name – he had hoped that he had put all that business behind him – but now that he had had time to evaluate Aphra's intelligence, he felt a good deal better. Narrey was unlikely to seek him out and try to do him harm. And Holcroft decided he would make no move against the Frenchman either. He would not risk provoking him. He would leave him to pursue whatever his mission was – it was no longer his concern, since he had forsworn espionage work on returning to England. Aphra would no doubt pass the word to Lord Sunderland, the chief minister, and he could take whatever action he saw fit to protect the realm and King James. In short, Holcroft decided, he would do nothing.

'We've got him up on the second floor,' said Widdicombe, shambling beside Holcroft along the dusty corridors, keys jangling musically at his belt. 'In your dear father's old chamber. I'm sure you remember it well, sir.'

Widdicombe had been one of the gaolers when Holcroft's late father Colonel Thomas Blood had been incarcerated in the White Tower for some weeks fourteen years ago, after his outrageous attempt to steal the Crown Jewels – and the grinning little turnkey never let his son Holcroft forget it.

'Ah, them were good old days,' Widdicombe screwed his face into a winsome, nostalgic expression. 'We had a better class of customer then, a much better class. Your father was a gentleman, sir, and if he landed in the durance it was for stealing a royal crown, not just a peck of dirty old powder, oh, no, he was a cut above, was your old Daddy, quite the gent, so charming, ever the swell, not some ten-a-penny pilferer like this nasty Matthews boy. A man of true quality, the old Colonel was. Always had a shiny shilling or two for me and the lads to drink his good health . . .'

Widdicombe looked at Holcroft expectantly. They were standing outside the door of the cell and the gaoler was jangling his keys, making a meal over finding the right one. 'Yes, it's thirsty work, running up and down the stairs all day, showing the gentlemen to the right cell. Right thirsty work. Back in the good old days, o' course, a senior gaoler such as myself would charge a whole half crown to admit a visitor . . .'

Holcroft looked at him coldly. 'Just open the door, Widdicombe.'

'Only I was wondering whether you might like to have some refreshments brought up; your father, if I remember rightly, was very fond of a glass of brandy or two of an evening. Or perhaps you might enjoy a cool can of ale? Perhaps, if you were to slip me a sovereign I might run across directly to the Red Lion and . . .'

The wretched little oaf was still fiddling with the bunch of keys and shooting acquisitive glances at the lieutenant. As a younger man, Holcroft might have punched him, knocked him down and kicked him till he opened the door. That remained an option – as did fetching a file of fusiliers and having the door broken down with their musket butts. But he decided on a more pacific course of action.

'You know, Widdicombe, I'm not sure I have time to visit this Matthews boy just now. Lord Dartmouth has given me so many commissions recently that I scarcely know where my head is. Perhaps I should busy myself today with the long overdue review of the accounts of the White Tower. My lord was particularly keen that I study all aspects of the Tower's financial affairs in detail and bring to his attention any shortfall in the accounting. He is looking for ways to save expense and he is most concerned about petty peculation by people in positions of authority. If I remember correctly, last time I opened the ledgers, there was a sum of five pounds, ten shillings and sixpence that was missing from the White Tower's books. Perhaps I should spend today chasing down the shortfall, finding the person or persons to blame . . .'

'Ah, this is the one, 'twas here all along!' Widdicombe had miraculously found the key, entered it into the lock and was pushing open the heavy door.

'Here's a most distinguished visitor for you, John Matthews,' he said as he walked inside. And to Holcroft: 'You take your time here, sir, make yourself comfy. And if Matthews doesn't answer your questions promptly, holler and I'll bring some of the lads to have a nice little chat with him, you catch my meaning, with their fists.'

'You are too kind, Jeremiah.'

'Not at all, sir, always a pleasure to have a member of the illustrious Blood family as our guest. Always a pleasure . . .'

By the look of things, Widdicombe's lads had already had a 'nice little chat' with John Matthews. His face was swollen and covered with red, purple and yellowish marks. He also flinched away from Holcroft's bulk, cowering and shrinking in on himself as the lieutenant walked towards him.

The young man was sitting on his unmade bed and Holcroft pulled up a stool and sat on it a few feet away. He said nothing for a while, leaning forward with his elbows on his knees and his big hands hanging loose between his legs, looking round the sparse cell and remembering his father's time in this very chamber.

The same smoke-blackened oak beams and stone-flagged floor. The same fireplace – unlit and empty at this time of year. The same barred window admitting weak shafts of pale sunlight. It had been in this bleak, soulless, anonymous chamber that he had recognised his father's weakness; seen, for the first time, his fallibility and understood his own burgeoning strength. It was here that he had worked out how he would save his father from the gallows, even though it meant opposing, indeed, outwitting men who were infinitely more powerful than him. It was in this cell, he now realised, that he had become a man.

'The Master-General of the Ordnance means to have you briefly tried for theft then hung by the neck until you are dead,' said Holcroft, in a quiet, conversational tone of voice, as if he were remarking on the weather. 'Probably next week, but maybe sooner if Lord Dartmouth can find the time. He's a busy man, you know.'

Matthews stared at him silently through bruised and fear-washed eyes.

'That will certainly happen if I walk out of this room unsatisfied. When I leave here, your course is set, and you will surely meet your Maker in less than a week.' Holcroft let his words sink in. 'But there is one slim chance of redemption. There is a way that I can save you. No, there is a way that *you* can save yourself a slow and painful death on the gallows.' He paused. 'Would you care to know how?'

Matthews stayed mute. The seconds ticked away. Holcroft was pierced by a sudden shaft of doubt: did this youngster seek martyrdom? Was he one of those whose faith was so strong that he truly had no fear of death? Or, indeed, one of those who welcomed it? Holcroft had met people like that before and, if this was one of that rare breed, he knew he was wasting his time here. He might as well go and pore over the dusty, leather-bound ledgers that made up the accounts of the White Tower and make Widdicombe and his cronies sweat for their petty pilfering.

Holcroft was not a cruel man; he did not wish this young fellow – thief though he surely was – to suffer. He stared steadily at Matthews and the look was returned.

He did not like to look directly at people, as a rule. But Holcroft forced himself to meet the young clerk's sad, steady gaze. He was about fifteen, Holcroft reckoned, maybe a year older, dark hair, sallow skin, poorly dressed, painfully malnourished and dirty beneath the bruises. Holcroft continued to watch him. The boy said nothing.

A long minute passed. *It's no use*, Holcroft thought. *He clearly wants to die, and I am not about to torture the answers out of him, even if that were in fact practicable.*

Holcroft straightened his spine, pushed back his stool, and began to rise . . .

'How?' said the prisoner.

Holcroft sat down again, very slowly. He looked at the prisoner. Counted to five in his head, to build the pressure. He said quietly, so quietly that the boy was forced to lean forward to catch his words: 'You might just possibly save yourself, John Matthews, by co-operating fully with me. By answering all my questions truthfully and without evasion or distortion. If you were to do that to my satisfaction, it may be that I could persuade Lord Dartmouth to commute your sentence to ten years' indentured servitude in the plantations. Transportation or death. You choose.'

Matthews surprised him by saying: '*Qui mori didicit, servire dedidicit.*'

As a child, Holcroft had picked up a good deal of Latin from his stern Presbyterian schoolmaster, a friend of his father's, who had also taught mathematics, grammar and rhetoric. He knew the tag: 'He who has learnt how to die has learnt how not to be a slave.' And indentured servitude was indeed a close cousin to slavery. Men and women thus condemned must labour for their masters without payment and many suffered appalling abuse at their hands. The only difference was that after ten years the indentured servant was freed, though few survived that long in the sickly heat of the West Indies. Still, it was better than being taken to the gallows.

'So you would choose death, then?' Holcroft said coolly, but inside he was shaken by the erudition displayed by the dirty skeleton of a boy in front of him.

Holcroft got up from the stool again.

'Wait, sir,' said Matthews. 'I do not truly wish to die. Do you swear, on your honour as a gentleman, that if I tell you all that I know, you will preserve my life?'

'I swear I will do everything in my power to help you; I will do everything I can to persuade Lord Dartmouth to commute your death sentence to transportation, that is, if you will answer my questions honestly. I cannot promise you any more.'

'It is enough, I think. Thank you. What do you wish to know?'

'You quoted Seneca to me just now. How come you to know Latin so well?'

'I was taught it at school.'

'I need full answers from you, John. Else I cannot help you. What school? Where? How did you afford it? I cannot believe that your family has much wealth.'

To Holcroft's surprise, the young man laughed. 'My mother is English; but she married a soldier of fortune from Genoa who came to live in London. But he died of a fever two years ago and she now lives in the Liberty of the Savoy, below the Strand. I went to the free school there, the school run by Father Palmer, for a few months before I was taken on here at the Tower. I was taught a little Latin there, your honour, which I found congenial and easy to master – it is not so very far away from my old dad's Genoese tongue.'

'This Father Palmer, he is a Jesuit?'

'He is a good man. A man of God.'

'That is not what I asked. He is a Catholic, yes, from the Society of Jesus?'

'The English and their obsession with religion – for you people a man who lives a good, decent Christian life, who selflessly helps the poor as Our Saviour taught us, who educates children for no reward, who tries to set them on the path to a better life, he *must* be a dirty criminal because he follows the True Faith.'

Holcroft kept silent for a while. He was pondering the phrase 'you people'. Did Matthews count himself a foreigner because of his father? Or did 'you people' mean Protestants or, more narrowly, Anglicans, members of the Church of England?

'Father Palmer must be a good Christian,' he said. 'You respect him, and revere him – rightly so – for his many good works.'

'I do.'

'And do you see much of him, these days? Since you have been employed here in the Tower on the far side of London.'

'I still live in the Liberty. I see him from time to time, walking in the streets.'

'Do you, perhaps, visit him at his home, or at your old school?'

'No, never. The school has many pupils, and I was there for only a few months before I was granted this position. I doubt Father Palmer has any recollection of me. I nod to him cordially, if we pass in the street, raise my hat politely, nothing more.'

'But he must be proud of you, surely. A poor local boy from his own school, who has become clerk in His Majesty's Ordnance. A plum post in the Tower of London, no less. I am sure he must be very pleased with your youthful success.'

'I doubt he remembers my name. Why should he know me, who merely attended a few of his classes, when he has so many other young souls in his charge?'

'So Father Palmer did not set you to steal the powder from the store? He did not instruct you to enter the magazine and fetch it for him – or for one of his friends?'

'No, of course not. Why would he do that? You, you *snake* . . . you are trying to make this into a plot, a conspiracy against that good man. It is not! I will not let you besmirch a true Christian and try to hang him with your vile lies and insinuations!'

Matthews was standing now, red-faced, shaking with anger. 'I will speak no more to you about Father Palmer nor about any other matter. I would rather hang!'

Holcroft lowered his head, he looked at his big hands, ignoring the threat of the angry boy standing over him and listening only to his words. He was not naturally skilled at this – the passion and poetry that resided in other men's hearts had always been something of a mystery to him. Yet he knew of his shortcomings and had trained himself, as far as it was possible, to listen to what men said and to test their words for truth or falsehood. To his ear, this was the voice of truth. The outrage was not false, so far as he could tell. This boy believed the Jesuit priest was innocent.

Holcroft looked up.

'Sit down, and calm yourself. Or I will see that you *do* hang. I have one more question for you before I go. Sit down, be quiet and listen to me.'

Holcroft waited. Eventually, Matthews subsided, and sat back down on the bed.

'Tell me then, John, *why* did you attempt to steal the keg of gunpowder from the magazine? Tell me truly and I will leave you here in peace, and do all I can for you with Lord Dartmouth at the court martial, as I have sworn on my honour to do.'

Matthews sat down, he took in a deep breath, then another. 'I behaved foolishly, nothing more. My sister fell gravely ill and I borrowed money to pay for a physician. I borrowed money from . . . some bad people in the Liberty. She soon died anyway, of the flux, but these people said I must pay them regardless and . . . and I cannot.'

'Who are these people – give me a name?'

Matthews hesitated.

'I need you to co-operate with me fully, John. Or I cannot help you.'

'They are very dangerous men, sir. If they knew I was naming them to you . . .'

Holcroft stared at him in silence.

'Their chief is called Patrick Maguire. He is . . . he is a kind of . . . kind of unofficial king of the Liberty. He has three brothers, they are very strong, violent . . .'

'Thank you. Go on, please. You needed to pay off Maguire and his brothers.'

'I saw that the door of the magazine was unlocked and unguarded and – God forgive me – I went in there to steal a keg. I thought I could sell it. There is an ale house, the Grapes, just off the Strand, a low place where the rank-riders all meet to drink. It is inside the Liberty so the law cannot touch them in there. I thought I could sell the black powder to these highwaymen and pay off my debt. That's all. A moment of madness, of foolishness, and it seems that I shall pay for it with my life.'

The boy buried his head in his hands and began to weep.

Chapter Eight

15 July 1685: Tower Hill, London

A square wooden platform surrounded on four sides by a rail had been built in the large open space a few hundred yards northwest of the grim walls of the Tower of London. The floorboards of the platform had been covered that morning with a thick layer of fresh yellow straw. By nine of the clock, the crowds were already gathered and multitudinous and the man who called himself Narrey, who thought that he was arriving in good time, had been unable to get his fine, gilt-trimmed carriage and six closer than fifty yards to the platform, and had been forced to climb on to the roof of his vehicle and sit with his legs dangling to get a proper view of the scaffold.

He had come to Tower Hill that morning to see the Duke of Monmouth meet his death. The man who would be king. The man who had raised his flag and beaten his drums and brought the men of the West Country to bloody ruin nine days ago on the field of Sedgemoor. The true King of England, James, second of that name, had not deigned to attend the execution of his rebellious nephew but Narrey had decided that it was his duty to witness the spectacle in order to measure the mood of the English populace, to determine what the citizens of London felt in their hearts for this Protestant pretender. There was some satisfaction in seeing a heretic rebel meet his well-deserved end, but Narrey took no pleasure at the sight of spilled royal blood. He was here to judge whether the English were ready to see the error of their ways.

It was a bizarre situation, Narrey reflected. England had an avowedly Catholic king, yet the vast majority of his subjects were Protestants. More importantly, the Houses of Parliament were almost entirely Anglican, both the Lords and the Commons. Indeed, Catholics and dissenting Protestants, Quakers and Baptists and the like, were not allowed by law to hold any positions of power in the kingdom – they could not be servants of the Crown, except by special royal dispensation, they could not be Members of Parliament, they could not be Justices of the Peace, they could not be officers in the Army, Navy or even the Ordnance. These positions were reserved solely for Anglicans. These laws, sometimes known as the Test Acts, had been passed in the previous reign and, while James might be very keen to overturn them now that he was on the throne, he did not have the power to do so. It was quite absurd, the Frenchman told himself. James might be King but in England the laws were made by their Parliament. And Parliament was resolutely anti-Catholic.

The Monmouth rebellion was a perfect demonstration of the deep religious divide between the King and his people. James Scott, the Protestant Duke of Monmouth, was the illegitimate son of King Charles II – although he maintained Charles had in fact married his mother, and so he was the legitimate heir as eldest son. Monmouth drew most of his support from those who feared Catholics, and for whom a Catholic King was an abomination. Many of his supporters believed or pretended to believe that Monmouth was the legitimate heir of King Charles, and thus should have been made monarch after his death in February this year, but the truth – as Narrey well knew – was that a large number of people in England, in Scotland, and even in Ireland, from the highest to the most humble, would back any Protestant man or woman with a half-credible claim to the throne as an alternative to James.

Well, God had surely punished those contumelious Catholic-haters. In just a few weeks, the rebellion had been utterly crushed by James and his well-trained troops, and hundreds of gibbets over Dorset, Somerset and Devon were adorned with the hanging bodies of the men and women who had dared to defy their rightful king. But had the brutal lesson been learnt? That is what Narrey wished to discover today. Were the embers of this foul Protestant rebellion finally stamped out?

A man selling hot gingerbreads walked in front of the carriage, pushing through the throng, crying his wares, and Narrey felt a twinge of hunger. He could smell the sweet cakes and their spices and his stomach growled; he had missed breakfast at the apartments of the French Embassy in the Palace of White Hall, where he and his servants had their lodgings, in order to bring the carriage across the city to this place in time for the execution. Although, of course, he had attended Mass in the private chapel before he left. He called down to the gingerbread man, and accepted a hot, sweet, sticky cake in exchange for a penny and, munching happily, he watched a group of men in black skull caps and white collars force their way through the crowds and clamber up on to the scaffold – four bishops, or what in this land passed for them. Prelates of the so-called Church of England. One of them even looked like a pirate chief, an elderly but muscular man with a patch covering a part of his face.

Now, he reckoned, it must be nearly ten of the clock – the appointed hour for the execution. He flicked open his gold watch – it was ten minutes before. The crowds had continued to swell and now with their combined weight they began to press in on the square scaffold platform. The air hummed with their voices, cheerful, robust, English voices, showing their excitement at the coming bloodletting.

A few hundred yards to the south of the platform, Narrey could see the battlements of the Tower of London, where the Duke was being kept prisoner. *And what was that?* The crowds parted for a moment and he glimpsed soldiers, redcoats. Two lines of uniformed musket-men jogging alongside a carriage painted blue and scarlet, the vehicle drawn by six horses, coming towards this place of death.

The carriage and the accompanying squad of soldiers came nearer, higher, climbing the hill – and now Narrey could see them clearly – the men in scarlet coats with yellow turn-backs and yellow mitre-shaped caps, clearing the way through the surging crowds of onlookers with their bayonet-plugged flintlocks. They drew up a dozen yards from the scaffold, creating a space in the centre of the crowd, a chain of armed men marking the perimeter. The carriage door opened and a slight, bareheaded young man in a golden coat stepped out, Monmouth himself, accompanied by a tall, strong-looking officer in a blue coat and a small black-clad Protestant priest.

Narrey's eye was drawn to the tall officer. He seemed somehow very familiar, the line of his broad shoulders, the unusual length of arm and leg . . . By the Virgin, it was him! It was Holcroft Blood.

Narrey took a moment to be sure. Yes, it was him. The man responsible for his recent humiliation. The traitor. The English spy. He was not mistaken this time.

He was, however, surprised by the surge of white-hot hatred in his belly and chest. Instinctively, he pulled the wide-brimmed hat lower over his eyes. He found he was breathing hard, panting almost. Calming himself, he leant forward and turned his head to the right, calling down to the man on the bench next to the driver.

'Guillaume, look who it is. The officer in blue on the scaffold.'

His factotum said nothing for a while. 'Is it truly him? He looks different.'

'It is him. I am sure of it.'

Well, well, Narrey thought. *Holcroft Blood in the blue coat of the Ordnance with a red officer's sash, commanding a guard of Royal Fusiliers from the Tower of London.*

Narrey watched as the redcoats formed a ring of men on the ground around the scaffold to keep the crowd at bay; he watched as Blood helped the Duke to mount the steps to the straw-covered wooden platform. He watched the Duke of Monmouth kneel and pray with his small black-clad priest and the four bishops.

The execution was about to take place.

Narrey had never set eyes on the Pretender before, although he had seen his likeness in several portraits. He was a very handsome fellow, he decided, if a little pale. It was a shame that such fine looks should be destroyed . . . He felt a sudden motion of the carriage, and clutched at the roof in near panic, but it was merely the press of men and women beneath him jostling each other and rocking the vehicle on its wheels. He glanced at Guillaume and the driver but both men seemed entranced by the unfolding drama. Then he heard a roaring sound all about him, like waves crashing on a beach. The English folk were shouting now, all of them, it seemed, and as if with one voice: 'Monmouth, Monmouth, Monmouth . . .'

The handsome young duke in the elegant golden coat got up from his prayers, smiled sadly and stepped forward towards the rail of the scaffold, a burly redcoat on either side of his frail form. The condemned Duke looked over the sea of shouting people. He raised his pale right hand in a calming motion and obediently the volume dropped. One man not far from the carriage called out: 'God bless our Protestant Duke!' Other voices echoed him.

They still love Monmouth, Narrey realised, *these stubborn English. Despite the rebellion's failure, they still love him.*

The crowd was shouting at random again, not just words of support for the little man on the scaffold now taking off his coat but also: 'Catholics all to Hell!' and 'Down with the Popish Prince!' even 'Death and damnation to the Whore of Rome!'

Narrey frowned. He had answered his own question about the loyalties of the London mob – even if he did not relish the answer. But there was no need for such blasphemy. These heretical folk were ignorant sheep – and like sheep who had been led astray, they could be herded by a firm shepherd back to the path of righteousness.

Narrey's eye was drawn by the axeman, a notorious fellow named Jack Ketch – a big man, hirsute, broad in the chest, with a vicious-looking short-handled axe hooked over one lump of a shoulder. He had not seen Ketch mount the platform but now the executioner was conferring with the Duke and Holcroft Blood in the centre of the scaffold. Narrey saw the glint of gold being slipped into his big hairy hand and the Duke was saying something to the man, smiling, urging him to strike cleanly.

Narrey leant forward and spoke quietly to Guillaume. 'When this business is over, I want you to make inquiries in the Tower,' he said. 'Discreetly, of course. But I want to know how Blood is occupying himself these days. Spread a little silver.'

'You want me to see to him?'

'No, don't touch him yet. Do nothing to draw attention to yourself – or to any of us. Just find out what you can about the man and report back to me tonight.'

Holcroft watched the crowds. They were too restive for his liking and a far larger number had congregated than he was expecting. Perhaps three or four thousand men, women and children in this open space north of the Tower, and more folk were crowded in the windows and on the roofs of the city, even hanging from the chimney stacks of the houses nearby. The gentry had brought their carriages and he could see half a dozen fine coaches with their rich owners standing or seated on the roofs. He listened to the words the mob chanted – universally in support of the man about to be executed and against the Catholic King who had ordered his public death.

Would the mob confine themselves to shouts and jeers? If there was trouble, a full-scale riot, his pathetic handful of Royal Fusiliers would be overrun in moments.

He put his hand instinctively on the officers' small-sword that hung at his left hip. He was reasonably competent with the weapon but it would be useless if things turned ugly. He hoped this whole grisly business could be accomplished quickly and with the minimum of fuss. He could see why nobody else had wanted this task and why it had been given to him as a punishment by Lord Dartmouth: quite apart from the unpleasantness of taking a man to his death, there was a real danger of being torn apart by an angry anti-Catholic mob.

The axeman Jack Ketch was an experienced man; Holcroft took comfort in that. He should do a quick, neat job and then they would whip the body and its head back into the carriage and he and the escort would return to the Tower as quickly as possible. With luck, once Monmouth was dead, the crowd would disperse peacefully.

James Scott, Duke of Monmouth, patted Jack Ketch on his meaty shoulder, walked to the rail and looked out at the sea of expectant faces. He raised one hand again, half acknowledgement of the crowd's love, half a final benediction for his followers. There was a sudden drop in the noise and the sound of urgent shushing, as neighbours quieted each other to hear the condemned man's final words.

'I shall say little,' the Duke said in a strong, carrying voice. 'For I come here not to speak but to die – to die as a Protestant in the Church of England!'

The crowd roared its approval, an ugly, menacing sound that crashed around the space like the war cry of an enormous, many-headed monster. Over it, Holcroft heard old Peter Mews, Bishop of Winchester – who was standing with three other bishops on the straw-strewn scaffold, and who had become something of a friend since the battery duel at Sedgemoor – shout out: 'You are no member of *my* church, sir!'

After a few last words with his own priest, Monmouth lay down in the straw and placed his neck on the scarred wooden block. He looked at Ketch and Holcroft heard him say: 'I hereby forgive you, my good man but, I do earnestly beg you, strike true. My servants shall give more gold if you do it quickly and well.'

Holcroft caught sight of Jack Ketch's face: it was pale and sweating, the stubbled cheek twitching slightly. It occurred to him that the executioner was more ill at ease than the man condemned to die. Was Ketch a secret follower of the Duke's? Did he fear that God would strike him dead for this gross act of *lèse majesté*?

Monmouth set his face down to the straw, his bare neck over the block; Ketch lifted the short axe high in the air, holding it with two hands. He looked at Holcroft for the sign, and the lieutenant nodded briskly. Ketch lifted the blade a little higher. A moment passed and nothing happened. The axeman seemed to be frozen. The crowd was quiet, not a whisper, not a murmur, awaiting the fatal blow.

'Strike man, strike, for the love of God!' Monmouth cried out at last.

And Ketch brought down the axe. Too fast. It was a poor stroke. The blade struck both the heavy wooden block and the Duke's neck at the same time. Blood flowed from a deep cut and Monmouth gave a shriek of pain. Ketch wrestled with the axe blade, which was now stuck fast into the wood. He put a boot on the block, struggled, cursing, and at last pulled the blade free from the grip of the timber.

Monmouth lifted his head from the wood. He turned and looked at Ketch with agony in his eyes. 'Have mercy man, for the Lord's sake. Strike true this time.' The blood from a long shallow cut under his jawline spilled down his neck, drenching the white linen chemise he wore. The crowd gave a drawn-out hiss of rage.

'Forgive me, sir,' mumbled Ketch. He lifted the axe once more. Monmouth placed his head back on the blood-smeared block. Holcroft could see that Ketch was badly shaken. The axe was wavering, vibrating in his hands like a fine ladies' fan. He brought it down again, a half-hearted blow, but Holcroft could hear the clunk of metal on bone. Monmouth gave out a terrible moan, clearly still alive and conscious.

'Again, man, do it again!' Holcroft shouted at the axeman, unable to control himself. Ketch was weeping now. He lofted the weapon, chopped down, but his eyes were filled with tears and his aim poor. The blade sank deep into the Duke's right shoulder. Bright blood bloomed on his white chemise. The victim screamed.

Ketch plucked the axe free and threw it to the straw-covered platform. 'I cannot do it,' he said, weeping. 'I cannot. My heart fails within me.'

Holcroft could hear the sound that the crowd was making change. The mob was now growling, loud and low, like a ravenous beast about to charge. He drew his small-sword, seized Ketch and placed the point against his neck. 'You will finish the job, man, finish it cleanly, or I will take your own life! I swear it.' Holcroft meant every word. Like the crowd, he was possessed by a terrible rage at the injustice of this botched task; he knew himself to be standing on the lip of actual murder.

'Spare me, sir, spare me,' Ketch was whimpering, tears running freely.

'Do your appointed task, and do it now or you will die!' Holcroft pressed the point of the blade into the fat under the man's jaw, a spot of red appeared, grew and a bead of blood trickled down his unshaven neck.

'Yes, sir,' Ketch was blubbering, 'yes, sir.'

'Give him to us,' one man shouted from below the platform. 'Give us Ketch and we'll show him how it ought to be done.'

'Throw that butchering wretch over the rail, soldier,' bellowed another.

But Ketch was burrowing in the straw for the short-handled axe. He found it and scrambled over on his knees to where Monmouth was still lying, neck on the block, covered in blood and moaning softly, appallingly. Holcroft could hear the victim saying over and over: 'God save me! Lord of Hosts save me! God save me now!'

Ketch got the axe up, held two-handed, and hacked down at the neck – and the blade found the flesh with a meaty *chunk!*

Yet Monmouth was still not dead, his left leg kicked out in response to the blow, scattering straw in the slight breeze. Bishop Mews stepped back a pace lest a flailing limb strike him. Ketch, still on his knees, still blubbering, swung and hacked again and this time, at last, he struck true. The head was hanging by no more than a scrap of tissue and skin, the blood pumping out on to the straw. Ketch released the axe and rolled away, knees pulled up into his belly, bawling like a child.

The crowd was shouting with rage; Holcroft could feel the surging crowd crash into the platform, the wooden scaffold was shifting and groaning beneath Holcroft's feet, the fusiliers on the ground pinned against the structure, unable to move. He saw a big, bald man in a leather jerkin, with a long unsheathed knife in his belt, was beginning to climb up the side of the scaffold. There was a line of white spittle at his mouth, which gnashed and worked silently – he seemed to be in the grip of a powerful and possibly murderous fit. A hundred other hands were grasping the rail, shaking it. From somewhere in the crowd, a musket shot rang out.

The bishops and clergy were huddled together, looking terrified. All except the Bishop of Winchester, who had his fists clenched, lifted and cocked, a bandage showing snow white on his left forearm. Bishop Mews was glaring at the madman, now in the act of climbing over the rail to come at them. Holcroft pulled the pistol from his silk sash with his left hand. He cocked the loaded weapon awkwardly, his right hand still gripping the sword, aimed the pistol at the bald man and without the slightest hesitation shot him in the centre of his red, screaming face, the heavy body flipping backwards over the rail with the punch of the bullet and disappearing into the crush of the mob. Holcroft shoved the pistol back into his sash, stepped over to the nearly headless body of the Duke, bent, and with the sharp sword, he cut through the last scrap of flesh and skin, seized the head behind the ears, his big hand encompassing it easily. Walking over to the rail, he lifted the bloody trophy high.

'Monmouth is no more,' he bawled, shaking the gory poll at the crowd. 'The Protestant Duke is dead! May God grant that he now rest for ever in peace.'

Strangely, this one atavistic gesture seemed to calm the crowd. The big man with a bloody sword in one hand and a severed head in the other was an extremely sobering sight. The mob gave out a long deep moan, a cry of scouring grief. Holcroft hefted the head a little higher so that all might see it. He shook it. It was surprisingly heavy. Warm fluid began trickling down his left arm inside his sleeve. Some people directly below him began to sob and weep. Others shouted out: 'God bless King Monmouth!' and 'May the Good Lord take our Duke to his bosom!'

Holcroft looked sideways at the victim's head that he held aloft. And to his horror, he saw the eyes in that blood-spattered poll move, both orbs sliding round towards him and seeming to regard him with a deep suspicion.

Chapter Nine

17 July 1685: Palace of White Hall

Holcroft sipped at the yellowish wine in the fine crystal goblet. The bubbles in the glass tickled his nose and he stifled the urge to sneeze. This was the wine of the French region of Champagne, he knew, and the fashionable new drink in the best London circles. But he wondered at the bubbles of gas that crawled up the inside of the delicate glass. Could it have gone bad? He had never had wine before that fizzed like this, even in all his years in France; it looked like half-fermented cider. It seemed unlikely they would serve bad wine at such a gathering. But Holcroft knew little of wine, he liked brandy when he wanted to drink properly, and ale on other occasions.

He had had no choice in the matter, the glass had been pressed into his hand when he arrived a quarter of an hour ago by his host Jack Churchill, who had then been whisked away by a gang of revellers to dance. He knew the wine was very dear and supposed he ought to make the effort to enjoy it. For Jack's sake.

He looked about him at the other men and women who had spilled out the old Cockpit Theatre to take a break from their exertions on the dance floor, and who were enjoying the fresh cool breezes of St James's Park outside the flung-open doors.

On the wide swathe of green, freshly scythed grass, tables had been spread with crisp white cloths, and set with food and drink, jellies and hams, fruits and cheeses, pies and roast capons. Liveried servants passed among the throng with trays laden with glasses of this odd Champagne wine and Holcroft wondered if he dared to ask one of the footmen he knew slightly – a fellow called

George – for a brandy. He was feeling nervous and uncomfortable in this merry throng. As he always did in strange company. But instead of demanding brandy he opened his throat and threw down the rest of the pale fizzy wine in one gulp.

He knew a few of the faces, officers from the Ordnance and other branches of the military. But there was no one he wished to speak to this evening. His eye fell on the high, octagonal building of timber and brick that gave this part of the King's palace of White Hall its name. The Cockpit was a collection of apartments at the western edge of the royal precinct, and he knew the place well. He had served as a page here for some months in the household of the Duke of Buckingham, when that nobleman had been in favour with King Charles. Its warren of corridors, kitchens, chambers and grand halls were imprinted on his memory.

The Duke of Buckingham's old apartments were now occupied by Princess Anne, the King's second daughter who, unlike her father, was a staunch Protestant. Sarah Churchill, the young princess's intimate friend, along with her husband Jack, had been allocated lavish chambers here, too, at Anne's insistence. And Jack was hosting this ball, two days after the botched execution on Tower Hill, to celebrate the death of the Duke of Monmouth and the end of the rebellion. Jack had implored Holcroft to attend the event and when he demurred, Jack said: 'How can you expect to rise in the world if you will not make connections who can help you?'

Lord Churchill and his pretty wife were at the centre of a laughing group of gorgeously dressed people; the men mostly in military coats, which were adorned with so much lace and silver braid that the scarlet cloth could scarcely be seen; the women even more in brilliant silks and taffeta gowns of every colour of the rainbow.

Holcroft suspected that he looked drab in his big blue Ordnance coat but he found it comforting to always wear the same clothes. It saved having to make any decisions about what to put on in the morning. The coat was not dirty; he brushed it carefully every night, exactly a hundred strokes of the clothes' brush, and hung it up in the wardrobe in his pokey suite of rooms in the Inner Ward of the Tower.

He had not bothered to wear his new periwig, a gift from Sarah Churchill; something she had commented on playfully when she and Jack had greeted him.

Jack's wife had taken an instant dislike to Holcroft from their very first meeting. He was too odd, too unworldly, too unambitious for her tastes. He always saw things only in black and white; for her the world was a range of fascinating shades of grey. She felt he was not the kind of man who could advance either her or her husband's interests and she resented, and could not understand, Jack's sentimentality about their long friendship. However, she was wise enough never to express openly her dislike of Holcroft Blood. She found other ways to make her antipathy apparent.

The periwig that Sarah had given him was absurdly expensive but it was also very heavy, it scratched his scalp most irritatingly and made his head exceedingly hot and sweaty – he was almost certain that Lady Churchill knew this and that the gift was unkindly meant. He could not see the point of wigs, anyway, when he possessed his own long, thick brown hair, neatly tied at the back of his neck with a green ribbon. But in this elegant, glittering, rainbow gathering Holcroft wondered if he ought not to have borne the discomfort and just worn the damn thing.

He plucked another glass from the tray of a passing footman. He would drink this down and then go home to the Tower. There was the report on the proofing of the most recently cast twenty-four-pounder that he wanted to look at. The huge gun had exploded in the testing at the Whitechapel proof-house some weeks before, unfortunately killing one of the engineers and maiming two matrosses who had been assisting the officer, and Holcroft wanted to go over the composition of the molten bronze in the cast again. Too much arsenic in the copper – tin mix, he suspected.

'Holcroft, Holcroft, come join us!' Jack was waving at him.

Holcroft mustered a smile and walked over to the gaudy, wine-flushed, chattering crowd around the victorious major-general.

'You know, of course, His Excellency Monsieur Barillon d'Amon-court, Marquis de Branges, the Ambassador of His Most Christian Majesty Louis XIV,' said Jack in excellent French, indicating a squat, powerful man with a bulldog's square head, scowling from under an enormous glossy black periwig.

Holcroft made his bow.

'I'm sure you must have encountered Monsieur Perigourd, the Comte de Maligny, First Secretary in the French Embassy and His Excellency Monsieur l'Ambassador's right-hand man.' This was a tall, dark-haired man, slim as a reed, elegantly dressed, with a faint but friendly smile on his strikingly handsome face.

'And the French military attaché, Major du Clos.' A muscular, brisk-looking fellow in an impeccable white uniform stared at him from the Ambassador's right, eyeing him from his wigless head, via his shabby blue Ordnance coat to the cheap silver-plated buckles on his worn shoes. The military attaché's eyes, Holcroft noticed, were dark brown, almost black, and curiously lifeless.

'Gentlemen, this is Lieutenant Blood of the Ordnance,' said Jack, managing to sound as if he were introducing a personage as great as the Emperor of China.

'Enchanted, Lieutenant,' said Barillon. The Ambassador inclined his ugly head.

'I am delighted to meet you too, sir,' said the Comte de Maligny, his blue eyes twinkling. 'But tell me, sir, your face seems familiar, have we perhaps met before?'

Holcroft shook his head. 'I do not believe so, Monsieur,' he replied in French.

'Deeply honoured,' muttered du Clos, without the faintest hint of sincerity.

'I was just telling the Ambassador of your extraordinary gunnery exploits at the Battle of Sedgemoor,' said Jack, smiling at his friend. 'The Duel in the Darkness.'

Holcroft smiled grimly and nodded, unable to think of anything to say.

'A most notable feat of arms,' said Maligny, shaking his head with respect. 'I salute your valour, sir. And skill. To destroy an enemy without the benefit of light.'

The other two French diplomats stared at Holcroft but said nothing.

Holcroft looked at his own shoes. *What was he supposed to say to these people?*

'Blood?' said the Comte de Maligny, after a long pause. 'There was a Blood, an Englishman, in our *Corps Royal de l'Artillerie*. Perhaps a relative, Monsieur?'

Holcroft found his tongue. 'That was I, sir. I had the honour of serving His Most Christian Majesty for a number of years.'

Maligny was beaming at him now like a long-lost nephew. 'I'm sure the honour was all ours,' he said. 'Why our Major du Clos, here, is an artilleryman just like you, sir. You must have many acquaintances in common in France. Perhaps you should meet up one day and compare notes on the mysterious arts of modern gunnery.'

Holcroft looked at Major du Clos. 'You served in the *Corps*, Monsieur?'

The French officer looked blankly at him. 'I trained at the *Corps* artillery school in Douai – but of late I have been detached on special duties for His Majesty.'

Holcroft felt a touch of unease at the man's cold expression. His round face was vaguely familiar. He felt that they might have met at some point but he could not remember the details of the encounter. 'It is an excellent school. I trained there myself for two years,' Holcroft said. 'I learnt a great deal in my time at Douai.'

Du Clos said nothing. He observed Holcroft with his curiously blank eyes.

There was another awkward silence.

'Let us have some more Champagne,' said Jack. 'George, bring that tray . . .'

'And now you serve the famous Board of Ordnance, Lieutenant Blood,' said Maligny – with a little forced jollity in his voice – 'and are clearly distinguishing yourself in King James's service. What a loss to French arms, sir, when you returned to your native land. Although I must congratulate His Majesty in his good fortune in securing your loyalty!' Maligny lifted his glass. 'I drink to your future success.'

'We all feel very honoured that dear Holcroft has returned to us,' said Sarah Churchill, arriving suddenly into the circle of men and putting a proprietary hand on her husband's arm. 'My Jack is quite enamoured of our lieutenant's skill with ordnance. Alas, though, I do not share his passion for gunnery. I find cannon to be ugly, cumbersome things, and their discharging to be appallingly noisy and smelly; indeed, I blush to tell you, but I secretly think them rather vulgar. I much prefer the cavalry, with their dash and style, oh, and those gorgeous uniforms! But then I am a mere weak and silly woman who knows very little of your manly military affairs.'

Major du Clos stared at Sarah as if she were a madwoman on the loose. But the Comte de Maligny began making noises to the effect that no, no, this was a perfectly reasonable opinion, why, he was a cavalryman himself; besides, it was his belief that such an exquisitely beautiful hostess could not possibly be wrong about anything.

Blood held his tongue. He knew better than to rise to Sarah's jibes.

'Holcroft? Holcroft Blood, is that really you?' An immaculately dressed young gentleman in a full suit of virulent lime green, with a froth of impeccable white lace at collar and cuff, sheer ivory stockings and emerald shoes with a three-inch heel, had eased past the three French diplomats and stood before him. 'And to meet you again here, of all places, in the Cockpit, our old playground! What a joy to see you again!'

Holcroft looked at the slim, absurdly foppish young man. Under a towering orange wig, a set of light brown eyes and sharp, fox-like features were aimed at him.

'Is it . . . is it Henri? Henri d'Erloncourt? How . . . how extraordinary.'

The young man, glowing with happiness, was heartily shaking Holcroft's hand, and speaking in almost faultless English. 'How do you do, sir? How *do* you do?'

Holcroft admitted that he was well but, privately, he was thrown off balance to suddenly meet someone fully grown that he had only known as a small child.

But Henri d'Erloncourt was chattering away to Jack and Sarah Churchill and the Ambassador and his entourage: '. . . of course, Lieutenant Blood and I were pages together in the Duke of Buckingham's employ, in this very place, the Cockpit, which of course the Duke had then, oh it must be nearly fifteen years ago, such happy times. And the games and shenanigans we got up to. You remember old Matlock, and the ferocious beatings he gave us, and poor old Robert Westbury, who disappeared so suddenly. Do you remember? And that marvellous game of whist that you played with the Duke of Buckingham, when you mulcted him of ten thousand pounds – with Lord Churchill, too, of course, as your partner. A famous victory at the tables! How that made our old master growl, we caught hell for months after that, I tell you . . .'

Holcroft remembered Henri d'Erloncourt, nicknamed Fox Cub, as a frightened weakling of a boy, completely at sea in a foreign land, caught up in the powerful currents, political, financial and sexual, of King Charles's decadent White Hall court.

'Have you seen our dear old Duke recently, Holcroft – you don't mind if I call you Holcroft, do you? Since we are old friends . . .'

'I believe he has retired permanently to his estates in Yorkshire,' Holcroft said. 'I understand his health is failing.'

'Ah, it must come to us all, I suppose. But he was a great man in his day, a truly great man. So wise. So very kind. I learnt an enormous amount from him . . .'

To Holcroft's relief, d'Erloncourt's witterings were interrupted by a trumpet blast and a footman bawling: 'My lords, ladies, gentlemen, His Majesty the King.'

James Stuart, second of that name, by the grace of God King of England, Scotland and Ireland, a tall, austere man, regal in crimson and ermine robes, stalked out of the double doors of the Cockpit Theatre amid a cloud of ministers, flunkies and hangers-on. He paused to accept the bows of the crowd with a cool nod and a cordial smile for Lady Churchill, who gave him the most elegant of curtseys.

Lord and Lady Churchill moved forward to greet the King. But Holcroft had no such ambition and began to look around for George the footman and his tray of fizzy wine. The Champagne was growing in his favour. It was, in fact, quite palatable. He beckoned the man over and exchanged his empty glass for a full one and found himself beside Captain Glanville of the Ordnance, who was also availing himself of the same. Glanville managed a barely civil nod. His face was flushed and angry: 'Blood,' he muttered, and turned away to look at the King. 'See you managed to make a God-damned mess of the execution,' he said out of the side of his mouth.

Before Holcroft could say anything he found Henri d'Erloncourt addressing him: 'My dear fellow, you simply must tell me what you have been doing these past fifteen years. I understand that you have been in France. If only I had known, I could surely have opened some doors for you. I have some excellent connections at Versailles. You must let me know if I can write some letters of introduction for you.'

'I am no longer in France, Henri. And I do not plan to return.'

'And so what are you doing now?'

'I serve Lord Dartmouth of the Board of Ordnance at the Tower.'

'How marvellous! Here in London. We must dine together. Shall we set a date?'

'No,' said Holcroft. Then, more politely. 'No, but I thank you.'

'But you simply must dine with me, I'm residing with the Ambassador here in White Hall and he has the most marvellous *chef de cuisine*. An absolute genius in the fine arts of the table. Say you will dine with me, old friend – say you will, and soon.'

'I will not say it. I do not want to have dinner with you.'

Henri d'Erloncourt stared at him, his mouth slightly open in surprise. He looked for a moment like the little boy Holcroft had known all those years ago, as if he would burst into tears at any moment. Holcroft suddenly became aware that what he had said might have been considered rude. Over the course of his life many people, people he liked and trusted, had told him that when he answered questions with complete honestly he sometimes offended people. He was trying hard to improve his behaviour. To be more like ordinary people. To lie.

'What I meant, Henri, is that, alas, I am kept very busy. I'm not sure that—'

'I cannot believe that the Ordnance keeps you at it all day every day. You must have time to eat, my dear fellow.'

Captain Glanville, who had overheard the remark, gave a kind of scoffing laugh.

'May I introduce Captain William Glanville, also of the Board of Ordnance?' Holcroft said, in an attempt to distract Henri from his persistent dinner invitations.

'Captain Glanville, this is Henri d'Erloncourt, a member of His Excellency the Ambassador Monsieur Barillion's establishment in England.'

Henri laughed. 'I am not so honoured, my dear Holcroft. His Excellency' – and Henri flopped a languid hand towards the diplomatic trio of Barillion, Maligny and du Clos, who were standing a few paces away with their backs turned watching the circus of courtiers, sycophants and petitioners around the King – 'is merely kind enough to offer me his hospitality as a guest when I have the opportunity to admire your beautiful country. But Captain Glanville, if you are also member of His Majesty's Ordnance, surely you can persuade our friend Holcroft to dine with me. He cannot be so terribly busy that he must forgo sustenance. I simply do not believe it.'

'Oh, we keep him busy enough with *menial* chores, my dear Monsieur,' said Glanville. 'The sort of things that gentlemen to not care to sully their hands with.'

Holcroft bristled. This was a clear insult. It was enough to warrant a challenge, if he chose to take offence. But did he? Lord Dartmouth had been quite explicit in his orders: he was not to quarrel with Glanville. He clamped his teeth and said nothing.

'At present, he is employed as a sort of grubby thief-taker,' said Glanville, chuckling. 'Making inquiries into popish plots. I hear he's been questioning a Catholic rogue called Matthews from the Liberty of the Savoy, who was caught red-handed stealing black powder from the stores. Though this one is no Catesby. That's for sure. However, it is most fitting – ha-ha-ha – and I'm sure you will agree, Monsieur – ha-ha-ha – that the son of a notorious thief should himself become a thief-taker. Sins of the Father, eh? Ha-ha-ha!'

Holcroft hit him.

It was a lovely, round, right-handed punch with the full weight of Holcroft's thickly muscled shoulder behind it, which smashed into Glanville's big laughing mouth, lifted him off his feet and hurled him sprawling to the close-cropped grass.

Glanville looked up from the lawn, dazed, blood oozing from between his teeth. He shook his head. 'I shall have satisfaction for that cowardly blow,' he said thickly.

The Ambassador and his colleagues, who had been listening to the exchange, were now gazing open-mouthed at Holcroft and his enemy sprawled on the grass.

'I am at your service, whenever you should require it of me,' said Holcroft.

'And I shall stand as his second,' said Henri d'Erloncourt loyally. 'It was a gross insult – one no gentleman could swallow who wished to keep his honour.'

Captain Glanville got slowly to his feet. He wiped the blood off his chin and looked at Henri. 'My second shall call on you, Monsieur, at the Embassy, to arrange a time and place for a meeting. Goodman's Fields is the usual spot.'

He swung around and glared at Holcroft. 'And you, sir, I shall gladly kill.'

Chapter Ten

18 July 1685: Tower of London and Hyde Park

'In front of the King? In the presence of the French Ambassador? You start a brawl at a party and accept a challenge to a duel – what in God's name were you thinking?'

Holcroft stood to attention before Lord Dartmouth's desk, feeling very low.

'He called my father a thief, sir, I could not allow—'

'Your father *was* a thief! Do you deny it? He made a desperate attempt to steal the King's Jewels not fifty paces from where we are now. Are you going to challenge me for saying that? Will you now fight *me*?'

Holcroft had rarely seen his commander so angry. Lord Dartmouth's face was almost purple with rage. And Holcroft knew that he was right. He had behaved with a stupid childlike impulsiveness, giving in to rage without a thought for anything else.

'And not five days ago I gave you an order to mend your stupid quarrel with Captain Glanville? Have you forgotten that? Or did you decide to ignore my orders as you have so many others? I do not know what to do with you, Mister Blood.'

Holcroft said nothing.

'I shall tell you what I am going to do. I am going to give you an order, a direct order right now. And if you do not swear to obey me, you are finished here. I shall have you discharged from the Ordnance without pay or references and with a recommendation to the King that you are not given a place in any of his forces, nor in any position over which he has authority. You can take yourself back to

France – or to wherever, as you please. So, tell me, Mister Blood, do you swear to obey my order?'

'Yes, sir.'

'Very well, you will humbly beg Captain Glanville's pardon for attacking him. You will tell him that you are thoroughly ashamed of your actions and that you offer your most heartfelt apology. I have already spoken to the Captain and he says he will accept your apology and we will hear no more of this nonsense about a duel.'

Lord Dartmouth gave Holcroft no time to think. He bawled at the redcoat on the door to admit the next visitor, and Captain Glanville came marching smartly into the room, boots crashing on the polished wooden floor, and snapped to attention.

'Captain Glanville,' the Master-General snapped. 'Lieutenant Blood has something he would very much like to say to you.'

Holcroft felt like a naughty child. His face flushed a deep red.

'I have this to say. Fuck you – fuck the both of you. Fuck you and your insults, Glanville. And I will be delighted to gut you like a fish at your earliest convenience. And fuck you, sir, with your sanctimonious horseshit about obeying absurd orders. I'm going to fight Captain Glanville. In fact, I'm going to kill the son of a bitch.'

There was silence in the room. Then Holcroft realised that, mercifully, he had not spoken these words aloud.

'Well, Mister Blood, what do you have to say to Captain Glanville?'

Expulsion from the Ordnance. Disgrace. No prospect of any future employment. Holcroft took a deep breath. Let it out.

'I crave your pardon, Captain. I had taken too much Champagne wine and I apologise for striking you in that ungentlemanly manner. I beg your forgiveness.'

Glanville was smirking. Holcroft could see the bruising around his blubbery mouth from last night's blow and he had the urge to add to the marks there.

'Well, what do you say, Captain?' Lord Dartmouth's tone was stern.

'Oh well, I accept, I suppose – at your command, sir. It was an ungentlemanly, sneaking blow worthy of a gutter brawler but *I* am gentleman enough to forgive you.'

'Very well, that will be all. Lieutenant Blood – I do not wish to see your face for the rest of today. You will absent yourself until my temper is restored. Dismissed.'

Blood turned on his heel, veins running with fire, and marched from the room.

The two horses were rented from a riding stables near Tyburn, a fashionable, expensive establishment within sight of the three-sided gibbet where London's criminals were routinely hanged. With a little forethought, Holcroft could have borrowed a pair of mounts from the Tower stables but, unusually for him, he did not begrudge the sizeable sum of money outlaid. The rented horses were magnificent: his animal a full eighteen hands of glossy black Arab stallion, and his consort's bay mare only a little less splendid. His companion, too, looked stunning that afternoon, and the sight of her on horseback, in a gleaming grey silk dress, high buttoned riding boots with a pert grey riding bonnet on her golden curls, soothed his turbulent heart.

Holcroft had stormed out of the Tower precincts in a fury that morning after the humiliating scene with Glanville and Dartmouth and found himself striding through the streets of London, hat pulled low, a grim expression on his face, cutting a channel through the city populace like a pike through a fish pond, citizens stepping smartly aside from the big man's arrow-straight path. He had walked, angry and aimless, for more than an hour heading west, aiming vaguely for Drury Lane and Aphra's grubby whorehouse, but had found himself in Holborn, at the junction with Gray's Inn Lane.

He had stopped, gathered his wits for a moment or two, and changed his mind. He knew that he leant too much on Aphra when things in his world were not going well. He did not want to whine at her again about the unfairness of his treatment by Lord Dartmouth – her career as a playwright was in the doldrums, she was near penniless and in poor health, and yet she never complained to him about her lot. He decided, instead, on a whim, to pay a visit to another lady of his acquaintance.

One with whom he was considering marriage.

Elizabeth Fowler was a young widow, the daughter of a barrister of Gray's Inn named Richard King. She was quite lovely, everyone agreed – a tall, fine-featured, peaches-and-cream blonde – and, while her father was not very rich, he was prosperous enough not to require financial support from a prospective son-in-law.

Holcroft knocked at the door of the large house in Gray's Inn Lane and a few minutes later he went out to find a Hackney coach to take the lady – without a chaperone, but with Richard King's blessing, since she was a widow of twenty-seven years and they'd be in public – to Hyde Park for an afternoon's ride in the sunshine.

Elizabeth rode well, appearing perfectly at ease in the sidesaddle. As they trotted, cantered then finally walked together along a track by a line of elegant elms along the northern edge of the park, he admired her straight spine, perfectly in line with the mare's, and the skill with which she controlled her mount. He also enjoyed her loud, cheerful talk, which reminded him of Aphra's loquacity when she had been at the brandy, and the fact that he could hear her clearly despite the stiff breeze that was shunting a flock of fleecy clouds across an otherwise blameless blue sky.

'. . . of course, we always spend Christmas at Biddulph Hall. That's my cousin Sir Richard Biddulph's place, wonderful old pile in Staffordshire, knocked about a bit during the late wars, of course, but always a warm welcome to be found there.'

Hyde Park was well populated that Saturday afternoon, the warm summer sunshine drawing out riders and pedestrians in equal numbers. It was the fashionable place to see and be seen – Sarah Churchill, who knew about such things, had once told him – at least in daylight hours. Gentlemen in bright coats and extravagantly plumed hats paraded with their rainbow-clad ladies; society mamas with pretty young daughters trotted in open-topped carriages along grassy, rutted tracks, hoping to catch the eye of dashing cavalry officers who passed them while out exercising their mounts. Parties had gathered in the sunshine, chattering, eating, drinking on blankets spread on the grass.

At nighttime, Hyde Park was another place entirely. In darkness it became the haunt of highwaymen and six-penny whores, footpads, outlaws, dissenting ministers and all manner of ne'er-do-wells who did their business when honest folk were abed.

'Such fun and games during the Twelve Days,' Elizabeth was still telling him about her aristocratic cousin in Staffordshire. 'The only drawback is that Lady Biddulph makes us all attend Mass in the chapel, supposed to be a secret, of course, but everybody knows she's an old stick-in-the-mud, loves her smells and bells . . .'

She raised and lowered her eyebrows at Holcroft in a comic manner. Holcroft was not sure if she had made a joke. He could see nothing amusing about attending a forbidden Catholic rite. He smiled at her anyway, in case she'd said something funny.

He had known, naturally, that she was from a Catholic family. He even knew that her brother was a Catholic priest, who lived in exile in France at the moment, and who used the false name Fitton when he was in England. Aphra had given him that particular piece of information. But Holcroft cared nothing for the idiosyncrasies of people's religious beliefs – nor very much for the names they adopted. His father had used a bewildering array of aliases during his lifetime. And he had himself used the false name of Leture, on occasion, when engaged in his covert activities in France.

Elizabeth's father, who was most desirous of a match for his eldest daughter, had sworn to Holcroft that all the King family now regularly attended Church of England services as they were required to by law. And to soothe any remaining qualms he might have about her religious background, he assured Holcroft that if Elizabeth were ever to marry again, she would do so in an Anglican service, as she had done when she married Captain Fowler, a handsome but penniless and avowedly Protestant naval gentleman who'd been killed in a duel two years ago in Flanders.

'I took Captain Fowler to Biddulph Hall one year – and he did not approve of the goings on there at all. Said the family was riddled with superstition and idolatry.'

She paused, and looked archly at him over her shiny grey silk shoulder.

Holcroft recognised that he was obliged to make some comment or other at this point, and managed to come up with: 'Indeed? Did he? How extraordinary!'

'But then Jane Pertwee always said the Captain was the most dreadful bigot.'

Jane was Elizabeth's closest friend, and as Elizabeth launched into a story about an importunate gentleman caller who was pestering Jane's pretty second cousin who lived in Manchester, Holcroft stopped paying attention to her exuberant prattle and gave himself up to admiring her lovely face and graceful figure. He liked the fact that she spoke so freely, with such a refreshing lack of restraint; she evidently did not often require much in the way of a response from him and, as he had almost no small talk, and no interest in acquiring any, when he was with her he felt relieved of the great burden of having to make conversation. He wondered what it would be like to be married to her. She did seem an eminently suitable candidate.

On returning from France, Holcroft had decided that he should marry as soon as possible, a decision driven in part by the craving he felt to have order in his life. He wanted to be conventional. He desperately wanted to lead a normal life. He hated change and surprises, and his greatest fear was that his life would one day collapse into a meaningless swamp of chaos. Marriage would anchor him securely to the world, and it would be pleasant, he was sure, to have his own household where he could arrange things just so, to have meals at regular times, and have the same familiar faces around him every day – and, finally, to be able to put aside the untidy, unpredictable, semi-nomadic life that he had endured for so long as a bachelor.

Accordingly he had looked around at his tiny circle of family, friends and acquaintances in England for help in finding a mate and it had been his youngest brother Charles, now all grown up and a barrister at Gray's Inn, who had introduced him to his colleague Richard King and his beautiful widowed daughter Elizabeth.

Holcroft had taken tea with the King family in Gray's Inn Lane twice and had escorted Elizabeth to the theatre once – with Mistress King joining them – to see a new production of *Macbeth*, for which Aphra Behn had helped to make the costumes.

At supper afterwards, Aphra and Elizabeth discovered that they loathed each other but masked their animosity with extravagant pleasantries. Holcroft failed to notice anything amiss at all. He had taken Elizabeth to dinner in the Cockpit with Jack and Sarah a few weeks after that, and Elizabeth had been nervous and rather over-awed to meet the couple who were so much at the heart of Princess Anne's glittering society. The dinner had been rather dull, Elizabeth for once subdued and demure, fearful of offending such an elevated couple, and even though Sarah and Jack kept the conversation spinning merrily along, Holcroft was aware as they drove away in the carriage afterwards that it had not been a thundering success.

He had dined once at Richard King's house – and Holcroft noted that in contrast to the Cockpit dinner, in that safe familiar setting her voice took on a rather carrying, nautical quality as she called to him down the length of the table. Afterwards, the two of them alone for ten minutes in the parlour while they drank their coffee, he had held Elizabeth's large moist hand and, at her urging, had kissed her briefly on the lips.

He was aware that some men enjoyed powerful emotions while kissing their lady-loves. Holcroft did not – but neither was he troubled by their lack: Elizabeth fulfilled all the criteria he had for a satisfactory spouse. And that was enough for him.

'She will make an excellent wife,' he remarked to Jack, as they had set off for the West Country on campaign a week or so after that kiss. 'She's pretty, strong and clean in her habits; she does not smell. And has hips suitable for bearing children.'

The anecdote about Jane Pertwee's second cousin's persistent admirer was not yet done and Holcroft happened to glance behind him and saw that there were two men on horseback approaching fast at the canter. He put a hand on Elizabeth's bridle and reined in himself, coming in to the side of the track they were on, to allow the other riders to pass by. But, to his surprise, instead of cantering on past them. The two horsemen also reined in. The nearer man was slightly breathless, clearly a gentleman, in a fine deep-blue coat embroidered with silver lacework, a slim small-sword, scarlet silk stockings and, under his black, gold-trimmed three-cornered hat, a silky, cascading, honey-coloured periwig that hung almost to his expensive saddle.

The gentleman touched his tricorn in silent salute and Holcroft realised that he recognised the man: it was the Comte de Maligny, the smooth French diplomat that he had met the day before at the disastrous party at the Cockpit.

Holcroft inclined his head and said: 'Good day, Monsieur.'

The comte nodded back, still too breathless to speak.

The second rider was a much rougher article, a muscle-bound type bursting out of a raggedy red coat with grey facings, with a scarlet cap trimmed with greasy brown fur on his big round head. A large white scar was cut into the left side of his face, giving him a menacing air, which was enhanced by the heavy cavalry sabre hanging from his belt, and the pair of horse pistols on either side of the horse's withers. He was too heavily armed, to Holcroft's eye, for a simple ride in the park.

Holcroft looked around him. There were no other people in sight. This part of the park seemed to be deserted and Holcroft was uncomfortably aware that the sun was beginning to sink behind the trees. Hyde Park was not a place to linger after dark. He suddenly felt the hair on the back of his neck rising. Some deep instinct was warning him that there was danger here. He put a hand on the butt of the big pistol that was shoved in the red sash around his middle. It was a Lorenzoni repeating flintlock pistol, sold to him in Paris by an impoverished Italian gentleman of fortune. Since his conversation with Aphra about Narrey's presence in London he had decided not to venture abroad without it, along with his usual officer's small-sword, a straight thirty-inch blade that always hung from a baldrick at his left-hand side.

The muscular man in the scarlet cap saw Holcroft's hand touch the pistol butt and his own brown hand leapt to the hilt of his sabre, half drawing the shiny blade.

'Lieutenant Blood, what a signal pleasure it is to encounter you again,' said the Comte de Maligny, smiling. He glanced left and right, then turned to the man in the scarlet cap, who miraculously had a naked length of curved steel in his hand. 'Put that away, man,' he snapped in French. 'This instant. We are among friends here.'

He turned back to Holcroft: 'How are you, my dear sir? Well, I hope. In the very pink of health, I am sure.'

Holcroft allowed that there was nothing wrong with his health.

'And I trust that matters between you and the other . . . the other gentleman of the Ordnance,' here the comte gave Holcroft a manly, sympathetic frown, 'have all been satisfactorily arranged? A discreet dawn meeting, perhaps?'

Holcroft said nothing. He looked beyond the two mounted Frenchmen and saw that a party of horsemen, four junior officers of Oxford's Blues, were fifty yards away approaching down the track, one of whom, Captain Redmond, he knew slightly.

'Are you not going to introduce me to the gentleman, Holcroft?' said Elizabeth.

He looked over at the slim, handsome French aristocrat. 'My dear,' he said, 'this is the Comte de Maligny, a secretary belonging to the French Embassy, whom I met yesterday at the Cockpit, and this is his, ah, friend . . .' Holcroft kept one eye on Scarlet Cap, even though he had instantly sheathed his sword at Maligny's command.

'Never mind about *him*,' said the Comte. 'What a joy it is to meet *you*, my dear young lady,' he said, eyeing Elizabeth like a house cat stalking a crippled sparrow.

'And this is Mistress Elizabeth Fowler, a dear friend of mine.'

'Alas, I see that you are a married woman, Mistress Fowler. That is indeed a great and terrible tragedy for all gentlemen of good taste . . .'

'A widow, sir,' said Elizabeth loudly, her hand toying with her curls. 'My husband, Captain Fowler of the Royal Navy, has been dead these past two years.'

'Indeed?' said Maligny, smoothing his moustache with thumb and forefinger. 'And I see you are fond of riding. Perhaps you might like to try a brisk gallop with me. My servants have set up a modest board in the copse yonder, with plenty of wine and food. We could gallop over together and you could join us for some refreshment. With Lieutenant Blood to escort you, of course. We would be deeply honoured.'

Holcroft suddenly felt an intense surge of rage. Elizabeth was nearly his wife and he was damned if he would allow this greasy Frenchman to whisk her off for a brisk gallop and then a glass or two of wine – or perhaps the other way around.

The four Oxford Blues officers trotted past and Captain Redmond touched his hat in salute to Holcroft, who nodded back rather more angrily than he meant to.

Elizabeth, he saw, was smiling, looking through her lashes at the Frenchman.

'I regret, Monsieur,' said Holcroft icily, 'that we cannot join you. The hour grows late and I fear I must escort Mistress Fowler home. At dusk I find that the park becomes populated with too many impudent blackguards. Good day to you, sir!'

Taking her reins, and turning his horse, all the while keeping his mount between Elizabeth and Maligny, he spurred down the track in the wake of the cavalrymen.

Learned nothing in France
Lively? Mask what you don't like

Chapter Eleven

20 July 1685: Liberty of the Savoy

The day after next, at about eleven of the clock on a bright but blustery Monday morning, Holcroft Blood rode out of the gates of the Tower, this time on an Ordnance horse, a very undistinguished dun-coloured beast, and set out west through the City. Once again he had the Lorenzoni pistol, fully loaded and primed, shoved through the scarlet officer's sash that was wrapped around his blue coat at the waist, and the small-sword at his left hip. As an extra precaution he had a pair of long horse pistols holstered on either side of his borrowed mount's withers.

The encounter with the Comte de Maligny and Scarlet Cap two days before had made him realise just how vulnerable he was to any well-armed enemies he might meet by chance – or through their evil design – although he now understood that there had, of course, been no danger at all from the French pair he had met, except perhaps a danger to Elizabeth's virtue. Scarlet Cap, while he had appeared menacing with a drawn sabre in his hands, was no more than a bodyguard, some veteran cavalryman, a Grenadier à Cheval, by the look of his uniform, who was now employed by the French embassy to protect the diplomats when they went about their business. He and Elizabeth had been at no risk from him – but if, for example, he had run into Narrey and his henchmen, the situation might have been far more serious.

The Lorenzoni was a unique weapon, or so he believed, a pistol capable of firing seven shots without needing to be reloaded. He had bought it from the Italian mercenary two years ago – not so much for protection but more out of curiosity. His mechanical mind was intrigued by its elegant design, the way the long lever rotated the steel cylinder beside the lock to feed a measured charge of powder and then a round ball into the firing chamber, cocking the pistol with the same action. Holcroft had practised with the Lorenzoni pistol for many hours on the Ordnance ranges and he could fire the weapon, reload and fire again in four or five beats of his heart. He had once fired seven aimed shots and hit a man-sized target at twenty-five paces with every single ball, and all that well inside a minute by his old brass pocket watch.

He doubted that he would have any need of the unusual weapon, or indeed any weapon at all, on this bright summer's day but, even if an attack by Narrey was most unlikely, he *was* heading into a notoriously dangerous and violent part of London – indeed, strictly speaking, not a part of London at all, but the Liberty of the Savoy, claimed by the Duchy of Lancaster.

The Liberty was a warren of narrow, filthy streets between the Strand and the curve of the River Thames around the old palace of the Dukes of Savoy and bordered by the Temple Bar to the east and the Charing Cross to the southwest. It was a place of sanctuary for rebels, highwaymen, thieves and rogues of all descriptions. The writ of the Crown did not run in the Savoy, for it was under the jurisdiction of the Duchy of Lancaster – even though James Stuart was in fact both Duke of Lancaster and King of England. Nevertheless, ancient custom dictated that royally appointed magistrates and constables from the surrounding parishes had no authority to seize a man in the Liberty who might be wanted a few streets away for the vilest crimes. As a result, it was a hive of lively debauchery, licentiousness and vice. His dead father had frequented the place, naturally, and today Holcroft was heading to an ale house called the Grapes, where he'd arranged to meet his older brother Thomas.

He was reasonably sure that the prisoner John Matthews was innocent of any crime more serious than stealing that keg of black powder. But he felt he must make sure his story was true by verifying it himself. Then he could report back to the Master-General of the Ordnance that he had investigated the poor fellow thoroughly and found nothing amiss, and hopefully thereby placate Lord Dartmouth with a demonstration of his professional diligence. With his master reassured, his own existence in the Tower could return to a happy state of orderliness and calm.

At half an hour before noon, Holcroft stepped down from the saddle and tethered his horse at the rail outside the Grapes. He paused at the door of the ale house, seized a grubby urchin lounging against the wall, lifted him to eye level, his thumbs in the boy's armpits, and, in a harsh voice recalled from his own childhood in a Shoreditch slum, ordered him to watch the horse, saying there would be a penny in it for him if the beast was unmolested when he had finished his business; but that if it were harmed or stolen, he would cut the boy's liver out and eat it raw with mustard.

'An'og,' demanded the child, meaning a shilling. He was quite unruffled by this rough encounter with a big, well-armed stranger. 'An' a tot of Barbados rum. Fer me service. Or I ain't responsible. A plague o' thieving coves in these parts, yer 'onour. A fucking plague. An' I'll suck yer cock for a crown, too, nosh it real good.'

They settled on three pennies, and only to watch the horse, a penny now, tuppence afterwards if Holcroft was satisfied with his wardship, and, content with the arrangement although still determined to keep a sharp look out through the grease-smeared tavern window, he pushed open the heavy oak door and went inside.

Thomas Blood was five years older than his brother and yet he had aged badly in the years since they had last met. When Holcroft first made him out through the fog of tobacco smoke, the stench of spilled ale, and the sweat of desperate men, he was seated at a table in the corner of the room, hunched over a pewter mug of ale. Holcroft thought he was seeing a ghost. For Thomas had come to resemble their dead father in an alarming fashion: the same long nose and drink-reddened cheeks, the same eyes, the same long chestnut hair turning to iron grey. Even his posture reminded Holcroft of the Colonel, although Thomas junior was a lesser man by all measures. Smaller, weaker, meaner-spirited. He had chosen the path of a rank-rider but had had little success in his chosen occupation and it weighed heavily on his soul.

In the course of a highway robbery some years ago, he had shot a pretty young gentlewoman dead in her carriage on Hampstead Heath when she refused to hand over her necklace. And while the criminal world shrugged at this misstep, a hazard of the trade, and took the view that she got what she deserved for resisting a man with a pointed pistol, Thomas had been so shaken by the murder that he had lost his nerve and existed now by cadging drinks and borrowing small sums from his fellow highwaymen and, some whispered, by acting as a paid informer.

Holcroft ordered two gills of brandy and went to the table to join his sibling.

'You're looking prosperous,' said Thomas sourly, accepting the mug of brandy and sinking it in a swallow. 'The Board of Ordnance must be treating you well.'

'Well enough,' said Holcroft, taking a small sip if his own drink. 'And you?'

'Times is hard, little brother, times is very hard.'

Holcroft turned to the barkeeper, a plum-nosed, squat-bodied rascal named Josiah Fitch, and signalled for another two tots. The man came bustling over at his command with the brandy jug, beaming obsequiously and refilling their mugs with the pungent brown spirit. He could smell money on the tall blue-coated King's man, even if he did mix with penniless tosspots like old Tommy Blood.

'So what brings you to this dismal shithole?' said Thomas. 'I got your note, surprised I was, very surprised – I see nothing of Charles either but he's an officer of the law these days and would not be welcome here. But you – you've been back from abroad for six months now or more, so I've heard, and I've not seen hide nor hair of you.

And now here you are. Yet, somehow, I cannot believe you sullied your boots with the filth of the Liberty for the pleasure of my company. So, what do you need?'

'I never had occasion to visit before.'

'Not even to see me. Not even to see your own brother, the man who raised you from a baby, fed you, wiped your arse, and your nose, sometimes even with different cloths, taught you everything he knew about how to get by in this wicked old world.'

Holcroft shrugged. Long ago, Thomas had taught him how to fight with his fists, that was true. He had done an excellent job. But his brutal method had been to knock the younger boy down repeatedly until he learnt to dodge the blows and hit back.

'I need some information,' he said.

'Thought it might be something in that line.' Thomas signalled again to the keeper, pointing at his empty pewter mug. 'Another one, Fitchy, if you would be so kind, my stinking-rich little brother has brought his money bags with him today.'

When the drinks were refilled, and Fitch had retreated, Holcroft said: 'There's a boy from these parts, a Savoyard called John Matthews who was in service with us in the Tower as a clerk. He got caught stealing a keg of black powder from the stores.'

Thomas laughed unpleasantly. 'What a ninny-hammer! So you caught him red-handed, did you? Well then, he's for the drop.'

'Transportation, probably. Do you know him?'

'Heard tell o' him. He's a Red-Letter-man, yes?'

'He's a Roman Catholic, if that's what you mean.'

'What do you want to know?'

'He told me that he owed money to some people here, and could not pay them. Four brothers, name of Maguire.'

Thomas went pale. He swallowed his brandy and rose from his seat.

'I've nothing to say about them. Nothing. Can't stay, brother. I must go.'

'Wait!' said Holcroft, seizing his arm. 'I'll pay you for your knowledge, Tom, and for your time, I'll give you half a crown.'

Thomas looked down at his brother, torn between fear and lust for the coin.

'Outside,' he said hoarsely. 'We'll talk in the street. Not in here.' He shot a fearful glance at the keeper Josiah Fitch and half a dozen lumped and shadowy forms drinking silently in the gloom on the far side of the ale house.

Holcroft paid his reckoning and joined his brother on the street. He was pleased to see that his horse was still there, apparently unmolested, and he slipped a couple of coins to the grinning boy, who turned and sped away. The brothers set off down the street, heading south towards the river, leading the horse between them.

The street was dirty and decrepit, even by London standards; the cobbled surface several inches thick with matted dung in some places, deeply pot-holed in others. The houses either side seemed to sag into each other, as if exhausted by their extreme age. Urchins flitted about the walking men, calling out services they could offer, until Thomas swiped one with his hand, catching him a heavy blow on the side of the head and rolling him into the filth. Women hung from the windows watching silently for the most part, though one scooped out her breasts and waggled them at the passing men. A drunk, unconscious and snoring, sprawled half in a dark doorway. Somebody had stolen his breeches, stockings and shoes, Holcroft noted, if he had ever possessed such items, for he was naked from the waist down.

'That name, Maguire – it's not one that you bandy about in the Liberty, brother,' said Thomas quietly. 'They are bad people, Patrick Maguire and his brothers. I mean, really *evil* people. They hurt folk. They *like* hurting folk. If the Matthews boy owed them money and couldn't pay it, he's better off facing transportation. Even the Tyburn jig. Least it'd be over quick. You should stay away from them, little brother.'

'Matthews said they ruled like kings here.'

'And so they are. Henry Killigrew is Master of the Savoy and chaplain to the King, he's another papist, or so they say.' Thomas gave a shiver of disgust. 'But while Killigrew rules the old Palace and its precincts, these streets round here are ruled by Patrick Maguire and his brothers. They have a finger in everything that happens here. The rank-riders, the filching-morts and whores, the purse-nippers, even the crimpers pay them. Patrick Maguire beat a man half to death a few days ago, then crucified him on his own front door. And not because he wouldn't pay, because he quibbled over how much. You see, brother, they *are* like kings here. And they always get their due. It's like a tax – a tax on thievery. And everyone pays. Everyone.'

'I don't care about the Maguires, Thomas, truly I don't. I just want to check that Matthews told me the truth. He said he stole the powder to sell to the rank-riders.'

'Could be. You can buy 'most anything in the Grapes you ask the right cove.'

'Where did you get powder and ball for your ... professional activities?'

'That would be telling.'

'That's why I'm asking, Tom. I want you to tell me. That's why I'm paying.'

'All right, you can buy powder, ball, pistols, blades here – anything you like if ye have the chink to pay for it. Your boy Matthews could have been telling you true. But if that was his game, stealing powder, the Maguires would surely come to know of it, and they would soon demand their rightful slice of the pie.'

The walked on in silence for a few paces. A patch of river opened up before them, visible through the tangle of a collapsed warehouse, a drift of brown sludge.

'What else can you tell me about Matthews?'

'Nothing. He wasn't part of a crew, I mean, he had no reputation as a thief.'

'Nothing else?'

Holcroft could faintly hear the sound of chanting, many voices, high, childlike.

'He has a mother still living, I think. I saw him once in the Grapes with an older sort fussing over him, Mary or Maria, something like that, I think it was; huge great pair of udders on her. Which no doubt came in handy in her line of work.'

'She was a whore?'

'No, though she'd have made a fortune. There's some rich gents who would pay handsomely to play with those great bouncers of hers. No, she was a wet nurse.'

They found themselves standing beside a long low building, reasonably new and built of timber planks. There were three large, chest-high plate glass windows in the front of the building. The sound of chanting was much louder. Holcroft went over to the building and peered through the shining glass. He found he was looking into a large room where about seventy children on wooden benches were reciting the declensions of irregular Latin verbs. A small, lean man in a shapeless black cassock was standing by a blackboard at the end of the room with a long wooden pointer in his hand, tapping it against the dark slate in time to the children's voices.

Holcroft turned back to his brother. 'Thank you, Thomas. You've been helpful.'

He fished in his coat pocket and from a handful of small coins he selected a silver half crown which he held out to Thomas.

Thomas kept his hands by his sides, he hung his head, looking sly and shifty. 'Couldn't make it a yellow-boy, could you brother? Times is very hard.'

Holcroft picked out a heavy golden sovereign and handed it over.

'Obliged,' Tom muttered and began to move away.

'Fare thee well, brother,' said Holcroft, stroking his horse's nose.

'Stay clear of those Maguires, mind,' said Thomas over his shoulder. He began to walk rapidly away up the street, back the way they had just come.

Father Michael Palmer was a little surprised to be confronted in his own classroom by the tall, healthy, military-looking man in a fine blue coat with a sword at his side and a big odd-looking pistol shoved in his waist sash. He hid it well, though. He had seen some extraordinary sights in the five months he had been living in the Liberty and he took this strange apparition in his stride. He had dismissed the pupils to their midday meal and was cleaning the chalk from the board with a cloth when the man knocked on the door and walked in without awaiting a summons.

'Father Palmer?' he said.

The priest admitted that it was he, and gave him a perfunctory blessing.

'My name is Blood, Father, and I'm here on the King's business,' said the big man. 'I want to ask you about one of your pupils.'

'Oh Jesus, Mary and Joseph, what have the young scamps been up to now?'

'I mean one of your former pupils: John Matthews.'

Father Palmer looked blank. Holcroft said: 'Small fellow, dark hair, fifteen years old or so, now works at the Tower of London as a clerk. Matthews.'

The priest looked none the wiser. 'And he was a pupil of mine? Forgive me, sir, but I have no recollection.'

'You don't remember him at all then?'

'No, but if he was one of mine, I'm sure he is an honest, upright sort of fellow. A clerk, you say? Does he need a character reference? Is he in some sort of trouble?'

'You might say that. He was caught red-handed in an act of theft at the Tower.'

'Merciful Father – that is bad. I shall pray for him.'

'You really don't recall him at all? A clever boy, slight in the body. One of your flock – by which I mean a Roman Catholic.'

A guarded expression came over the priest's face. 'Mister Blood, I have a licence from the Duchy of Lancaster to minister to my parishioners here in the Liberty; it is signed by the King himself along with Dr Henry Killigrew, Master of the Savoy. I can show it to you, if you require it. We have a chapel, yes, dedicated to the Blessed Virgin Mary. Some of the people follow the True Faith, and worship without fear of arrest. Some do not. But your Protestant laws do not apply to us.'

'I have not come here to persecute you, Father. I have no interest in your soul. I merely wish to know about John Matthews, a former student of this school.'

'I am afraid I cannot help you. I have four hundred pupils here, half Protestant, half Catholic. And as we only began to teach classes in March this year – with the kind permission of His Majesty – your boy cannot have studied here for very long.'

'Do you mind, Father, if I take a quick look around your school. I have to report to my master that I have made a thorough investigation.'

'Of course, of course. We have nothing to hide. I will have one of the teachers show you around. And now, if I cannot be of any further service to you . . .'

A young man in a similar baggy black cassock, one Father Williams, was summoned and, after leading Holcroft's horse into a stable block, he took the Ordnance lieutenant on a long and seemingly meandering tour of the many school buildings. It was a bigger place than Holcroft had first imagined, with five separate classrooms of a similar size to the one he had already seen. There were even some empty rooms, quiet, neglected and dusty, that they passed through on the way to others that were in use. At the heart of the school, there was a large central courtyard, next to the kitchen, where hundreds of boys aged between ten and fifteen were being served out a grey slop from steaming cauldrons. The noise was horrendous. Father Williams guided him through the throng, shouting out pieces of pertinent information and pointing to the various different buildings around the open space.

Holcroft found himself feeling uncomfortable: he hated crowds at the best of times, and this vast jostling pack of grubby slum children, shrieking and shoving and slurping their soup and bread, made him feel slightly ill. It reminded him too much of his own Shoreditch childhood. He pulled himself together when he caught a glimpse, through the shutters of a window they passed, of the unmistakable square wooden frame of a printing press and half a dozen inky folk hard at their work.

I wonder if they have a licence for that, too, he thought. The press was probably illegal but hardly the stuff of a grand conspiracy – there were dozens of unlicensed presses all over London putting out pamphlets that ranged from the mildly seditious to the stark raving mad. You could find an illicit news sheet on the table of any coffee house in the city. And he cared not a jot if the priests here made up and distributed unlicensed material promoting their own faith. What he'd said to Father Palmer was true: he wasn't there to persecute them. Their souls were their own business.

There was a whipping post where one unfortunate lad was receiving chastisement from another priest with a birch rod. They passed a small brick chapel, and Holcroft caught a sickly, unfamiliar whiff of incense, and Father Williams waved vaguely at a weed-slimed wharf that led out to the brown river, where stacks of paper were being delivered from a barge: fodder for the press, Holcroft assumed.

This was a noisy, crude, dirty place and full of exuberant life. But, despite the obvious Catholic stamp, Holcroft got no sense that this might be a place for plots and treason. Father Palmer and his fellow priests were trying to do God's work, to educate the poor, and without feeling the need for any secrecy or shame.

Holcroft thanked Father Williams, collected his horse, mounted and pointed its nose toward home. As far as he was concerned, John Matthews, clerk of the Tower, had become a thief only because he saw the opportunity to steal a keg of powder and was in desperate need of the money. Now, he had to persuade the Master-General of the Ordnance to show the poor fellow the doubtful mercy of transportation.

Chapter Twelve

21 July 1685: Tower of London

Holcroft was awoken the next morning by the bells St Peter ad Vincular in the northwest corner of the Inner Ward calling the Protestant faithful to matins. He quickly washed, dressed and, ignoring the call to prayer, took his breakfast alone in the almost deserted officers' mess.

As he ate, he kept a sharp lookout for Captain Glanville. He had no desire to encounter that officer, fearing that anything the fat little man might say to him would cause him to lose his temper. Even the thought of Glanville's well-fed smirk made his blood seethe. After his meal, he went to the little Ordnance office where he kept the ledgers and papers, and began looking at the reports on the proofing of the new twenty-four-pounders, including the one which had exploded and killed the officer of engineers.

He was deep in his reading when the door banged open and Enoch Jackson stood on the threshold. Unusually for the master gunner, he was pale and shaking. Even his bald, sun-tanned pate seemed to be unnaturally blanched.

'You'd better come, Mister Blood. Better come now. I've sent a boy for the doctor but there's quite a to-do in the White Tower. The gaolers think the plague has struck again. Best if you come now, sir, before somebody does something silly.'

A few minutes later Holcroft stood in the doorway of the cell in the White Tower. For once, the gaoler Widdicombe, who had conducted him from the entrance up to the chamber, had not reminded him that it had once held his father. Holcroft looked through the doorway, with Widdicombe cowing behind his bulk, and Jackson hanging back in the corridor. The chamber was in disarray, the stool and chair knocked over, papers from the small desk in drifts on the floor. There were sticky, foul-smelling pools of liquid here and there. Vomit streaked with blood. The bedsheets and blankets were tangled around the body of Matthews, which lay half on and half off the bed. The remains of a meal – a pie of some kind, pork or ham, a bowl of radishes, a chunk of cheese, a half-drunk pewter mug of ale. A curl of orange peel.

Holcroft went over to the corpse – there was clearly no life here – but he felt the neck for a pulse anyway. Matthews's skin was a blueish-grey colour and cold and it was clear from the contorted muscles of his young face that he had died in agony.

'Is it the plague returned?' asked Widdicombe, his voice trembling. Holcroft pulled open Matthews's shirt and peered at his armpits. No swellings, no buboes.

'No, not the plague, thank God,' he said.

'I'll be the judge of that,' said a high voice, and the scrawny form of Arnold Whicker, a gentleman who was licensed to practice medicine in the city by the Bishop of London himself, wormed through the thick press of bodies in the doorway.

The little doctor, an elderly grey-haired man in a stained black coat, knelt beside the body and peered at it. He lifted one of the corpse's eyelids, and sniffed at the mouth. Then, like Holcroft, he pulled open the shirt and examined the armpits.

'He clearly died of a convulsion, sir, but—' Holcroft began, but before he could say any more the doctor leapt to his feet and held up a hand to silence him.

'It is *not* the plague,' the little man pronounced, and there was an audible collective exhalation from the crowd of gaolers, soldiers and servants at the door. 'Looks very much like apoplexy, to me,' the doctor said briskly. 'The distortion of the body, the facial expression, skin tone *post mortem*. Yes, apoplexy.'

'Do you think it is possible, sir,' said Holcroft, 'that this might be—'

'I have made my diagnosis, young man,' said Doctor Whicker. 'And I am almost never wrong in these matters. I shall direct my bill to Lord Dartmouth, and now if you will excuse me, sir, I have a pressing engagement in Cheapside.'

The doctor brushed past Holcroft and walked out of the door.

The dwarfish Widdicombe decided it was time to exert his authority.

'Right then, Hodges, Simpson, get in there and let's get this place cleared up. Take his body up to St Peter's. We'll let the padre say a few words and get him into the ground. Just like Matthews to give us all a scare like that. No consideration.'

Holcroft stepped aside as the two assistant gaolers bustled into the cell. He put a hand on Widdicombe's arm: 'Tell me, Jeremiah, the food. Who brought it for him?'

'The pot boy brings it from the Red Lion on Tower Hill, same as for all the others. Those who can pay, at least. Fine grub there, if you don't mind the prices.'

'Are any of the other prisoners sick?'

'No, fit as fiddles, sir. All of them. Save for old Sir Francis – but he's got the consumption. Cough, cough, coughing away. The poor old soul. He won't see the month out, and such a fine and generous old gentleman, too. It's a damned shame.'

Half an hour later, Holcroft was once again standing before Lord Dartmouth's desk in his cosy wood-panelled study. He reported the death of John Matthews. And also added that his inquiries had discovered nothing that might suggest that the boy had been involved in a plot of any kind or that he had been anything other than a thief.

'Well, the fellow is dead now. So I believe we can close the book on him. Saves us hanging him. Give me a brief written report, if you will, by this evening and then I want you to pack your bags and be ready to move out in the morning.'

'Sir?'

'I know that you have apologised to Captain Glanville – and that it cost you a great deal to do so. But I'm posting you away from London for a while to let things cool down between the two of you. I'm sending you to Sheerness. I want you to take command of the garrison there and to strengthen the fortifications. The Dutch burnt the fort to the ground in '67, as I'm sure you remember, and coastal defences are one of the few things that the King is now willing to spend money on. So off to Sheerness you go – to make the Thames Estuary impregnable to our sea-borne enemies; I'll have the detailed orders on your desk by this afternoon.'

'Sir, I should prefer to remain here. I am concerned about the manner of poor Matthews's death. It looked to me as if it could just possibly have been poison.'

'You think he was poisoned?'

'I don't know, sir . . .'

'Did Whicker think he was poisoned?'

'No, sir, he said it was apoplexy.'

'Do you think you know better than the good doctor? He is a Fellow of the Royal College of Physicians, you know.'

'Yes, sir.'

'Who would want to poison Matthews?'

'I don't know.'

'Look, Holcroft, I like you, I think you know that. And I understand that you don't want to go off to the wilds of Kent. It's a miserable, dreary place and the wind whips off the North Sea something cruel. But you can come back to London from time to time to see your friends, attend parties and so on. Sheerness is not very far away. It's just that I don't want you living here in the Tower for a year at least. I am fairly certain that if I allowed you to stay, you would kill Captain Glanville or he would kill you within a matter of days or weeks. So you are going to Sheerness and I would be obliged if you did not give me any more nonsense about mythical poisons.'

'I'm not refusing to go, sir. I would just like a few days to investigate—'

'The orders will be on your desk this afternoon. And you will leave tomorrow morning. Is that understood, lieutenant?'

'Yes, sir.'

As Holcroft walked across the Inner Ward, heading for his rooms to begin packing, he realised, to his surprise, that more than anything, he was feeling a sense of relief.

Matthews may or may not have been poisoned. Probably not, it was likely just apoplexy – the doctor was, as Lord Dartmouth had pointed out, one of the most respected medical men in London. And who could have poisoned him? Narrey? Why? In God's name, why would the Frenchman, on an important mission for his King, want to murder an innocuous thief? A thief who was to be hanged in a week or so. It made no sense. It came to him that he had been conjuring absurd and terrifying fantasies inside his own head. The news from Aphra that Narrey was in London had shaken him more than he liked to admit. It had made him suspicious of everyday, ordinary things. The French bodyguard in Hyde Park with the scarlet cap. The poor boy Matthews, facing a horrible fate, and dying of a sudden fit – as dozens did every day. Holcroft realised that he was beginning to start at shadows.

Sheerness would doubtless be a grim, miserable place, a place of disgraceful exile, but he found that he was relishing the chance to get out of London. He could put all his fears about Narrey behind him – there was little, in fact almost zero chance of meeting the shadowy French spymaster in a small, sparsely populated town on the wind-swept Kent coast. He was also, he dared to admit to himself, rather angry with Elizabeth. The way she had been so open to a flirtation with the Comte de Maligny in the park: it had been shameless. He would send her a note telling her of his new posting, and leave her to stew for a little while. Then, when some time had passed, he might forgive her. Or not. He would decide that later.

He quickened his step across the cobbles. He lifted his head, straightened his spine. He would be leaving it all behind. His jealousy over Elizabeth, his fears about Narrey, the conflict with Glanville – everything would be in left behind in London.

He was going to Sheerness.

Part Two

Chapter Thirteen

23 October 1687: St Pancras Church and Gray's Inn Lane

'Dearly beloved, we are gathered here together in the sight of God, and in the face of this Congregation, to join together this man and this woman in Holy Matrimony, which is an honourable estate . . .'

Holcroft paid scant attention to the rector of St Pancras Church as he droned out the words of the marriage ceremony. He was looking at his bride Elizabeth, who was standing beside him in a pale blue silk dress that matched the colour of her lovely eyes, and considering her sweet face through the gauzy white lace veil.

It had taken him two years to bring her to the altar – mainly because his visits to London from the garrison town of Sheerness were at best intermittent. She had complained that he was neglecting her – which he was – although he claimed that it was only his duty that took him elsewhere. After a year's betrothal, in which he saw her only three times, he had finally agreed a wedding date with her father, Richard King. And now, she was here, on this chilly Sunday in late October in the old church in the parish of St Pancras, north of the sprawl of London town.

She had become more beautiful, he thought, in the two years he had been in Kent. Which seemed odd: he had been under the impression that women became less attractive the older they got. Nevertheless, he suspected that he should be feeling more than a detached sense of satisfaction at her perfectly regular features, her unblemished skin, her sparkling eyes and her sweetly upturned nose.

Marriage was a good thing – everybody said so. And while the marriage portion that Holcroft had received had been a mere two hundred pounds, with King pleading poverty and the possession of two other unmarried daughters, Holcroft was pleased with the match. The soon-to-be Mistress Blood would be an adornment to his new life, and she was still of an age, three years younger than Holcroft, to bear him children. She was a big, strong girl, almost as tall as he was, with broad shoulders and capacious hips. With God's blessing, she should be able to push out a healthy son or two for him in no time. Holcroft did not enjoy children, finding them noisy, dirty and chaotic, but he did feel that they would bring stability and a certain prestige to him, which he hoped would make him feel less adrift in the world.

There was a small congregation to witness the nuptials, for Holcroft had few close friends: Lord and Lady Churchill were standing two paces behind him, Jack beaming, Sarah looking on with a cynical smile. His barrister brother Charles stood at the back of the church looking solemn in an inky black suit of clothes. Ensign Rupert Pittman and Sergeant John Miller commanded an honour guard of a dozen Royal Fusiliers. Enoch Jackson had attended and presented Holcroft with a tiny brass model of Roaring Meg, exact in every detail, made from scraps of metal but which could be carried in the palm of his hand. Aphra Behn was there too, wiping her eye with a lace rag, and even Lord Dartmouth had condescended to attend, now that Holcroft's penance in Sheerness was over and he was reinstalled in the Tower.

He had laboured hard over the past two years in that windswept corner of Kent, thickening the walls of the fort that overlooked the River Medway and installing six enormous naval thirty-six-pounders on the two sides facing water. These armaments were tricky items, not just because of their huge weight – 6,200lbs each – and the difficulty of transporting them the twenty-odd miles from the naval base at Chatham, but also because of the danger of them exploding from the huge charge of black powder that they required for each thirty-six-pound shot. But he had tested them to his satisfaction, many times, over many months, and stocked the magazine at Sheerness with a sufficiency of ball and powder, and he had trained the garrison gunners mercilessly until he was confident that any enemy flotilla that approached the mouth of the River Medway would suffer in an appropriate fashion.

Lord Dartmouth, making a tour of the fortress in the summer, and witnessing a demonstration of the thunderous barrage, had been impressed. And, a month or so later, Holcroft had been allowed to relinquish his duties to a more senior officer and return to the fold. His replacement as commander in Sheerness was one Captain William Glanville, who arrived in the windswept Kentish garrison two days after Holcroft left it. The timing was no coincidence; Holcroft knew it was designed to keep the two officers from meeting. And while Glanville was bound to visit the Tower from time to time, and their paths must eventually cross, they would not be labouring side by side in the proof-house, or seeing each other daily in the officers' mess or on parade in the Inner Ward – and Holcroft was grateful to Lord Dartmouth for arranging things so deftly.

'Wilt thou have this man to thy wedded husband,' said the rector, 'to live together after God's ordinance in the holy estate of Matrimony? Wilt thou obey him, and serve him, love, honour and keep him, in sickness and in health; and, forsaking all others, keep thee only unto him, so long as ye both shall live?'

'I will,' said a hearty female voice that seemed to echo round the church.

The voice, yes. Holcroft would have to speak to Elizabeth about that. Her first husband had been partially deafened by cannon fire aboard his frigate and, apparently, had habitually conversed in a bellow to his wife. And she, understandably, had bellowed right back. But the roar of consent she gave in response to the vows was unseemly. He desperately hoped she would moderate her tone once they were wed.

And then, in what seemed like no time at all, Holcroft was lifting her delicate veil and tenderly kissing his bride and the guests were applauding, and Jack was slapping him hard on the back and wishing him all the joy in the world.

They signed the register in the vestry and, as man and wife, exited the church arm-in-arm, beneath a silver arch of drawn fusiliers's swords, while being pelted somewhat painfully with grains of wheat by the sparse but enthusiastic congregation.

A short carriage ride followed to the Gray's Inn Lane, where Richard King's house stood, handily close to the Inn of Court through which he earned his living.

The proceedings in King's parlour passed in a slight blur, at least for Holcroft; he drank his own health in brandy with a large number of exuberant neighbours and relatives of Richard and Mistress King, as well as with his own few friends. And he did not have time to eat much, such was the crowd of strangers wishing to congratulate him. However, the spread put out by Mistress King was very creditable – Aphra Behn, he noticed, slipped a large wedge of yellow Dutch cheese into her bag just before she left, and he made a mental note to pay her a visit soon and leave her another purse of money. By the time of the bedding – when Elizabeth's bridesmaids had undressed her and put her in the big wooden four-poster bed in the main bedroom of his new father-in-law's house and his bridesmen (Pittman, who was still a bachelor, and one of Elizabeth's unmarried male cousins) had done the same for him and laughed themselves almost to tears by repeating ancient priapic witticisms to him – he felt rather drunk.

When all the traditional wedding night rites had been performed – the pins removed from her hair and nightdress to ensure good luck, their stockings stripped off and blindly flung at the entourage, the posset drunk to make him lusty – and the bridesmaids and bridesmen had finally drawn the bed-curtains and retired, gig-gling, Holcroft found himself alone with Elizabeth for the first time that day.

However, as he leant over to embrace her in the huge bed, he was not thinking of the joyful conjugal task at hand but rather less romantically considering the last words Jack Churchill had said to him before he made his farewells and drove off with Sarah in his new fine, gilt-covered carriage.

'I want you to dine with me this Friday, Hol. I want you to meet some friends of mine at the Rose Tavern in Covent Garden. We're a sort of club. Can you get away?'

'I'm perfectly happy in my post at the Ordnance, Jack.'

'I'm sure. But I want you to meet these men. To discuss some political matters. Serious matters. And, ah, slightly delicate matters. I know you will be discreet.'

'What sort of club?'

'I would rather not say.'

'Who are these people?'

'You will meet them on Friday. Two of the clock. Rose Tavern, yes?'

It was not like Jack to be so mysterious: serious political matters, delicate matters, he had said. And why would he not tell him who he was about to meet?

'Holcroft! Come along, my dear,' Elizabeth boomed. 'Let's get this done.'

That voice! Holcroft had never realised before how irritating it was. It was like she was using a speaking horn, although their faces were only inches apart. Every man, woman and child in the house-hold must be able to hear her, clear as a bell!

He had not, in fact, spent much time conversing alone with Elizabeth before the wedding. She had always spoken exuberantly, and clearly, and her voice had carried somewhat at gatherings – but he had presumed this was a result of gaiety or nervousness.

When they had taken rides together, he thought she was speaking loudly to be heard over the wind and the sounds of the horses. He had not expected this volume of noise in the intimacy of the bedroom.

'Don't doze on me, Holcroft. Attend to your duty. I'm going riding with Jane Pertwee after breakfast, then shopping at the Royal Exchange – so we must get this business over with. If I don't get my eight hours, I'll look like a hag in the morning.'

Holcroft kissed her – partly to make her stop shouting. His hand caressed her large bosom through the cambric nightgown. He felt her strong hand burrow under his own nightshirt and grip his half-erect member and begin to jerk it vigorously.

'Come along, man! Captain Fowler was always a lot brisker than this. Boarders away! There we are. That's my hard handsome husband. That's the ticket!'

So Holcroft rolled on top of his wife and did his duty.

Chapter Fourteen

28 October 1687: The Rose Tavern

The upstairs parlour of the Rose Tavern in Covent Garden might have been designed for conspiracy. It was dimly lit, low-ceilinged, windowless and the background hum from the busy taproom downstairs made it difficult to overhear the conversations at other tables.

Jack had met Holcroft downstairs, greeted him briskly and conducted him up to a large table in the corner of the parlour at which sat eight men, many of them known to Holcroft and most of them military gentlemen of one kind or another. Holcroft felt a prickle of apprehension run up his spine at the serious nods he was given. He could not put his finger on what it was – not immediate danger, he was sure of that – but there was something underhand about this gathering of men and he felt a spike of anger at Jack for including him in whatever this mysterious meeting was about.

'Whatever is said at this table is not to go any further, Hol,' said Jack. 'Do you understand me? Don't mention to anyone what you may learn this afternoon. Yes?'

Holcroft grudgingly gave his word that he would remain silent. And sat down.

Jack poured him a glass of wine and began to make the introductions. 'You will know Colonel Percy Kirke, of course, from the Monmouth campaign and the fight at Sedgemoor, as you must also remember Colonel Charles Trelawny, from the same.'

Holcroft nodded at the two senior officers: he was not a close acquaintance of these men, although he had dined in the same mess with them many times on the three-week campaign. The two older men inclined their heads to acknowledge him.

'I think you must have made the acquaintance Colonel Charles Godfrey, of the First Foot Guards, at some point – he's a very fine card player,' said Jack.

Holcroft had indeed met the man several times but he did not consider him a fine card player at all. In fact, he considered him a near idiot, and possibly slightly mad. He taken more than a hundred pounds in gold off him a few weeks ago at whist – and with pitiful ease. '. . . and Colonel Thomas Langston, over there, who was with me in the Tangiers garrison.' This fellow on the far side of the table was a stranger to Holcroft. He made a formal sort of bow, ducking his bald head forward.

'This is Captain George Byng of the Navy – and Captain John Cutts of the Anglo-Dutch Brigade, whom you may not have met before since he has been serving in Holland for more than a dozen years.' Two more strangers – although he had heard Lord Dartmouth, in his capacity as Admiral of the Fleet – speak glowingly of young Captain Byng, a most courageous young officer, his master had said. 'And over there,' continued Jack, 'is His Grace the Duke of Grafton – who was also with us at Sedgemoor, as you will surely recall. He had the First Foot Guards there. However, forgive me if I am wrong, but I am not entirely sure whether you have previously encountered the Earl of Danby, at the head of the table there . . .'

'Oh, we have certainly met,' said the Earl. 'But not for a very long time.'

While the other men murmured their greetings to the newcomer, and Holcroft made an automatic reply, he looked hard at the Earl of Danby. Yes, they'd met before.

'My lord,' he said coolly.

'Mister Blood,' said Lord Danby, smiling crookedly, 'what an honour to make your acquaintance again,' and the nobleman even looked as if he meant it.

It was clear to Holcroft, from the moment he sat down, that Lord Danby was the leader of this group of men, and he wasn't sure how comfortable he felt about that.

They had first met during his period as a lowly page in the service of the Duke of Buckingham, and Lord Danby – or Sir Thomas Osborne, as he had been then – had been one of the Duke's right-hand men, a fixer, a man who could manage dark and difficult affairs for his master and who was not at all scrupulous about how the ends were achieved. Holcroft had disliked him, and feared him. His father had told him that old Tommy Osborne had even once sent an assassin to kill him when he was locked up in the Tower. But Holcroft had faced up to Osborne, as he stood beside the King in the Banqueting House, when Holcroft had demanded that his father be pardoned. And Holcroft had triumphed then – so he no longer held the man at the head of the table in the same awe. But nothing would persuade him to trust him.

Holcroft was not alone in his wary opinion of the earl. Few men in London or the country as a whole trusted Lord Danby. He had risen like a Chinese rocket as a young man, attaining majestic heights under the late King Charles after the fall of his own mentor the Duke of Buckingham – which was partly engineered by Osborne himself. He used his power ruthlessly: ruining his enemies, and rewarding his toadies with positions at court, always in exchange for a fat fee. His corruption, the huge scale of the bribes he demanded from supplicants, was gross even for King Charles's deeply avaricious court. He amassed vast wealth in a short time. But if his rise had been swift, his own fall from grace a few short years later had been as sudden.

His political enemies had gathered themselves, and Danby had been forced to resign his positions. He was impeached and imprisoned in the Tower for five years while Holcroft was in France and, these days, he was not much regarded as a political force – indeed Holcroft was surprised that in this gathering he should be deferred to.

But he was deferred to. It was Lord Danby who called the table to order when the wine had been poured and who gave a brisk order to the waiter for oxtail soup and oysters, followed by mutton chops, beef steaks, then herring pie and cheese.

'Gentlemen,' he began, 'we have not gathered these past few months and it seems right to me that we should review some of the aims and designs of this club, for the benefit of our guest and perhaps future member, Lieutenant Blood, here.'

There were murmurs of agreement. And every eye was fixed on Holcroft. He turned to his right and looked at Jack, who smiled and nodded reassuringly.

'We are an Anglican dining club, no dissenting Protestants or Catholics are welcome, and we call ourselves the Rose Taverners and meet from time to time for the purposes of conviviality, fellowship and discussion of current political and military matters that are close to our hearts. There is no conversational subject which is banned from the table, although we are all gentlemen here and gentlemanly conduct is expected, and the one rule is that private matters discussed here are not to be repeated elsewhere, indeed we discourage all mention of the club to outsiders . . .'

A secret political cabal, thought Holcroft, his heart sinking, *anti-Catholic in nature, militaristic in spirit.* He wondered how long he would have to endure their odious company before he could politely take his leave. What was Jack thinking by inviting to this gathering of smug, self-important, probably deeply seditious fools?

Lord Danby was still speaking '. . . and I think that it behooves us to raise a glass and congratulate our guest on his gallant action at Sedgemoor – Lieutenant Blood, gentlemen, I give you "The Duel in the Darkness". 'The men around the table dutifully drank their wine and Colonel Kirke said loudly: 'Hear him, hear him!'

The proceedings were interrupted by a pair of waiters bringing food and, while the conversation around the table became general, Holcroft occupied himself with his oxtail soup, keeping his face low down over the bowl.

'It's a damned disgrace!' he heard Colonel Trelawny saying to his neighbour. 'Good Protestant men thrown out of their regiments, some made destitute, by that scoundrel Tyrconnell. Replaced by papists, some of whom are barely soldiers at all.'

Captain Cutts chimed in from across the table: 'The officer roll of the Irish Army is now fully two-thirds Catholic, or so I'm told.'

'Do you count yourself an Irishman?' said Lord Danby, smiling at Holcroft.

Holcroft thought carefully before he answered, wiping his lips with his napkin to cover his mouth. 'My father was one, all his days, and I was born there,' he replied.

'So you do?'

'Mmmm, no. As I have lived in England or France most of my life, I'd hesitate to make that claim. I'd also say it doesn't make much difference. We have the same King.'

'Indeed? What do you make of the Earl of Tyrconnell's treatment of the Army in Ireland?'

Holcroft paused and took another mouthful of his soup. He knew he had to tread carefully. 'It certainly seems unjust that these Protestant officers have been dismissed from the Army without recompense – I know of many for whom the investment in their commission is all the money they have in the world. Many men, indeed, may have borrowed to buy their positions. One, two thousand pounds. Considerable sums. And now that is all gone on a whim of their commander-in-chief.'

'Quite right,' said Trelwany. 'It is bare-faced theft. Outrageous!'

'But, on the other hand,' said Holcroft, 'the Earl of Tyrconnell is Lord Deputy of Ireland, appointed by the King, and presumably is executing his royal wishes . . .'

'So you would blame the King,' said Lord Danby.

'No, sir, I would not make so bold a charge,' said Holcroft, turning away, and rather rudely giving Danby his shoulder. 'Could I trouble you, sir, to pass me the bread basket,' he said to the young sailor, Captain Byng, at the far end of the table.

Lord Danby said no more. Holcroft finished his soup in silence, wiped the bowl clean with a piece of bread and listened attentively as Richard Talbot, Earl of Tyrconnell, was roundly damned for his policies, his high-handedness in power and, of course, his idol-atrous Roman Catholic faith.

'It's this damned Declaration of Indulgence, I swear that the King has gone too far this time . . .' Percy Kirke was growling away on the far side of the table. 'By circumventing our laws against Catholics, the King would not just be letting papists have access to positions of power, he would potentially be letting Jews, Mussulmen, even cow-worshipping Hindoos, God help us, into the highest offices in the land.'

'Do you know many Hindoos who seek high office?' said Jack.

'That's not the point,' huffed Kirke. 'The laws of England are made by Parliament – or they should be. But the King has seen fit to dissolve the House and seeks to make laws himself by declaring an Indulgence for this man or that one, allowing men to hold office even if their religion should by law preclude it . . .'

'There's a great seething nest of them down in the Liberty of the Savoy,' said Colonel Godfrey, 'with a papist chapel, a free school to educate their brats – rats I call 'em – and a printing press spewing out idolatrous superstition and filth day and night. And all just a bowshot from White Hall and the court of our royal master.'

'Send in the troops,' said Kirke, 'burn them out of there. My Lambs would do it in a trice, just for the fun of it. That's what we did in the old days – burn them all.'

'And risk another Great Fire?' asked Jack, mildly.

'It would be worth the risk,' said Godfrey. 'Just as the Great Fire stopped the Great Plague, so another fire would cleanse London of this foul plague of papists.'

'You jest, Colonel, of course,' said Jack, shooting a nervous side-ways look at Holcroft, who was silently chewing his beef and avoid-ing eye contact with anyone.

'Do I?' said Colonel Geoffrey. 'Yes, I suppose I do. But something must be done about them, and soon – our country is in serious danger of being overrun.'

There were many more comments of this ilk. And Holcroft, frankly, was bored. He was interested in neither religion nor politics – nor in rank bigotry, for that matter – except insofar that he devoutly wished to see no more bloody rebellions like the attempt by the Duke of Monmouth to seize the throne for the Protestant faith. He did not seek change; he wanted to maintain the status quo. He did not particularly care who was king, nor what his royal conscience told him about religion. Holcroft wanted peace. He merely wished never to have to slaughter his countrymen again.

At one point, while the herring pie was being carved up and distributed, Holcroft was asked by Lord Danby about Lord Dartmouth's political position, whether he was, as he was said to be, completely loyal to the King.

'You know Dartmouth well, I'm told. Indeed, some people say you are rather an intimate, even a favourite of the Master-General.'

Holcroft was irritated by the question. He avowed that Lord Dartmouth was loyal to James. In the following question from Danby, Holcroft answered that he believed that all or certainly most officers of the Ordnance were equally loyal to Dartmouth. Holcroft added, a little too dramatically, that he personally held the Master-General in the highest regard and would follow him into Hell, if asked.

The Duke of Grafton, overhearing the remark, snorted with disgust but said nothing. Some years ago, Grafton had been removed from his position as Admiral of the Fleet and replaced by Lord Dartmouth and there was bad blood between them.

The uncomfortable meal wound on, course after course, and Holcroft ate until his waistcoat protested. The rancorous tussle between the King and the Fellows of Magdalen College, Oxford, was briefly discussed – how the King had forced a Catholic President on those staunch Protestant clerics. Jack, he noticed, made little contribution to the debate, merely smiling and nodding and refusing to allow himself to be drawn into the condemnations of

James. Which was only right, Holcroft noted. Jack had been a pro-
tégé of James since he had been a boy page in White Hall all those
years ago. His rise in the military and his elevation to the House of
Lords were the result of his royal patron – as well as his own charm,
energy and merit, too, of course. But without King James's influence, Jack Churchill would still be a lowly officer in some dead-end
post. Rather like Holcroft.

One statement caught his ear, and it sounded to him as if the
boundary between legitimate complaint about government policies
and outright treason had been crossed. It was over the cheese, a
great yellow moon of cheddar, that the Duke of Grafton said: 'Well,
this situation will not last for ever, let us take comfort in that. The
King has no living son – and the succession will pass to his daughter Mary, who we all know is a good Protestant. There will be no
Catholic princeling to continue a royal line of papists. All men are
mortal – even kings. We must all possess ourselves with patience. It
is merely a question of time.'

Grafton, the bastard son of the late King Charles and his legendary mistress Barbara Villiers, had not said that he wished his uncle
King James dead – which *would* definitely have been barefaced
treason. But the disloyal sentiment made Holcroft feel uneasy, and
he wondered if the Duke of Grafton – like the Duke of Monmouth,
his half-brother – harboured some grandiose ambition of his own.

'Why did you bring me to this place, Jack, with these people?' he
said as they departed in the late afternoon, walking though the wide
streets and elegant squares of Covent Garden. Both men heading
east to the Tower where Jack had Army business with Dartmouth.
'Surely you did not think I would make common cause with them?'

'Of course not, Hol. I know that you are admirably loyal to King
James. But I introduced you there because I wished you to understand what men of influence are saying behind closed doors. People
are angry with the King – very angry, as you saw at dinner today.

His policies of toleration towards his fellow Catholics are tearing the country apart. Danby is leading the charge and I do not think it would hurt if you remained friendly with him. He is by no means without influence. His goodwill could be valuable one day. Political change may well be coming to England – and sooner than you think – and you would do well to prepare for it.'

'Well, I thank you for my dinner, Jack – and I shall endeavour not to offend Lord Danby, nor any of his friends, but I *am* loyal to James and I will thank you if you do not again bring me into the company of your little Treason Club.'

'As you wish, Hol, but I hope you will consider your options. These men might one day be in positions of great power and it would be good for you to know and understand them. Several of them, including Lord Danby, expressed a desire to dine with you, to sound you out. You are not without a certain renown in military circles, after the part you played at Sedgemoor. They see you as a man who is prepared to act without fear to do what he knows is right. They see you as a rising star in the Ordnance – someone with Lord Dartmouth's ear and perhaps also someone who might be called on to occupy a higher position. If things were to change, that is.'

Chapter Fifteen

10 December 1687: Palace of White Hall

The King was determined that he would not allow his ill-temper to show. But the wretched man was infuriating. Sir Herbert Johnson was a fellow of at-best mediocre talent and he had been shown nothing but love, care and kindness by his God-given sovereign. He had been granted the post of Marshal of the High Court of the Admiralty, a plum worth two thousand pounds per annum, for which he was expected merely to show his face in the Admiralty Building a few times a year and sit on a committee or two. It was a lucrative sinecure granted by a generous monarch with only the expectation of loyalty in return. And *this* was how his generosity was repaid.

'All I am asking, Sir Herbert,' said James, slowly, 'is whether you would willingly support a vote to repeal the Act and others like it, should you be summoned back to Parliament. I only wish to know where you personally stand on this issue.'

'I could not say, Your Majesty. It would depend on so many varied factors . . .'

'I think you could say. Indeed, I insist that you *do* say.'

'If you compel me to answer, Your Majesty, if you were to wring an answer from my lips, then I must tell you that no, I would *not* vote to repeal the Test Acts, nor the other penal laws against Catholics.' Sir Herbert, gave a low, obsequious bow, a gesture that contradicted his words. 'My conscience would not permit me to do so. England is a Protestant country, and the laws enacted by Parliament are designed . . .'

'And if I should tell you that I will not have disloyal men in my House of Commons, men who plan to go against my wishes – what then would you say?'

'My answer would remain the same. If I am not called to Parliament at the next session as the Member for Overton, in the county of Berkshire, it would be a matter of the greatest regret for me. But I cannot promise you something, sire, which I cannot in good conscience deliver when – or if – I am ever recalled to the House.'

'What if I commanded you to do it?'

'Alas, Your Majesty, it sorrows me deeply . . .'

'You're also a Justice of the Peace for Overton, are you not?'

Sir Herbert gave another flamboyantly humble bow.

'No longer, I think. You may consider yourself dismissed. And I shall be forced to find another Marshal for the Admiralty High Court, too. Now, get out of my sight.'

Sir Herbert bowed again and withdrew from the Red Audience Room.

King James turned to his old friend and most trusted servant, Major-General, Lord Churchill: 'What is wrong with these people?' he said.

Jack Churchill said nothing but smiled sympathetically. He hated these sessions of what the King called 'closeting', in which he invited prospective Members of a new Parliament to meet him in relative privacy and sounded them out on their views on relaxing the laws against Catholics and dissenters holding office.

James had been doing this all summer and autumn, when he could spare the time from his other duties and, even now with Christmas fast approaching, he was still summoning worthies from the shires for these little semi-private chats. Yet very few of these 'closeted' gentlemen had acquiesced to the King's demands, no more than a handful. Not nearly enough to fill the House of Commons.

However, there were a few ambitious types, such as the Earl of Sunderland, the King's chief minister, who wholeheartedly supported the King's plan to sweep away the legal restrictions placed on those who did not belong to the Established Church of England. Lord Sunderland, born into a Protestant family, had gone so far as to convert to Catholicism merely, some said, to confirm his position as the power beside the throne.

Unprincipled toady, thought Jack. But, in truth, most of the men of substance that James had 'closeted' had refused to accommodate their monarch, pleading their consciences, even though it meant losing their positions at court or seats in a future Parliament, or even their magistracies and town offices in the countryside. It was a remarkable display of unity by almost all the gentlemen of consequence in England.

The men who defied their King were duly dismissed and, as a result, more and more official roles were filled by Catholics and dissenters. James would probably get what he wanted, eventually, Jack reflected, but there was a good chance he might provoke an insurrection by the great mass of Anglican landowners large and small long before then. And no one wanted a repeat of the appalling slaughter of the Monmouth rebellion and its equally bloody aftermath.

The court's composition had changed, too, since James's accession to the thrones of the Three Kingdoms a little under three years ago. There were many new faces in White Hall, foreign faces, Catholic faces – if there could be such a thing. There were still a few staunch old Protestants round the King – Lord Dartmouth and Lord Feversham, for example, and, of course, himself – but the Catholic contingent had now swollen to alarming proportions. Father Edward Petre, the King's confessor, was a very prominent man these days. The Pope had even sent an ambassador to England, the papal nuncio Ferdinando d'Adda, a smooth-mannered and wily Italian aristocrat, who seemed to be constantly in attendance.

John Drummond, the Catholic Earl of Melfort, was now firmly in favour with James Stuart, too, and constantly urging the King on to greater excesses – pushing him to make ever bolder declarations in favour of his co-religionists, to issue more inflammatory decrees. And then there were the French, half a dozen of them huddled around Paul Barillon d'Amancourt, Louis XIV's veteran Ambassador to the Court of St James. Barillon, an extremely able and subtle man, had almost daily private conferences with the King, just after the royal breakfast, and even whispered in his ear at public audiences offering advice and support from France.

If nothing else, thought Jack, it looked very bad to have a Catholic King of England, with such a close and influential French adviser. The Ambassador's colleagues, the slim, handsome Comte de Maligny and the muscle-bound Major du Clos, the military attaché, were almost always in attendance, too. And the perpetual gaggle of French hangers-on, black-clad priests, guests of the Ambassador and high-born royal servants and so on, gave the court a very unnatural, European feel.

However, there was no getting rid of them. Louis XIV had been most generous to James with subsidies – he had received 500,000 *livres* immediately upon his accession, a vast sum. But again, it did not look good, even viewed dispassionately, it gave the impression that James was in the pocket of the Sun King. That His Most Christian Majesty, who was his paymaster, was also his puppet-master. That was guaranteed to make even his most level-headed Protestant subjects fearful for their faith.

Jack recalled his own disastrous conversation with James on the subject of religion two years ago in Winchester. The King had been performing the ceremony of the King's Evil, touching those poor folk afflicted with scrofula, which some believed could be cured by the laying on of royal hands. The King was attended by a gaggle of Latin-chanting Catholic priests swinging incense-burners, and he'd asked Jack what he thought the people made of this ancient ceremony being carried out this way.

Jack, in a moment of unguarded candour, said: 'I think it makes them uneasy, sire. They fear you are paving the way for a forcible restoration of Catholicism.'

The King had lost his temper immediately and shouted angrily at him, calling him a Protestant dog, and a viper, and questioning his loyalty. When he was calmer, a few minutes later, he said: 'All I seek, Jack, all I want is a little more toleration for those who adhere to the Old Faith. They have been persecuted in this land long enough. That's all. I swear to you, on my honour, that is all I am trying to achieve.'

Jack had mollified him, apologising, saying he only hoped to make James aware of the deep aversion, of the age-old suspicion that people felt for the Roman faith.

'Nine tenths of all your subjects are Protestants, sire,' he pointed out.

James had then asked him if he, Churchill, would consider converting to the Catholic faith, the True Faith, and Jack answered his King with a brutal sincerity: 'Sire, I have been bred a Protestant and I intend to live and die in that communion.'

Jack had been lucky – the King had not taken too much offence, neither had he dismissed him from his court. But he and Jack had a relationship going back twenty years. And, mercifully, James had never again raised the issue of his personal faith.

Is it too late, Jack wondered, *to steer James from this disastrous course?* He was alienating the very heart, lungs and backbone of the country, the Tory squires out in the shires, the Anglican bishops, the Whiggish university Fellows, the grand Protestant landowners, too – and, as his dinner at the Rose Tavern in October had shown him, a proportion of the Army and Navy officers was against him now as well.

Narrey watched the unfolding farce with contempt but nothing more than a bland smile on his face. The mutton-head petty bourgeois Sir Herbert Johnson resisted the King's blandishments and was duly dismissed from whatever fat sinecure he had held. It would have been amusing if it had not been so pathetically absurd.

The King was too soft with his subjects. It should not have been the case that a potential Member of this English Parliament could refuse the King's command. A proper King would not be bound by any sort of free Parliament in the first place – the idea of Louis XIV being forced to bribe and cajole one of his own subjects into voting the way that he wanted was laughable. The choice given should be obey or be removed. And men like Narrey existed for such a reason. It was regrettable, much of the time, to take a human life. But it was sometimes regrettably necessary.

He would have removed Sir Herbert in a heartbeat.

The death of the boy John Matthews in the Tower had been necessary. And Guillaume had managed it with his usual deftness. Narrey knew that he could not afford to take even the smallest chance that his grand design would be discovered. And Matthews had, by his pathetic pilfering, attracted the notice of Authority – in the shape of that inquisitive snake Holcroft Blood – to the Liberty of the Savoy. Blood had poked his nose into the free school there, asking questions. And, had he discovered anything of note, Narrey would have had him swiftly dispatched, too. Either with poison, or other means. That would have been a pleasure. But, in the event, it had not proved necessary. Blood had found nothing and had gone away satisfied with his inquiries, or so it seemed – indeed he had gone off to a posting on the distant coast of Kent, Narrey learnt – and the risk attached to the killing of a king's officer, in Narrey's sober judgment, far outweighed the risk that Blood had discovered anything significant in the Savoy in one brief visit at the early stages of the mission's development. If Matthews had lived, he might have told Blood more. But that potential leak was pinched off. For a week or so, while he waited and watched to see if anything more would come of Blood's investigations, Narrey had revelled in the thought of taking his revenge on the Englishman. He longed to do it, frankly; he longed to dispatch Guillaume to accomplish the task. After his humiliation before the King at Versailles, he imagined the pleasure of his enemy's death as an almost sexual release. But nothing more had happened. Blood was clearly quite unaware of his scheme. Nobody in authority was interested in the free school – as far as he could determine – or in the momentous event that he had been tasked with. And killing Holcroft Blood might awaken interest, and provoke a fresh inquiry. No, Blood must be allowed to live. For now. Anyway, urgent business had called him back to France, a spy had been located, trapped, and had to be be dealt with. But Narrey had promised himself one thing. If Blood should ever again show the slightest curiosity about the school or the activities therein, he was a dead man.

Narrey had now been back in England for only a few weeks, after more than a year's absence in France, but he had been struck on his return to the Court of St James by the change in the tenor of the King's circle. The grand Protestant noblemen, who had made up the majority of the court in the King's first year of rule, were now a remnant. Two or three stalwarts remained and the rest had been swept away. And as far as he knew, this beneficent change had not come about by any design of Man – certainly he had not engineered it himself – it was clearly God's will. And King James's will, too. England was returning to the True Faith, slowly, but surely. And all the saints would rejoice when the heretic nation was at last welcomed back into the fold.

The Frenchman was pleased, too, with the progress made in his own mission, the sacred task that Louis XIV had entrusted to him. Nothing had come of Holcroft Blood's interference. There had been no other investigations; there had been no discreet surveillance, Guillaume had assured him. The stage was set for the final act that would ensure that God's plan, and Louis XIV's design, was played out satisfactorily. He would enjoy reporting this to his master when he returned to Versailles in a month or so. In the meantime, it was vital to keep King James from falling under the spell of his leading

Protestant commoners – men like the oafish Sir Herbert Johnson. If these stubborn gentlemen of the shires would not obey their monarch in this simple matter of a vote, they must not be allowed political power at all. They must be kept on the sidelines – permanently. It was clear that the English Parliament could not be recalled now. Perhaps it need never be recalled again.

The Comte de Maligny leant forward and whispered at some length in the French Ambassador's ear. Paul Barillon listened attentively to his First Secretary, turned, smiled and nodded his agreement to the tall, good-looking aristocrat. Then His Excellency lifted his head, caught the King's eye, bowed and stepped forward, walking across the black and white chequered floor and making for the large carved-oak-and-red-velvet throne on which James was slouching, scowling at his lap and cutting slices off an apple with a jewelled ceremonial dagger, popping the pieces in his mouth and crunching loudly.

'Your Majesty, might I make so bold as to ask a foolish question?'

'Monsieur l'Ambassador, *oui* – yes, what is it?'

Out of the corner of his eye, Barillon saw the soldier, Lord Churchill, the King's friend, take a discreet step closer to the throne so as to be able to hear more clearly.

'I am only a simple Frenchman, sire, but might I ask Your Majesty, why you require your Parliament to be summoned *at all*. If they will not comply with your wishes, if they will not do as they are told, surely they are of no use to you. And since you have dismissed them, why not continue to rule without their aid? You are the King!'

'King, I am, but unfortunately I do not have the power to make the laws in this land, Your Excellency,' said James glowering at the Ambassador. 'I believe I have had this fully explained to you more than once. I wish to abolish the Test Acts, to change the laws of the land, and to do so I must call a Parliament and have them enact the changes. I can give special royal dispensations, Indulgences, as they are called, to this individual or that one, and allow them to hold office and practice their faith in the manner of their choosing, but that is expensive and time-consuming, there are sheaves of papers to be signed off by the many different departments of state. And my Protestant officials prevaricate and drag their feet most damnably in the process. But I can do that, yes. I have *that* power. What I cannot do is to change the iniquitous laws that state that no man of the True Faith may hold public office. There is also the matter of money. My revenues are provided by Parliament, they must vote on the annual subsidy I receive from the Treasury. In short, they hold the purse strings and therefore I must recall them at some point, whether I wish to or not!'

'If it is a question of money, sire, I believe that my master Louis would look most kindly on a request for a loan, or perhaps even another substantial subsidy—'

'His Majesty has ample funds for the moment,' interrupted Jack. 'You have already been more than generous, sir. And the King thanks you for your kind offer.'

'Is that so, sire?'

'Yes, yes, Barillon. Thank you but I am not in desperate need at this present time, not quite yet,' said the King – but his expression was that of a wistful child.

'Only let me assure you, Majesty, that if you should choose to do without your troublesome English Parliament for an extended length of time, the King of France would be glad to stand with you in your hour of need and provide the necessary financial support. Or any other kind of support that Your Majesty might require. Indeed, sire, should your own countrymen prove to be unruly, should they be so rash as to take up arms against you, as did the traitor Monmouth, then may it please you to know that the Sun King would be equally honoured to provide you with a few of his regiments of guards – if required – merely to help you enforce the King's peace.'

'That,' said Jack Churchill firmly, 'will not be necessary. His Majesty has some twenty thousand men under arms and, as I have the honour to be a senior commander in his Army, I may tell you that I can conceive of no situation, *no situation at all*, which might require the presence of large numbers of French troops on British soil.'

That would be the last straw, Jack thought, *a certain recipe for catastrophe.* An unpopular King, funded by French money, surrounded by Catholic priests, papal envoys and various foreigners, who brought in French troops to oppress his subjects.

It would be a lit match dropped in a barrel of gunpowder.

Yet as Paul Barillon d'Amoncourt, Marquis de Branges, representative of His Most Christian Majesty, Louis XIV, bowed and moved away from the English King's throne, he noticed that James's long, sad face was lit with a little gleam of hope.

Chapter Sixteen

11 December 1687: Mincing Lane and
The Liberty of the Savoy

Holcroft turned the letter in his big hands, feeling the cheap fibrous paper with his fingertips. He had already opened and read its contents – it had not been sealed – and examined it minutely, looking between the lines, paying attention to the weight of ink used, the variations of colour, even warming it gently over a candle to see if it contained a secret message written in egg white, lemon juice or alum.

It did not. And Holcroft was certain that it was no more than it purported to be. Anyway, the person who wrote it had been dead for more than two years so any secret message it contained would probably be long out of date.

It was just a letter, written by a boy who knew that he was soon to die on the gallows and addressed to his mother. He told her he loved her, of course, and berated himself for his stupidity for attempting to steal a keg of gunpowder from the unguarded magazine in the Tower of London. He told her that she would not be allowed to see the hanging, that it and the trial would be done in private, and that he was happy in that. He hoped that God would have mercy on him in the next life and that He would keep her safe and well until she joined him in Heaven.

It was signed John Matthews.

Holcroft was sitting by the fire in the withdrawing room of his small, tall, newly rented house at the south end of Mincing Lane, near the junction with Tower Street. He had eaten his dinner with Elizabeth and he was drinking a dish of hot coffee by the fire, blissfully alone, and wondering what to do about the letter in his hands.

On his return from Sheerness, Holcroft had been commissioned by Lord Dartmouth to make a survey of the Tower of London and draw a map of the fortress and its liberties and he had recruited Sergeant Miller and a file of his fusiliers to help him with his measuring tapes and sight-line poles. The whole of the Tower was to be mapped and detailed plans drawn up of the buildings, towers, gates and rooms.

In the course of the survey, Miller and one of his corporals had been measuring the now-empty cell in the White Tower in which the young clerk John Matthews had died of apoplexy. They had discovered a loose stone by the fireplace, with a small hollowed out space behind it containing the letter. It had probably been used by generations of prisoners – perhaps even by his own father – but Holcroft felt that, in a small but strangely unforgivable way, he was invading the privacy of the dead boy by removing the note and examining it so closely.

However, the letter had cleared up one matter satisfactorily: John Matthews was not involved in any Catholic plot, so far as Holcroft could tell. His appropriation of the gunpowder was what he had said: an opportunistic act of theft. But that left Holcroft with the problem of what to do with the letter. He could, he knew, toss it into his drawing room fire and forget about it. No one would blame him, no one would know he had disposed of it in this casual, cruel manner.

But some feeling, some sense of guilt, perhaps, at the way in which the boy had been treated while imprisoned, and in which he had died, stayed his hand.

He looked at the outer side of the letter, where the words Maria Matthews were inscribed. Outside the room he could hear his wife discussing the proper cleaning of the silver with the maid. Her voice! It seemed to echo all around the tall house.

He had asked her to speak more softly on several occasions, and each time she had laughed merrily, as if he were making some jest, and said she would try, for the sake of his delicate little ears – although, she pointed out, she had nothing to hide, she was not ashamed of what she had to say and could not see any reason why she should not speak up clearly and candidly like an honest Christian woman. Captain Fowler had appreciated her fine, clear voice. Nothing was worse, her sea-captain former husband had claimed, than a God-damned mumbler.

How Holcroft wished that he had married a mumbler!

He looked at the letter in his hand. It was a rainy Sunday afternoon in December, a little after three of the clock, and the prospect of a long and loud evening with his wife lay before him. She would join him for coffee and they would sit and sip by the fire and converse – or she would read him something edifying from the *London Gazette* or the Bible, bawling the words across the short space between them – until it was time for a little light supper and then upstairs to bed, where he knew he must do his marital duty and attempt to make her pregnant. As he had done every night since the wedding. Domestic bliss, he had heard it called.

'Holcroft, my dear!' There she was, at the door of the little room, calling to him like one stag roaring to another across a wide Scottish glen. 'I thought I might read you some of Mister Bunyan's wonderful new book this afternoon – *The Pilgrim's Progress* – Jane Pertwee lent me her copy. Would not that be simply wonderful?'

Holcroft's literary tastes ran more towards natural philosophy and, if reading was the order of the day, he would have preferred to settle down in front of the fire with a copy of an intriguing book he had bought recently by a Fellow of Trinity College, Cambridge called *Philosophiae Naturalis Principia Mathematica*. He felt sure that he could learn a great deal from this treatise on the motions of cannonballs in flight – a subject close to his heart. But if his wife insisted on reading to him from John Bunyan, he knew it would be difficult to decline.

Holcroft was trying to train himself not always to speak the truth. Lying did not come easily to him, despite his former role in France, and his usual trick was to pause before answering, think carefully about what he was going to say, and then say it.

'Would not that be wonderful?' his wife yelled again, sitting down in a chair.

Holcroft paused, took a breath, but before he could get a word out, Elizabeth was off on a new track, banging away about the maid, and the way she cleaned the silver, disgraceful, slovenly, they must think about giving her notice and finding someone more suitable. Holcroft was aware that every word must be audible to the servant in question who moments before had been outside the door.

'My dear,' he said loudly. 'Pay attention, Elizabeth. I'm afraid that I cannot listen to you . . . uh, read this afternoon – I must go out. I have a letter to deliver.'

'Go out?' Elizabeth went over to the window and looked out at the grey, dismal, drizzly London street. 'Go out on a Sunday . . . on a foul day like this?'

'I am afraid so, my dear. I must deliver this letter, you see, and—'

'Can't you do it tomorrow? Or send a boy round to deliver it?'

'I shall be fully engaged tomorrow with the Tower survey. And the boy would not be able to find the addressee, there is a certain amount of enquiring to be done. And I feel it is my bounden duty, you see . . .'

'Duty, eh. Well, never let it be said that Elizabeth Blood does not respect a call to duty. Fowler was very keen on it. It's a shame, that's all! I was looking forward to a cosy afternoon, just the two of us. Never mind. But, fair warning, I shall probably have to start Mister Bunyan's new book without you. Will you be long?'

'Not too long, dearest, an hour or two at most.'

Half an hour later, Holcroft pulled off his sopping hat and cloak and, dripping more than a little, pushed his way through the crowd of drinkers in the Grapes and to the wooden counter. He had wanted to stretch his long legs so, rather than borrowing a horse from the

Tower stables, which would have meant a twenty-minute detour, Holcroft had walked the two miles from Mincing Lane. The rain had become heavier on his journey and by the time he arrived at the Liberty, he was regretting his decision to come out of his warm house in this weather.

He was given a decent amount of space at the bar, partly because of his size and dampness, and partly because the Ordnance coat proclaimed him as a king's officer.

The landlord, Josiah Fitch, came bustling over in good time too, and wiped the rough wooden boards in front of Holcroft with a greasy rag – he clearly remembered Holcroft's previous visit and the healthy amount of silver he had spent.

'What will it be, yer honour?' he said, smiling ingratiatingly at his customer.

'A quart of your best ale,' said Holcroft, 'and some information.' The fingers of his left hand resting on the counter played with a bright silver coin – a half crown.

'Not looking to have another sup with your brother, then?' said Josiah, turning away to fill a quart pot from the tap.

'No.'

'Where is old Tommy these days?' asked Fitch. 'I haven't set eyes on his for a month or more.'

'He's living up in the north now, I think,' said Holcroft. 'York or Durham, I heard. Maybe even Scotland. But it's not him I want to see.'

'There's a few folks in the Liberty who would like to have a little chat with old Tommy Blood. More'n a few. And not in a friendly way, if you catch my meaning.'

Holcroft became aware of a dark-haired man staring at him from the corner of the bar; a big fellow, with a deep scar on his cheek, not tall but lumped with solid muscle at the shoulder and forearm. The man was clearly listening to the exchange.

'Whatever Thomas has done, or hasn't done, it is nothing to do with me.' He said the words neither to Josiah Fitch nor to the dark stranger glowering at the corner but to the air somewhere in between. His hand slipped to rest, obviously, on the hilt of the small sword hanging at his left side. It was his only weapon. He suddenly wished he had thought to bring a pocket pistol with him – or even his Lorenzoni repeater. Too late now, and besides, he was not seeking any trouble, just wishing to deliver a two-year-old letter to a poor woman whose son had died in his keeping.

'Here you are, sir,' said Fitch, banging the quart pot down in front of Holcroft. He reached for the coin in his customer's hand but Holcroft closed his fist around it.

'Not quite yet, Fitch,' he said. 'A little information first.'

'Passing information can get you killed, Mister Blood – I think you know that. Tommy knew it. Which might explain why he's no longer residing in these parts.'

'Nobody is going to get hurt by this, Fitch, I simply want to know the whereabouts of Maria Matthews. I have a letter to deliver to her. No tricks. A simple delivery. Do you know her? It's not official business, I'm just passing on a note.'

Josiah Fitch looked suspicious. 'Now see here, Captain, you can't expect folk in these parts to go peaching on each other, telling any old king's man who asks about a person's whereabouts, spilling secrets to soldier-boys. It's as bad as telling the law.'

'Lieutenant.'

'What's that?'

'I'm a lieutenant not a captain.'

'Lieutenant, captain . . . what's the difference?'

'Five shillings.'

'What?'

'A lieutenant of the Ordnance gets five shillings a day, a captain gets ten.'

Fitch said: 'Ten shillings a day? It's all right for some, isn't it?'

Holcroft suddenly felt tired. He had no wish to discuss the Ordnance rates of pay with this irritating jackanapes. He wanted to hand over the letter to John Matthews's mother, make a small apology, and go home. And if Elizabeth insisted on talking loudly at him all evening, he would plead a headache and go off to bed.

He tried the straightforward approach.

'Do you know Maria Matthews? Yes or no?'

'I know old Maria.'

'And will you tell me where she is, so that I can give her a letter from her dead son John? Yes or no?'

'How about you give me the letter, an' I deliver it to her – for a suitable fee, of course. Call it a sovereign. Postage, if you like. You can afford it – *lieutenant, sir.*'

'No, but I will give you this half crown if you tell me where she lives. Right now. And if you don't, or if you lie to me, I'll come behind that counter, cut off your cock, and stuff it down the wide hole I'm going to slice in your gullet. Then I'll piss over your mangy, pox-ridden body and burn this foul bowze-house to the ground.'

Holcroft smiled nastily and held up the coin between his forefinger and thumb.

Fitch gave him a hurt look, but he snatched the silver from his fingers and said: 'She lives down at Palmer's free school, right at the back, where all the babies's cries won't be heard. End of this street, by the river. Can't miss it.'

And he turned away grumpily to serve another lucky customer.

On a Sunday, he had not expected much activity at Palmer's free school – the one he had visited two years ago when he was investigating John Matthews – but the place seemed to be full of life. He could hear a bell tolling softly somewhere in the complex and streams of people, scores of them, were coming out of the school through the wide open double front doors. It struck Holcroft belatedly that this must be time for Vespers, the evensong of the Romish faith. And that the papists from all over this part of London had just finished their Sunday evening devotions.

He waited until the stream slackened and pushed his way against the throng of people in their best coats and hats, bonnets and frocks into the central courtyard where he had seen the children being fed their noon-time slop on his last visit. By the red-brick chapel off to the left, Holcroft saw a man in a black cassock, with a gold crucifix and amber beads standing by the open door of the House of God. It was the young priest who had shown him round two years ago – Father Williams, was it?

Holcroft walked over and explained his mission to the priest.

'Maria? Oh yes, of course, she's with us, she lodges in St Mary's Foundling Hospital with her charges. Would you like me to give her the letter?'

'Thank you, Father,' said Holcroft, 'but if you don't mind I should prefer to hand it to her personally and apologise for the length of time it's taken to reach her.'

Father Williams looked doubtful. 'I suppose it would be all right,' he said. 'But a swift visit, we do not wish to disturb any mothers or babies who might be sleeping.'

Father Williams led him once again across the central courtyard – this time, it being Sunday, the space was devoid of all the running, clamouring children – and through a door, down a long corridor and into a long, narrow, high-ceilinged hall lit by several tall windows. He had passed through this hall last time he was here but then it had been empty. Now it was laid out with rows of beds of varying sizes – from tiny cots to full-sized adult pallets on stout wooden frames – all along both long walls. On the short wall at the far end of the hall was a huge painting of the Virgin Mary in a white gown and blue cloak, standing palms spread wide on a white cloud in a shaft of sunlight. She appeared to be smiling down on everyone in the hall.

After the vast painting, the next sensation to hit him was the smell – a waft of sweet milk, blood and faeces, womanly sweat and warm baby flesh. It was not, in fact, unpleasant. Holcroft noted that there were seventeen beds along the left-hand wall and sixteen along the right. Some beds were occupied, some with tiny forms, swaddled and sleeping – nine tiny infants, he counted – and some which contained nursing mothers with babes at the breast; some were occupied by resting women, whose grossly swollen bellies indicated they were in the last stages of pregnancy.

Many of the women moving about the hall looked as if they were no more than three or four months gone, their condition hardly showing. The middle space between the lines of beds was kept clear for traffic and Holcroft counted fourteen young women, no fifteen, there was one coming in through a door at the back, all in simple grey sacking-cloth dresses, moving about, some sweeping the shining floor with age-worn brooms, some carrying jugs of warm water, bowls of milk-pap, piles of napkins or clean bedding and what-have-you from here to there.

'You have all these people in your service?' said Holcroft. He was taken aback at how many women there were. He had never seen so many females gathered in one room – there were thirty-two of them, his quick-counting brain told him – he and Father Williams were the only men.

'St Mary's is not only a home for foundlings,' said Father William. 'Although that was our original function, and we do receive a dozen or so babies every year, left on the doorstep, usually. St Mary's is *so* much more than that.' The priest spoke quietly and calmly but there was an unmistakeable note of pride in his voice.

'Father Palmer felt that since we have been blessed with such a generous patron,' he continued, 'we should extend our work beyond rescuing of foundlings and give succour to unfortunate girls who have fallen into sin with men, and who find themselves with child, but who are unable to care for the baby after it's born.'

'Where do all these pregnant women come from?' Holcroft was still reeling.

'Most from London,' said a new voice and Holcroft looked down and saw a small round woman, with an enormous shelf of a bosom, a cheery red face and tiny, twinkling blue eyes smiling up at him.

'But we've had women from Kent and Essex – even had a lass come all the way from Lincolnshire to us one time.'

Holcroft was fascinated and a little horrified. He looked round the room, gazing at the women and children while the priest conferred with the fat little woman.

'What do you do with all the babies?' he asked.

'Oh, we try to find good homes for them,' she said. 'Gentlewomen who find they cannot conceive with their husbands come to us, choose one they like and raise 'em as their own. Or respectable craftsmen from the Guilds, those who're looking for apprentices or household servants, they come and take their pick. And the great religious houses in France have taken a number to raise to serve the good monks and nuns, praise God – some of them might end up as clergy themselves. We get orphans coming here too. Children who turn up looking for a hot meal and a bed. We take them all in. We like to think that we do God's work here.'

'I believe you do,' said Holcroft. *This place is like a manufactory*, he thought. But instead of producing tables or baskets or swords, it produced human beings. Women came in to this hall, stayed a while in peace and comfort, until their babies were ready to come, produced their unwanted offspring, then left and returned to their lives. The children, instead of growing up unwanted in the depravity of some foul London slum had the chance of a good, happy life – and an education, to boot. He was impressed. It was a deeply Christian enterprise, compassionate and loving.

'I'm Maria Matthews,' the fat little woman said. 'I'm the Matron of St Mary's Foundling Hospital. Father Williams said that you came here to speak to me.'

Holcroft realised that the young priest had disappeared. He fumbled in his coat pocket and produced the crumpled letter.

'I am Lieutenant Blood of the Board of Ordnance,' he said, a little pompously. 'I questioned your son John in the White Tower after he had been caught stealing from the stores.' He saw that Maria's face had fallen. She looked near to tears.

A little blond boy, an elfin creature of about seven years, with bright green eyes, appeared by her side, tugging her apron: 'Why so sad, Auntie Mary? Don't be sad!'

'Not now, Samuel, not now. Go and play in the courtyard, there's a good boy.'

Maria wiped her eyes with a dirty kerchief and said: 'You were saying, sir?'

Holcroft cleared his throat. 'After I spoke to him, he died suddenly, as you know.' He paused for a heartbeat, unsure how to proceed. 'We think it was apoplexy. And I am sorry to say that we did not discover this letter, which as you see is addressed to you, until quite recently. He had hidden it in his cell and . . .'

Maria had taken the letter out of his hands and, opening it eagerly, she looked at the spidery black writing inside. Her merry blue eyes were brimming with tears.

'I . . . I cannot read as well as I should, sir,' she said. 'He was trying to teach me, my good boy John was. But I am still not very clever with written-down words. As a great kindness to me, sir, would you be so good as to read it aloud?'

Holcroft took the letter, tilted it up towards the last of the daylight coming in from the tall windows. He cleared his throat noisily and read: 'Dearest Mother, it is with a heavy heart that I write these lines, perhaps the last I ever shall write . . .'

Chapter Seventeen

11 December 1687: The Strand

He was being followed; he was certain of it. Three men, probably. The one behind him, he'd identified him first. His pace was almost exactly the same as his own. The man stopped when he did – once to cross to the north side of the Strand, and once again to peer in the black window of a closed chophouse he liked to frequent. There was a man on the far side of the road, too, walking parallel with him, also matching his speed in a way that was unnatural. There was likely to be another fellow ranging ahead, too – that would be the minimum professional surveillance pattern, with Holcroft in the centre of the triangle. But he had not yet spotted the advance man.

Holcroft rebuked himself bitterly. It had taken him at least ten minutes to notice the followers as he made his way home – the foot traffic on the Strand was light, there were only a handful of people about, most of them middling sorts hurrying to their warm hearths on this dreary Sunday evening. A few scurrying servants who had been granted leave to visit their own families on this holy day and were returning to the cramped garrets in grand houses where they toiled all week. He had been thinking about St Mary's Foundling Hospital, about the children whose lives had been salvaged, and when he had quit the Liberty of the Savoy and turned right up the Strand, Holcroft hadn't even considered that he might have company.

Footpads? Perhaps. Casual thieves looking to waylay a rich-looking king's officer? That would be no surprise, coming as he was out of the lawless Liberty. But surely they would have fallen on him in the narrow, pitch-dark streets there, not followed him into the broad, better-lit and busier thoroughfare of the Strand.

Darkness had fallen on London but householders on the better streets were encouraged to hang lanterns outside their houses and the taverns and alehouses often had flaming brands outside their doors to attract customers. Nevertheless, the wide street was dark enough in places for an ambush. Holcroft pondered what to do. Did they mean him any harm? It was difficult to say. Perhaps if he continued all the way home to Mincing Lane, these men would merely watch him all the way there.

That did not seem likely. These people were not friends; they were not guardian angels. Whoever they were, they meant to do him harm. Could he fight? Three against one – and he without a firearm. God, how he wished he had the Lorenzoni!

No, was the answer, he would likely end up dead or badly injured. Could he flee from them? If he suddenly ran north ... Aphra Behn's house was in Drury Lane, and he could seek refuge. No – that would mean bringing trouble to her door. And, on the way, the streets were narrow and dark – the slum of St Giles was up there too, hardly a place a respectable man would wish to run towards. However, to flee south would take him back into the Liberty, but also towards the river. Could he escape by boat? No, there'd be no time to hail a wherry.

All these considerations flashed through his head as he continued to plod onward up the north side of the Strand, giving no outward indication that he knew he was being shadowed. He saw a coach and six approaching up the Strand, the horses' hooves clopping on the cobbles, and in that vehicle he saw his salvation. It was well appointed, glossy black with gold leaf on the pillars and an intricate gold design on the doors. The curtains were also black and tightly drawn against the evening chill. There was a black-cloaked coachman sitting in front, well wrapped in his layers against the December cold as he drove the three pairs of black horses, and twin lamps illuminated the night on either side of him. Holcroft stepped into the mud of the street and hailed the vehicle, raising his hand and calling out to the coachman to halt.

The coachman reined in the black horses, calling 'Whoa, whoa!', and hauled on the hand-lever brake to bring the big vehicle to a halt.

It stopped beside Holcroft, with the driver still calling to his beasts, calming them and bringing them to a snorting, stamping standstill. The door of the carriage swung open. Golden light spilled from the interior, almost blinding Holcroft.

He put his hands up to shield his eyes and saw two men inside the vehicle. One, he recognised in a spilt second as the dark man with the scarred face who had been listening to his conversation with Josiah Fitch in the Grapes. Now, for some reason, he was wearing an expensive but badly fitting blond periwig. The second man, a gingery type with vast whiskers, was pointing a large cocked horse pistol at his head.

The red-headed man pulled the trigger, the cock snapped down and Holcroft saw a blue spark struck against the frizzen ignite the powder in the pan.

Then nothing.

Misfire.

Holcroft was already hurling himself backwards into the mud of the street. He landed with a splash. He rolled and leapt to his feet, clamping his long scabbard with his left hand and hauling the small-sword free with his right. The ginger man in the coach hurled the useless horse pistol at him, and it crashed against his cheek, lights flashing in his head, the lock cutting deeply into the skin below his left eye. Holcroft went back a step. The man with the ridiculous wig and scarred face was already out of the carriage, he had a short axe in his right hand and a long dagger in the other.

Holcroft stepped in and lunged with his small sword but Scarred Face knocked the point away with his dagger blade and swung the axe at Holcroft's neck.

He got his left forearm up and half blocked the axe swing, but only half, the wide blade thumping hard into the thick, heavy material of his wet Ordnance coat at his left shoulder. Holcroft punched with the sword hilt, a good solid blow, and caught Scarred Face full in the mouth with the metal guard, the knuckle-bow. With a jolt of satisfaction, Holcroft heard the snap of breaking teeth and felt the hot spurt of his enemy's blood across the back of his right hand.

Scarred Face dropped immediately and behind him loomed the ginger man, a fresh horse pistol in his hands, which he was in the act of cocking.

Holcroft lunged with the small-sword. The blade lanced out and slid into the darkness under the ginger man's chin. The sword plunged deep into the man's throat, going in easily, passing through the skin and flesh, the tip bursting a good six inches out the other side and nailing into the black painted wood of the coach wall. The ginger man was gurgling, scrabbling with his hands at the blade beneath his jawbone. Holcroft paused for a heartbeat, took a huge breath and ripped the blade free, sideways, the steel laying open his victim's neck in a waterfall of splashing blood.

Scarred Face was up again and snarling bloodily, to his left, by the open coach door. Holcroft surged towards him, using his weight to shoulder him against the side of the carriage, then he whipped his forehead forward, smashing it into the bridge of his opponent's nose. The man slumped, stunned, his absurd blond wig slipped off his shaven head, and Holcroft, stepping back, jabbed the point of his sword deep into the man's belly, skewering down towards his pelvis, the blade scraping on bone.

The ginger man was still clawing at his bloody, ripped throat, still holding the heavy horse pistol. And above and to the left, Holcroft could see the coachman, standing up on his bench and peering down at the fight, a squat musket-shaped weapon, probably a blunderbuss, in his hands. He could hear the pattering of running feet and the shouts of the man who had been following him, approaching fast.

He had to get away. He had to leave now.

Holcroft reached out with his left hand and ripped the blood-slick pistol from the ginger man's slack fingers. The man was falling anyway, breath bubbling and puffing wetly from his frothing throat. The piece was already cocked and Holcroft pointed the weapon with his left hand at the looming black shape of the coachman, aiming for the centre of his dark mass. He pulled the trigger, the flint snapped down.

No misfire this time. The flint ignited the spark in the pan, and fired the charge in the barrel, the pistol boomed, the coachman gave a cry, half turned and tumbled backwards and away, his weapon clattering as it fell into the driving footwell.

Holcroft turned to his right, there was a shape there and a glint of steel. The man who'd been following him. He slashed wildly with his sword, heard a clang, and lunged at the shape. He felt the steel go into flesh, and a curse, and the shape backed away. He could hear other men calling to each other on the other side of the coach.

London voices. Savoyards.

'Did they get him?'

'Is he down?'

No, Holcroft was not fucking down. And now he was properly angry. He dropped the empty pistol and stepped to his left, found a footing in the darkness against the side of the coach and swung up to the driver's seat. The horses were skittish, jerking against the secured reins and the brake on the carriage – the banging of pistols, the angry shouting and the smell of blood was upsetting them. They were close to panic.

Holcroft fumbled for the reins with his left hand, his fingers brushed the warm wood of the blunderbuss stock. He could see two men in the light of the carriage lamps approaching fast to the left of the horses, in the lee of the houses on the Strand.

One called out, 'Bartie, are you all right?'

There was a shape behind his shoulder, someone nimble climbing over the roof of the carriage. He turned and saw a flash of angry, brown-bearded face speckled with gore. Holcroft slashed overhand, up and across his body, the slim steel blade arcing through the lamplight. The blade thudded into the head of the climbing man above, cutting on down, slicing into his scalp and cutting away a large flap of skin and hair. The fellow howled and rolled away, elbows and knees thumping across the wooden roof and his heavy body splashing down into the mud. The two men in front of Holcroft were shouting, calling their friends, cursing their enemy, Holcroft could see a long glint of steel under the foremost man's dark cloak . . .

But now Holcroft had the coachman's blunderbuss in his left hand, lifted free of the footwell. He dropped his small-sword, point first, into the foot rest where it stuck into the wooden board, and holding the blunderbuss in his left hand, he cocked it swiftly with his right. It was an ugly, clumsy gun with a two-foot brass barrel ending in a broad trumpet-shaped mouth. Holding it awkwardly in just his left hand, butt braced against his pelvic bone, he pointed it at the two men, bunched together by the horses' flanks, no more than two yards away, both armed with knives.

In almost the same moment, he released the brake with his right hand, scooped up the leather reins from the curled metal holder, and pulled the trigger of the blunderbuss. The big gun exploded, jumping wildly and jabbing painfully into his waist as it belched a lethal storm of rusty nails, broken glass, musket balls and small stones in a wide pattern off to his left. The blast swept the two attackers off their feet, knocking them into moaning huddled heaps on the cobbles.

The horses screamed, bucked wildly and lurched forward, terrified by the explosion behind them, the carriage shot away down the Strand, with Holcroft fighting to keep his seat, not making any attempt to control the panic-stricken beasts, glad to be moving away from his enemies and at such a fine speed . . .

'My dearest, what has happened to your face?' Elizabeth held the candle a little higher and peered at Holcroft's left cheek, looking over his shoulder into the mirror.

He was in his nightshirt, washing his face with warm water in the porcelain ewer on the stand in his bedroom, preparing to go to bed. The thrown pistol had given him a deep cut and a big, painful bruise under his left eye.

'It is nothing, my love, I carelessly walked into the corner of a building in the darkness as I came out of a public house. Sheer clumsiness. Nothing to worry about.'

He finished patting the small, crusted wound, threw down the cloth, and hefted the bowl over to the window, resting it on the sill and pushing up the latch with his elbow, before opening it and pouring the bloody water out on to the cobbles below. His shoulder was paining him, too, where the axe had struck him, and under the thick linen nightshirt was a large angry red bruise but mercifully no laceration.

'Too much brandy!' she bellowed. 'Should have guessed that's what you were about, Holcroft – carousing! Men, why can't they stop at home with a dish of tea.'

'Yes, dear,' said Holcroft, sliding into bed. 'You are quite right. But it has given me something of a headache. Do you mind if I forgo my marital rights – just for this night? I'd prefer, if you don't mind it, dearest, merely to go straight to sleep.'

'Nonsense, Mister Blood, we can't let a surfeit of French brandy and a little headache hold us back. Buckle to, my bonnie lad. Captain Fowler never let a drop of brandy get in the way of his duty. Come along, Holcroft, we've a baby to make . . .'

Chapter Eighteen

15 December 1687: Palace of White Hall

'They want me to make a commitment,' said Jack Churchill to his beautiful wife.

They were dining together, *à deux*, a rare occurrence for a couple who were as sought after as they, eating a simple meal – chicken soup, cold mutton and boiled asparagus, gooseberry fool – in the parlour of their quarters in the Cockpit.

Sarah took a sip of her wine: 'And what did you say to them?'

'I prevaricated, of course. I told Lord Danby that, on the one hand, I was a good Protestant Englishman and the avowed enemy of all dictatorial, absolutist French-style government, but, on the other, that I was bound to James by ties of affection, loyalty, duty and – well, gratitude, to put it bluntly. I have served him for nearly twenty years and he had raised me up to be the man I am today. I pointed out – as the Duke of Grafton is so fond of saying – that James would not live for ever, and that Mary of Orange was the heir, and she was Protestant to her marrow.'

'How did he react?'

'Danby said that there would come a time, and it would come very soon, when every gentleman of means in England would be required to make a hard choice – a choice between his King and his religion. But, the thing is, Sarah, I don't want to make a choice – I love them both. And I am determined to try my utmost to steer James into a less confrontational position. I wish I could make him listen to me.'

'If it does come to a choice, and you love them equally, as you say, then you must choose whichever is more advantageous for us as a family, for you personally.'

Jack moodily speared a thick slice of cold mutton, spread mustard thickly on and popped it in his mouth. 'I know that, my darling,' he said, his words muffled.

'Then ask yourself, which side will help us – which will help our family most.'

'Can we talk about something else,' said Jack. 'I am heartily sick of designs and deceits, plots and politics. Tell me, my love, how fares your princess?'

Anne, Princess of Denmark, the King's second daughter, was Sarah's good and intimate friend, and she, her husband George and her retinue occupied most of the private apartments and state rooms in the Cockpit. The Churchills had the rest.

'Not in the very best of spirits, my darling. I try to cheer her but in truth she is very low. After she gave birth to that poor dead mite two months ago, since then she has got it into her head that she is cursed never to see a child live to adulthood. I tell her it is nonsense and that she and George will surely make another one. But she has lost three children this year, poor soul. Did you know that, dearest? You remember how distraught I was when . . . when our own dear Harriet . . . so I grieve with her. I pray with her daily for their poor little souls.'

Jack swallowed the last of his wine. 'Is there nothing at all cheerful that we could discuss? Tell me something amusing.'

Sarah, who was sitting opposite her husband at the small table, wiped her damp eye and straightened in her chair. She smiled at her handsome husband – by God she was lucky to have him, and she knew it – and slipped her silk shoe off before sliding her stockinged foot up under the table and thrusting it into her husband's crotch. Jack sat up with a start and raised his eyebrows.

'Would your ears be offended by a little salacious gossip, my one true love?'

'Not in the least,' said Jack. 'Tell me everything, the more salacious the better!'

Sarah began sliding the small silk-clad foot over Jack's groin and upper thigh.

'You know that young Foot Guards officer, Ensign Richard Campion, the very handsome one with the green eyes?'

'Ye-es. I know him, Sidney Godolphin wanted me to take him on as an aide, he's a Cornish relative, I gather. Pretty as a petal but no cleverer than a clod of earth.'

'Well, he has taken up with Lady Dorothy Whipple, the Countess of Sligo's youngest daughter. Quite head over heels in love with her. Or so Lady Dorothy believes. They say she has already been most generous to him with her favours.'

Sarah's silk foot was now rubbing at Jack's parts with a steady insistent stroke.

'Hmmm,' he said, 'do go on, my dear . . .'

'But she may be in for a rude awakening,' Sarah continued.

Jack abruptly got up from the table. He walked round and seized Sarah by the wrist, pulling her up from her chair, embracing her hard and kissing her deeply.

As Jack began to caress her back through the silk of her bodice and gently kiss the side of her neck, he mumbled, 'Rude awakening, yes, go on . . .'

'Because . . . oh darling, Jack . . . Because, handsome, green-eyed Richard Campion – darling, shall we go into the bedchamber, yes? Now? – because Ensign Campion was seen yesterday morning, before dawn, coming out of the apartments of that Major du Clos fellow, who's attached to the French Embassy, and looking quite disgracefully *deshabillé*, shall we say, tucking his shirt into his breeches – aagghh, oh, hmmm, darling – or at least that is what my little spies tell me.'

'Really?' Jack looked up from his work. They had reached the bedroom and were both half out of their clothes. 'That's Major du Clos's line of country, is it?'

'Oh yes, all the ladies tell me so. Some of the pages, too.'

For a long while neither of them uttered a recognisable word. Then, when they were finished, panting, glowing with joyous perspiration and lying side by side on top of the embroidered covers of the four-poster bed, Jack drawled: 'And so tell me, my dove, did your little spies have any other juicy morsels to share?'

'I do have one more item, yes.'

Jack levered himself up on one elbow and looked down at his flushed wife's lovely face: 'Another pretty boy who is sadly indiscriminate with his affections?'

'No, I had this from one of Anne's chamber maids, who has a girl-cousin who serves Queen Mary over in the royal apartments. Apparently, they sometimes meet up in the laundry for a gossip to pass the time while the bed linens are boiling.'

Jack sat up. Mary of Modena was an Italian princess who had married the King in the year 1673, after the death of James's first wife Anne Hyde – who had given him his two daughters, Mary of Orange and Anne of Denmark. The Italian lady was a shy, unhappy woman disliked by the public for her Catholicism, with no living children, who kept to herself in her apartments and was seldom seen about the court.

'Go on, my love.'

'Mary's maid told Anne's girl that the Queen had not had her womanly bleeding for two months in a row now.'

Jack stared at her. Neither said a word for a several long heartbeats.

'And she is not yet thirty,' said Sarah. 'Still quite young enough.'

'It could mean nothing,' said Jack. 'A few missed months. There could be several explanations. Anyway, even if she is with child, she could miscarry. Or the baby could be stillborn. It might be a girl. It most probably changes nothing at all.'

'Or,' said Sarah, 'it just might possibly change everything.'

Chapter Nineteen

17 December 1687: The Strand

Holcroft did not often dwell in the past. He did not like to rake over things that he had done badly – or that he had done well, for that matter. He found dealing with the present, the brightly coloured, shimmering, fast-moving, unpredictable *now*, quite difficult enough without going into hypothetical questions of what might have been, if a particular set of circumstances had been different.

On the other hand, unfinished things, uncompleted tasks irked him. They gave him an uncomfortable sense that the hidden forces of chaos in the world were in the ascendant, that order was quietly slipping away and the universe as he knew it would very soon be plunged into darkness. Mysteries made him feel uncomfortable. Puzzles needed to be solved, if he was to have peace of mind. And as he walked along the Strand on a cold December morning six days after the attempt on his life in this very street, he contemplated the attack and tried to solve the puzzle that lay behind it.

The man with the scarred face and the silly wig, who had overheard him talking to Fitch in the Grapes, had gathered his friends and attacked him an hour or two later, obviously trying to kill him. Why? Robbery he could understand – he was likely to be carrying a purse, and his clothes, boots and sword would have been worth something. But murder made no sense. It was risky. Holcroft was a large, strong, armed man – and a soldier by profession. And even if he *were* killed, and the murderer could shelter from the law in the Liberty, the victim's friends or relatives might seek private vengeance. A soldier's commander, his fellow officers and some of the enlisted men would be unlikely to let it lie. Anyway, what would be the point of murdering him? What advantage did it give?

On his way here, he had passed the spot in Fleet Street where he had jumped from the carriage – the horses had been tiring of their headlong panic and the vehicle was slowing – and he had landed safely and sprinted away into the dark side streets, still clutching the empty blunderbuss and its pouch of powder and shot, cutting down Salisbury Court, only pausing at the Queen's Theatre in Dorset Gardens by the river, trying to stifle his panting, listen for any pursuit, and reload the firearm – all at the same time. But there had been nobody following him. He waited fifteen minutes in the darkness and then stepped calmly on to the wharf at Dorset Stairs, tucking the blunderbuss inside his coat, and hailed a passing wherry to take him homewards.

As the boatman rowed him downstream, it was the sight of the theatre, tall, black and deserted on a grim Sunday night, that gave him an idea of how he might unravel the puzzle of the murderous Savoyard with the badly scarred face.

Now, six days later, on this cold, bright, Saturday morning, as he headed back along the Strand – the pavement thronging with strollers and shoppers, loud-crying food vendors, running urchins, pedestrians of all sorts and the thoroughfare filled with scores of high-stepping horse-riders, puffing chairmen and fine carriages clattering past – he felt that he were in a different and more benign city all together.

Nevertheless, he had taken some necessary precautions. As well as his officers' small-sword, the right hand pocket of his big blue coat held the comforting weight of the fully loaded Lorenzoni repeating pistol. And a dozen yards behind him, sauntering along in a bright green civilian coat and pulled-down black felt hat adorned with an emerald plume, was a slyly grinning Sergeant Miller, who carried a veritable arsenal – two pistols in his broad leather belt at the front, only half hidden by his swinging green coat, a third pistol wedged in the small of his back, a pair of small steel pistols, one in each coat pocket, and one tucked up his left sleeve; a thick-bladed cutlass hung from a baldric at his left side, a razor-like skinning knife sat in the top of his right riding boot and a final steel pocket pistol shoved into his left boot.

He swaggered – and clanked a little – as he walked and, while he might have looked like some diminutive buccaneer, Miller was the finest pistol shot in the Royal Fusiliers, regularly winning prizes at regiment's annual shooting competitions.

On the far side of the Strand, a disreputable old man, hatless and as bald and brown as a boiled egg on top, was shambling along, roughly but not exactly at the same rate as Holcroft. Master Gunner Enoch Jackson wore a voluminous blue cloak that covered his body to his knees – but if that garment had been lifted it would have revealed that the veteran was also unusually heavily armed, with pistols and a cutlass at his waist, and in one hand a coachman's blunderbuss loaded with a full charge of two drams of Number Three black powder and a dozen half-ounce pistol balls.

Holcroft did not expect to be attacked again – not in broad daylight – but he was not prepared to take the chance of an encounter without the means of striking back. He recalled that he had not expected to be attacked the last time either. The presence of Jackson and Miller, both of whom had been delighted to be asked to act as paid guards, was a precaution. Holcroft was a cautious man. He had been lucky last Sunday night, and he knew that, if ginger man's pistol had not misfired, he would now be a dead man. So he had spent a little of his own money, squared it with their commanding officers, and privately hired the two men in the Ordnance that he trusted most. Between them, he reckoned, he, Miller and Jackson could successfully fight off an attack by any force smaller than a dozen armed men.

Holcroft paused at the door of Thomas Pettigrew's chophouse. He looked at Miller and nodded, and Miller grinned back, winked for good measure, and took up a position leaning against the brick wall, his hat pulled down even lower over his eyes, his right hand resting casually on the butt of one of his belted pistols. *He's truly enjoying this*, realised Holcroft, surprised by his own insight.

Aphra Behn was already seated at a table at the back of the dining room and Holcroft made his way to her and bent for a kiss. He caught a waft of her smell – raw spirits, stale tobacco and rancid sweat – and recoiled at its pungency.

Aphra saw his reaction, and laughed.

'Came straight from the Grapes,' she said. 'I didn't bother to go home to bathe in French perfume, change my petticoats and prettify myself just to meet you, Holly.'

Holcroft saw that she looked thin and tired and was wearing a disreputable, low-cut dress of some cheap material, which exposed a good deal of wrinkled upper chest flesh. However, she was animated, carrying an air of quiet excitement, even of triumph.

'On that subject, you'd better show old Pettigrew some chink or he won't let us eat. He thinks I'm a penniless ne'er-do-well who'd steal the cloth from the table.'

Holcroft took off his hat, sat down and waved over the scowling old man who was lurking in the shadows. He looked around and saw that the restaurant's candle sconces had been adorned for Christmas with sprigs of holly and fronds of green ivy.

'We'll have a dozen mutton chops, Thomas. Quick as you like. Bread, butter, green beans, a dish of buttered turnips and a jug of your best claret.'

Once the order had been given, and the proprietor had hurried away looking relieved, Holcroft looked at his old friend on the far side of the table.

'You do, in fact, look just like a ne'er-do-well,' he said, smiling at her.

'I'm sure that is a generous complement,' she replied. 'You saying that my finely honed skills as an actress, as an artiste who has performed for dukes, kings and emperors, have not deserted me. Not that I look like a poxed-up buttock-broker.'

'A what?'

'A buttock-broker – didn't they use that low term when you were growing up in Shoreditch? Or have you forgotten your humble origins? It means a person who brokers, or sells "buttocks", a thieves' cant word meaning prostitutes. A prostitute, I suppose somebody had to tell you one day, is a kindly female who offers men—'

'I know what a prostitute is, Aphra. I've just never before heard of these buttock-breakers—'

'Brokers. They are called buttock-brokers, Holcroft,' Aphra said these words deliberately loudly for, at that moment, old Thomas Pettigrew came to the table bearing a basket of fresh bread, a slab of butter and a large jug of red wine. Pettigrew glared at him. Holcroft blushed. Aphra laughed and poured him a glass.

'I'm sorry, Holly. Forgive me. I passed myself off as a' – and here she stage-whispered the word – 'buttock-broker . . . a bawd or madame, when I was at the Grapes. A bawd from Wapping, that was my legend, looking to get some fresh young girls for the docks' trade. It was a ruse, a subterfuge. And a useful one, I think.'

Four days ago, Holcroft had visited Aphra and had asked her to make some discreet investigations on his behalf. He asked her to see if anyone she knew could tell her the identity of the bewigged man with the scarred face, giving her a good description, and telling her what had happened last Sunday evening. He had thought she might ask some of her acquaintances in the seedier parts of London, theatre folk, after all, mixed with all sections of society, and she lived in a bawdy house herself in Drury Lane, but he'd not expected her to invent a new identity and risk her life by entering that nest of lawless murderers, asking questions.

'That was very dangerous, Aphra. I wish you had told me that was what you were planning to do. These people are prepared to kill if you cross them.'

'Well, it is done now and no harm has come to me. Don't you want to know what I found out?'

Holcroft took a sip of his wine and reached for a piece of bread.

'The man with the scarred face is called Michael Maguire – or he *was* called that. He died of his wounds on Tuesday. Does that name mean anything to you?'

'The name Maguire does. A family of criminals in the Liberty are called Maguire. They prey on the other crews. Everyone seems to be terrified of them.'

'They have a fearsome reputation, for sure,' said Aphra. 'Taxing the Savoyards – squeezing them for everything they can. Feared but not much loved was my understanding. I spoke to your man Josiah Fitch at some length about this – in bed!'

Holcroft gaped at her. 'Aphra, there was no call for you to—'

'Calm yourself, Holly, he was ill. He was laid up with the gripe and I bought him some soup, sponged his brow, brought him some rags to blow his nose on. A nip or two of brandy. But I'm shocked you should think I would lower myself—'

'What did he say?' Holcroft interrupted her. Sometimes he found Aphra's teasing a little tiresome.

'The Maguires, their whole organisation, thirty bravos or more, had been hired by another man – a very powerful man – to protect his interests in the Liberty. This took place nearly three years ago. In February of 1685. Lots of silver has since been paid to the Maguires, and more has been promised when their task is done.'

'Who is this man? What interests?'

'A Frenchman from Paris. A Catholic. And his interest is in a school down at the end of . . .'

'Palmer's free school,' said Holcroft. 'What did this Frenchman look like?'

'Ah-ha – hardly anybody seems to know. Only Patrick Maguire, the patriarch of this clan of rogues, Father Palmer and maybe some of his assistants, have actually seen his face. He always wears a hat pulled down low in company, apparently, and his lieutenant, another Frenchman, arranges the day-to-day business for him.'

'Oh Aphra!' said Holcroft. 'You *have* done well.'

'Haven't I.'

'Do you think it could really be . . .'

'I do. We had word that he was in London two years and a half ago. And I believe we have stumbled upon his base of operations here, his lair, if you like.'

They sat in silence for several minutes as Pettigrew brought their chops and they began to eat – Aphra attacking her plate like a starveling.

Narrey, thought Holcroft. *Right here. Perhaps, even now, not three hundred yards from where I'm eating my mutton.* He looked out of the big front window and caught a glimpse of Sergeant Miller at his post, still leaning against the wall, still smiling and now puffing a long white clay pipe of good Virginian tobacco. Beyond him, on the far side of the Strand, Holcroft could make out the form of an old bald beggar, draped in a voluminous cloak and seeking alms from every passerby.

It seemed clear to Holcroft that the attempt to murder him was the result of his enquiries in the Savoy after Maria Matthews. Narrey was doing something in the Savoy that he did not wish Holcroft, or any figure of authority, to discover. Holcroft had no idea what it was that he was up to, he had genuinely only meant to deliver the letter to Maria. But Narrey or his Savoyard allies would not know that. Narrey, or perhaps Patrick Maguire, had reacted explosively, sending the man with the ill-fitting wig and scarred face – Michael Maguire – and the others to kill him.

'Do not go into the Savoy again, Aphra,' said Holcroft. He had a sudden pang of terror for her. It occurred to him that his own blundering investigations might be leading her into mortal danger. That must not happen. 'Don't go anywhere near the Grapes or anywhere in there again. I want you to promise me that.'

'I have no plans to, Holly. I can promise you that. I have no wish to run foul of Narrey. The question is – what should we do with this intelligence?'

'What intelligence? All we know for sure is that a mysterious Frenchman has been free with his money to a gang of Savoyard rascals. We suspect he's Narrey, but we have nothing more solid than a suspicion.'

'So we do nothing?' Aphra Behn frowned at him.

'I will send a note to the Earl of Sunderland, telling him that we suspect that a notorious French spy known as Narrey is operating out of the free school in the Liberty of the Savoy. Sunderland must have heard of him from his own people in France. He has plenty of capable men who can look into such matters. But I think it would be best, Aphra, if you and I left Narrey and these murderous Savoyards alone.'

'That seems like an excellent way of dodging our responsibilities.'

'Aphra, I'm not employed to hunt spies. Since King Charles's death, I no longer have any connection with intelligence at all. Neither do you, in fact. And what could we do anyway? Do you want me to take a company of fusiliers into Palmer's school and start tearing the place apart looking for Narrey and his henchmen? I'd spark a riot – and, even if I got out of the Savoy alive, I'd be court-martialled by Lord Dartmouth for using the King's troops without authorisation. I say we tell Sunderland everything we know and suspect, and stay well away from the Savoy – as like as not, if we leave him be, Narrey will not come after us. He does not know of your involvement and I shall not be in London for some months after Christmas. I'll be in Yorkshire, in Hull, to be exact, in the King's fortress there, surrounded by his soldiers, and well out of Narrey's path. I should be perfectly safe in Yorkshire while Sunderland looks into the matter.'

'Are you not at all curious about what Narrey is plotting?'

'I'd like to know what he's doing here, sure,' said Holcroft. 'And I'll make my own enquiries in Yorkshire. But I don't want to know badly enough to risk my life – or yours – in uncovering the truth. My suspicion is that Narrey is running an illicit press from the Savoy. Propagating his religion. Pamphlets, news-letters and so on. I'll mention that to Sunderland. It's illegal and seditious. But pamphlets are not life-threatening – nobody will be killed unless we try to interfere with his operation and he sends his bully-boys after us. Leave him be, I say, let Sunderland deal with it.'

'Narrey serves Louis XIV. We should ask ourselves what the Sun King wants.'

Holcroft shrugged. 'Total hegemony? To rule the whole of Europe unopposed?'

'I think we need to narrow it down just a little more than that – does Louis seek to harm the King? Is James Stuart at risk from him? If so, we cannot do nothing and leave it all to Sunderland's men. It would be our duty to warn the King in person.'

'I don't think he means to harm James,' said Holcroft. 'What advantage would it bring to France if, say, our King were to be assassinated? The throne would pass to Mary of Orange, and Dutch William would be her consort. No benefit to the French there, in fact, quite the opposite. England and Holland would be united against them.'

'Haven't you heard all the rumours?' said Aphra.

Holcroft looked blankly at her.

'The Queen is said to be with child. If that baby is a boy it means a Catholic succession. A Catholic King to follow James. A Catholic dynasty.'

'A Catholic England,' said Holcroft.

Chapter Twenty

18 May 1688: Palace of White Hall

'Absolutely not!' said Lord Dartmouth. 'I must make clear my strongest opposition to the idea. As Admiral of the Fleet, I may tell you categorically that the Royal Navy needs no help at all from the French service. The idea is preposterous – indeed it is insulting. We are perfectly capable of patrolling the Channel without the assistance of even a single French sloop. No. Never. Joint operation, joint command, forsooth!'

The Red Audience Room was surprisingly hot. But it was not merely the dense crowd of courtiers and ministers around the King's throne that made it so warm that spring morning. The twin fireplaces had been lit at dawn when it was chilly. But now, at eleven of the clock, the sun had come bursting through the clouds and, although it was only mid-May, the shafts of strong, bright sunlight lancing in through the big audience chamber windows made it feel more like the middle of a blissful August.

'It was merely a suggestion, your lordship,' said Monsieur Barillon, with a smile and a disarming Gallic shrug. 'I was merely suggesting that a joint Anglo-French naval force would make a better job of guarding these busy sea lanes. Merely as a means of guaranteeing your protection, Majesty, if, for example, the Dutch were to attempt to raid England again, or even, Heaven forfend, to attempt an invasion.'

'We are quite capable of protecting ourselves,' snapped Lord Dartmouth, 'if the Dutch – or, indeed, if any *other nation* – should attempt to breech our defences.'

King James frowned. He had listened carefully to the French Ambassador's proposal and it had seemed quite reasonable. According to Sunderland's spies, there was increased activity in the large port of Hellevoetsluis, the home of the Dutch grand fleet, twenty miles southwest of The Hague. It looked as if the United Provinces were fitting out ships and might be contemplating another raid on the coast of England, as they had done successfully in the past. But then, perhaps the Dutch were not planning anything of the kind: Sunderland's agents were notoriously unreliable, indeed, some had been discovered to be supplying information to both King James's chief minister and the Dutch Stadtholder, William of Orange; some grossly exaggerated the information they had; and some, apparently, fabricated their reports entirely to extract easy money from their gullible English paymasters.

In truth, James was not concerned about the threat of a Dutch raid: despite their continued rivalries, the two countries were not at war, nor were they particularly hostile to each other. More concretely, James had spent a good deal of money over the past three years improving the defences of the coastal forts in the Thames Estuary and in all the major ports along the eastern seaboard. If the Dutch fleet did decide to venture out of Hellevoetsluis and cross the North Sea in arms, they would receive a shock when they came into range of the powerful new cannon in the English fortresses.

What did interest James was the evident hostility between Lord Dartmouth and the always helpful French Ambassador, Monsieur Barillon d'Amoncourt. Was this just a manifestation of the pride of his friend the English Admiral, who felt his service had been belittled by the French suggestion today? Or was there a religious element to their animosity? Dartmouth was stubbornly Protestant, James knew – was that why the Admiral continually resisted help from Catholic France? James hoped not. These religious divisions could ruin the harmony of the court. Perhaps it was time to remove Dartmouth from his naval duties. He could still have the Master-Generalship of the Ordnance – but, maybe, he was stretched a little thin with both of these huge, sprawling organisations under his command. James's deliberations were interrupted by a white-wigged footman bowing, approaching the throne and telling him that their lordships, the bishops, had arrived and begged for admission.

More religious argument, thought James. *What is wrong with these people?*

He sat up straighter in his high padded chair and attempted a gracious smile as seven elderly men in the black and white garb of bishops of the Church of England shuffled into the Red Audience Room and made their bows before their monarch.

James inclined his head in acknowledgement, noting immediately who was present in this little delegation, and who was not. The Archbishop of Canterbury, William Sancroft, of course, was not among their number. The Primate of All England had fallen out badly with his king over James's policies to tolerate freedom of religion – which, naturally, undermined the Anglican orthodoxy – and such was the acrimony between them that James had forbidden him the court. The King well remembered the day when Sancroft had blurted out rudely, to his face, that he believed that the Roman Catholic Church taught 'doctrines destructive of salvation'.

So William Sancroft was not part of this delegation today, for obvious reasons, but it did not mean that he was not the driving force behind ... behind whatever this was. *Whatever this was?* James knew exactly what this was. Insurrection, plain and simple. The Archbishop of Canterbury sat in his palace in Lambeth like a spider in the centre of his web and schemed and plotted against James's policies: and this was the result. This delegation had all the marks of a Sancroft ploy, only a fool would think otherwise. And one day the royal patience with the outright disloyalty of this troublesome Archbishop would come to an end.

Maybe that day would be today.

'Your Majesty,' said the leading bishop, a muscular, energetic-looking fellow in a black skull cap, with a large black patch over his wrinkled cheek, 'we come before you in all humility, fresh from a service of prayer and thanksgiving in Southwark Cathedral for Your Majesty's long life, and with exhortations to the Almighty to preserve you in continued good health still on our lips. Before any more words are spoken this day, I wish Your Majesty to know that all these men of God here assembled have prayed for you and your family today, as Defender of the Faith and leader, anointed by God, of our Established Church of England, and that each of us has instructed all the priests and clergy, in all the churches and organisations under their purview, to do the exact same. We are your loyal servants, Majesty, know this, and we wish nothing more than that God Almighty may guide you in the just ruling of our nation, and keep you safe and sound in His loving hand until you are called, many, many years from now, we earnestly pray, to receive your Heavenly reward.'

It's going to be bad, thought James. *With this heavy slather of honey coating, it's going to be very bad indeed.* This old fellow who looks like a Caribbean pirate – Peter Mews, was his name, Lord Bishop of Winchester – he had evidently been chosen to speak for them all. That meant he was probably the bravest of the pack of them. He scanned the rest: that overfed oaf Francis of Ely, stern old William of St Asaph; girlish John of Chichester; Jonathan of Bristol, the hard-faced intellectual and Thomas of Peterborough whose family, some whispered, came from French Jewish stock, and only converted to Christianity three generations past.

'I am most gratified, my lords, that you should come to my court to tender such noble expressions of piety and godliness,' said James with a cold fixed smile. 'But was there perhaps another matter, something more urgent than your good wishes for my health, that you wished to mention? If so, please be so good as to speak of it.'

Bishop Mews cleared his throat; he scratched briefly at the scar under his face patch; he straightened his spine. 'It concerns Your Majesty's Declarations of Indulgence,' he said finally. 'The royal proclamations that you have commanded to be read this Sunday from every pulpit, in every Anglican Church, in every corner of the nation. The, ah, the thing is, Your Majesty, we think, that is we all feel . . . we have in fact all put our names to a document, that makes clear that, ah . . .'

Of course it was about the Indulgences, how could it be anything else? James felt the first glow of anger begin to warm his belly. A little over a year ago he had issued a Declaration of Indulgence, an announcement that granted broad religious freedom in England (he had issued one for Scotland, too) and this message stated that his subjects would henceforth be allowed to worship in their homes or chapels *as they each saw fit.* It also ended the requirement for men to take oaths of loyalty to the Established Church of England before taking any public office. It meant that Roman Catholics – and dissenting Protestants, and other non-Anglicans – could be magistrates, or Army officers, or hold official positions in the corporations. The Declaration had been ignored, indeed it had been actively opposed by the Church of England, the Justices of the Peace, the Army – more or less anyone with any power. Its opponents had claimed it was unconstitutional, that the King could not change the laws of the land by royal decree. Only the two Houses of Parliament could make the laws that bound the people of the Three Kingdoms, they argued, and a King could not announce to his subjects willy-nilly what he decided was legal and what was not.

In April of this year, 1688, James had reissued his Declaration. He was out of patience with his Protestant subjects and determined to impose his will on the Three Kingdoms. This time he had insisted that his proclamation be read out to every congregation in every church all across the country. He wanted everyone in Britain to know that Catholics and Calvinists, Quakers and

Baptists, non-Anglicans of all and any stripe, would no longer be persecuted for practising their particular faith.

It was a fine vision: one these hidebound Anglican bishops were trying to spoil.

'We humbly wish to present to Your Majesty with a petition,' said Peter Mews, finding his voice. He kept his head bowed, and James saw that he was holding a vellum scroll. 'A petition that has been signed by seven senior bishops of the Church of England, including The Most Reverend William Sancroft, Archbishop of Canterbury, in which we humbly ask Your Majesty to withdraw his Declaration of Indulgence and rescind your policy, for we cannot in good conscience allow this—'

'Enough! I have heard a sufficiency already on this subject from your master, my lord Archbishop of Canterbury. I do not wish to hear any more on this matter.' James's anger was at boiling point. 'I reject your God-damned petition. Here and now. It is rejected. The Declaration of Indulgence stands – and if you will not implement it in your churches, I shall have you all arrested and tried for sedition.'

'Your Majesty, we speak for the whole of the Church of England, the Established Church of this your kingdom, we speak for all Anglicans in your—'

'I said: *Enough!*' James rose from his throne. 'I am King of England. I am also the Supreme Head of the Church and I say that you shall read out my Declaration.'

Bishop Mews said nothing; he continued to stand there holding out his scroll.

If James had had a sword in his hand at that moment, blood might well have been shed on the black-and-white chequered floor of the Red Audience Room. The King calmed himself with an effort of will. He was conscious of the eyes of the French Ambassador on him, watching, looking for weakness, ready to report his lack of self-discipline to his master in Versailles. James took a deep, cleansing breath.

'I have changed my mind,' he said. 'I shall, in fact, accept this foul petition – for it is evidence of a seditious libel. You hand to me, my lord Winchester, not a document signed by the bishops of England, but a warrant for all of your arrests.'

A footman stepped forward and took the scroll from Bishop Mews's hands.

'But Our Lord taught us to be merciful,' said James. 'And so I shall give you one final chance to recant. Will you, or will you not, instruct your priests to read my Declaration to all their congregations this Sunday, and the next Sunday as well?'

'Alas, your Majesty,' said Peter Mews, his face drawn and grey. 'We cannot countenance that illegal action, not now, not ever, and so, it is with great regret that on behalf of the seven of us, I must humbly refuse to obey your royal command.'

'Last chance, your lordships, or I shall have you taken directly to the Tower to await your trials. If you seek a martyrdom, I shall be more than content to provide it.'

Bishop Peter Mews made a low bow, but said no more.

'You – none of you – have anything to say on this matter?'

Jonathan, Lord Bishop of Bristol took a step forward. 'We are all of one mind, Your Majesty. We must obey our consciences – and the rightful law of this land.'

'Very well,' said the King. 'Guards! Remove these men from my sight!'

Chapter Twenty-one

25 May 1688: Mincing Lane

The carriage was a marvellous affair of sky blue and scarlet paint, with touches of gilding on the pillars and windows, and a magnificent coat of arms with a pair of foxes rampant gules on an azure field on the door. It drew up to the corner of Mincing Lane and Tower Street and came to a halt beside the blue-painted front door of the narrow brick house. A white-wigged groom stepped off the seat at the back of the vehicle, pulled down the folding steps, twisted the handle and opened the coach door.

A vision in a blue and gold suit of clothes stepped delicately out into the mud of the street on scarlet calfskin high-heeled boots. A ginger wig was piled on the top of the gentleman's head under a broad, ostrich-plumed hat, and a clever pair of beady brown eyes examined the tall, thin house with great interest.

The gentleman walked carefully up the three stone steps and rapped loudly on the door with his silver-headed cane. He turned fully around, while he waited for his knock to be answered, and surveyed the street, noting the middle-class dwellings, the shops and all the small places of business in this thoroughfare in the heart of the City of London: the high, narrow, almost Dutch-looking houses, their front rooms fitted with lace-curtained sash windows looking out on to the traffic; the apothecary's window diagonally across the street, which was filled with coloured bottles of unguents, dried bundles of herbs and murky pickled creatures in huge glass jars; the coffee house, two doors further down, a place occupied by wafting smoke and noisy bustle, the gentlemen clearly seen through the big windows, gesticulating happily as they talked, the

aroma of a freshly roasted brew wafting across and cutting delight-
fully through the usual street smells.

He turned back and looked up with approval at the fashionable
and expensive fan-shaped panel above the front door, hinged at the
bottom and filled with triangular segments of glass in every hue of
the rainbow so it resembled a male peacock's tail.

'Good morrow to you, sir,' said the maid peering out of the open
door.

'I am Henri d'Erloncourt. Is the master of the house at home
today?' he said. 'Or the mistress? I am a very old and dear friend of
Lieutenant Holcroft Blood.'

He advanced without invitation and the girl made way for him,
flustered, saying that the master was away, but that the mistress was
at home, then taking the ostrich-plumed hat and gorgeous crimson
and sky-blue cloak from this unexpected visitor.

D'Erloncourt seated himself in a large oak chair, while the maid
disappeared to summon Elizabeth. He observed the layout of the
ground floor with interest; the narrow central hall, in which he
now sat, well illuminated by daylight from the peacock-fan window
above the front door, and with a room on either side. By craning his
neck around, he could see that one was a study of some kind, with
a writing desk and comfortable leather-covered chair, and the other
was a dining room with a long, shining wooden table. The stairs ran
up from the hall on the right-hand side, and on the left a dim corridor led towards a kitchen, and presumably a pantry and scullery
and so on for the servants. He tried to imagine what the house must
cost to rent – a hundred and fifty pounds per annum, perhaps – his
old friend Holcroft was doing well. Certainly, he was richer than
the penniless, awkward boy he had known as a page in the Duke of
Buckingham's service. But that had been a lifetime ago – much had
changed and they were both different men now.

'My dear Monsieur d'Erloncourt!' The booming female voice
almost shocked him out of the chair. He took in the large blonde

woman, fashionably dressed in a violet taffeta gown, who was advancing on him down the hall stairs. 'You are most welcome in our humble home – but alas, my dear sir, Lieutenant Blood is away in the north at present on Ordnance business. Nevertheless, you simply must come into the parlour and share a pot of chocolate. I meet so few of Holcroft's friends.'

Henri allowed himself to be conducted up the stairs, and along a corridor that doubled back towards the street side of the house. The mistress's first-floor parlour was on the left. And there was a large chamber, Henri noted, a formal withdrawing room, off to the right, and another set of stairs leading up to the second floor, where there were presumably bedrooms and chambers for the servants. As they turned left into the parlour, Elizabeth prattled away at an astounding pace and volume, jumping from topic to topic, and Henri found it difficult to follow what she was saying. *She's nervous*, he thought. And wondered why.

While Elizabeth rang to summon the maid, and ordered chocolate and pastries, Henri peered out of the parlour window, looking down on the street below, and saw that his carriage had become an object of interest to the local urchins, and his coachman was pretending to act all fierce and threatening them with his whip.

Ensconced with Mistress Blood in the parlour, with a pot of chocolate poured out, and a cup in his hands, he gave an amusing and embellished account of his time with Holcroft in Buckingham's service, and it was made clear to Elizabeth that he and her husband had been the best of friends under their dear old Duke.

Then Henri set out to make himself agreeable to his hostess, telling her about his aristocratic family, again with a few touches of imaginative fiction, of his gilded life in their hôtel in Paris and at the Palace of Versailles, where all the nobility of France was gathered at Louis XIV's glittering court. Recognising immediately that she was the type to enjoy this, he let slip a few salacious and fabricated snippets of gossip about the libidinous court of the Sun King.

'My goodness! Three women in the King's bed all at the same time. I don't think I should like that very much if I were Madame de Maintenon, his mistress!'

'Madame knows how to love the King,' said Henri, with a saucy wink. 'When to indulge him and – most importantly – when to bite her tongue and say nothing.'

Elizabeth was enjoying herself. She had not realised how lonely she would find married life. When Holcroft was in London he worked long into the night at the Tower – the survey and map-making task had occupied him entirely – and he came home late and dog tired almost every evening, wanting only to eat and sleep before he went off early the next morning back to the Ordnance. Some nights they barely talked. And when she tried to engage him in a jolly conversation about this or that, he looked annoyed and broke off their chat or complained of a headache and said he wanted to be left in peace. For the past few months, he had not been home at all, staying up in Yorkshire on some tiresome King's business in Hull.

Now that she reckoned up the time, she realised that she hadn't laid eyes on him since January. Elizabeth was lonely and feeling more than a little neglected. She was used to the busy, warm, noisy family house in Gray's Inn Lane, with her two sisters and her mother and father and all the servants. Here in this cold, narrow house in Mincing Lane, with only her dull maid and cook to talk to, she was truly bored.

'You must have some more of this chocolate, my dear Henri,' she said.

And when she had poured out the thick black liquid, she continued: 'And do tell me, sir, how are the ladies of fashion wearing their hair this season in Paris? Is it still all tumbling curls at the temple, like our own Queen Mary, or have things moved on?'

She would not be so bored, she was sure, if they would only go out a little more. But Holcroft seemed to have no interest in either attending or throwing parties – nor did he invite his fellow officers and their ladies to dine with them. And there was his parsimony – he was quite well off, everybody said so, but he lived like a pauper. Or like a bachelor. She would dearly like to have more money to spend on clothes but when she had bought a new silk gown a few weeks into the marriage, Holcroft had discovered how much it had cost and had insisted that she send it back to the dressmaker. Neither her tears nor her anger had moved him. Back it went.

On the other hand, this handsome French gentleman, with his beautiful clothes and exquisite taste and his glamorous tales of life in the Palace of Versailles, was much more to her taste – she was excited that Holcroft had such a wonderful friend, and surprised that he had never mentioned him. She arranged herself on the chair, pushing her shoulders back to display her bosom more prettily. She wished she had had time for the maid to arrange her hair properly. Not that she wished to start an *affair de coeur* with this handsome young Frenchman, no, no, she was a respectable married woman, but a little flirtation never hurt anyone.

When the chocolate was gone, she asked Henri if he'd care to stay for dinner.

'My dear Elizabeth, I would simply adore to take up your kind invitation, but alas, I am spoken for. I am to dine with the Ambassador today – indeed, I am already rather late. Such has been the pleasure of our conversation that I completely lost track of the time. I must bid you good day, my dear, and reluctantly take my leave.'

'But you must call on us again, Monsieur – promise me that you will pay me the compliment of another visit. And soon!'

Henri d'Erloncourt looked at her – this sad, lonely woman was quite appalling, her voice alone made her *insupportable*, but he knew that if he wanted to he could easily make her his mistress. He suppressed a shudder. The thought of bedding her!

He said: 'That would be delightful, my dear. Perhaps I might be permitted to visit again when your husband is back from his travels in the north. It would be an honour to dine with you and renew my acquaintance with dear old Holcroft. Or, if you prefer, we could dine in the suite of apartments in White Hall that the Ambassador has been kind enough to assign me when I am visiting your beautiful country. We do have a simply marvellous chef at the Embassy.'

'That does sound wonderful. We would not be imposing, I hope?'

'Not at all! It is settled. It will allow me to repay you for this perfectly delicious chocolate. You will come to the Embassy when Holcroft is back. Yes? When do you expect him in London again? Do you know the date when he will return?'

'Holcroft will be back at the beginning of next month. I believe he said in his last letter the third or the fourth of June. He said he had nearly completed his duties in Hull. And I know that he would be delighted to dine with an old friend.'

'I shall send you and Holcroft an invitation at the earliest opportunity, my dear Elizabeth, and I shall anticipate our next meeting with the greatest of pleasure.'

Chapter Twenty-two

3 June 1688: Yorkshire

Ten miles south of York, on a pot-holed road that led north towards that city from the market town of Selby, Holcroft Blood walked his tired horse along in the gloom of early evening and pondered his wasted day. He had been riding alone on the roads around Yorkshire, on the Great North Road mostly, all of this day and the last, up as far as Darlington in the north and Doncaster in the south, without achieving his aim.

After a busy five months, the fortifications of the port of Kingston upon Hull were in as good order as could be expected given the amounts of money that had been allocated by the Board of the Ordnance for the task and now, under the supervision of a master gunner, the cannon were being cautiously test-fired into the grey waters of the Humber. Holcroft had absented himself from the firings – knowing that Enoch Jackson, who he had brought north with him as an assistant and to a certain extent bodyguard, would be thorough and careful, and would make a detailed report – but not without a twinge of guilt at this small dereliction of his duty.

In truth, he was tired from long hours of hard labour over many months; indeed almost since he had been recalled from Sheerness the summer before he had been working like a dog. As well as his normal duties casting, proofing and testing the King's cannon, he had been given the task of surveying the Tower for an accurate bird's eye view of the royal palace, which he had completed to Lord Dartmouth's satisfaction before Christmas. However, instead of being allowed a short respite, Dartmouth had told him that he was to be sent to Hull to review and rebuild the fortifications and, additionally, he had asked that, in his spare time, he undertake a review of the accounts of the expenditure of the Ordnance Department over the past three years with an eye on identifying areas of overspending and finding some offices where significant savings might be made.

'The King is complaining to me again of the vast sums he has to outlay on the Ordnance,' Dartmouth had said. 'See if there is anywhere we can trim the fat.'

So, by day, Holcroft laboured on the walls of the fortress, and by night, burning candle after candle, he had examined the accounts of the Board of Ordnance for the past three years, poring through more than a ton of papers and ledgers tied up into fat bundles with red tape and shipped up north to Hull by Royal Mail coach.

A barn owl hooted from a dark and menacing oak tree to the left of the main road, thirty yards ahead. Holcroft lifted his head, listening. He put a hand on one of the pistol butts in the holsters on his horse's withers. But it *was* just an owl.

Holcroft's close examination of the Ordnance papers over many months had revealed something rotten at the heart of his beloved organisation. Corruption: regular, systematic, small-scale corruption. Or peculation, as it was sometimes called.

Holcroft himself was honest, but that was almost by default – corruption, peculation, theft, the taking of small bribes for turning a blind eye, or accepting discreet emoluments for breaking this rule or that one; these things were not in his nature. He viewed the world in black and white. Rules should not be broken. He *liked* rules, rules brought order to a chaotic world. People who broke the rules, in his view, should be punished. Peculation and other forms of sharp practice meant stealing from the Ordnance, which meant stealing from the King – even if the amounts in question were relatively small and the King would never know about it.

Holcroft stood resolutely against it.

After several months of nightly labour, the patterns of regular corruption inside the Ordnance had now become clear to Holcroft.

He had written up his findings in a report that he called *A Review of Various Corrupt and Immoral Practices in His Majesty's Ordnance* and sent it with ample evidence and examples in a fat buff-coloured folder to Lord Dartmouth in the Tower of London. He had named the principle men involved and he had demonstrated, in the simplest terms, comprehensible to even the meanest intelligence, how they had cheated the King on a regular basis. There were those men who stole sundry items such as picks and shovels and mallets and wooden buckets and who sold them on to civilians in the City – there was a ring of sergeants and corporals involved in this – but that was not the most serious crime, to Holcroft's mind, and in truth he scarcely concerned himself with this pilfering. The offence that irked him most was the false musters. This crime was perpetrated over long periods by the well-born, often wealthy officers and the gentlemen of the Ordnance.

It worked like this: a full strength company of Royal Fusiliers might, in theory, contain sixty men listed as private soldiers – including half a dozen corporals and sergeants and two drummer boys. There would also be an ensign, a lieutenant and a captain in command of the unit, who were paid separately. The company captain or his lieutenant would fill in a claim for pay with the quartermaster, which would be passed on every month to the Board of Ordnance, and on to the Treasury, and it would demand pay for all sixty men at approximately eight pence a day (with more for the noncommissioned officers and less for the drummer boys). The private men did not of course receive eight pence a day, they received a lesser sum after amounts for food and equipment had been deducted. Nevertheless, approximately eight pence a day was demanded from the Board of Ordnance for each serving private soldier. For a company of sixty men, this was a sum of four hundred and eighty pennies, or two pounds a day. In the course of a year, the pay for the sixty privates would come to seven hundred and thirty pound. A considerable sum. Holcroft ran these figures over in his mind easily, fluidly, a gift he'd always enjoyed.

The peculation came when a corrupt captain or lieutenant reported an inflated number of private men as serving in his company and pocketed the difference in pay. For example, the 4th company of the Regiment of Royal Fusiliers, Holcroft happened to know, was sadly under strength. They had had a number of desertions in recent months, four men had been killed in an accident when a large barrel of black powder had exploded, or had died of their wounds afterwards, and one man had succumbed to a mysterious sickness. On the most recent muster report he had seen in Hull, dated February 1688, their captain claimed that his company strength was sixty-one private men but Holcroft knew, for certain, that the correct number was, in fact, fifty-two. The captain was retaining the pay of nine men a day for himself – although he was probably paying off his lieutenant, and the senior sergeant. Over a year, the captain was defrauding the King of the sum of a hundred and nine pounds and ten shillings.

This was one company, and the Royal Fusiliers boasted twelve, although not all of them were corrupt. And Holcroft's investigations demonstrated that this had been going on unchecked for the past three years. There were other similar outrages across the Ordnance, some going back for longer, Holcroft was certain. But since James had come to the throne, the officers of his new fusiliers regiment had defrauded His Majesty of a sum approaching three thousand pounds – a vast fortune.

And at the centre of this web of corruption was the Ordnance quartermaster. He was the man who signed off on the fusiliers' muster rolls, the man who affirmed that the numbers of the men who claimed their pay from the Treasury were accurate. The quartermaster was not only in charge of the pay of the Royal Fusiliers, but also of the wages for the gunners, matrosses, civilian drivers, farriers, blacksmiths, stable boys and all other kinds of servants, as well as the salaries of the gentlemen of the Ordnance.

That quartermaster's name was Captain William Glanville. At the moment the officer was commanding the windswept military fortress in Sheerness – although Holcroft knew that, at least once a month and sometimes more frequently, he returned from the wilds of Kent to the Tower of London to attend to his duties there.

After sending his report and waiting a week to allow Lord Dartmouth to read and digest it, Holcroft had excitedly made the long journey to London to confer with his superior officer. The false muster arrangement was the tip, he felt, of a large and dirty iceberg. There was also money being skimmed from the King's coffers for the men's food, which was execrable, and for forage, horse shoes, nails and fuel for the Ordnance blacksmiths, a proper accounting of all powder and shot in the stores was also long overdue – if that poor boy John Matthews had not been caught with the keg of powder in his hands, its loss would never have been noticed.

Holcroft had been shocked, however, when he arrived at the Tower of London by Lord Dartmouth's response to his report.

'Yes, it makes interesting reading, Lieutenant,' he said, when he had been summoned to hear his master's verdict. 'I congratulate you on a very thorough piece of work.'

'Do you think then, sir, that we should widen the investigation, as I suggest? I'm sure I could get to the bottom of the discrepancies about the men's beef rations.'

'Not at this time, Holcroft, not just now. There are strange political currents stirring at the moment. High affairs in White Hall and other places that may affect us all. No, I think the sensible thing to do is to hold fire. I will keep this report for the time being, and when the time is right we shall thoroughly clean our house.'

'You mean to do nothing, sir?' Holcroft goggled at the Master-General.

'The truth is, Mister Blood, we risk angering a group of powerful people with this review. I think the more prudent course is to bide our time until we see how things turn out. I thank you for your hard work but I must ask you to keep your findings to yourself. I wish you to be discreet. I can count on you for that, can I not?'

That had been a month ago and a day after the meeting, Holcroft, disappointed, angry, and more than a little confused by his master's response, had returned to Hull.

His stomach rumbled loudly. He had not eaten since breakfast that morning in the filthy guest house in Doncaster. And it was full dark now on the Yorkshire road. He would stop for the night at the next inn he came across, he decided, and eat there. If there was none, he would find food and accommodation in York when he arrived in a couple of hours. Tomorrow he would travel the roads north of the city. And if he still had no luck he'd begin the dismal circuit all over again.

Dartmouth's continued silence in the matter of the false musters exposed in his report was a puzzle and Holcroft did not like unsolved puzzles. But he came to the conclusion that Lord Dartmouth must be waiting for something, a bigger crime to be revealed, perhaps, which would make his report more devastating. He clung to the great man's promise that when the time was right they would thoroughly clean house, as he had put it. Which Holcroft took to mean that they would sweep all the dirt and rubbish, the corruption, out of the Ordnance, the house. He was rather proud of himself for working that metaphor out without assistance.

So, as his tired horse clopped along the lonely road, he turned to the other unsolved puzzle in his life. That of the French spymaster Narrey and whatever foul scheme he was up to in the free school in the Liberty of the Savoy.

In April, he had received a letter in Hull from Aphra Behn telling him that she had had news that Narrey was back in Paris – or at least that he had been after Christmas and during the cold early months of the year. That was good news and made Holcroft feel a good deal safer.

At least until he read the next part of the letter.

In February, Aphra wrote, Narrey had tracked down and murdered the agent known as Jupon who was living in that city. He was not a man that Holcroft knew personally but Aphra had a long-standing connection with him and his death had been gruesome. Narrey had fed the English spy a fast-acting and lethal poison. It had been mixed with sugar and sprinkled on a pastry left for Jupon to find and eat.

Jupon had died in the arms of his English clerk, Benedict, who was also an old acquaintance of Aphra's. The clerk reported that with his last desperately gasped words, the old spy Jupon had tried to tell him something about Narrey's true identity.

Aphra had written this letter to Holcroft in an old code that they both knew well, a substitution of numbers, sometimes marked with asterisks or dashes, for the letters of the alphabet. It was not a terribly secure means of communication, and the code was of some antiquity, having been used by the Royalist spymasters in the civil wars between the first King Charles and Parliament. Holcroft and Aphra indulged in its use more as a private joke between them than a protective measure – nevertheless, it added a layer of security to their correspondence, and one that was guaranteed to baffle the casual reader.

Aphra wrote that her young clerk friend had reported that Narrey's true name was something connected with poetry, or perhaps with play-writing.

'Narrey's identity should be sought "in verse", at least that is what Benedict reported to me as Jupon's last words,' Aphra had written to Holcroft.

Holcroft thought hard about that. And got nowhere. He had, as promised, written to Lord Sunderland in December explaining what he and Aphra had discovered and what they suspected about the French spy and his activities in the Savoy. But Lord Sunderland had not written back and Holcroft had gone off to Hull and occupied himself day and night with the Ordnance review and the refurbishment of the sea defences. He had let the problem of Narrey, the Maguires and the printing press in the Savoy sit unexamined for the past few months at the back of his mind.

Now, on the eve of his return to London, he began to consider it again with the utmost seriousness: he had been told that Narrey's identity was connected with poetry. All right. Good. It would be useful to know who Narrey really was. Very useful. Exposing him, blowing on him, as it was called in the trade, would neutralise him as a secret operator. But Narrey's connection to verse meant nothing to him. He did not much care for poetry, and French poetry he liked even less than the English variety. He had written to Aphra, saying it was more her line of country, and she should try to call to mind any patriotic French heroes who had been immortalised in rhyme – Roland, perhaps, or Oliver. Or to look into the works of that fellow Molière, who was now so popular. Holcroft went so far as to attempt a jest: start by reading *The Misanthrope*, he wrote to his friend, for that described the humanity-hating Narrey perfectly.

He was proud of that literary quip – he had made a joke, a proper funny joke, and he was sure Aphra would laugh most heartily when she read that. But he did not see, honestly, how poor Jupon's dying words could advance them . . .

'Stand, sir!' said a gruff voice. Holcroft was jerked out of his thoughts. 'Stand and deliver over your fat purse to me, sir, or I shall be obliged to shoot you down!'

Holcroft's horse had already halted. He looked at the mounted figure at the side of the road in the dark, voluminous cloak covering his body, and pulled-down broad-brimmed hat hiding his face, a pair of pistols glinting in the faint starlight.

Holcroft lifted his hands from the saddlebow, palms out, fingers spread.

'I would be most obliged if you did not shoot me!' he said.

'Hand over your purse, sir. Or I shall surely blow you to Hell,' said the rider.

'There is no need to be like that, Tom,' said Holcroft. 'If you want to borrow a few shillings from your little brother, all you have to do is ask.'

'Holcroft?'

'I've been looking for you over half of Yorkshire, Tom.'

'Well, now you've found me. You damn buffle-head – I could have killed you.'

'Is there somewhere we could get food and drink? Perhaps a bed for the night?'

'If you've got the chink for it, there is.'

The inn on the outskirts of York was almost as squalid, dimly lit and unwelcoming to strangers as the Grapes – and for many of the same reasons. Holcroft realised, a moment after he entered, having to stoop because of the low, grimy ceiling, that this inn was little more than a thieves' den. Men in groups of two or three sat at greasy elm-wood tables and sipped silently from pint pots, or engaged in low, muttered conversations, shooting suspicious glances here and there. There were a pair of slatterns lounging on the counter, half-dressed, drunk, bored – for none of the customers sought female company this night. Or none of them could afford it.

Thomas Blood, it seemed, was well known here. He exchanged short, gruff greetings with a tall, bald, fish-belly-white man behind the counter, who looked to be the proprietor, and they found a table and were served two pints of a dark, strong ale and a strong-smelling pork pie with one side greenish with mould.

Holcroft cut himself a slice, nonetheless – he was extremely hungry and he had eaten worse than this in his time – scraping off the unsavoury parts of the pastry and washing the tangy, gristly, grey-meat filling down with the strong dark ale.

'So this is where you bide now,' he said to his brother, casting a glance around the dank, musty-smelling parlour of the inn.

Tom looked at him suspiciously. 'Here . . . and other places too. I like to move around. Free as a bird, that's me. Roost where I like, wherever the fancy takes me.'

Holcroft thought of telling his brother that he had no intention of betraying his whereabouts. But if his brother didn't trust him, insisting he was trustworthy wasn't going to change anything. He remained quiet and ate some more of the disgusting pie.

'Was there any reason why you were looking for me?' said Tom. 'Or was it to enjoy the magnificence of my hospitality and the wit of my discourse?'

Holcroft realised that he had been silent for some time.

'Tell me straight, Tom, I beg you. Are you hiding from Patrick Maguire? Are you up here out of fear of that Savoyard?'

Tom had twitched in his chair at the mention of the name. He regained control of himself. 'What's that to you?'

'I killed his brother Michael some months ago. Put my sword through his liver.'

Tom looked at him for a moment. Then he laughed. A nasty, dry rasping sound.

'Perhaps, then, it should be you roosting up in Yorkshire. If you killed Mickey, then Patrick Maguire will surely flay you alive. Surprised you're still breathing.'

Holcroft flapped a long arm at the counter man, signalling for more ale.

'I *have* been billeted up in Yorkshire for a while now, in Kingston upon Hull, as it happens,' he said. 'I'm on legitimate Ordnance business. Maybe that's why I'm still alive. But I'm heading to London the day after tomorrow.'

'My advice would be to stay up here. Stay as far away as you can from the Maguires. That's what you should do, little brother. If you want to live a long life.'

'I do want to live a long life, Tom, I surely do. That's why I want you to help me. I want you to tell me everything you know about the Maguires and their operation in the Liberty. Will you do that for me? Just tell me all you know about them, and about the school run by Father Palmer, and about a Frenchman who came to see the Maguires about two years ago, a man with a great deal of silver to spend.'

Tom was looking at him, aghast. His skin so unnaturally pale it looked green.

'You don't understand, Holly; you can't peach on the Maguires. You just can't. And that rich Frenchman you mentioned, he's a bucket of pure poison, too.'

'As I understand it, Tom, the Maguires are planning to kill you if they catch hold of you, isn't that right? They already believe that you are an informant.'

Holcroft stopped talking as the counterman approached and put two fresh pint pots on the table, then waited a little longer till he was out of earshot.

'You're a dead man, Tom, by your own reckoning, if the Maguires lay hands on you. So – what will they do to you if you tell me more about them. Just a little general information. You have nothing to lose. They can't kill you twice over.'

Tom had his face buried in his pint pot, gulping furiously. When it was emptied, he said: 'I'm not a fucking informant, little brother. I'm not a spy – yours or anyone else's. You can get that right out of your head for a start. Tommy Blood don't peach. All I did was have a little chat with a friend of mine, a bailiff of the Duchy of Lancaster, one of Henry Killigrew's men, and we had a few drinks, had a few laughs, and chewed over what was what and who was who in the Liberty. He lent me a shilling or two, as well, that's all – but those Maguires, they took it the wrong way.'

'I know you wouldn't peach, Tom. Never. But if you could tell me a little of what you know, I'll use that information to hurt them. I promise you. I killed Michael Maguire. They want me dead, too. Probably more than they want to kill you. When I get back to London, I expect them to come after me. It would be much better if I were to strike first – you taught me that when I was learning to box, d'you remember? Strike hard, strike fast, strike first. Help me, Tom, like you used to when we were young chickens, help me by telling me what you know. Help me now and I'll deal with Patrick Maguire – and any of the other Savoyards who get in my way – I'll do it, I swear, and then you will be free to come home to London.'

Tom stared at his younger brother, weighing him. Then he nodded slowly.

'I'm going to need a large amount of brandy for this,' he said.

Chapter Twenty-three

4 June 1688: Liberty of the Savoy

Patrick Maguire entered the small brick-built chapel of St Mary the Virgin, inside the compound of the free school in the Liberty of the Savoy. He dipped his massive right hand in the basin of holy water, blessed himself, and genuflected towards the altar at the far end of the aisle and the large crucifix hanging on the wall before shuffling into a pew at the back. There were three other men already in this small house of God. One of them, Father Palmer, was standing by the altar; the other two were on their knees in front of him receiving the Blessed Sacrament from the old priest's hands.

Maguire pulled off his shapeless knitted woollen hat to reveal a large, lumped and scarred head with a grey dusting of stubble. He had had his poll shaved once a week, every week since he was a brash young man, fighting for prizes in bare-knuckle matches at county fairs in Ireland. The combat was in a style called 'stand down', in which the two opponents moved their bodies very little, and were obliged to keep one foot at all times on the scratch line, and must smash at each other with their fists until one man fell. Maguire had been trained at a tender age by a Tinker hardman, an old friend of his father's, in the noble art of *Dornálaíocht* and he was a champion at this most brutal of country sports before he was twenty years of age. But his glory days at the markets and Romani horse fairs had been thirty years ago – and since then drink and soft living had sapped his will and thickened his waist.

Not that anyone today would dare to call him soft.

Maguire sat quietly and waited for the private Mass to be over. He knelt, an awkward manoeuvre for a man of his bulk, and prayed a little for the soul of his brother Michael, listening to the familiar, soothing, but entirely incomprehensible Latin words that the priest said. He closed his eyes and asked God's forgiveness on the sins he had committed, so many of them, and for the sins he was planning to commit. For the grave sin of murder.

There would be forgiveness in Heaven, the Frenchman had assured him. He was a loyal, faithful son of the Church. Had he not paid for the huge crucifix that adorned this very House of God? Did he not regularly make his confession to Father Palmer? The Almighty knew that he only did what he did to feed and protect his family.

Patrick Maguire was the leader of a clan of more than half a hundred poor and hungry folk – and that was only those directly related to him by blood and marriage. There were hundreds more in the Liberty who were bound to him by service and debt or merely by their co-existence in this filthy little corner of London.

His three remaining brothers and their women, his two sisters and their husbands and families – they looked to him, for employment, for sustenance, for leadership. And they all had their hands out to him, looking for money, begging for his help. They called him a king – and he *was* a ruler of sorts. People asked him for justice, for aid in hard times, for protection too, from the Stuart King's law and from the other brutal creatures of this London jungle. What manner of man was that, if not a king? But he was also, in a sense, a prisoner of the very kingdom he had created with his own two fists. He was watched constantly by the folk of the Liberty, observed every day by a thousand eyes, his actions judged, weighed and sifted by those who were waiting for the lion, king of this jungle, to show a hint of weakness.

His people, his immediate family, ate and were clothed, and slept under dry roofs because the rest of the Liberty rabble feared him. They paid him their tithe for everything he did for them – but almost everything that came in went straight out again, the children who needed shoes, the men who could not ply their trade because of injury, the lavish feasts he was obliged to throw, the drinks he had to buy to maintain his prestige as leader of this tight criminal world. And Henry Killigrew, Master of the Savoy, intimate friend of the King, that *gentleman* took his cut every month – a bribe to allow the Maguires to operate without interference. Patrick Maguire had a small amount put by, a little pile of silver, but no great wealth. And after all his largesse, did the people love their uncrowned king? They did not!

There were many among the Savoyard rabble who outright hated him – he had caught one or two of his own brothers giving him foul, envious looks. They said he was cruel. They said he was a vicious monster. He had to be harsh, on occasion, yes, when his authority was challenged or to maintain good order in the Liberty. He had been obliged, in the right season, to kill and maim men. Many men. How else would he have the respect of these thieves and murderers, these cut-purses, rank-riders, beggars and whores? Strength was all that these violent scum understood.

And if they thought him weak – if they ever detected the merest whiff of frailty – it was over for him. The common thieves and casual killers who grudgingly paid him his rightful due would rise up, arm themselves, and end his kingly rule with blood and violence. He would be a dead man, a body in the gutter, and those who depended on him would be dead too. To show the slightest weakness in public was to invite death and destruction into his own house. To be weak was to die.

That was why he must kill this man – the tall soldier in the blue coat, who had killed his younger brother Michael. If he did not take his revenge he would be seen to be weak. Blood was his name, he had been told, and his end would indeed be bloody. There was no other way. The man must die. And Patrick must be seen to do it.

Michael had been a fool. He had used a hired coach to ambush the soldier, which was a stupid, needless complication. Michael did it, Patrick knew, because he wanted to pretend, even for a short while, to be a gentleman – not just the gutter-born cut-throat that he was. That ridiculous blond wig, the fine, golden clothes he sometimes wore when he was with his friends – they were examples of his foolishness. Three good men were dead and another would never walk again.

Simplicity was best. Michael should have killed him in the Liberty. Just shot him down from the shadows as he walked along through the dark, narrow streets. Maybe stabbed him a dozen times for good measure. Cut his throat, just to be sure. Simplicity was the key. Simplicity – and a few more men, just in case. The plan this time would be simple. Patrick Maguire would see to that.

The Mass was over and the priest disappeared out of a door in the darkness at the back of the chapel. The Frenchman, his patron, stood with his back to the body of the chapel, clapped on his broad-brimmed hat and pulled it low over his face. He conferred briefly with his lieutenant, a hard, brawny type who answered to the name Guillaume, then turned and beckoned Patrick Maguire forward to the altar.

'Sit,' said Narrey, gesturing at the front pew. No greeting, no respect. Just as if he were commanding a dog. Patrick knew that, if he wished to, he could snap this slim Frenchman's spine like a twig. He would have to deal with his guard-dog Guillaume first – but that would hardly be problem. Instead, he found himself settling his bulk in the front pew and smiling ingratiatingly up at the French fellow. All he could make out of the man's face was a sharp nose and chin and two animal-bright brown eyes staring at him from the darkness under the hat brim.

'Before I left for France, I ordered you to kill the king's officer who has been poking around this school, did I not?' said the man. 'Yet he still lives and—'

'We tried, your honour. But we could not find him . . .'

'Don't interrupt me. *Never* interrupt me.'

Patrick was shocked to find he felt a tinge of fear at the Frenchman's instant anger. It had been so long that he almost did not recognise the emotion.

The other man, Guillaume, frowned at him from the Frenchman's elbow. Patrick hung his head. He knew that he did not have to accept this rebuke. He could get up and walk away. Or maybe crush both of these men then walk away. But there was the money to consider. A lot of money. This foreigner had chests of it, and he was generous, too. Better to sit like a good doggie and listen to what he had to say.

'You tried to find him and you failed. Why did you not try harder?'

'We went to the Tower precincts, bought a few drinks in the Lion, had a word with some of the locals; asked, very discreet, like, for the whereabouts of this Lieutenant Blood fellow. They said he had been sent up north, to Yorkshire . . .'

'And you did not think to go after him in the north?'

'The Liberty is mine, your honour. I say who breathes in here. And London, too, I can take down any man in this city, if I choose to. But Yorkshire, well, there's odd folk living there, they're all foreigners, they talk strange, have strange customs. I wouldn't know who to trust in that neck of the woods. Who might peach on me . . .'

'Their reach does not extend so far, Monsieur,' said Guillaume.

'Evidently,' said Narrey. 'Well, I have news. Blood is back in London. Or will be in a day or so. You will finish the task you were given. You will not fail. I shall pay you double the agreed amount when you bring me his head. His head, hear me?'

'As you say, your honour,' said Maguire.

'I shall provide you with the location,' Narrey continued. 'I shall conduct you there in safety, hide you and your men till the time is right; I shall give you the means to enter the place. If you require arms, they shall be provided. All that will be required from you is that you kill Blood and bring me physical proof of his demise.'

The door of the chapel creaked and all three men turned to see who the intruder was. Maria Matthews dipped her hand into the Holy Water, blessed herself and came down the aisle towards them. Behind her, like grubby little ducklings following her bustling form, came four boys aged between about six and eight years.

'I hope I'm not disturbing you, Mister Guillaume, or your nice gentlemen either,' she said. 'But your message said to meet you here at this hour, with the boys. These are the only ones in the Hospice of the age and size you asked for, sir.'

The four boys were lined up before the altar and slowly Narrey walked down the rank of them, examining each carefully.

He reached out a hand and gently stroked the soft downy cheek of a pretty-featured blond child with startling green eyes.

'This one,' he said. 'I like this one. You can take the rest of these brutes away.'

The green-eyed child looked terrified; staring up at the Frenchman, he started to snivel. Maria, distressed, began to herd her remaining charges towards the door.

Guillaume said to Maguire. 'You'll teach the boy what he must learn to do?'

Patrick nodded. He was about to speak when Maria spoke from the chapel door.

'Forgive me for asking, gentlemen, I don't mean to pry into your private affairs or nothing like that – but when might I expect young Samuel back at home with us?'

Narrey looked at her from deep beneath his hat-brim. Then he looked at the pretty boy. His voice seemed to deepen, darken and echo around the chapel.

'He will not be coming back.'

Chapter Twenty-four

10 June 1688: outskirts of London

Holcroft took his time on the two-hundred-mile ride from Kingston upon Hull to London. He wanted the leisure to think, and he was aware of a reluctance to return to the no-doubt warm embrace and hearty welcoming bellow of his wife.

He sent his luggage ahead by cart and spent five days on the journey, enjoying the mild sunshine of early June, and stopping at coaching inns in the evenings, eating and drinking well, and sleeping as soundly in the dormitories as ever he did at home in Mincing Lane. On the afternoon of the third day, somewhere outside Northampton, he thought he finally understood what Narrey was doing in the Liberty of the Savoy. But it took him until the outskirts of London, two days later, before he could believe the reasonings of his own oddly constructed brain.

During that long, brandy-splashed night, Tom had told him everything he knew about the operations of the Maguire clan, the free school set up by Father Palmer, and the involvement of the mysterious Frenchman with the chests full of silver.

Palmer's school had been set up by a group of English Jesuit priests – Father Palmer was their leader – in the spring of 1685, a month or so after James's accession to the thrones of the Three Kingdoms. Father Edward Petre, the King's Catholic confessor, had been involved, too, smoothing the path of the Jesuits in White Hall and obtaining for them the permissions and licenses from the King that would allow them to freely practise their religion in the Liberty. The free school itself was a legitimate enterprise, born of a Christian desire to help the poor and less fortunate and give them an education at no cost beyond the price of quills, paper and ink – at least that is what Tom had been told – and cynical as he was, he believed it.

But within a few months things began to change. In the late summer of the first year, the Maguire clan, who had hitherto ignored the free school as something from which no tribute could be wrung, began to spread the word that it was now under their protection. In September, a thief called Mallory broke into the school one night after a drinking session and stole a pair of wooden chairs from one of the classrooms. He was hunted down, made to bare-knuckle fight Patrick Maguire in public and was beaten to a bloody pulp. He was then doused in hot tar and burnt alive on the stolen chairs in front of the school. Even for the Maguires, it was a harsh punishment.

They were sending a message to the Liberty.

The Frenchman, and a henchman, a muscle-bound military man of some kind named Guillaume, had arrived at about the same time the Maguires laid claim to the school and that was when the establishment began to alter its nature. Narrey did not stay long but after his visit – which was much gossiped about in the Grapes and elsewhere – the spirit of the free school changed. Over the next two years, the numbers of pupils began to decline, schoolchildren left and were not replaced. Rooms were given over to another kind of enterprise: St Mary's Foundling Hospital.

Holcroft vividly remembered his own visit to the Hospital, his meeting with Maria Matthews, mother of the dead thief John, and the feeling of great goodness that he had detected in her.

He asked Tom about the printing press, the one he had spotted, but Tom did not know much about it. It was sometimes used, he said, to run up cheap pamphlets and it was probably illegal. But the material it produced was not alarming. It was mildly seditious, encouraging Catholics to meet together and celebrate Mass, not to abandon the True Faith, reminding people of holy days, and so on. Occasionally it would reprint a popular sermon by some Jesuit big-wig or recount the life of a saint. Tom didn't read the pamphlets thoroughly, he admitted, but the ones he had glanced at, found ale-damp and disintegrating on tables in the Grapes, were harmless enough.

Holcroft had been disappointed. He had hoped Tom would reveal something extraordinary about the school and Narrey's operation but he could find nothing interesting or heinous about it. He was missing something.

Narrey had spent many hundreds of his royal master's *livres* on this enterprise – and he would not do that to print off a few tame religious pamphlets. French money was flowing into the Savoy. And Narrey never spent a penny without calculating a return. Tom told Holcroft near the end of the evening that Michael Maguire had bought a tot of brandy for everyone in the Grapes on at least two occasions, and had boasted of his family's lavish new source of income.

It was not until Holcroft embarked on his long, leisurely ride home to London, and began marshalling all the facts in his head, assembling all the impressions he had formed, that he realised what must be taking place.

It was the number of women in St Mary's, and the progress of their pregnancies when he visited them, that finally gave the game away.

He had visited the Foundling Hospital in December and he had seen thirty-two women inmates: twenty-nine in various stages of pregnancy and three women who had recently given birth. He had noticed that fifteen of those pregnant women were three or four months gone. And, as he thought about it, he realised there was something odd about that count. There were too many of them.

Holcroft liked numbers, he liked to play with them in his mind. He asked himself, why were there so many women at *that* stage in the process? If a woman found herself in this sort of difficulty, and she went to St Mary's, she would probably go at about three or four months – when the baby began to show, when people might begin to ask where her husband was. She would presumably stay there till the birth, say, six months later. More women would come in over the next six months; others would have their children and leave St Mary's. There should, then, be a roughly equal number of women at every stage between being three months pregnant and being a nursing mother. He remembered saying to himself that it was a manufactory from which babies were produced at regular intervals. A baby farm. Pregnant women coming in one end, mothers and babies coming out of the other. Not counting the three women with babies at their breast, there were twenty-nine women present and there should be a roughly equal distribution of women at three months, four months, five months, six months . . . and so on. But there wasn't. There was an unnaturally large number – more than half of the twenty-nine – at three or four months.

He might have written that off as an anomaly, a freak of chance. But for one thing. There was one very important person also pregnant at the same time. A person who, while she was as socially removed from those penniless Savoyard girls as it was possible to be, was not, in fact, very far removed in terms of physical distance.

Holcroft went over it again in his mind, step by step. Yes, it made sense. Yes, he was sure. And with that knowledge, suddenly there were bells pealing in his head.

He was astounded by this mental reaction. He could actually hear church bells ringing out to celebrate his solving of the puzzle. He knew that he had an unusual mind – but this was unprecedented. Was he going mad? He halted his horse, shook his head to clear it. But the bells continued to ring. He was in a narrow street with houses on either side, and he recognised where he was, at the beginning of the North Road, not far from where he had lived as a child in Shoreditch. He looked ahead and saw the square tower of the Church of St Leonards, which he had attended many years ago, and at the top of the tower he could see the big brass bell swinging in the belfry.

He was not mad. Real bells were ringing all over London, a joyous noise.

He called out to an old woman, walking towards him with a great basket of dirty linens on her bent back, asking what was the meaning of this celebration.

'Why, sir, don't ye know? The whole town is a-buzzing with the news. The Queen has been delivered of her baby. A healthy boy, God be praised.'

Part Three

Chapter Twenty-five

14 June 1688: Palace of White Hall

It felt strange to be walking up the lane off the Street in White Hall, heading towards the porter's lodge that guarded the entrance to the Cockpit. It was not the first time Holcroft had returned to his old haunt since leaving the Duke of Buckingham's employ all those years ago. He had been here half a dozen times, in fact – to see Jack and Sarah, once to deliver a personal message to Princess Anne from Lord Dartmouth, and on other occasions, too. But each time he walked up this narrow, cobbled lane, with the same trickle of dirty water running down the middle, past the old tennis court with the red-tiled porter's lodge looming ahead of him, he was transported back to the days when he was a lowly page struggling to comprehend the currents of power that flowed through the Palace of White Hall.

Even now, in his thirties and a player on the world's stage, Holcroft was not sure that he understood what drove men's passions in this seat of royal power. Religion, and the ardour it aroused, was still something of a mystery to him: he was an Anglican, and had always been, content to abide by the Book of Common Prayer and attend the church of St Peter ad Vincula in the Inner Ward of the Tower of London almost every morning. The Church of England, as far as he was concerned, understood the correct interpretation of the Divine Law. No question. Therefore all other interpretations were wrong. Yet he still did not understand the hatred so many of his co-religionists felt towards those of the Catholic faith.

He knew vaguely that it stemmed from a fear of the foreign and an urge to cling to what was familiar. A crony of his father's had once told him that Catholicism meant absolutism, the abolition of a free Parliament, and dictatorial rule by the monarch, who greedily seized all power for himself and trampled over good men's rights. Like the system they had in France under that Most Christian King, Louis XIV. And he knew that this bleak view was widely shared among his countrymen.

Englishmen (and Scotsmen, Welshmen and Protestant Irishmen) feared that if the King allowed Catholics to worship freely, their own faith would be undermined, they would ultimately be forced to change their religion, and popish slavery would follow. It would mean a return to the dark days of Bloody Mary, when Protestants were burnt at the stake by the score, by the hundred. Therefore, all right-thinking Englishmen agreed that papists must be kept down, excluded from the workings of the state, punished for their adherence to an incorrect faith. This doctrine, however, made no sense to Holcroft. If these folk were wrong, they'd go to Hell. That would be their punishment. No need to punish them in this life too.

Nevertheless, he did recognise that almost nothing incited a greater vehemence in the hearts of his fellow countrymen than religion – and he knew that what Narrey had done, his cunning scheme with St Mary's Foundling Hospital, could bring the Three Kingdoms to the brink of civil war. That was why he had to tell someone he trusted what he had learnt – and seek his advice – as soon as possible.

That had not been all that soon. He had been swept up by Elizabeth when he had arrived home, and kissed and cosseted and fed and bedded. His wife had told him all that had occurred since he had left, and had spent a considerable amount of time complaining that the sum of money he had left her had not gone nearly far enough. She had been forced to seek credit with some of the tradesmen and shopkeepers. Holcroft spent two days visiting creditors and settling her bills. Then he had had to make his report on the works at Hull to Lord Dartmouth – that and writing up his assessment of the new guns and fortifications had taken almost two days – and it was not until one Thursday morning in the middle of June that he found himself with an hour or two spare to visit Jack and tell him what he knew.

The porter was a young Scotsman called Mackay who had only one arm. He had lost the other at Sedgemoor standing firm with Dumbarton's regiment under the withering rebel fire. Holcroft knew that the man was lucky to have this position, as so many of his wounded comrades had been abandoned by their regiments and ignored by their officers, and that he might feel obliged to curry favour with visitors to retain it, but he was still rather surprised by the effusiveness of his welcome.

'Lieutenant Blood, sir, greetings! A pleasure to see your bonny face this fine day. We all remember the Duel in the Darkness, oh yes. And how you served that rebel gunner out on the moor that was causing we Dumbarton's boys so much grief. How may I serve you, sir? Name your lightest wish. What is your command, sir?'

'I'm here to see Lord Churchill, if he can spare me to the time.'

'I'm sure his lordship can make the time for such a distinguished visitor.'

Mackay rang a bell, a spotty page was summoned and ten minutes later Holcroft found himself in a plush study that had once belonged to the Duke of Buckingham, being handed a glass of secco by his old friend Jack. The walls were papered in the same blue and gold, the oriental blue carpet had the same geometrical design adorned with tigers and dragons. Even the furniture was the same. That was another strange sensation. The ghost of Buckingham seemed to be everywhere.

'I can't give you very long, Hol,' Jack said. 'I'm playing whist with Percy Kirke in a half hour. But sit yourself down, and tell me what you have been doing these past few months. I feel I haven't seen you in an age. Are you quite well?'

'I'm well, Jack, as I trust you are. I've been in Hull, as it happens. Working on the sea fortifications. I've also been reviewing the extent of corruption in the Ordnance. False musters, and so on. What I've discovered would utterly shock you, I'm sure.'

'Really, I doubt that, but tell me anyway – what have you found out?'

'I gave all my findings to Lord Dartmouth in a special report but I'm supposed to keep my mouth shut for the time being. But that's not why I'm here. If you are short of time, I'll come directly to the point. The Queen's child may be a changeling.'

'What? You think the baby is . . . What? You think that fairies . . . *What?*'

'Jack, forgive me, I chose my words poorly. I think the child believed to be the heir of the King James and Queen Mary, the princeling known as James Francis Edward Stuart, may not be the offspring of the royal couple. I hope that's clearer.'

'If by clearer you mean completely nonsensical, idiotic, ridiculous . . .'

'I'd better begin again.'

'Yes, you had. Are you feeling all right? You are not ill or suffering from a brain fever or something.'

'No. I'm fine. Now, pay attention, Jack. You remember, a few weeks after Sedgemoor, I was asked by Lord Dartmouth to investigate a man called Matthews?'

'Yes, a Catholic, caught with a stolen barrel of black powder from the Tower of London magazine. Just a common thief, I think you told me.'

'Yes, I told you that – and he *was* no more than a sad unlucky thief. But he was poisoned to death by Narrey anyway.'

'Narrey – the French spymaster. Louis's most powerful intelligence man poisoned a London thief. You *sure* you've not suffered some sort of head injury?'

'Just listen, Jack. I investigated John Matthews's background in the Liberty of the Savoy. I went to a free school there. A licensed Catholic school. I found nothing to trouble me. Nothing that I thought was a threat of any kind. But because of that inquiry, Narrey, who was in London, poisoned John Matthews. Slipped something into his food – probably pure arsenic powder – that was delivered to his cell. I didn't realise at first. Then I remembered that Matthews had no money for food . . .'

Jack opened his mouth.

Holcroft held up a hand. 'Let me tell you the whole thing,' he said.

He realised that he had been babbling with too many ideas trying to get out at the same time. He calmed himself.

'I originally thought Matthews, the thief in the Tower cell, had died of apoplexy. The doctor confirmed it. Then I remembered he had been imprisoned for stealing because he was desperate for money. So he could not have paid to have food sent in. Somebody else sent the food to him, as charity for a hungry man – and it was poisoned. And the poisoner was Narrey – or one of his people acting on his orders. They were trying to shut up Matthews because his mother worked with them and they feared that by investigating Matthews I might be led to his mother in the Savoy – and so to Narrey and his baby scheme. I only worked it out when I heard how Narrey had poisoned another man in Paris.'

Jack sat back in the armchair and took a draught of his secco. 'So Matthews's mother worked with Narrey,' he said, nodding. 'Is she a French spy then?'

'No, of course not, she's just a wet nurse.'

Jack frowned.

'More than two years after he died, I discovered a letter from Matthews to his mother, which had been hidden in his cell. I delivered that letter to Matthews' mother, who is a wet nurse by trade, but whom I discovered had been made the matron of something called St Mary's Foundling Hospital attached to the free school. The Hospital contained a number of pregnant women – that is its *raison d'être*, not foundlings, primarily, it actually shelters unmarried women, who have accidentally become pregnant, until the babies are born, then it finds homes for the children.'

Holcroft took a sip of his own wine. Jack seemed to be following him.

'I thought St Mary's was a fine Christian institution – a force for good in the world – even though it happened to be run by Catholic priests. But once again my inquiries provoked a reaction – I was attacked on the way home, in the Strand, by a gang of men and forced to kill some of them in the fight. I spoke to a friend after that and discovered that a mysterious Frenchman – Narrey, I believe – was the secret paymaster behind the free school and St Mary's Foundling Hospital.'

'I heard something about the affair in the Strand,' said Jack, 'a number of dead bodies were found – we believed it was some sort of war between gangs of Savoy criminals – but why did you not come to me? We could've brought them to justice.'

'Maybe. I may have made a mistake. But I thought it might be difficult to persuade White Hall that Narrey was behind the operation in the Savoy. We had scant evidence, save for our instincts and long experience of his methods. Not enough to move White Hall to action. But I may have erred badly there – as you will see.'

Jack nodded but said nothing.

'As you know, I've been in Hull recently, on Ordnance business in the old port, but I managed to find my brother Thomas in Yorkshire, after a couple of days of searching the highways. He used to live in the Liberty, and he told me a few things that brought me to this conclusion. Are you ready? Pay attention to this, Jack. The women in the Foundling Hospital were *not* a random group of unfortunates who accepted the charity of the kindly priests. I believe they were selected – or many of them were – because they were at the same stage of pregnancy as Queen Mary. They were brought there by Narrey so that a healthy baby boy might be produced at the same time as the Queen was delivered of her own child.'

Jack sat up straight at this point.

'Now I know what you will say, Jack, how could Narrey guarantee that a suitable baby boy would be born to one of the Foundling Hospital women . . .'

'How could he?'

'With numbers, Jack. Simply, with numbers. I saw fifteen women in the hospice who were at the same stage of pregnancy as the Queen. At that time they were at the beginning of the second trimester. Perhaps three or four of the women might have miscarried during their term – I'm looking at the worst case here – and maybe four or five babies might have been born dead or impaired in some way. Even with that wastage rate, that would still leave, let us say, six live babies. The chances of one of them being a healthy boy are good, very good, if not an absolute certainty. Do you follow me, Jack?'

Lord Churchill nodded grimly.

'Now consider the proximity of the Liberty of the Savoy to the Palace of White Hall,' said Holcroft. 'The Foundling Hospital is beside the river and only a few hundred yards away by water from the Privy Stairs, which lead directly up into the private royal apartments. I do not assert that this is what happened, mark you, but just imagine, for a moment, if you had a newborn baby, born at the same time as the Queen might be expected to deliver her own baby, and you concealed it in – oh, I don't know, a bed-warming pan, something that might be brought into an expectant Queen's bedchamber without causing comment. The baby, carried by a trusted nurse, is rowed upstream from the Liberty to the Privy Stairs in a wherry or a skiff – ten minutes' work – and then smuggled inside the Queen's apartment in a bedpan.'

Jack stared at him – speechless.

'The maids and attendants would have to be in on the game, of course,' said Holcroft. 'But don't you think it possible, Jack?'

'Possible, I suppose so. But improbable. And what of the Queen's own baby?'

'If she herself bore a healthy boy, a fine Catholic heir for James, there would be no need for all this tricksy substitution business. Narrey could abort the plan – sorry, please forgive my clumsy choice of words, Jack – and no one would be any the wiser. On the other hand, it is possible that the Queen never had a baby in her womb. And it was all a conspiracy from the start,' said Holcroft.

'Or if she did conceive a baby,' he continued, 'it is possible that, like so many of the Queen's other pregnancies, it ended in disaster. The Queen is sickly and has been unsuccessfully trying for a child with James for some years. I apologise for being blunt, Jack, and I would not say this in front of Sarah, but the Queen's children all seem to die inside her, or die shortly after their birth. She may have some deficiency of her womb – I don't know. But does it not seem at least plausible that someone like Narrey, with a reason to wish for a Catholic heir for King James, might hatch a plan to introduce a healthy boy from another mother into her birthing bed?'

'It is fantastical, to be sure,' said Jack. 'But perhaps just plausible. And if it is true it could bring the temple crashing down about our heads. There is something else to consider, too, which in fact supports your notion. Sarah told me that the Princess Anne was excluded from the bedchamber for the birth – even though she petitioned the King for the honour of being present. No reason was given. From what I can gather, the only people present when the Queen was delivered of her baby were Catholics and foreigners. Anne, who would be the baby's half-sister, was put out, she complained to Sarah at length. Yes, it's plausible. I think, Hol, you'd better come and meet my friends, Kirke and the others.'

'I do not say that this is what happened,' said Holcroft. 'I only suggest that this is a possibility and, as such, an alarming one.'

'Oh, I understand the gravity of your possibility,' said Jack. He called to a page and told him to have the carriage made ready as soon as possible. 'I earnestly pray, Hol, that it is untrue. But we cannot do nothing. We must take counsel immediately.'

*

Holcroft had promised himself that he would not associate again with the group of men that he called the Treason Club yet somehow, with Jack on his heels, he found himself once more climbing the stairs to the dim, low-ceilinged, upper room in the Rose Tavern where these people frequently gathered.

When Percy Kirke saw Holcroft Blood emerge from the stairwell, with Jack coming up behind him, the first thing he said was: 'No! Absolutely not. I am not playing against him. I mean no insult to you, Blood, no disrespect at all is intended, but I will not play at cards with you! We didn't agree to this, Jack. I shall not play.'

'Calm yourself, Percy, I have not brought Holcroft along to play cards. My brother Charles will be my partner, that is if we decide to play at all after what my friend has come here to tell you.'

When Jack had assembled the members of the Treason Club – Lord Danby, Colonel Trelawny, Colonel Kirke, Charles Churchill, who was another colonel who had fought at Sedgemoor, Captain Byng and the rest of that disloyal fellowship, Holcroft ran through again what he'd told Jack an hour before. This time the response to his words was more explosive. He stressed that this was a hypothetical scenario but the men in that low room seemed to think he had proved beyond doubt that the royal child known as James Francis Edward Stuart was an imposter.

The King was damned to Hell and back. The Queen called a harlot and worse.

'I say this again,' said Holcroft loudly, trying to be heard over the hubbub. 'I have no proof at all that a substitution has been made – the Queen may have been delivered of a healthy baby boy in the usual way – all I believe is that a plot did exist, orchestrated by the spy Narrey – but whether it was carried through I cannot say—'

'Course it was carried through,' shouted Colonel Kirke. 'It's clear they were up to no good when they excluded all Protestants from the birthing chamber. And now we have a Catholic heir to the throne, a Catholic dynasty to rule over us for ever. . .'

'The country won't stand for it, the Army won't stand for it, the Navy . . .'

'The bishops, the whole of the Church of England, they'll put a stop to this . . .'

'We have no choice,' said another sweating, red-faced military man.

'Oh, come now, that is not quite true,' said Lord Danby quietly. 'We do have a choice. But it's not one to consider lightly. But, if we stand together . . .'

Chapter Twenty-six

16 June 1688: Mincing Lane

From the dark window of the room above the apothecary's shop in Mincing Lane, Narrey looked out at the blue-painted front door of the house diagonally opposite. Below his feet in the back room behind the shop lay the bodies of the apothecary and his wife, both Huguenot immigrants from Paris, whom he had befriended over a number of weeks and persuaded to allow him to rent, for a generous fee, the room in which he now sat. That had been a waste of money, he could not really conclude otherwise, for the man he wished to watch had not been in his home across the street for most of the time that he had been renting this small, musty-smelling room.

Now, however, his target – Holcroft Blood, Lieutenant of His Majesty's Ordnance – was back in his residence, and it was time to bring the operation to fruition. He had killed the apothecary and his wife easily, with a gift of expensive crystallised ginger, liberally laced with the old crone's inheritance powder, which he had insisted that they both taste. The look on the old Huguenot's face, after he had eaten that single piece of ginger, when his professional knowledge allowed him to realise what was happening, had been comical in the extreme. Narrey felt little remorse at their deaths: it had been necessary. Beside, these were French folk who had abandoned the True Religion and their own homeland, and chosen exile in this land of filthy heretics. God would judge them harshly, he was quite sure of it.

Narrey had watched in the early evening as Holcroft had returned from his labours at the Tower, been greeted by the maid and admitted to the house. He had waited patiently as the hours passed and the lights came on in the square windows across the street. Now they were in the downstairs dining room; now the parlour on the first floor. And yes, now they were retiring to bed on the second floor. He would give it an hour or two, and then send in Patrick Maguire and his Savoyards.

The bells of St Dunstan-in-the-East had rung midnight some time ago. Neither Blood nor his wife would be venturing out anywhere till morning's light. Narrey waited. He'd always been a patient man. He had learnt how to wait quietly when he was a little boy and the skill had never left him.

At a little before two, Narrey went downstairs into the apothecary's shop and pulled open the door of the storeroom. Inside, a dozen sets of eyes stared back at him. The air was foul with old sweat and stale breath, the faint smell of pickling brandy, which lay over the yeasty odour of dried herbs, acrid dusty powders and other harsher alchemical scents.

'It's time,' he said.

Eleven men, most of them large-bodied, rough-looking types, shuffled out of the storeroom. And one beautiful boy. Patrick Maguire kept a huge hand on Samuel's slim neck as he was marched out of the store and into the shop. Narrey went over to the window and gazed through a crack in the shutters out into the street: it was only intermittently lit by lanterns hung by householders outside the larger businesses and dwellings. All quiet. Not a soul to be seen. A lone mongrel was sniffing at a pile of stinking refuse at the corner where Mincing Lane met Tower Street.

Narrey turned to Patrick Maguire, who was looming by the door, checking the seating of a flint in a large horse pistol.

'He will play his part?' he said, nodding down at the whey-faced boy, his lovely eyes huge and black in the half-dark, who stood by Maguire's massive right leg.

'He had better – or I will cut all the skin off his backside,' rumbled Maguire.

The boy looked terrified.

Narrey looked over the other ten men: they seemed competent enough. Most were armed with pistols and knives, though here and there a man had an elegant small sword or an axe or cleaver, and one scarred fellow carried a long, new-looking flintlock musket. They were only facing one enemy, who would be fast asleep in his comfortable bed. His wife, the maid and cook were of no account. For a moment, Narrey wondered if he had overestimated his target: he knew Blood was a fighter – he had killed Michael Maguire and two of his friends – but was sending eleven men against him too many? Would they get in each other's way? No. And that did not matter anyway. Better safe than sorry.

'Be careful,' he said to Maguire. 'And, remember, I want his head.'

'This is for Michael,' said the big man. 'I've waited a long time for this. I'll fetch his head, don't fret, your honour. I only wish I had time to make him suffer.'

'Do not tarry. In, out, and back here before the hue and cry is raised. Yes?'

'I think I know this kind of business a little better than you.'

Narrey looked out at the deserted street one last time. 'So then . . . Go.'

He went over the door of the apothecary's shop, turned the key in the lock and pulled it wide open, standing back to allow Maguire and the child to hurry past him. The rest of the men remained where they were, by the open door, some hefting their weapons, licking dry lips. They were tense, alert, ready for battle.

Like swift, slinking shadows, Maguire and the boy crossed the street. They stopped outside the blue-painted door, and Narrey saw the child lifted smoothly on to Maguire's shoulders. The boy fiddled with the latch on the fan-shaped window above the portal, sliding a thin knife blade into the gap between the frame and the window case to slide the tongue back. The window yawned open and Maguire boosted the child up through the gap, keeping a grip on the boy till his whole body was through. Then released him. A long minute passed.

He's struggling with the bolt, thought Narrey. *He's too weak to slide it back. Or the key is not on the hook by the door.*

Another minute, and Narrey thought seriously about abandoning the mission.

And then the blue door opened from the inside.

'Go,' said the Frenchman, slapping a hand on the shoulder of the nearest man. 'Go now.'

He saw Maguire, still outside the door, looking expectantly across at the dark apothecary's shop doorway. And the men were gliding out, all ten of them, and running the few dozen yards across the street to the open portal of the house and being ushered briskly inside by the uncrowned king of the Liberty of the Savoy.

Holcroft jerked upright in bed. He thought he had heard something, the squeal of a metal hinge. His mind was clear; he concentrated his hearing. There! Another wrongful sound. The soft scrape of wood against wood, coming from downstairs, and now the shuffle of heavy feet. A whispered angry word. He slipped out of bed, wearing only his nightshirt. Bare feet on the cold floorboards. For an instant he thought about waking Elizabeth. And decided against it. One bellowed question from her could ruin everything. It was best if she stayed here anyway, awake or asleep. His groping hand reached to the table beside the bed and closed on the cold metal of the Lorenzoni repeating flintlock pistol. He hefted its weight in his right hand and, as quietly as he could, he pulled back the dog-head hammer to full cock. Then he began to walk, cautiously, slowly, nearly blind in the darkness, towards the bedchamber door.

In the hall outside, a single, fat-bodied candle was burning in a sconce on the wall. By its light he could see the staircase plunging into the darkness of the first floor. He thought of taking the light but realised that he needed two hands to work the Lorenzoni. He would fight in darkness, then. He turned and snuffed the candle with his finger and thumb. He did not care to have the light behind him, outlining his form for an enemy to clearly make out. He crept down the first staircase to the landing on the first floor and paused outside the parlour, his back flat against the wall, to listen. He could hear them clearly now, whispering, jostling each other, the creak of floorboards under the weight of several big men. There was a shaft of light, not bright, a dim beam. Somebody opening the door of a dark lantern. *Good*, he thought, *they will be in light, and I shall be in darkness.* He moved to the head of the staircase that led down to the hall and the front door.

There was the shape of a man, backlit by the lantern's beam. He had his foot on the first step and what looked like a sword in his hands. The step creaked under his weight and someone behind him muttered a curse and there was another low call for silence. Holcroft could see many moving shapes behind the man on the first step, people crowded into the small hall between the stairs and the front door, which he could see was now open, the street lighter than the hall, with a gigantic, bald-headed man only just fitting under the lintel. Holcroft sank silently to his knees, and lay flat on the floor, his chin hanging over the top step, making his body into the smallest possible target. They were sure to return fire. With luck they would fire high, as most people did.

He held the Lorenzoni in both hands, aimed at the dark shape that was stealthily climbing the stair, one step, two steps, a nervous pause when it creaked.

Holcroft pulled the trigger.

The pistol fired, the shot shockingly loud in the confined space, the lancing jet of orange light illuminating the tableau below him. He saw a startled man in a patched russet coat, cutlass in his hand, take the bullet to the centre of his chest and be hurled backwards by the force of the shot. Behind him, glimpsed in an instant, a crowd of men, nine or ten of them, packed like fish in a net in the hallway between the stairs and the front door, the long hall table and comfortable visitors' waiting chair compressing them even more in that narrow space. Holcroft took it all in in a moment, and turned his attention to the Lorenzoni.

He thanked God that he had spent so much time in the Ordnance range practising with this piece, for the movements to reload it came naturally to him, even in darkness. He tilted the pistol downwards, twisted the loading lever through half a circle to rotate the central spindle, an action which due to the genius of its maker Michel Lorenzoni, dropped power and shot into the barrel of the pistol, primed the frizzen pan, even cocked the weapon. He twisted the lever back to the starting position. He was ready to fire again.

It took Holcroft less than three beats of his racing heart to achieve this and now, once more, he had a loaded pistol in his hands. He could hear shouts of rage and alarm below him, someone, a booming bull bass, was shouting at the other men to get up the stairs: 'It's only one man! Get up there, or I'll have your fucking balls!'

Holcroft felt, rather than saw or heard, the next man try to come up the staircase in a bounding rush. He lifted the pistol, carefully shot him in the middle of his dark mass, and immediately set about reloading. Below him, a musket fired. The bullet passing a yard above his prone body. A pistol barked from the hall, too. He heard it smash into the wall behind him. He loosed another shot down the stairwell, unsure if there was anyone attempting to climb, but unwilling to take the chance of being overwhelmed. His wife was screaming 'Holcroft!' from the bedroom above.

And then the whole hall was lit by a gigantic blast from a blunderbuss.

Twelve pistol balls erupted in a spreading pattern from the trumpet-mouth of the coachman's weapon, smashing into the flank of the men crowded in the hall with brutal efficiency. Several men were blown off their feet. The air was filled with the screams of the wounded and the stench of blood and burnt powder. Enoch

Jackson stood in the open doorway to the dining room, now lit by an open dark lantern on the sideboard in that room. Jackson dropped the empty blunderbuss and pulled a horse pistol from his belt. From across the hall, Sergeant Miller stepped into the doorway of the study, grinning like a diminutive devil, a cocked pistol in each hand. He blew the top off the head of one man, and shot down a second fellow who lunged suddenly at him with a knife. He dropped his smoking pistols and drew another gun from his waistband, cocked it smoothly, hunting a new target.

A big scarred fellow pointed a long pistol at Miller but before he had time to fire the small sergeant shot him through the throat. From the other side of the hall, Jackson fired his pistol into the side of a man with a musket, and hauled another loaded piece from his pocket. Holcroft fired the Lorenzoni once more into the mass of struggling, falling, shouting, blood-spattered Savoyards, but the big front door was wide open now, and the bald giant was gone, and those in the hall who could were running, fighting each other to get out of the house, away from the three smoke-wreathed fiends who fired as fast and as accurately as a company of Guardsmen.

Holcroft got to his feet, fired once more at the disappearing Savoyards, and turned to find Elizabeth at his back, milk-faced, and clutching a silver candlestick, with three blazing candles.

'Oh my God,' she said, and for once her voice was close to a whisper. Holcroft turned back and surveyed the battleground: there were six dead bodies on the hall floor, and one living man with his stomach torn open, blue-grey entrails bulging through his fingers, who was sitting, sobbing in a lake of his own and others' blood.

Enoch Jackson intoned from the doorway: 'He stood in the midst of the ground, and defended it, and slew the Philistines: and the Lord wrought a great victory.'

Holcroft automatically muttered: '2 Samuel, 23: 12.'

Then, feeling somehow sick and ashamed, he looked over the carpet of carnage. At the blood and the bodies. One of them caught his eye. It was smaller than all the rest, about half the size of the men, and half hidden under the long hall table. He went down the stairs, walked towards it, and crouched beside the small corpse.

The boy's eyes were still open, still a startling, brilliant green, but a fist-sized hole in the side of his skull had allowed all the young life to ooze out of him.

Chapter Twenty-seven

26 June 1688: Yorkshire

Thomas Osborne, Lord Danby, read over the letter in his hand one final time and placed the large piece of paper on the desk top in front of him. He squared it neatly with his fingertips on the leather surface in line with the edge.

He was sitting alone in his large comfortable study in his grand house on his estate near Whitby, North Yorkshire. It was past midnight but a sense of excitement, of impending destiny even, meant that he felt not the slightest urge for sleep. There was a page on duty outside this chamber, should he require anything, but the rest of the servants and his wife were all abed.

'This is my personal Rubicon,' he muttered to himself. 'Once crossed, there can be no going back.'

The letter was high treason. No question about it. It was addressed to His Majesty, Prince William of Orange, Stadtholder of the Republic of the Seven United Netherlands, and it baldly invited the Dutch ruler to come to England, depose the Catholic monarch James and to seize the thrones of the Three Kingdoms by force.

Treason it might be, but Lord Danby believed it to be a justified treason. William, a good Protestant, had a decent claim to the thrones: he was married to Mary, James's eldest daughter, who until the past two weeks had been his heir apparent. He was also the grandson of the first King Charles, whose head had been hacked off by the Parliamentarians in the late civil wars.

The document made passing reference to this – not that William needed to be reminded of it – and went on to outline the many grievances of James's Protestant subjects, beginning with the overruling of the Parliament-made laws, which ensured that only Protestants could hold public office, by the King's indiscriminate use of Indulgences. It then cited the arrest of the seven senior bishops of the Church of England, including the Archbishop of Canterbury, who were even now languishing in the Tower of London awaiting trial for refusing to order that James's decrees on toleration for all religions be read from every pulpit across the land. The letter claimed that the newborn Prince of Wales, James's longed-for Catholic heir, was suppositious – that is, that the baby had been smuggled into the birthing chamber and was an imposter. No true heir at all.

The letter assured the Prince that Englishmen of wealth and power, and all who supported them, would rise to fight for William should he come across the sea.

It promised rebellion, once more, in the name of the Protestant cause. For an instant, the fate of the Duke of Monmouth and his botched execution was conjured up in Danby's mind. Odd, he thought, that the brat of that old villain Colonel Blood, the boy who had overseen that execution of the traitor Monmouth, should also be the fellow who had informed them about the baby-factory in the Savoy and exposed the criminal subterfuge in the birthing chamber.

Danby could not make his mind up about young Holcroft: he was highly regarded in the Ordnance, a rising officer in that service with the patronage of Lord Dartmouth, and Jack Churchill never ceased to sing his praises. But Danby had not forgotten his blatant blackmailing of the old king to save his father from the noose and his refusal to be reasonable when pressure was applied. What would he do if – *when*, he hoped – William were to cross to these shores with his Dutch army and challenge James? Could Blood be counted on to come over to the Williamite side – and bring the other officers and men of the Royal Train of Artillery with him? Or would he be mulishly stubborn and insist on remaining loyal to Catholic James?

Lord Danby had no answer to his own questions. But that odd young officer would be one to watch when the time came. Which way would he jump?

Danby picked up the letter again. It was not the first communication of this nature that he had indulged in with The Hague, with the ministers and servants of Prince William. He and several other prominent Englishmen, lords, bishops, Army officers, even some local landowners and Justices of the Peace, had been writing and receiving letters from Holland for months. But this was the first explicit, formal, written invitation for a foreign army to invade these shores. If this letter were to fall into the wrong hands, Lord Danby, for all his wealth and titles, would be tried, found guilty, and beheaded like poor Monmouth. It was, then, appropriate that he should consider long and hard before adding his signature to the bottom of the page.

He looked at the other names listed, powerful men, all committed to the Protestant cause. All swearing loyalty to William and beseeching him to come over and save them from the tyranny of a Catholic succession: the Earl of Shrewsbury, the Earl of Devonshire, the Viscount Lumley, the Bishop of London, Lord Russell, a naval captain and son of the Earl of Bedford, and Henry Sydney, the son of the Earl of Leicester, a friend and confidante of Prince William, and the man who, with considerable urging from Lord Danby, had actually written this treasonous letter.

A Rubicon, then. And one that had to be crossed.

Lord Danby dipped his quill in the pot, shook off the excess ink and signed his name at the bottom of the letter below the others, with a flourish. If he dispatched it this night, it could be in Holland, in Prince William's hands, within three, four days.

'*Alea iacta est*,' he muttered as he shook a fine sand over the fresh ink.

Chapter Twenty-eight

27 June 1688: Palace of White Hall

'You say these men, this gang of criminals from the Liberty of the Savoy, broke into your house in Mincing Lane, in the dead of night, in an attempt to murder you and your wife in your bed, have I got this right?' The King's tone was incredulous.

It did sound a little fanciful, when put like this, Holcroft realised, but it *was* the truth. There was no other way to tell it.

'Yes, Your Majesty,' he said, looking at his shabby shoes.

'And you, and your comrades, a veteran master gunner of the Ordnance and a sergeant of my Royal Fusiliers, lay in wait for these villains and, when they broke in, you killed half a dozen and wounded many others before they ran off into the night.'

'Exactly as you say, Your Majesty.'

'Well, the question I have for you, Lieutenant Blood, is . . . why? Why should these cut-throats be so keen to murder you? Why – or rather how – did you know that they would be coming for you that night, so that you could lay your murderous trap? I feel there is something vital that you are not telling me. What have you to say, sir?'

This was the question Holcroft had been dreading.

'The man behind the attack is, I believe, a Frenchman, an agent of France. He and I have, ah, crossed paths before, in France, while I was . . . while I was living there, serving in His Most Christian Majesty's *Corps d'Artillerie*. I knew he was in London and I suspected that because of our long enmity he might seek to harm me.'

'That is not an answer. That just raises a host of more questions.'

The Earl of Sunderland stepped forward, and leant in to the King to whisper at some length in his right ear.

'Indeed?' said the King. 'So you were in the . . . ah . . . service of my late brother Charles, as well as in the Sun King's service.'

Holcroft said nothing. He felt a furious anger at his secret past being bandied about in this indiscreet manner. He looked about the Red Audience Room, and noted that the French Ambassador and his coterie of hangers-on were at the far end of the room talking to Jack Churchill. And, he very much hoped, out of earshot. Not that it mattered. He was thoroughly blown on as an agent. If he ever went back to France, he would almost certainly be arrested and shot as a spy.

He had been summoned by the King after the night of carnage in Mincing Lane had become common knowledge. There had been no way to keep a noisy gun battle in a small London street in the middle of the night a secret for very long, not to mention all the blood and the dead bodies. The neighbours, in their night shirts and caps, had swarmed over the street outside the house within minutes of the attackers' departure, the local constables had been summoned. Sir Henry Firebrace, one of the two sheriffs of London, had arrived the next day and ordered Holcroft to explain himself or face imprisonment and trial. Naturally the King was told of it, too.

And now, eleven days after the battle, Holcroft found himself in the Red Audience Room in the sprawling royal apartments in White Hall, trying to answer his sovereign's questions satisfactorily without mentioning that he believed that the man behind the attack might possibly have substituted a Savoy whore's child for the Prince of Wales, the much-celebrated heir to the thrones of the Three Kingdoms.

'So you are claiming that this is a private feud between spies?'

Holcroft was close to losing his temper. 'I am saying, Your Majesty, that I was attacked in my home by a number of men, criminals and thieves from the Liberty of the Savoy, who serve a French master, and that I defended myself and my home with an appropriate amount of force. I also humbly request that I be allowed to take a force of armed men, Royal Fusiliers, into the Savoy to seek out the man behind this attack and bring him to justice. I did, in fact, send a note to Lord Sunderland about this matter some months ago, alerting him that a French agent was operating here under our noses. I received no reply. I understand no action was taken at the time.'

'Is this correct, Sunderland?'

'I received a rather odd note from Lieutenant Blood at Christmastide ranting about Catholics in the Savoy, something to do with Father Palmer's free school.'

The King frowned. 'I will not have them molested. No, sir, no Lieutenant Blood. You may not take my soldiers into the Savoy to harass this free school and the good Fathers who teach the poor there. I have given them a special licence to practice their religion freely and I have had enough of my Catholic subjects being hounded for their faith. No, sir. You shall leave them be. Lord Sunderland and his officers will make the appropriate inquiries into this matter.'

Holcroft said nothing.

The King let out a breath. 'However, I shall dismiss the charges of affray against you, Lieutenant Blood, and your men, as it seems that you *were* merely protecting yourself. But I doubt that this French spy, if he is even still in London, will trouble you after you massacred so many of his men: what was it? Seven killed.'

'Six, Your Majesty, and one innocent boy – from the free school.'

'Be that as it may. I think your shadowy Frenchman will have learnt not to disturb you in your dwelling again. That is all. You have my leave to retire, sir.'

Holcroft made his bow and retreated from the throne, leaving Sunderland and the King in earnest conversation. He was halfway down the room, almost at the big double doors, with the footmen preparing to open them, when Jack stopped him.

'You are unhurt, Hol, yes? And Elizabeth too?' he said, looking concerned. 'I heard about the bloody business at your home. Sarah and I were shocked. If you like, I can give you a file of redcoats to keep watch on the house. Unofficially, of course.'

'Thank you, Jack, but there is no need,' said Holcroft. He was still fuming at the stupidity of the King and his chief minister. 'I have moved Elizabeth and the servants into my old quarters in the Tower. We'll be staying there for the time being – and we will be safe, I think. Jackson and Miller will continue to watch over me, too.'

Before Jack could reply, Henri d'Erloncourt's face appeared at his left shoulder.

'My dear Holcroft, I am appalled, quite appalled at this outrage. You must be shocked to the very core by this gross barbarity. How are you nerves, my dear?'

'I am well, thank you, Henri,' said Holcroft wearily. 'This is not the first time someone has discharged a pistol at me.'

'But in the sanctity of your home, your hearth, it is all quite, quite ... monstrous. Do you have any idea who could have perpetrated this foul crime?'

Holcroft looked at Henri D'Erloncourt; his long pointed nose was almost twitching with excitement, his brown eyes were darting all over, seemingly trying to assure himself that his old friend was unharmed. To Holcroft, he resembled even more than usual a young fox, sniffing the wind, scenting for danger.

'We know they came from the Liberty of the Savoy. But not much more. My Lord Sunderland is going to make some further inquiries,' he said. 'And now if you will forgive me, I must get back to the Tower, my duties call ...'

'Of course, of course. You must be terribly shaken. But you can tell me all about it, every sword blow and pistol shot, every gout of red gore, on Sunday.'

'On Sunday?' said Holcroft.

'Yes, Sunday, the first of July, I think we said. You are dining with me here in my White Hall apartments. Your lovely wife Elizabeth arranged everything. Surely you have not already forgotten?'

'Ah, no, of course I hadn't forgotten,' Holcroft lied. 'Till Sunday, then.'

And with a vague sense of approaching doom, he made his fare-wells and left.

Chapter Twenty-nine

28 June 1688: Tower of London

This might well be considered theft, and Holcroft knew it. In one sense he was no better than Captain Glanville and all those others who robbed the King with their petty peculations and false musters. One the other hand, it was only food and drink set out for the officers' dinner, fare that he might have eaten himself if he were hungry. And if he did not take it, the cooks and the mess staff would have disposed of it themselves, sold it, eaten it or taken it home to their families.

Well, he was doing this anyway – theft or no. He shoved the roasted chicken into the sack, and followed it with a loaf of fresh bread and a couple of apples. He put a silver half crown on the sideboard that held the remains of the dinner, mainly as a salve for his conscience, swung the sack over his shoulder and, seizing a bottle of brandy decanted from the barrel, walked out of the mess and headed across the Inner Ward towards the White Tower.

A few minutes later he was sitting in a small, dank cell with his friend Peter Mews, the Bishop of Winchester, unpacking the meal and setting it out on the prelate's table. This ground-floor cell was a far cry from the spacious one on the second storey where his father had been held, it was cramped and damp, no fireplace, and only one tiny window, high up on the left side, that let in a thin beam of afternoon sunlight from the warm late-June day outside. But these miserable conditions did not seem to depress the spirits of the cells' elderly occupant.

'How perfectly splendid! May God shower His blessings upon you, Holcroft Blood,' said Peter Mews, tearing off a chicken leg and attacking it with his teeth. 'The food in this ancient stronghold has been, up until this point, execrable,' he said with a full mouth. 'Your man Widdicombe serves us nothing but slop and sour ale twice a day and I cannot bring myself to put silver in that venal old homunculus's pocket for better fare.'

Holcroft poured himself a glass of brandy, and sat back in the cell's only chair. The bishop sat on his narrow cot, squeezed in on the other side of the table, such were the chamber's meagre dimensions.

'Are you keeping well, my lord? No gaol fever, no chills?'

'I'm splendid, thank you. Fit as a fiddle. Never better.'

Holcroft speculated how an inanimate wooden musical instrument could be either fit or unfit. But he said nothing. The bishop was evidently in good health.

'What news of the trial?' he asked the older man.

'We go before the Lords tomorrow, I'm told, a full session. And I think it likely that we shall be exonerated in short order. Seditious libel – it's a ridiculous charge. Everyone recognizes it. The Lords are with us, the Church is united, in fact, the whole country is behind us. The King has overreached himself and will be sorely humiliated, I believe. I and my fellow bishops will be free men within the week.'

'Will the King act against you once you are free, do you think?'

'No-oo, I doubt it. James has behaved very badly – and he knows it. Did you hear that there were angry mobs out all across London when they took us into custody? Chanting terrible things about the Pope. Blackguarding the King and his ministers. Behaving disgracefully, I must admit. But it is gratifying to feel we have the support of the common people. The trial will be the end of this business, you mark my words, Holcroft. James has got bigger concerns than a few contumelious priests. You'll have heard the news about the Dutchman, William of Orange.'

'What about him?'

'Really? I *am* surprised, the Tower is such a splendid anthill of gossip. I should have thought you would have heard days before me. I had it from Widdicombe, he came round here trying to ingratiate himself, greasy little monkey – didn't think to feed me proper victuals but he was quick indeed to share his apocalyptic news.'

'I have been somewhat caught up in my own affairs,' said Holcroft. Indeed, he had been too busy for gossip and he had chosen not to mix much with the other officers in the Tower since his return from Hull. Captain William Glanville had been recalled from Sheerness, he had heard, and Holcroft was hoping to avoid another disastrous confrontation. He had also quarrelled with Lord Dartmouth, who told him to stop badgering him about the corruption report he had written while in Yorkshire. On top of that, he had had his hands full settling Elizabeth and her maid – the cook had been dismissed – into the tiny Tower quarters he'd occupied before marriage.

'It seems that Dutch William is preparing for war. He seeks to invade us,' said the bishop, without seeming alarmed at this information. 'He is gathering ships and men at Hellevoetsluis and he is planning to come over here at the end of the summer, or in early autumn, before the seas become too dangerous. Apparently, he has been invited by several high-ranking noblemen to take the throne.'

'No! Do you believe that is true?'

'I have no idea. Probably not. But it is something to occupy the mind of our dear old sovereign, and with luck he will leave his bishops alone for a little while.'

'I am pleased that you will be getting out soon,' said Holcroft.

'So am I. But enough about this old fool. I heard that you faced down a marauding army of Savoyard villains who attacked your home. I heard you defeated them and caused much righteous slaughter of the paynim. Is it true? Excellent!'

Holcroft didn't care for the relish that the bishop showed for the murderous affair in Mincing Lane. But he admitted that it was true and gave a brief account.

'I've had to move my wife here for safety,' he said sadly. 'She follows me during the day, when I am about my duties, asking questions in her, well, in her rather *carrying* voice. It is distracting and un-officer-like. I suspect the men have been laughing about it behind my back. I have begged her to keep to our rooms but she says she gets bored with nothing to occupy her and she wants to learn about my Ordnance duties. She says she wants to get to know me and my work better.'

'Did she really?'

'Yes, I thought she might be interested in the guns because, well, because I love them so. I took her to the armoury yard and had the cannon wheeled out. I showed her the biggest one, Joshua's Trumpet, the great thirty-six pounder, you should see it my lord, it's a magnificent beast – bigger than anything you would have used in all the wars against Parliament. I took her over to the Demi-Culverins, Screaming Sally, Chained Lighting, Lawful Murder and all the rest. I even showed her Roaring Meg, of course, and explained that she had fought nobly in the late civil wars and that she had once been commanded by a future bishop of the Church of England. Which would be you, my lord.'

'Thank you, I did manage to guess. So, what did she say? Was she struck dumb with amazement at this display of military marvels?'

'No, not at all. Strangely. She said she found guns boring. Boring! As if anyone could find cannon dull. It's inexplicable. To make it more interesting, I explained to her in great detail their respective weights, the charges of powder they each took, the size of ball, the amount of windage each could tolerate, the number of horses required to pull the gun carriage. She actually yawned! I was taken aback. I make no claim to understanding the minds of young ladies but I was astonished by her indifference. Frankly, my lord, I don't know what to do with her. I'm at my wits' end.'

'These things are sent to try us,' said the bishop. 'You could send her away. Or do you think she would still be in danger from these murderous Savoyards?'

'There is still a danger, yes. And she must stay here for the time being. But that is one of the reasons why I wanted to come and see you, in fact . . .'

'Do go on, my dear boy, if I can be of any service at all . . .'

'You studied at the University in Oxford, isn't that right, my lord? You studied literature, poetry, verse and so on? Perhaps some French writers, as well as English?'

'It was many years ago now, but yes, St John's College. I read a good deal back then. I also continued my studies for some years in Paris after the wars were over.'

'I am trying to find out the identity of the man behind the attacks on me and my household. I am persuaded that he is a Frenchman, an intelligence agent, known only by the codename Narrey. However, I did receive an indication of his true name. A man in Paris, an agent of the English Crown, was murdered by him. Poison, it seems. And with his final breath he said that the French spy's identity could be found in verse. It is not very much to go on but I wondered if there were any French spies or intelligencers who could be found in French poetry, or in a famous play perhaps.'

'What did this poisoned man say, exactly, as he was dying?'

'He said Narrey's identity should be sought in verse.'

'Hmmm. Let me think. Not much comes to mind, to be honest. Pierre Corneille wrote a play called *The Liar*. But it's not really about spies, more about lying to women in order to bed them. Harpagon, the wealthy protagonist in Molière's *The Miser*, thinks the valet has been sent to spy on him. Does that help?'

Holcroft said nothing. It didn't help. And neither, he realised, did a vague instruction to seek Narrey's identity in poetry. It could mean anything. Or nothing.

'He said "in verse", did he? This poor poisoned soul.'

Holcroft nodded.

'Well, this could be leading us up a blind alley, but when I was in Paris, more than twenty years ago, there was a new kind of slang that the young gallants were using about the court. They called it 'the inverse' – it was a way of being witty, and also of disguising the meaning of your speech. You switch the syllables in a word or phrase, so the second one comes first. *Verlan*, they called it, being *l'envers* – the inverse – of the original word. There was one fellow, Comte de Mal-something or other, who was most amusing, quite the verbal trickster . . .'

Holcroft vaguely remembered people talking in this peculiar way when he had been in France. It had irritated him greatly when he had been struggling to learn to speak the French language correctly. At that moment, the door of the cell opened.

'Begging your pardon, Mister Blood,' said Widdicombe, poking his misshapen head around the door. 'But Lord Dartmouth has been asking after you. He wishes to speak to you, at your earliest convenience, about the new saltpeter receipts.'

'I'd better go,' said Holcroft, rising to his feet. 'Thank you, my lord, for your advice. And I wish you luck with the trial tomorrow.'

'No need for luck,' said the bishop. 'Do not forget your Deuteronomy 3:22. The Lord will fight for us! And if He is with us justice must prevail.'

Chapter Thirty

30 June 1688: Liberty of the Savoy

Patrick Maguire sprawled in the front pew of the little chapel in Palmer's school, staring at the huge crucifix that he had paid for with his own hard-wrested money. Behind him, the other frog-eater, Guillaume, was prowling up and down the central aisle of the chapel, tense, angry, distracting. In front of him, the slender French arseworm who called himself Narrey was staring coldly at him from under his brim.

'The true mark of a man,' said Narrey, in a grating, schoolmas-terish tone, 'is not shown by his successes. No, no, not at all. God sends troubles to test us, to test the strength of our faith. The path is never smooth. The true mark of a man is how he responds to these setbacks, these failures. Whether or not he has the courage to overcome the obstacles placed in his path and see the task through to the end. That is when character is displayed, that is when a man shows his true mettle . . .'

Maguire let the words wash over him. He was tired. He had not slept well for days. His youngest brother Francis's death burdened him greatly. Just twenty-two years old and he had been butchered with all the others in that chamber of fire and death in Mincing Lane. Patrick had had to explain to his widow why young Francis was in the house of a stranger on the other side of London, and why he had been cut down like a dog by the bullets of the soldier and his two men. He'd not done it well.

Maeve had said nothing when he told her. She had wept silently and waited for him to say his piece and go. He had little if any comfort to offer her, little for himself either. Two of his younger brothers had been lost in the space of half a year, and nearly a dozen good Savoy men had gone down too – and all because this damned Frenchman kept pitting his clan against this man Blood. Sending them into the fire of battle without proper information about what they would face.

'. . . this is why we must rise above the slings and arrows of outrageous fortune, as your own immortal Bard puts it. A man learns from his mistakes and goes forward, secure in the knowledge of eventual victory, in the rightness of his sacred cause . . .'

'No,' said Patrick. He said the word loudly, forcefully in his booming bass. The word ricocheted around the chapel like a musket ball.

Narrey stopped his long speech in mid-sentence in his surprise. 'What?'

'No more. I have had my fill. This fellow Blood is a killer, a soldier, and he has the whole King's army behind him, and I will not send any more of my family and my men against him and his comrades to be slaughtered like so many bleating sheep in a shambles . . . So, no. To whatever it is that you are working up to, I say no.'

That morning a woman had spat on his shadow and cursed him. Patrick had been walking down the street, coming back from the Grapes after a liquid conference with his lieutenants, and a woman, Elsie Johnson was her name, had hawked up a gob of phlegm and spattered the cobbles behind him as he passed her, a dark imprecation was muttered too, just out of the range of his hearing.

Elsie's man Davie was one of the half dozen bravos he had left for dead in the house in Mincing Lane. By the time his brain had registered the insult, by the time he had recognised the gross disrespect, he had walked on three paces and when he turned, Elsie was gone. It had been so long since he had been challenged that he had not recognised it for what it was. Rebellion. He knew he ought to seek her out and punish her. Make an example of her. But he had not the will. Tomorrow, perhaps.

'Mister Maguire, do I need to remind you of the substantial amounts of money that I have paid over to you?' Narrey had stepped in closer to the seated giant. 'Do I need to remind you of who I am, of who I represent, who my master is?'

If the Frenchman was attempting to be intimidating, he failed miserably.

Patrick Maguire stood up, towering over Narrey. He could sense the Frenchman's muscular factotum closing in on him from behind. He turned around fast. 'You stay where you are,' he said to Guillaume, pointing a huge, sausage-like finger at him. 'Take another step and I will end you. And if your hand so much as touches that pistol in your belt, I'll take it from you and shove it so far up your arse that you will be able to spit fire out of your fat French gob. Hear me?'

Guillaume stopped dead. He stood still, his hands spread wide from his sides.

'I *have* taken your money,' said Patrick. 'I've *earned* your money. I have protected your little baby-farm for whatever disgusting scheme you had in mind. That's now over. I have sacrificed two of my brothers and a dozen of my men to your designs. And I do know who your master is. But if you think I'm afeared of the King of France you are sorely mistaken. *I am king in the Liberty. I rule here.*'

He roared the words and the chapel shook with his pain, grief and anger.

Narrey took a step backwards, he put out his hands as if to ward off the giant Irishman.

'Let us not be hasty,' he said. 'I have more silver, much more, as much as—'

'*Be silent!*' Patrick felt the old bare-knuckle madness stir inside him. He wanted to snatch up this slippery little French sodomite and pound him in a bloody mush.

'This is my kingdom,' he said quietly, when he had control over himself again. 'If this soldier, this Holcroft Blood, ever shows his nose again in the Liberty, I shall visit my vengeance upon him. And it shall be terrible. I will grind his flesh and bones into the dust. He will beg for death. But I will not seek him out. I will not risk any more of my family, my own blood, nor any more of my men in your pointless feud.

'I am finished with you – with both of you. And I would urge you to pack up your possessions, take your pregnant hags and your mewling babies, if you still have a use for them, and leave *my* kingdom with all haste before I decide to take the blood price of my brothers from your flesh. Go back to France – or to Hell, for all I care.'

Patrick stepped past the hooded man, roughly pushed aside Guillaume, and stamped off down the aisle towards the doors. He needed a drink, a bloody great big one, to wash the foul taste of these filthy, scheming foreigners from his mouth.

Narrey watched him leave. He looked at Guillaume and said: 'Well then, old friend, you heard him. If the mountain will not come to Muhammad . . .'

Chapter Thirty-one

1 July 1688: Palace of White Hall

In the fine coach, bathed and shaved, in clean linen, sporting freshly polished shoes and an itchy chestnut periwig, with his blue coat thoroughly brushed, Holcroft sat next to his wife Elizabeth – who was similarly beautified in a new salmon-pink gown and matching wrap – and contemplated the agony of the Sunday afternoon ahead. On the front of the hired coach, next to the driver, sat Enoch Jackson, vigilant and armed with the captured blunderbuss and a cutlass, and behind in the pillion seat at the back of the vehicle lolled Sergeant Miller, adorned with his usual arsenal of pistols and blades and carrying a loaded flintlock musket. There was not much chance of the coach being waylaid in daylight, as it drove from the Tower, west across London, to White Hall, but Holcroft did feel a prickle of apprehension as they passed along the Strand, the road that ran across the north of the Liberty of the Savoy. This uncomfortable sensation did not leave him until they had reached the Charing Cross and turned left into the broad street that led to White Hall.

'What I cannot understand, my dear, is why we *must* go to dinner with this importunate French fellow. I do wish you hadn't arranged it without asking me.'

'If I had asked you, you would have said no. You never want to go out, Holcroft, you never want to do anything but work. You must try to get out into society, at least once in a while. Besides, he is a dear friend of yours, husband, and so far as I can reckon you have far too few of those. He is charming, very well bred, and a count, a genuine French aristocrat. You need to be moving in more elevated circles.'

'I knew Henri d'Erloncourt briefly as a child and since then I have not given him more than a moment's thought,' said Holcroft. 'Anyway, I have plenty of friends: there is Jack, and he's a genuine lord now, and . . . there is Aphra Behn.'

'Oh *her*,' said Elizabeth. 'She is hardly respectable. She's a *writer*. A woman writer – whatever next? And she lives in a house of . . . well, extremely dubious repute. No, no, she is not at all the sort of person we should be seen mixing with.'

'Lord Dartmouth is my friend. And so is John Miller . . . and Enoch Jackson.'

'Lord Dartmouth is your *patron* – which is not the same thing. And Jackson and Miller are . . . well, they are not exactly of the *noblesse*, are they my dear?'

The coach paused at the lofty, castle-like gatehouse at the entrance of the Palace of White Hall, and a red-coated soldier peered into the window of the coach, nodding at Holcroft's Ordnance uniform and officer's sash before waving them through.

They alighted in the Street, and leaving Miller and Jackson to mind the vehicle in the warm July sunshine, they made their way through the Privy Garden to a cluster of buildings, north of the warren of royal apartments, which housed the French embassy.

There were redcoats from the King's First Foot Guards at every door he passed, and Holcroft spotted a file of them, under an ensign, marching smartly across the immaculate gardens. The King, he had heard, was much concerned about the danger posed by the anti-Catholic riots, which had flared up across the city for several nights in a row now – the London mob had been celebrating since the release of the seven Anglican bishops from the Tower, lighting bonfires, drinking extravagantly and dancing around burning effigies of the Pope and Louis XIV. The presence of the red-coated soldiers was to guard the French Embassy, in case the exuberant and lawless citizens took in into their heads to attack all Catholic foreigners and their priests.

Holcroft was comforted by the sight of so many disciplined English soldiers. He knew that Narrey would have allies in the Embassy – he was Louis's most powerful spymaster, and as such the Embassy would always offer him covert help, if required – and to a certain extent he felt he was walking into the lion's den.

However, he had taken the precaution of informing Lord Dartmouth, and Jack Churchill, where he would be and if Narrey were to attempt another attack that afternoon or evening, he calculated that it would not be in or anywhere near the Embassy. The resulting scandal would be so great, so damaging to the King's reputation and French political interest, that Narrey would never contemplate it.

Nevertheless, the soldiers made him feel more comfortable. All he had to do was sit through this tedious formal dinner, be pleasant to Henri d'Erloncourt and his legion of dull guests, eat his food, drink his wine, smile, nod, and listen to his host's cheery prattle, and then they could go home. Duty done. And, at a reasonable hour of the day, he hoped. If he was lucky he might even get some work done that afternoon.

He was surprised – when they presented themselves at the door of the Embassy, at the fashionably late time of one o' clock, after acknowledging the stiff-standing Foot Guards on either side of the door – to be conducted not into the Ambassador's vast reception hall nor into the grand ballroom but up a discreet staircase and along several corridors and to a small door somewhere in the bowels of the Embassy.

The door was opened by a villainous-looking footman wearing an eye patch, a black coat and white wig and Holcroft and Elizabeth were ushered into a suite of well-lit rooms and into the presence of Henri, Comte d'Erloncourt himself.

The young man was resplendent in a perfectly cut suit of clothes in a pale lavender, ivory stockings, purple shoes and a wig that was tinged a light blue.

'My dear Holcroft, welcome, welcome, a thousand times welcome, and here is the lovely Elizabeth, my English angel! How delightful to see you both again.'

The room was a smallish, comfortable withdrawing room, lined with oak panels and with a cheerful bouquet of bright flowers in the fireplace, and a good many indifferent oil paintings adorning the walls and displayed on almost every surface.

The one-eyed footman brought in a tray of Champagne, and while Holcroft sipped the fizzy liquid, Henri asked solicitously after his health, and that of Elizabeth, and even Lord Dartmouth. Was all quite in order at the Tower of London?

A dark, muscular man walked into the room, taking off his hat and cloak, and Henri laid a hand on his arm and said: 'My dear Holcroft, permit me to name my friend, Major du Clos, lately of His Most Christian Majesty's *Corps d'Artillerie.*'

Holcroft mumbled something about having already met the gentleman – he briefly mentioned Jack's victory celebration at the Cockpit three years before.

'Of course,' said Major du Clos, 'how could I forget. That impudent fellow grossly insulted you and you knocked him down with a single blow. I hope you killed him, sir, for his discourtesy. Although I heard nothing subsequently about a duel.'

'A duel, Holcroft, what's all this?' called out Elizabeth. Holcroft noticed with amusement that Major du Clos flinched slightly at the volume of her remark.

'It was all smoothed over,' he said. 'There was no need to fight.'

'I assume the cowardly cur apologised abjectly to you,' said du Clos.

Holcroft said nothing but he could feel a hot flush suffusing his neck and jaw.

There was an awkward silence, into which Henri said: 'Do you like art, my dear Holcroft? Oil paintings? Allow me to show you some of my creations?'

Henri conducted Holcroft to the wood-panelled wall where a large framed picture had been hung. It was an image of an ugly, squat-looking church nestling in a lush valley. There were several stupid-looking black-and-white cows grazing in the foreground and a half-naked man in what appeared to be a blue cloak or perhaps a Roman toga was gesturing towards the building as if to say: *Voila!*

'Do you like it, Holcroft? I painted it in Germany on a journey there last summer. I'm so proud of it. Tell me what you think? You must be completely honest.'

Holcroft bit his tongue. He had been caught out in this way before. He'd learnt painfully over the years that when people asked him to be completely honest, they almost never meant it. Behind him he could hear Major du Clos answering questions from Elizabeth about the bunched sleeves of the dresses that ladies of fashion were favouring at the Sun King's court in Versailles that summer.

'It is very artistic,' Holcroft said, 'Very, very . . . ah, very artistic.' He looked at Henri, who was gazing up at him with a kind of moist-eyed yearning – like one of his cows. 'I did not know that you were such a . . . such a *painter*, Henri,' he said.

'It is my passion,' he said simply. 'I paint on my travels, whenever I have the time. I have painted many of the wonders of the English countryside. I have been told – although I do not like to boast – that there are echoes of the great Poussin in my works. See here, this one, you will like this one, as a military fellow. It was inspired by the great Hannibal crossing the Alps to wreak his vengeance upon the Romans.'

Holcroft dutifully peered at another picture of a sickly looking, horse-like elephant, which carried a man with an extravagantly plumed helmet waving a sword.

'It is very . . . very life-like,' he lied. 'I can almost believe myself to be there.'

'Do you think so? Do you honestly think so?' Henri was blooming with joy.

'Monsieur, the dinner is served,' said the villainous one-eyed footman, to Holcroft's relief. The four of them trooped through to the adjoining room where a table had been laid out for them, gleaming with polished silver.

When they had sat down, and a chicken soup with leeks and cream had been served, du Clos began to question Holcroft about his work at the Tower and the state of the Royal Train of Artillery. Holcroft answered guardedly. He was aware that he was talking to a soldier of a foreign power and he kept his answers vague and short.

'The main problem with His Majesty's Train, as I see it,' said du Clos, 'but you must, of course, correct me if I am wrong, my dear Lieutenant Blood, is that your drivers, and carters, and farriers and so on are mere civilians. And, as such, do not come under military rule. They are not soldiers, they do not comprehend military discipline, and in the event of a battle, they cannot always be trusted to do their duty.'

'I invited Major du Clos to join us this afternoon,' said Henri, 'not only because he is a particular friend of mine, but also because he is an artillery man, just like yourself, Holcroft. I thought you might find that you have interests in common.'

'In the French service,' continued du Clos, 'as you well know, Lieutenant, we attempt to keep the number of civilian contractors to a minimum.'

A dish of roasted ducklings was brought in and served to the diners.

'It's a question of expense,' said Holcroft. 'Our system is to hire the civilian drivers when and if needed. In times of peace, we do not have to carry the cost of having them on the strength. It is considered more economical this way.'

'If you will forgive me, sir, that appears to be short-sighted,' said du Clos. 'If war should break out, suddenly, and the Train was ordered to march, you might find yourself lacking the personnel needed to transport the guns to where they must be.'

Holcroft shrugged. The French artilleryman was making a valid point. But his deep sense of loyalty to the Ordnance meant that he did not wish to acknowledge it.

'Tell me, Henri,' he said, wishing to change the subject. 'What are your plans for this summer. Will you remain in England for a while?'

'Alas, my time here is nearly over. I have painted my last idyllic English vista – for the time being. My task is done. I must return to France in only a few days time.'

'But surely you will be visiting us again?' said Elizabeth, who was genuinely distressed by the news that Henri was departing.

'I cannot keep flitting like a swallow between France and England,' said Henri, with a gallant smile, 'but I may be back in a few months, in the autumn or early winter, perhaps, if only to have the pleasure of your company, my sweet Elizabeth.'

There was a fish course – a roast salmon – then a baron of beef, followed by gooseberry sorbet, and finally many different kinds of cheese, fruit and sweetmeats. There were, of course, wines from the French regions to match each course. The food was perfectly delicious, evidently the best provender available. And both Major du Clos and Henri went out of their way to make their guests feel comfortable.

Henri must be extremely rich to afford to be this lavish, thought Holcroft, easing open the lower buttons of his waistcoat and sinking his glass of delicious red in one long swallow. He realised that he was, against all the odds, enjoying himself.

'You must tell me, my dear Holcroft, about this famous battle at your house,' said Henri, 'all of White Hall is quite a-twitter at your heroics.'

Holcroft dutifully gave an account of the fight in Mincing Lane, saying that it was a gang of criminals who had attacked him, desperate men whom he must have unintentionally offended while making inquiries for Lord Dartmouth in the Liberty of the Savoy.

Given the company he was in, he made no mention of French spies, or fiendish Catholic plots involving bed pans and switched babies.

'It must have been utterly terrifying for you, Elizabeth,' said Henri, 'why does the King not do more to extirpate these rascals living in the heart of London?'

She looked noble and bawled: 'A true Englishwoman never shows her fear!'

Holcroft set out for Henri the peculiar nature of the Liberty of the Savoy – explaining that it was a separate legal entity to all the other wards of London, under the jurisdiction of the Duchy of Lancaster, and thus was immune from the usual laws.

'But how did you know *when* these villains would attack you, what gave them away?' asked Major du Clos. 'I understand that you cleverly lay in wait for them.'

'Not exactly,' said Holcroft. 'When I came back from Yorkshire, I asked Miller and Jackson to stay with us in Mincing Lane. It was a simple precaution, and one we were glad of in the event. These two brave men still watch over us, they are outside this house, even now! Although I believe the danger has largely abated. I doubt those Savoyard villains who survived will be eager to make another similar attempt.'

'I applaud your foresight and the skill at arms that you showed,' said Henri, his face alight with admiration. 'Your courage is an example to all of us. I should have nightmares for the rest of my life, were I to suffer such a foul attack on my person.'

The conversation turned to politics and talk of a possible invasion by Prince William's forces. 'It will never happen,' said Major du Clos. 'The Sun King will not allow it. I shouldn't be telling you this but, since we are among friends, I may inform you that Louis has sent a letter to the Prince of Orange threatening war with the United Provinces, if its fleet is to set sail. And the wealthy merchants of Amsterdam will never allow William to take the risk. Trade would suffer. And, as I am sure you know very well,

Lieutenant Blood, James has sufficient regiments in hand to be able to counter any invasion force the Dutch could muster. You may all sleep comfortably in your beds. The invasion will not happen.'

'Have another piece of the crystallised ginger, Elizabeth,' said Henri. 'I can see that it is to your taste. I have a confectioner in Paris who makes it for me specially.'

She took a piece of the candied sweet and chewed with evident pleasure.

They took coffee back in the withdrawing room, and Holcroft submitted to another viewing of the dreadful oil paintings. And then they made noises about leaving, Elizabeth exclaiming at the magnificence of the fare and the lavishness of the hospitality they had received. It was nearly dusk, and Holcroft took Henri aside and enquired discreetly if he might make use of the house of ease before they left.

'Certainly, certainly my dear fellow,' said Henri. 'Down the corridor on the right, there is a little room expressly for that purpose. Guillaume, perhaps you would be so good as to steer our good friend in the right direction.'

Major du Clos ushered Holcroft out of the room and pointed to a gilt-edged door at the end of a narrow passageway.

As he was leaving, Holcroft heard Henri saying to Elizabeth: 'I wish you would take this with you, my dear, as a small gift. I know how much you enjoyed the ginger. The box is camphor wood and it will preserve the sweetmeats for months. A small memento of our delightful gathering today.'

In the house of ease, as Holcroft relieved his bladder into a large porcelain bowl designed for that purpose, he found himself looking at an elegant framed print on the wall of Reynard the Fox, the French folk character, lolling on a pile of furs having finished a sumptuous meal of meat and drink. He knew how the legendary trickster must feel, for after the magnificent repast he had just enjoyed he felt sleepy and wished for nothing more than to return to his quarters and rest for a while.

He smiled to himself as he looked at the human-dressed animal and remembered that Henri's nickname as a child in the Cockpit had been Fox Cub.

Back in the less comfortable environs of his quarters in the Tower, Holcroft drank a pint pot of well-watered small beer and wondered how soon it would be seemly for him to go to bed. Elizabeth had chattered loudly and incessantly all the way though the uneventful coach ride home – how refined the Comte d'Erloncourt was! What exquisite taste, what grace . . . and Holcroft had been tempted to block his ears with his fingers. Now she was threatening to read to him from the poet John Dryden's latest slim volume.

'His verse is so haunting, so lovely . . .' began Elizabeth.

Suddenly, like the cogs of a house clock coming into place, something chimed in Holcroft's brain. 'Verse, in verse, inverse,' he said out loud, 'Reynard the Fox . . . and even, God save me . . . Guillaume. His lieutenant's Christian name is Guillaume. Why am I always so completely stupid!'

He leapt to his feet, snatched the empty pint pot in one hand, seized Elizabeth by the wrist with the other. He dragged her though to the tiny pantry at the back of his quarters, she protesting violently. 'No time to explain,' he said, pouring half a cup of salt into the pot and filling the rest with water from the jug. 'Drink this!'

Elizabeth refused. Holcroft grappled her – she was surprisingly strong – seized her jaw and, forcing her mouth open, he poured half the contents of the pint pot into her mouth. 'You must be sick,' he said. 'Henri is Narrey! He's Narrey!'

'It is you who is sick!' she mumbled before retching and puking massively into a porcelain washing-up bowl.

Holcroft drank the rest of the salted water and joined her in coughing and spewing into the sink – the magnificent feast, soup, fish, beef, gooseberry fool, cheese, the whole half-digested lot came gushing out of him. He was left, gasping, slumped over the half-full bowl, his senses reeling.

'Again,' he said, straightening up and pouring more salt into the pot.

Elizabeth slapped him, a hard, almost stunning blow with her left hand that knocked Holcroft against the counter and caused him to drop the pint pot.

'You beast,' she said. 'You brutal monster!'

She slapped him once more. Another tooth-rattling full-force swipe across the jaw. She swung at him again but this time with her right hand, and he was ready, his arms up – he half blocked the strike with his forearm but, even so, her palm painfully clipped the back of his head. His right hand clenched automatically, the fist shooting out in the counter strike, and made it halfway towards her face before he stopped himself. Just in time to prevent the powerful blow smashing the bridge of her nose.

'You monster. You would strike a woman! You coward.'

She slapped him again, and he rode the blow, dropping his arms and allowing her palm to smash his face to the side. Then he stepped back, well out of range.

'Calm yourself, Elizabeth! Be calm now! Or I *will* be forced to hit you.'

'You animal! You filthy beast! How could you do that to me!'

'My dear, listen to me. Henri d'Erloncourt is Narrey. He is the one who sent those men to attack us. The dinner, the meal he gave us, might have been poisoned.'

Elizabeth dropped to the floor, in a puddle of her skirts, and began to weep.

'Why do you always have to spoil *everything*?' she said.

Chapter Thirty-two

4 July 1688: Palace of White Hall

There was nothing much he could do about his left eye, which even three days after the tussle with Elizabeth was so swollen that it was nearly closed. But at least neither he nor Elizabeth had been poisoned – which was a vast relief. They had felt no ill effects that night or the next day except for a certain sourness of stomach caused by the salt. Holcroft was still quite certain that Henri d'Erloncourt was Narrey but either the food had not been tainted or they had managed to vomit it out before it could have an effect. The eye was more of a problem – he looked as if he had been brawling – and he had an important visit to make this day. Aphra had been kind enough that morning to apply some of her theatrical make-up, a little white powdery compound, to the rest of his bruised face before he went into White Hall. But he still looked pale and bruised, like a blue-water sailor after his first night of shore leave.

Sitting uncomfortably on a high-backed chair in the antechamber outside Lord Sunderland's lavish state apartments, he was reminded of his days as a lowly page in the Duke of Buckingham's service when he had been regularly told to sit quietly until he was required. He had been waiting for nearly an hour for a private audience with the King's chief minister, and he began to suspect that the man was deliberately making him sit longer than necessary in order to humiliate him. Well, he would wait then. This was too important for him to walk away from in a fit of pique.

He had sought out Aphra Behn the morning after the dinner with Henri, or Narrey as he supposed he must now think of him – taking the heavily armed Jackson and Miller with him – and found her alone in the shabby, dusty, sweat-smelling changing rooms at the back of the elegant Theatre Royal in Drury Lane.

'Not another attack,' said Aphra immediately, as he walked into the dim space where she was sat on a stool with a needle and length of thread hanging from her mouth, apparently making an adjustment to an elaborate black and red gown. He had left Jackson and Miller outside the door. He pulled up a three-legged stool and sat close to her. 'Not another attack – this is just small a disagreement with Elizabeth.'

Aphra raised an eyebrow but said nothing.

'I know who Narrey is,' he said. 'He is Henri, Comte d'Erloncourt, a French aristocrat and most indifferent painter, who is somewhat loosely attached to the French Embassy in White Hall.'

'I know him,' said Aphra, eyes sparkling. 'I know the man. I met him once after a performance of *Hamlet* here, in this theatre, in fact. There was a grand dinner for the cast and, well, even though I was not in the play, I came anyway, and I met him here – a foxy little fop, as I recall, quite clearly not a man for the ladies . . .'

Holcroft was aware of Aphra's poverty, and that she eagerly took any opportunity for a free meal. He wished he had remembered to bring her something. A gift of some kind or some money. But he had left his purse in the Tower that day.

'A foxy little fop – indeed.'

'How did you unmask him, and more importantly, does he know that you know his identity? You must be aware of how dangerous that knowledge is.'

'I know and it was thanks to you that I discovered who he is. Your man Jupon said that his identity could be discovered "in verse" – but that doesn't mean in poetry. It means in the inverse. The French have a kind of slang, which I encountered in Paris. It is called the *verlan* – *l'envers*. The inverse. When they want to be clever they say things like *laisse baytom* for *laisse tomber*, meaning 'let it go' – you invert the sound of the two syllables of the word.'

'I don't understand. How does that make Henri, Comte d'Erloncourt, our French master spy?'

'It's not the inverse of his true name, but rather his nickname. We used to call him Foxy or Fox Cub when I knew him as a child. As you mentioned, he resembles a fox in features and colouring. Reynard is the famous French fox character in the children's stories. I suspect that was Henri's nickname – Reynard – as a child. Or perhaps his code name in his first days in the spy trade. Elizabeth told me that his coat of arms, on the side of his coach, has foxes on it. He has a charming picture of Reynard the Fox in his privy. The *verlan* for Reynard would be Narrey.'

Aphra looked unconvinced.

'There are other more subtle indications, too,' Holcroft continued. 'My brother Thomas told me that the mysterious Frenchman who came to the Savoy with his chests of silver, that is to say, Narrey, had an accomplice, a lieutenant, called Guillaume. Henri has a particular friend – a Major du Clos – whose given name is Guillaume. And there's more: the timings fit. When you reported that Narrey was at Versailles, Henri d'Erloncourt was also back in France. When Henri was in England, Narrey was here too. D'Erloncourt was beside me at Jack Churchill's party when Glanville mentioned that I was investigating a Catholic plot involving the powder thief Matthews. I think that Glanville's sneering at me triggered Narrey's murder of Matthews, to stop the boy telling me anything about his mother Maria, who works for Narrey. Also, the men who attacked us at Mincing Lane knew exactly how to get into the house, and that I had returned from Hull and would be there on that night. They had clearly done a good deal of reconnaissance. Henri d'Erloncourt was in my house with Elizabeth only two weeks before the attack. None of these things would point to d'Erloncourt on its own but, if you put them all together, it suddenly becomes clear. These two are our men. D'Erloncourt and du Clos. I am completely sure of it.'

'Well – that is quite something. But does Narrey know that you know?'

'I don't think so. He invited me and Elizabeth for dinner yesterday . . .'

'You went to dinner with Narrey? Are you mad? You sat in his parlour and ate his food? Drank his wine? I am surprised you still breathe.'

'I didn't know at the time. And I think my ignorance saved me – and Elizabeth. Narrey did not attempt to poison me then, although he clearly could have done so; he saw that I was ignorant of his identity and only attempted to extract information. Also he must have known that if he poisoned me in his rooms, he'd be taking a huge risk.'

'So . . . what should we do?' asked Aphra.

They discussed briefly what to do with this knowledge.

'You must take this to Lord Sunderland,' said Aphra. 'It is the only thing to do. His lordship can have Narrey arrested, and interrogated. With any luck, he'll be tried and hanged as a spy. You had better go and see Sunderland as soon as possible. And don't accept any more dinner invitations from Narrey! Now, let me look at that eye.'

So Holcroft had sent a note by a messenger to Sunderland, asking for an audience, but he had been occupied with his duties in the Tower for the rest of that day, and the next. He had not been able to extricate himself. Glanville had jeered at him during the officers' morning meeting, and asked him if he had been brawling in the gutter once again. Holcroft had clamped his jaw, refusing to rise to the fat man's jibe.

But, on the third day, an appointment had been made. En route to White Hall, accompanied by Jackson and Miller, Holcroft had paid a visit to Aphra, where he allowed her to apply the thick theatrical white powder to his bruised face. And although he had arrived ten minutes before the appointed hour, the chief minister's servants made him wait for an hour or more outside his office.

'Ah, there you are at last, Mister Blood,' said Sunderland, who was standing at a tall sash window, half turned from the room and staring out at the muddy waters of the Thames. His words made it sound as if Holcroft had been wilfully late – a childish slight – but the Ordnance lieutenant was determined to take no offence.

'You requested an audience with me, yes? What is it that you wish to discuss? Although, I warn you I can give you only a few minutes of my time.' Sunderland did not turn to greet Holcroft, he kept his eyes fixed on the river craft outside.

'Might I begin by asking, my lord, how your investigations are progressing into the French spy known by the codename Narrey?'

'A French spy? I recall you said something of that nature to the King a week ago. After that disgraceful business at your house. He's called Nero, is he?'

'He is called Narrey. Might I ask, most humbly, whether you have, in fact, made any progress in this urgent matter?'

'Investigations are in hand. We are busy establishing the facts of the case.'

It was on the tip of Holcroft's tongue to say that Sunderland had not even established his quarry's correct codename. But he managed to hold his peace.

'I am very pleased to hear that, my lord. And I am even more pleased to be able to tell you that I have identified the spy Narrey. His true name is Henri d'Erloncourt. I may tell you that he is now in residence not a hundred yards from this very room.'

Sunderland turned to face Holcroft.

'What are you saying, sir?'

'Henri d'Erloncourt is the French spy Narrey. This is a man who has been a thorn in our flesh for many years. This is the man who ordered the attack on me and my wife in our home. He has been responsible for a good deal of mischief while he has been in England, including the murder of a prisoner held in the Tower, whom he poisoned. He has an accomplice called Major Guillaume du Clos, a military attaché.'

'I shall look into it.'

'My lord, with the greatest possible respect—'

'I have answered you. I have said that I shall look into it.'

'My lord, I do not think you understand—'

'What *you* must understand, Mister Blood, is that the French are our allies. Yes, they have their spies. Yes, there are unquestionably intelligencers in their Embassy – spies even, of course they have people like that. Just as we have our own people in Versailles, as you know very well from your time in the service of the late king. But the greatest danger to this country does not come from the French! We must not seek to alienate King Louis, nor his compatriots – nor even his spies – at this time. Louis is our ally and our strong bulwark against the Dutch. I note your information, which may be useful in future. And I tell you again that I shall look into the matter. Now you will kindly leave me in peace. I have more important matters to occupy me.'

'I give you fair warning, sir, if you will not act then I shall take matters into my own hands.' Despite all his efforts at self-control, Holcroft found he was shouting at the chief minister. 'Henri d'Erloncourt sent armed men into *my house*, he threatened not only me but my wife as we were sleeping in our marital bed—'

'You forget yourself, sir!'

The door had opened and a large-framed footman poked his head round it.

'If you will not deal with Henri d'Erloncourt, sir—'

'Wait, sir, wait one moment, Mister Blood. Be quiet! You will hold your impudent tongue.' Sunderland was moving towards the desk. The footman had entered and another big fellow too. They were advancing menacingly on Holcroft.

'What was that name again?' Sunderland was rummaging in the piles of papers that were strewn over his broad desk.

'Henri. Comte. D'Erloncourt. Codenamed Narrey.'

Sunderland brandished a piece of yellow paper. 'Here! Yes, I thought I had seen that name. He scanned the paper. The burly footmen put a hand each on Holcroft's two shoulders. He stifled the urge to shrug them off, punch them both into oblivion.

'Henri, Comte d'Erloncourt and one Major du Clos. Yes, they have both been given passports to depart these shores. It says here that they left yesterday morning.'

'They've gone?'

'It would appear so. Back to France.'

Holcroft had forgotten what Henri had told him at the dinner. That they were leaving England in a few days' time. Apparently, among the lies, there had been truth.

'And if they return to England, you will arrest them?'

'*I shall look into it, sir.* If, on balance, they merit arrest, and if it seems expedient to do so, I shall do exactly that. Now, if you will forgive me, sir, I must ask you to leave me in peace. My servants will escort you to the door. Good day to you!'

Chapter Thirty-three

21 September 1688: Tower of London

Sometime that summer, and in later years Holcroft would never be able to put a finger on the exact date, it became clear to him – and to almost everyone in the Three Kingdoms – that the Protestant Prince, William of Orange, was preparing to invade. The talk in the months of July and August was of little else. When would he come here? And what would occur when – very few people now said *if* – he did?

In September, the King issued a general proclamation confirming what almost all of his subjects already knew. That an invasion of England was likely, even imminent. James ordered loyal men and women to prepare to defend with all their might their rightful King, themselves and their homeland against this foreign foe.

William was readying a powerful fleet of ships and an army under the famous soldier, General Friedrich Herman von Schomberg. Holcroft had heard many tales of this grizzled half-English, half-German warhorse, whose exploits stretched back to long before his own birth. Schomberg had fought everywhere and for everyone. He had fought for the Dutch, and then for the Swedes; he had even served the late king of England, Charles II, commanding his royal army at a time when it seemed likely that England would invade the Dutch provinces. He had fought in Portugal and Spain. Schomberg had also served Louis XIV – as, of course, had Holcroft, though their paths had not crossed – and he had risen to the supreme rank of Marshal of France. But with the persecution of the Huguenots, following the revocation of Edict of Nantes in 1685, which outlawed the Protestant religion in France, Schomberg had been forced by his proscribed faith to flee to Germany.

Now, it seemed, the old warrior was coming to England, and with him an army of Protestant Dutchmen and other European allies of the powerful House of Orange.

The morning after King James's call to arms, Lord Dartmouth summoned Holcroft to his office. The Master-General of the Ordnance seemed to be agitated, he paced up and down on the rich Turkish carpet in front of his long oak desk.

'I'm going to sea,' he said to Holcroft, in between issuing commands to his servants and some of the junior Ordnance officers, which ranged from ordering his domestic affairs, the packing of his belongings, arranging a personal supply of wine and fine foods, to the casting of more cannon balls, ordering the stocks of powder in the Tower's magazines to be increased, and the hiring of more drivers for the guns.

Holcroft knew that, as well as his position as Master-General of the Ordnance, Lord Dartmouth was England's most senior naval commander – Admiral of the Fleet.

'The King has informed me that I must take personal command of the Channel Fleet tomorrow, I am superseding Sir Roger Strickland—' He broke off mid-sentence. 'No, not that one, the other one,' he said, redirecting a servant to a different chest.

'I'm bound for the Medway in the morning. James wants me to mobilise the Navy and stop the Dutch fleet, destroy it or drive the buggers off, before it can land their army. Our secret reports from The Hague suggest that the northeast coast is the most likely spot for their disembarkation – and if they come anywhere near the Humber, I promise that your fine work in Hull will not be wasted, Lieutenant Blood.'

'That is very gratifying, sir,' said Holcroft. He was feeling uneasy in the midst of this chaos and was fighting the urge to return to the peace of his own quarters.

The situation with Elizabeth after the evening of the dinner with Narrey had only grown worse. He had tried to explain to her why he had acted as forcefully as he had but Elizabeth had refused to believe that their charming, aristocratic host was in fact a murderous French spy. She had begged to return to the house in Mincing Lane but Holcroft had forbidden it. Narrey might have returned to France but he did not yet feel safe in that place. Some of the Savoyards had escaped with their lives the night of the fight in the hall and might seek vengeance.

Elizabeth had wept and said that he was unreasonable, a monster, and that she could not spend another moment in their cramped rooms in the Tower. Holcroft said she must; Elizabeth said she would not – and had taken herself and her maid off, tearful and trumpeting her disapproval of Holcroft's intractability, to her parents' house in Gray's Inn Lane. Holcroft was dismayed at the swift breakdown of their relationship – but it did allow him to pass his evenings in a blissful silence.

'I say Lieutenant Blood, but I am incorrect in that appellation,' continued Lord Dartmouth. 'At my request, the King has graciously consented to grant you this.' He handed Holcroft a stiff sheet of paper. He looked at it with disbelief. It was his royal commission as a Captain of Pioneers in His Majesty's Ordnance. Promotion! He had never sought it but, now that the commission was in his hands, he was extremely pleased. Captain Blood! It had a fine ring to it. And it hadn't cost him a single penny!

'I don't know what to say, sir. But thank you . . .'

'You can thank me by giving Dutch William a damn good pounding, if the opportunity presents itself. Your promotion comes at a price, you know. I want you to be second in command of the Train, under Sir Henry Sheres – you will have heard that they've given him a knighthood – if His Majesty should order it formed. Try to keep Sir Henry in line, won't you? He's not a well man, you know. Don't let him make a fool of himself if he . . . Well, you know what I mean. We don't want a repeat of his conduct at Sedgemoor. We don't want another fiasco, do we?'

'I'll do my best, sir.'

'You *do* understand, Holcroft, don't you, that you will be, in effect, in command of the Train? Sir Henry will be the Comptroller, of course, but you will be *de facto* in charge. Keep him informed of all your decisions. The niceties of rank must always be maintained. And any order you give must be in his name. But you are the responsible officer, do you hear me? The Train is yours. I am relying on you.'

'I understand, sir. And, may I venture to ask, who will remain in command here, in the Tower, if the Train is sent out to give battle? Who will take *your* place?'

Lord Dartmouth was suddenly avoiding Holcroft's eye. He cleared his throat. 'Major William Glanville will be in full command of the Tower garrison, he will act as my deputy, and as constable of the Tower in the event of Sir Henry's prolonged absence on campaign or otherwise.'

Holcroft's heart sank. 'Major? The King raised him up to be a major? But, sir, the review I wrote, into the false muster business, surely if the King knew about . . .'

'The King has decided to reward a good many officers at this troublesome time – a cynic would say that it was to ensure their loyalty. However, Major Glanville purchased his step, Captain, in the usual fashion. He was not awarded the promotion by the King, *gratis*, as you were. Be grateful, sir. I don't want any difficulties from you about this. Our country is about to be plunged into a brutal war, a foreign enemy is almost at our gates, and we need every competent Ordnance officer we can muster. I know there is bad blood between you and Glanville but you must work together for the common good. Can you do that, Holcroft? For me?'

'Yes, sir. I can do that. And, once again, thank you, sir. I am truly grateful.'

Chapter Thirty-four

23 November 1688: Salisbury Plain

Holcroft walked along the row of the guns in the early dusk. His charges, his bronze beauties, were lined up neatly along the east bank of the River Avon, a few miles north of the city of Salisbury in Wiltshire, and they, and five full companies of Royal Fusiliers, comprised the extreme left flank of the Royal Army.

Lieutenant Rupert Pittman was officer-of-the-day. He had fired the blank signal Falcon not ten minutes ago, and Holcroft trusted the young fellow – who had been permitted by Lord Dartmouth to purchase his promotion at the same time that Holcroft received his – to perform his duties satisfactorily in his absence. However, he could not stop himself from making his own unofficial inspection of the twenty-six pieces that he had brought so far and with such difficulty.

All was in order, so far as Holcroft could tell, and here was Enoch Jackson, fussing over one of the Sakers – it was Roaring Meg, of course – carefully cleaning out the burnt powder residue from the touchhole with a long thin knife, known as a gunner's stiletto, for its resemblance to the famous Italian assassins' dagger.

'All well, Enoch?' said Holcroft.

'All well, sir,' said Jackson. 'Just giving Meg a little care and attention. She's been showing her age, recently. Misfiring in practise sessions. When we get her safe back home, I'm going to give her a good and proper overhaul. Perhaps bore out a completely new touchhole for her.'

'Just as long as she can shoot straight for this campaign, Enoch.'

'She will, sir, I know she will.'

The orders to form the Train had come the day after Lord Dartmouth's departure, and Sir Henry Sheres had been content to delegate the hurried assembly of the guns, men, horses and wagons to Holcroft, while he retired with several bottles of Lord Dartmouth's finest claret. It had been brutal, exhausting work – Holcroft had previously only partially recognised before what an enormous task it was to get twenty-six cannon, four mortars, two hundred and fifty vehicles ranging from massive oak gun carriages to light, two-wheeled wagons and several hundred men and horses, with fodder and food for all of them, out of the Tower and on the road.

The Train, once assembled, stretched for more than a mile, and Holcroft, with Sir Henry snoring all day in his own fine carriage, led this vast cavalcade to Finchley Common, northwest of London, to make camp and await further orders. From Finchley they could move the Train north or west with equal ease – which is to say not very much. The abysmal condition of the roads in winter made any movement of the heavy guns and wagons snail-slow. But they would face that problem when their orders came from the King's commanders. In the meantime, they had parked the guns, billeted the officers in the local houses, pitched the men's tents on the grassy common and waited.

It had not been clear, in October and even into early November, where the Dutch invasion fleet would make its landfall. Many believed that Hull would be the destination. Holcroft secretly hoped that, if the Prince of Orange must land at all, it be at that old port on the Humber. His diligent work on the fortifications meant that any hostile fleet would be severely mauled, shot to pieces, with many ships sunk, before any troops could be landed on the Yorkshire coastline.

It would be best, of course, if the invading Dutch fleet was destroyed at sea by Lord Dartmouth's powerful Royal Navy squadrons. But alas . . .

Lord Dartmouth's intentions had been pure, Holcroft was sure of it when he heard the dismal news in the second week in November, he was no traitor, absolutely not, yet he had failed in his duty to King and country to keep the enemy fleet from England's shores. His fault, it seemed, was partly indecision, partly bad luck and partly the prevailing autumn winds.

Assuming that the Dutch fleet, a mighty force totalling four hundred and sixty three ships – sixty of them warships, and with forty thousand men aboard – would take the shortest route across the North Sea and land on the eastern coast of England, Dartmouth kept the English fleet in the Medway, ready to sail north and intercept William and destroy his vast fleet en route.

William had set out in late October but a storm scattered his ships and they were forced to return ignominiously to port to refit. Lord Dartmouth then considered sallying out and blockading the Dutch in their home port of Hellevoetsluis but he hesitated – the crueller news pamphlets suggested he was scared – and decided that respect for the wild weather should keep him in the Medway. To be fair, Holcroft reflected, the coast of the Low Countries was a notorious lee shore on which a fleet might well founder if the changeable winds shifted to the west.

On the first day of November, when the wind swung around to the east – anti-Catholic pamphlets in London called it a 'Protestant Wind' – William of Orange with a stiff blow behind him set out once more, again heading northwest. Lord Dartmouth found to his dismay that, with all the weather coming from across the Channel, and with an unfavourable tide, he was penned in the Medway, unable to get his warships out of the Thames estuary and into battle.

The initial Dutch course proved to be a feint, and when the wind changed again and came around to the north, William's fleet also changed direction and headed due south. Dartmouth was again slow to react and the Dutch ships were already passing through the Channel before the English Admiral could bring his forces into play.

Sitting in the parlour of a large farmhouse off Finchley Common, Holcroft read a long, almost gloating report in the *London Gazette* that said the Dutch force was so large that it was able to salute both Calais and Dover at the same time as it passed through the Channel. Troops lined the decks of William's ships and fired off their muskets, military bands played jaunty tunes and the Prince of Orange's colours flew from every Dutch masthead.

The sea chase began. William heading round Kent and down the south coast of England, with Lord Dartmouth trailing behind him, lagging the invasion force by two full days. With each fleet equally matched and travelling with much the same speed, the two forces moved along the coast of England in tandem. However, on the fifth of November – an auspicious day for Protestants, on which they joyously commemorated the death of Catholic Gunpowder Plotter Guido Fawkes – bad weather forced Lord Dartmouth to abandon the chase and shelter in Portsmouth harbour.

A hundred nautical miles west, untroubled by the Royal Navy, the Prince of Orange also made for shore, and landed his army at Brixham, near Torbay in Devon – a force of fifteen thousand horse and foot, spearheaded by his elite Blue Guards, and containing troops from countries as diverse as Lapland and Switzerland.

As well as a well-stocked supply column containing food and ammunition – and arms for those Englishmen who might wish to support him – William brought with him a powerful Train containing a score of twenty-four-pounder cannon. Holcroft, reading the intelligence reports, recognised that the two Trains were of roughly equal strength.

On the sixth of November, after six weeks of inactivity on Finchley Common, Sir Henry Sheres received his written orders from the King – which he had mutely passed on to Holcroft. They were to take the Train to Salisbury with all speed, the orders said, where the Army would muster in all its strength and oppose the invader.

It had taken two bruising, mud-drenched weeks to move the guns less than a hundred miles to Salisbury. Holcroft and his men had occasionally had to manhandle the heavy ordnance over the worst stretches of road – sometimes recruiting idle and occasionally reluctant fusiliers to help with the task.

Sir Henry Sheres claimed that he was unwell and spent his days in his gilt-trimmed, canary-yellow carriage alone with his many clinking bottles. His sole contribution had been to summon Holcroft near Windsor and complain to the exhausted mud-spattered captain that the roads were too rough and that a particularly deep pothole had made him spill his breakfast glass of sack. But now it was done, here they were, assembled on Salisbury Plain – King James himself, his courtiers, servants and ministers, and twenty thousand of his best fighting men – horse, guns and foot – once more under the overall command of the ageing Lord Feversham.

'What news of the enemy, sir?' said Jackson, sliding the gunner's stiletto into the sheath on his belt, and wiping the shining barrel of Roaring Meg with an old rag.

'They say William is still at Axminster,' Holcroft replied. 'But his German scouts have been seen as near as Shaftesbury – only forty miles away.'

'So when will we fight them?'

'I don't know, Enoch. In a few days, I suspect. This is a good position; we block any advance on London. But we may have to move west again. The King can't afford to let William alone in the West Country for too long; he can't let him get too comfortable. We can't let him look as if he is winning – that we're afraid of him. You will remember that bloody Monmouth business. And the men of Devon, Dorset and Somerset have surely not forgotten their treatment after the last rebellion. Hundreds hanged, hundreds more transported in chains. If they decide to rise up again for *this* Protestant prince, we'll find ourselves in a very uncomfortable spot.'

'If we have to fight those West Country folk again, sir, we'll all do our duty.'

'I'm sure we will. But I cannot say I relish the thought, Enoch. I had a bellyful of slaughtering our own people at Sedgemoor. And I can tell you that I fear another foul bloodbath. May not happen, of course. I'll know more after tonight. I'm going to see Jack, to play cards in the command tent. I'll understand it better tomorrow.'

'It's a damned disgrace, that's what it is,' said Colonel Percy Kirke, playing an ace of spades, which was immediately trumped by Holcroft. They were playing whist, but only for pennies at Kirke's insistence, in the newly promoted Lieutenant-General Lord Churchill's sumptuous, multi-roomed tent half a mile north of the artillery park. Colonel Kirke had been fulminating about the failure of Lord Dartmouth and the men of the Royal Navy to prevent William's landing two weeks earlier.

'Sheer bloody incompetence,' said Kirke. 'I'd have the silly old bugger court-martialled. Shot on the deck of his flagship. He's made us look like cowardly fools.'

'He cannot command the winds,' said Holcroft. He too had been dismayed by Dartmouth's performance but he was not prepared to join in the ridicule of his patron.

'If he doesn't understand the winds, then Lord Dartmouth has no business being Admiral of the Fleet,' said the Duke of Grafton, who had once held that very office.

Holcroft's partner, Colonel Trelawny, played a low spade, as did mad Colonel Godfrey, of the First Foot Guards. Holcroft scooped up the cards, having won the trick and the game. It occurred to him that all of the men who were sitting around the table with him had fought at Sedgemoor. Between them they commanded a significant proportion of James's troops. And all of them were members of the gang who gathered in the Rose Tavern in what he privately called the Treason Club.

'You will have heard about the events in Yorkshire,' said Godfrey, smiling slyly as he dealt out a new hand. 'Lord Danby has openly declared his support for William and called out his militia – three hundred men, I'm told. Furthermore, I hear the Princess Anne has left London, James's own daughter! She's gone north to join with Danby. For her personal safety, she said, to get away from the London rioters.'

'Lord Delemere has raised the standard of rebellion in Cheshire,' said Trelawny, picking up his cards and scowling at them. 'And Lord Cornbury has gone over to the Dutch, too.'

The air in the tent was sour and gloomy: every man, even Holcroft, was aware that England stood on the brink of a catastrophe that might prove to be more terrible than the bloody decade-long wars between the first King Charles and Parliament. William and James were more or less equally matched in strength, although William seemed to have the upper hand in morale and quality of troops – and if enough Englishmen rallied to his cause he would have the advantage in numbers, too. On the other hand, if Louis XIV decided to weigh in on King James's side, and sent over a few regiments of his crack French Guards, that could tip the balance the other way and the coming war could soak the land in blood for years.

At that moment, the flap of the tent opened and Jack Churchill walked in out of the gloom of early evening. He was soaked, raindrops glistening on his cloak and hat.

'How does our noble King?' sneered the Duke of Grafton. 'Full of his customary fire and fighting spirit?'

'The King is not well,' said Jack, taking off his hat, shaking it and handing it to a servant. 'He had a nose bleed that would not stop, no matter what we tried. But worse than that, he cannot decide what to do. Whether to advance into the west and attack William or retreat to London and consolidate the defences of his capital. If we went back to London, we could at least put a stop to these damn riots. The mob is burning churches, for God's sake – Catholic churches – and besieging the houses of foreigners. I said we should march west and confront William, defeat him before the rebellion spreads. Lord Feversham wants to go back to London. Nothing is decided. James dismissed us all and said he would take to his bed and pray for guidance.'

'Maybe it is time,' said Percy Kirke. And the rest of the men shared a look.

Holcroft had been studying his cards. He looked up in the suddenly crystalline silence. He was not at all adept in deciphering the expressions of other men but it was clear even to him that there was something strange and dangerous in the air.

'Yes, with great regret, I must agree that the time has come,' said Jack.

'Tonight?' said Godfrey.

Jack nodded.

'What about him?' said Kirke, inclining his head at Holcroft, who was looking from face to face, trying to divine what was afoot. 'What about the artillery?'

'Hol, could I have word with you in private?' said Jack. 'Through here.'

Holcroft put his cards down on the green baize in front of him and got up.

He followed Jack into the side chamber off the main room of the tent, and Jack poured them both a glass of wine.

'I'm going over, Holcroft,' he said. 'I'm going over to William. And so are all those men out there. And many hundreds more besides.'

Holcroft stared at his friend. 'No. You cannot mean it,' he said. 'After all that James has done for you? You cannot betray him. He raised you up from nothing . . .'

Churchill looked as if he had been punched hard in the stomach. 'Yes, it is true. James made me. And I served him well. But I can no longer serve him. Not now. He is not fit to rule, Holcroft.

Surely you can see that? His obsession with his damned religion
has undone him. And he will not listen to reason. The bishops
are against him – indeed the whole Church of England, after he
unjustly locked the Seven in the Tower. The House of Lords will
not support him, not now, and if he ever recalls the House of Commons, he would have to pack it with so many Catholics and dissenters and other strange creatures of that ilk that it would bear no
resemblance to the previous House, nor would it truly represent
the country.

'The Army is against him, most of it anyway. And there are many
Williamites among the Navy, too. The common people do not love
the King, Holcroft. They fear him. They fear he will force his damned
Catholicism upon them. The corporations of the towns, the Justices
of the Peace, the solid men of the shires: all of them are against him.
You heard about the response in Exeter when William rode in on
his showy white horse? The West Countrymen cheered him in the
streets. They praised him to the skies: called him a saviour. The King
is finished, Holcroft. It is time for James to accept that hard fact and
abdicate. He can no longer rule over us.'

'It is not up to us to choose who rules over us, Jack. God places
the King on the throne. If we go round changing our kings whenever we feel inclined we end up with nothing but anarchy, revolution, a mad world without order or rules . . .'

'That may not happen. The country is united against James. If we
act now, united in purpose, then we can stop this war in its tracks.
If all good men abandon James, he will have no one to fight for him.
He can then be made to see reason.'

'You are asking me to commit treason, Jack. I never expected that
of you . . .'

'It will not be treason if we win. If William wins, then our side
will . . .'

'I do not wish to hear another word, Jack. It sickens my heart to
hear you speak this way. I beg you do not do this terrible thing. It's
unworthy of you.'

'I will do this. I am doing this. We are all doing this – and not just for ourselves, not just for that. It is what is best for our country, too.'

Holcroft turned his back on Jack. He stared hard at the grubby canvas wall and he heard his friend draw in his breath in a soft shocked whoosh at his rudeness.

'Hol, come with us! I ask you this for the last time. Come with us tonight. Bring the Train with you. With the regiments that I and my friends command, and with the officers loyal to us, we will deal such a blow to the Army by our departure that there can be no possible victory for James. If you bring the Train with us, it will make certain there can be no fight – no battle, no war, no blood need be shed. If you stay and fight for James, you, and whoever else is foolish enough to remain with him, will all be slaughtered. You and I, Holcroft Blood, shall be on opposite sides of the battle. Think on that. Your beloved cannon might cut me down. One of my dragoons might shoot you dead with his musket. Come with us, Holcroft! I beg you.'

Holcroft took a deep breath. He kept his back to his friend, slowly let out the air. Then he spoke: 'We have been friends for a good long time, Jack, and out of respect for that friendship, I shall not speak to anyone about your plans for this . . . this gross betrayal, until you have made your . . . escape. But I shall not go with you. The Train is the King's property, the guns, the carriages, the cannon balls, the wadding, every single speck of powder . . . and if I were to hand it over to the enemy, I should be guilty not only of the foulest betrayal, and black treason, but also of common theft. I shall not go with you, Jack. I will not be a thief. Neither can I wish you godspeed. But I shall keep my silence about your actions, I swear it, until dawn.'

'Are you sure you will not come, Hol?'

'I am certain. Furthermore, I do not consider us to be bound any longer by any ties of friendship. It is finished between us. I will therefore bid you goodnight, sir.'

Holcroft turned and, without looking at his old friend, marched past Jack Churchill, pushing through the flap, and stepping into the other room where the three senior soldiers were sitting wide-eyed at the card table.

It was evident that they had heard everything that had been said through the thin canvas wall. Holcroft glared at them: 'You gentlemen are a disgrace to your service,' he said. 'A disgrace to your families, a disgrace to your country. Every one of you.'

And with that parting shot he marched out of the tent and into the night.

Holcroft walked south through the encampment of the Royal Army towards the artillery park on its extreme left flank. He scarcely noticed that the rain had stopped for his cheeks were wet, and hot tears were dripping down his chin. He trudged along beside rows and rows of grubby tents, hundreds of them, past dozens of campfires where men stirred pots of soup or stew, his boots splashing in the puddles; he heard snatches of singing, saw two men, bare-chested, wrestling with each other on the muddy ground by flickering torchlight, both cursing, and one man, naked from the waist down, rutting with a pretty red-haired whore on a pile of empty sacks.

How many of these men will still be here come morning? he asked himself. *How many will have slunk away over the next few hours of darkness, encouraged, perhaps even led, by their officers, their generals, to go over to the enemy?* He felt sick, but also in a sleep-like daze, as if his recent conversation with Jack Churchill had been some horrible dream. Perhaps he would wake tomorrow in his own tent and all would be well. But he knew this could not be – this was no dream; this was a waking nightmare. He had never suspected that Jack might be capable of such base behaviour, even after his friend had taken him to Covent Garden to meet those appalling men of the Treason Club. These men had obviously been plotting together for months, if not for years. But Jack, no, never, he could still scarcely believe it was true. It was so unlike Jack, so unlike him to behave in such an underhand way. He knew it must be Sarah who had persuaded him. That grasping, amoral witch.

As he had heard tonight, Sarah and her intimate friend Princess Anne, James's younger daughter, had fled the Cockpit and joined Lord Danby and his rebel militia in Yorkshire. And if Sarah Churchill had joined the Williamite side, how could her husband Jack not do so too? It was all so wrong. And yet he knew, deep down in his belly, that what Jack had said was correct. James *was* doomed. His Army officers would melt away tonight, ride away into the darkness and make for William's lines; and these soldiers, sitting round their campfires in the darkness, singing, laughing, drinking, would be left leaderless. Without the majority of their officers they would provide no effective opposition to William's crack Blue Guards and his hard-bitten European mercenaries. William would win. James would, after an ocean of blood had been uselessly spilled, find himself at the mercy of the victorious Dutch prince – would the King meet a gruesome fate like Monmouth's, or indeed like that of his own father, the first King Charles?

James was doomed. But first there must be a battle. A vast blood sacrifice. The Train would bring the big guns into play on the field – and, as Jackson had said, they would all do their duty – and his men would fight bravely, bloodily for their doomed King. At Holcroft's command, they would slaughter their own countrymen in their droves – those who had gone over to William's side, and perhaps the men of the West Country, too. They would blast his own compatriots apart with case shot, smash their attacking files with cannon ball. They would mash brave English, Irish and Scotsmen into a hellish bloody pulp. And worse, Holcroft would be firing his twenty-six deadly cannon at his former best friend, trying to kill or maim him, blow his limbs off, just as Jack had described it in that treacherous bloody tent. The thought made Holcroft's gorge rise. *But there must be a battle, mustn't there?*

'Halt, who goes there?' said a deep, rough, military voice. 'Stop right there, stranger, else I'll blow your fucking head right off!'

Holcroft had walked through the Army encampment and had come back to the artillery park on the southern side. There was a low palisade erected around the long line of guns, the wagons, the horse lines and the tents of the officers, gunners and civilians, and in the gateway stood a tall figure with a flintlock musket across his chest and the mitred hat of a Royal Fusilier.

'I'm Captain Blood of the Ordnance, man, let me pass.'

'I think I can vouch for him,' said another voice, and Sergeant Miller appeared with a burning pine torch in his hand. The sentry stood back, a jumble of apologetic words on his lips, but Holcroft ignored him and stared bleakly at the little sergeant.

'Had a good evening, sir?' said Miller. 'Win some chink off those Army sods?'

'No. And no. Listen to me, Sergeant Miller. You are to get word to all the officers, both Ordnance and Fusiliers, and the headman of the drivers, too, I want every man of rank in the officers' mess at dawn. Don't bother about Sir Henry Sheres, I'll tell the Comptroller myself, when he, ah, wakes in the morning. Make sure you inform all the others. Dawn tomorrow, everyone in the officers' mess. Yes?'

'Yes, sir – but may I ask, what's afoot, sir?'

'Keep this to yourself, Miller, that is an order. I'll make the formal announcement tomorrow. But, between you and me, we're on the move in the morn.'

'Going into battle, sir?' the sergeant's eyes gleamed eagerly in the darkness.

'No, the very opposite. We are going home.'

Chapter Thirty-five

9 December 1688: Tower of London

When the heavy guns of the Royal Train of Artillery rumbled through the gates of the Tower of London, Major William Glanville, acting Constable of the fortress, deputy to the Master-General of the Ordnance, was watching the arrival from the top of the Byward Tower. As the Train passed below him to enter Water Lane, he called out to the weary, mud-smeared officer in charge: 'You, sir, Captain Blood. Where is the Comptroller? Where's Sir Henry Sheres?'

Holcroft looked exhaustedly up at the rotund black-wigged figure in the gold-embroidered blue coat standing straddle-legged on the battlements.

'He's taken a leave of absence, sir. He says he's not well, indeed he believes he is seriously ill, and has returned by carriage to his house in Deptford to recuperate.'

'Then you shall report to me in an hour's time, Mister Blood, when you have housed the guns, unharnessed the horses, dismissed the men . . . and so on. In my office, sir, in no more than one hour. I shall require a full explanation for the disgraceful and cowardly actions of the Ordnance on this shameful campaign.'

Holcroft looked up under the brim of his hat at Glanville, trying to hide his glowing hatred. 'Your office, sir?' he said. 'Or the office of the Master-General?'

'Same thing, fool. While Lord Dartmouth remains with the Fleet, I command here. Be there in one hour, sir, and be prepared to explain yourself thoroughly.'

Two weeks earlier, Holcroft had addressed the gathered officers of the Ordnance and the Royal Fusiliers at dawn and informed them briskly that they would be taking the Train to London immediately. He had been to see Sir Henry Sheres in his tent before first light, and had told him that, in his opinion, it was best for the Train to withdraw from the field. He had been prepared to make a case for his refusal to fight his guns in a futile battle – in fact, he had been prepared to knock the old sot over the head with one of his own bottles, if necessary – but Sir Henry was in such a poor condition that he had merely waved his agreement and said next to nothing.

'Whatever you think best, my dear chap,' he said, nodding, drooling a little, over the half-empty brandy glass he was cuddling to his chest. 'I am not well, Captain Blood, not well at all. You must do whatever you think is right for the Train.'

As he had walked out of Sir Henry's tent heading towards the officers' mess, he had looked over the artillery park palisade at the rest of the Army encampment.

It was a scene of utter chaos. Large numbers of the soldiers' tents had been trampled flat, the cook fires were out, and there were crowds of men wandering about aimlessly. Some were gathered around speakers, sergeants and corporals, mostly, who were standing on boxes and haranguing the men and shaking their fists. Others appeared to be hefting their packs and muskets and walking away, going back to whatever part of the country they came from. There was no one to stop them. There was barely an officer in sight, certainly none above the rank of captain.

It seemed that Jack Churchill, and all his Treason Club friends, had indeed departed, ridden west to join William, and they had taken most of the officer corps with them. Holcroft could only wonder what James would be doing in the headquarters in the grand house in Salisbury on this grim winter morning: would he be full of royal anger, shouting about betrayal and promising dire vengeance? Would he be quiet, resigned to the loss, in effect, of his whole army? What would the ministers and priests, the French diplomats, all the sycophantic men that James surrounded himself with, what would they have to say this morning? What would all the Catholics who had urged him to follow this course, to choose this policy of tolerance, what would they have to say, seeing the fell crop their advice had yielded their master? Most of all, Holcroft wondered, what would James *do* now?

But that was not his primary concern – the Ordnance officer's responsibility was to get the Train, all the guns, all the wagons, all the men, safely back to London.

The roads to the capital had been thick with refugees, soldiers who had deserted King James's ranks and hordes of country folk who were fleeing the advance of William's troops. That made forcing a passage for his cumbersome mile-long Train even more difficult. But the news among the refugees of the conduct of the Prince of Orange's men-at-arms was encouraging: it was not the behaviour of a victorious invading army, laying waste to all in their path. William and his half-German general, the ferocious old warhorse Friedrich von Schomberg, had them tightly controlled – any man found looting was hanged on the spot. Holcroft knew that Jack, for all his base treachery, if he now had any authority in the Dutch forces, would never let these foreign troops despoil the lands and property of Englishmen.

The Prince of Orange had issued a declaration saying that he had no wish to be King, but that his father-in-law James had been led astray by bad advice, and that all Prince William wished to do was remove these unnamed evil counsellors from the King's side. Holcroft, when he heard this news, in a hay barn somewhere near Windsor, cheered it silently. However, few English people believed the Dutchman's words. James was finished. All now agreed. The Prince of Orange and his wife, Mary, James's eldest daughter, would take the reins of power, even though no one knew what form the new government would take. And no one seemed to know exactly where King James was. He was no longer on Salisbury Plain, that was for sure. And he wasn't at his castle in Windsor. Perhaps he was already fleeing the country.

It took Holcroft two difficult weeks to reach London – during which he was twice menaced by enemy cavalry, and once had to form the fusiliers and drive off a body of German mercenaries with a couple of crisp volleys – and he was dismayed by what he discovered when he got there. The capital was even more chaotic than the roads leading into it. In the absence of strong government, the citizens had come out in force and were displaying their disdain for the King and his ministers and revealing their deep hatred of all things Catholic. They surged through the streets shouting slogans and smashing windows. Any man suspected of being a papist was set upon and beaten to death. Old scores were settled as neighbour accused neighbour and the mob wreaked destruction.

As Holcroft moved the mile-long Train through the western suburbs, and into the long street known as Piccadilly, he saw grand houses aflame and celebrating crowds hundreds strong dancing and drinking in the street. Passing through the Strand, the Train was pelted by stones from the roofs of the houses in the Liberty of the Savoy. Enoch Jackson was struck by a half-brick on his bare brown bald head and rendered semi-conscious amid a flood of bright scalp blood.

Holcroft had him put in an ammunition cart, poll bandaged up tight, on a pile of clean straw, and the master gunner lay there between boxes of wadding, barrels of powder and coils of spare rope, muttering something about a man called Samuel.

'Did you see who flung the missile?' said Holcroft. 'It came out from the Savoy, didn't it? Was it hurled by somebody whose face you recognise?'

Jackson smiled wanly. 'No, sir. First book of Samuel, chapter 17, verse 50.'

It was a mark of how exhausted Holcroft was that he could not for a moment recall the passage. Then he laughed: 'You are no Goliath, Enoch. A deadly fellow with a Saker, for sure, but no Philistine giant. And whoever flung that wicked stone is no David – just a Savoyard villain. Nor has he slain you. You rest here, man; we'll be home at the Tower soon. You'll be on your feet in a day or two.'

'Let me see if I understand this. You, Captain Holcroft Blood, entirely on your own authority, decided to deprive His Majesty the King of the services of his Royal Train of Artillery and the several hundred men of the Ordnance and Fusiliers. You bypassed the Comptroller Sir Henry Sheres, barely even consulting him, and ordered the Train to depart from the field, on what might have been the eve of battle, and to return to the Tower without a shot being fired. Is that right? Do I have it correctly?'

Holcroft could think of nothing to say in his defence. He nodded wearily. 'Yes, sir. Broadly speaking, that is correct.'

Major Glanville's glee was coming off him like the heat from the large fire in the corner of the Master-General's office. He had his feet up on the big desk and was rubbing his hands together like a miser surveying his cash bags. On the oak surface in front of him was a fine polished steel and chestnut-wood pistol, which was weighing down a buff-coloured folder, stuffed with papers. Glanville flicked the butt of the pistol with a finger and it rotated on the card, spinning like the spoke of a wheel.

'You freely admit to, um, let's see . . . dereliction of duty, desertion in the face of the enemy, unauthorised removal of His Majesty's property – so, common theft – as well as usurpation of the command of a superior officer. And let's add cowardice, too, high treason, conduct unbecoming an officer, and several other charges that I'm sure I'll manage to come up with before I very shortly preside at your court martial. I don't think there will be very much doubt about the verdict.'

Holcroft stirred himself. It was true. A court martial, particularly one convened by William Glanville, would almost certainly find him guilty. The major would find five senior officers – at least one of them of general officer rank – to sit on the board of the court; the evidence, which no doubt would be hastily procured by Glanville, would be listened to; the final judgment would be swiftly made and a sentence of death would be pronounced, which would be implemented almost immediately. A firing squad at dawn the next day up against the inside wall of the Inner Ward.

'I did what I thought was right, sir, in the circumstances. Half the Army officer corps had gone over to William that night; without officers to control them, most of the private men were packing up and heading for home. There was no order in our lines, there was in fact no Army left, and there seemed no point in remaining there and allowing the Prince of Orange to come up and capture the King's guns at his leisure. I thought it best to bring them safely back to the Tower. I'm pleased to say that I managed that feat despite a deal of difficulty and no little danger en route.'

'I do enjoy watching you squirm, Blood. Why don't you plead for clemency from me, from the acting Master-General. I believe I would enjoy that very much.'

Holcroft said nothing. But there was one glimmer of hope.

'Are you sure that you would not like to beg for mercy – perhaps on your knees or grovelling on the carpet? It might even do some good,' said Glanville, with an almost drunkenly happy expression. 'For some reason, I'm in a fine mood today.'

'No thank you, sir.'

'Quite sure, Mister Blood? I might be minded to save your miserable life.' Glanville had risen from his chair and was prowling behind the desk. He stopped by the generous coal fire in the grate and unnecessarily poked the blaze with a poker.

'I think it only fair to warn you, sir, that at my court martial, I shall inform the board of judges that you hold a personal grudge against me because of the blow that you received at the Cockpit victory party.' As he spoke, Holcroft kept his voice quiet and even. But inside a molten rage was charring the walls of his stomach. 'I shall remind them of that fine punch that I gave you – which laid you out, and which you subsequently forgave – and I will suggest that you are not only a coward but also that you are bringing these charges out of sheer malice and hatred of my person.'

Glanville snickered. 'That horse won't run,' he said. 'You humbly begged my forgiveness, here in this room, in front of Lord Dartmouth. As a man of gentle breeding, what could I do but forgive you? You will appear as the brutish gutter-brawler that you are. Besides, the removal of the Train of Artillery from the lines on Salisbury Plain without proper orders is quite enough to hang you ten times over.'

Holcroft stared at him. All his instincts told him to leap at the man and smash at him with his fists until he was no more than an oozing mound of mush. He restrained himself with some difficulty. There were two armed fusilier sentries outside the door, and a charge of assault on a superior officer might be the final nail in his coffin.

'I shall say that your malice comes from the fact that I made a report for Lord Dartmouth that exposed your corruption. That business of the false musters. I know all about it, Glanville. I have delivered the review to Lord Dartmouth and he is considering what action to take. He said we would clean house in the Ordnance. Thoroughly clean house. Those were his very words.'

Glanville let out a howl of laughter. 'Oh, ho-ho, the review, oh yes, *A Review of Various Corrupt and Immoral Practices in His Majesty's Ordnance*. Ha-ha! That's what you called it, is it not? Dartmouth allowed me to read it weeks ago. In fact . . .'

Glanville lifted the pistol from the pile of papers and picked up the buff folder that lay underneath.

'. . . in fact, this is that very report, if I am not mistaken.'

Holding the folder awkwardly, with the pistol in one doughy hand, he opened the card cover and scanned the first page.

'This is the one, here it is. And you seek to threaten me with *this*?'

Glanville took a step backwards and shoved the whole file into the fire, where it burst into flames.

'No!' shouted Holcroft and leapt forward.

'You stay exactly where you are, Mister Blood,' said Glanville. 'Do not move so much as a hair.' The pistol was cocked and pointing at Holcroft's chest.

He watched in anguish as the buff folder consumed itself on the hot coals.

'Did you honestly think that Dartmouth did not know about the false musters and all our other little games? Did you really think that he would not be taking his portion? A full twenty per cent of the money goes into his pocket. He makes a cool thousand a year from this and all the other schemes. And you thought he would forego the money and punish the guilty men. Clean house, as you said. What a fool you are! What a ninny-hammer! Why, I almost feel sorry for you in your innocence.'

Holcroft dropped his eyes and stared at the carpet. He had been a fool. No wonder Lord Dartmouth had been reluctant to act on his review. But he was also aware of a deep sadness. The great man he admired, a fine upright man who he had been proud to serve, had been discovered to have feet of clay. After Jack's betrayal, it was a doubly hard blow. *Were there no straight-dealing men left in this world?*

'Well, I must not keep you, Captain Blood. Much as I should like to convene a court this afternoon and have you condemned out of hand, I must postpone the pleasure. It may take some days or weeks to summon enough senior officers to complete the task. In the meantime, I shall put you to work. Your career may be finished but there is no reason to be slothful while you still draw your pay from us.

'So . . . you may well have noticed as you passed through London that the mob has taken to the streets and is running riot, burning the homes of known Catholics and ransacking the foreign embassies. Yes? You did notice that, did you?

'As well as that, a number of Ordnance gentlemen have shown themselves to be black traitors and have quit the Tower to go off and serve the invader, William of Orange. Accordingly I am very short of personnel. Even gutter-born, cowardly incompetents such as you must be usefully employed. You will go back to your quarters and clean yourself up, and this evening at dusk you will lead the eighth company of Royal Fusiliers to the western edge of London and patrol the Covent Garden area between the Strand and Long Acre, keeping the King's peace, and putting down any insurrection with appropriate force. The First Foot Guards are protecting White Hall, so do not stray west of Charing Cross. Don't go below the Strand into the Liberty of the Savoy, that's definitely off limits. Nor should you venture north of Long Acre into the slums of St Giles. A troop of Royal Dragoons went there yesterday and was swallowed up. Only one horse, mad with fear, emerged alive this morning. Stick to your brief: patrol between the Strand and Long Acre, enforce the King's peace – you may arrest anyone found looting and fire into any riotous crowd that refuses to disperse in a timely manner – and have yourself back here in the Tower by dawn. Do you understand your orders, Captain Blood?'

'Yes, sir.'

'This may be a chance for you to redeem yourself, Blood. Do your duty well, make sure that all those charming new houses in Covent Garden are unmolested by *hoi polloi*, protect the gentlemen and ladies there and their households and maybe the court martial will show you a degree of clemency. I make no promises, but do your duty tonight and we shall see.'

It was difficult for Holcroft not to display the burning hatred he felt for this wretched man in his face. And he knew he would never in a hundred years be able to keep it out of his voice. He gave a curt, 'Sir!' and turned on his heel to go.

'Don't get any ideas about skipping away to escape your doom, Captain Blood,' Major Glanville's voice was full of mockery. 'If you're not back by dawn, I'll have you posted as a deserter. I'll even put a reward out on your head. A hundred pounds should be enough. You're not worth much more than that.'

Back in his quarters, now so wonderfully quiet with Elizabeth lodged in Gray's Inn Lane with her parents, Holcroft found a note that had been shoved under his door.

He stripped off his muddy coat and sweat-stained shirt, but kept on his breeches and riding boots. After he had washed his face and torso in the big porcelain bowl and found a clean shirt, he poured himself a glass of brandy and opened the note.

It was from Aphra Behn, and it was composed in their usual number substitution code. As he scanned it, Holcroft translated the message effortlessly in his head.

His friend had written:

My dearest Holly,

Now that you are off to the wars with your beloved Train, ready to blow the upstart Dutchman back into the sea, I do not know when you will receive this letter. I pray that your servant or perhaps a fellow Ordnance officer will forward it to you on campaign for I believe this information, once received, might well preserve your life.

Narrey is back in London again and residing in the Liberty of the Savoy. He returned to Versailles in the summer but the invasion of Dutch William has brought him running back and he bears with him a vast sum of money, a subsidy of 300,000 livres from his master Louis XIV to our own King James to aid him in his struggle with the Prince of Orange. My source of information is none other than Benedict, the young clerk who worked for poor Jupon. He has apparently taken up the reins of his late master's work and has asked me to undertake certain inquiries for him here in London, which I am delighted to do, since he is paying in hard cash and that most generously. My play writing, which you admire so much, does not bring in the riches I had hoped and so the money is most welcome. Benedict has a private income and has conceived an abiding hatred of Narrey, since he killed his master Jupon. He has sworn to devote his life to the destruction of his enemy.

I trust that you will take all necessary precautions to protect yourself against Narrey while he remains in London – I have asked Benedict to keep us abreast of his movements across the Channel, as best he can – and I further beg that you will stay out of the path of any musket balls, cannon fire, cavalry sabres and other perils of that ilk while you are destroying the enemies of our rightful King,

   Your friend,

   Aphra.

Holcroft put down the letter. He noted that it was dated one week ago. There was something odd about it but he could not put his finger on it. He sank the brandy in one draft. His quarters were cold, unheated since he had left with the Train more than two months ago, and the December chill had sunk into the brick walls. It was nearly dusk, though the day was little more than half done by his pocket watch. Nearly time for him to parade the fusiliers and begin his patrol.

He felt the brandy warming him. Narrey was in London again. That was an alarming thought but also, perhaps, it presented him with a unique opportunity. If Narrey was in the Savoy, he was likely in Palmer's school. And if he was there . . .

For a brief instant, Holcroft considered going to Lord Sunderland with this new intelligence. No. Sunderland would do nothing. He had had his chance – had the wretched man not said to Holcroft, in so many words, that he did not care if London teemed with French spies? No. Holcroft would do this alone.

Not exactly alone. He would take with him some of the best-trained troops in the British Isles. The men of the Royal Fusiliers. He put on his big blue and gold Ordnance coat and buttoned it up. He wrapped a long scarlet silk sash tightly around his waist, and after rummaging in a drawer, he found the Lorenzoni, checked it was loaded and shoved it in the sash over his belly. His small-sword he slung at his hip. He put on his hat, with a jaunty magpie's feather in the band. He was ready to go.

He put all thoughts about the court martial, Glanville's gleeful triumph and his insults and taunts, his imminent disgrace and possible death by firing squad to one side. He had an opportunity to deal with Henri d'Erloncourt, codenamed Narrey, once and for all. An opportunity that might never again present itself. He would be disobeying his orders – Glanville had told him to stay north of the Strand – but it would hardly be the first time he had ignored his superiors and followed the beat of his own drum. And Glanville meant to have him shot anyway. His vague talk of clemency was nonsense. It was time to go on to the attack. Holcroft recognised it. It was time to strike against the man who had sent killers into his home. It was time to take his revenge on Narrey – before his own sad fate was sealed.

Chapter Thirty-six

9 December 1688: Liberty of the Savoy

As Holcroft marched down the Strand, with sixty red-coated, flintlock-armed men at his back, he reflected that the London he had known almost all his life now seemed alien. They had passed more than a dozen burning houses in the city, and an equal number of ash-stinking, smoking ruins, the product of many days of unchecked riot. There was not a magistrate or a parish constable to be seen – almost no gentlemen of means visible either – and no other troops about save the fusiliers marching behind him. They had come across several knots of men and women – many extremely drunk – singing crude songs about the Pope around *ad hoc* bonfires built in the middle of the street or bawling out popular anti-Catholic ditties as they staggered along, sloshing tankards in hand. But these Londoners melted away before the fusiliers' determined advance. There were bodies, too, here and there, the dead and the dead drunk. Holcroft had noticed one skinny young girl in Fleet Street, weeping over her torn blood-wet skirts in the lee of St Clements Church, a servant who had clearly been violated, perhaps by more than one brute. And from time to time, Holcroft saw furtive, shadowy figures darting out of broken open shops and warehouses, their arms piled with looted goods.

Holcroft did not waste time on any of them.

They marched in the centre of the streets, boots beating the cobbles in unison, lit by their own pine torches, in a rectangular formation six men abreast and ten men deep. Holcroft and Lieutenant Rupert Pittman were in front and the two sergeants, the diminutive Miller and the huge, bear-like Masterson on either flank. The eighth company's commanding officer, Captain Lawhead, had deserted his post more than a week ago and was now rumoured to be an aide-de-camp to the Prince of Orange himself. This was why Holcroft, a gunnery officer, a gentleman of the Ordnance and not a Royal Fusilier, had been assigned to fill that officer's role by Glanville this night. Lawhead was a mild soul, religious, who had been friendly to Holcroft in the officers' mess. He liked him. He wondered whether the captain was with Jack Churchill in a sumptuous tent with the Prince of Orange, somewhere on the outskirts of London where William had agreed with emissaries from James to halt his advance. He wondered if his name might be mentioned in that tent, perhaps even fondly.

He stopped himself.

It was still too raw. Jack's betrayal of his King and his country. The way they had parted. Holcroft had known that he must end the friendship. He could not be in the company of someone who would behave in that manner. Strangely, he realised now, he did not blame Lawhead nearly so much for the same crime. Why was that?

There was no point thinking about it. It was done. His friendship with Jack was over and, most likely, so was his own earthly life. There was no time for remorse or self-pity – and he had no appetite for either. He wanted to concentrate on the task at hand. The firing squad would be easier to face if he knew that he had dispatched Narrey to Hell and perhaps even that bully Maguire, too. His brother Thomas would be a good deal safer if he did manage to kill the king of the Savoyards, as he'd said he would. But that aim was secondary: Narrey was the target. Narrey was the prize.

He halted the company. 'Lieutenant Pittman,' he said. 'You will kindly take four files of men and patrol up St Catherine's Street yonder.'

Holcroft pointed at the dark narrow street to the right leading northwest off the Strand. 'You will proceed to Long Acre. Then turn left and follow that street until you meet St Martin's Lane. Go slowly, go carefully. You are showing your presence, letting the mob know that the King's soldiers are here. Turn left on St Martin's and come to the bottom end of the lane and we will rendezvous at the Charing Cross in, say, one hour's time. Do you have that clearly?'

'Are you sure, Holcroft?' said Pittman, his smooth, angelic face crinkling in worry. 'Ought we not stay together? For safety, I mean, the rioters may be armed.'

'You'll be fine, Rupert. No need to be scared. Sergeant Masterson knows what he is doing. If you come across a large, dangerous mob then leave them be. Retreat.'

'I'm not scared! How dare you suggest that! I'm just concerned for you.'

'I apologise, Rupert. Of course you're not scared. Be a good fellow and do as I say. Meet us at the Charing Cross in one hour.'

'As long as you understand that I'm not afraid. Anyway, what are *you* going to do. Why can't we all patrol together?'

Holcroft felt a twinge of guilt at lying to the boy but he overrode it. 'We can cover more ground this way. I'll take the Strand and investigate the side streets; you make a long loop northwards and we will meet in an hour. Don't take any risks!'

Holcroft watched as a reluctant Lieutenant Pittman, assisted by his massive veteran sergeant, marched his forty men up St Catherine's Street, until the column was swallowed by the darkness and the sounds of their boots died away.

'Sergeant Miller – gather the men. No ceremony, just gather everyone around.'

Holcroft looked at the semi-circle of faces under their soft golden mitred hats: twenty young, eager men; fit, tough, lean and full of excitement.

'I have no authority for this action,' he said. 'And therefore I cannot order you to follow me into what may be a dangerous situation. But I am going into the Liberty of the Savoy to seek out a French spy who I believe is hiding there. He is a murderer, he has killed many innocent men, and he has been plotting in this country and meddling in our affairs of state. I cannot say more than that. But I am going into the Liberty' – Holcroft pointed to the dark roads leading off the southern side of the Strand – 'where I will seek him out, arrest him or, if he will not surrender, kill him.'

There was a chorus of fierce growls from the red-coated men.

'I take full responsibility for this mission, myself, alone. And if any man does not wish to play his part in it, he must speak now, and he may stand down – wait here until I return. There will be no repercussions, no penalties, there will be no black marks against his name. I swear it. But he must speak up clearly now.'

There was a silence, and then one man spoke. He was a tall fellow, a corporal, with greasy, black hair poking out on either side of his mitre cap, his voice was pure Dublin: 'This spying cove, sir, the fella you're hunting. This the same fella who sent his villains into your own house in Mincing Lane, sir. Trying to murder you and your good lady wife in your bed, sir?'

'Yes, that's who I seek.'

'Well, I'm your man, sir,' said the Dubliner. 'Can't abide a fella who would send men to attack a young lady in her bed. And I've no time for Frenchmen either.'

'Thank you. Does anyone else wish to speak up?'

'We're all with you, sir,' said Miller somewhat impatiently. 'Me and all the lads, sure we are. This is not a town council meeting. We're fusiliers. Let's go.'

They formed a column of twos, and led by Holcroft and Miller they jogged fifty yards up the Strand, turned left and plunged into the heart of the Liberty of the Savoy. They ran hard. There was little attempt at stealth. Twenty sprinting men, in brass-buttoned red coats, heavy boots, clattering with accoutrements, muskets, plug-bayonets and swords, was a sight and sound that was impossible to avoid. But Holcroft was more concerned with speed. He needed to get to Palmer's school before word of the soldiers' presence got there. His greatest fear was that Narrey – forewarned by whatever methods of communication prevailed in the Liberty – pigeons, roof-top torch signals, or just swift-running boys – would escape before he could be taken. The school was on the bank of the Thames and it would take only a moment or two for a skiff to be launched and the French spy to slip away over the dark water. *Why did I not send men by boat? What a fool!*

They ran. Twenty men puffing and pelting down the dark, narrow street.

They ran across the spill of yellow light coming from the front windows of the Grapes and Holcroft thought he caught a glimpse of the ugly, plum-nosed face of Josiah Fitch gawping at him through the greasy glass.

A hundred yards from the school at the very bottom of the pot-holed street, the missiles started to rain down from the rooftops on either side. Some of them were harmless, soft rotten fruit, and chamber pots full of liquid and solid matter. One of the fusiliers in the third rank was drenched and he could be heard cursing and spluttering, while his mates laughed like monkeys. The hard Savoyard voices of men, women and children called out mocking insults from the darkness, seemingly from all sides. But they caused no injury. The tiles, bricks and shards of sharp flint were another matter. A small fusilier was caught by a shower of stones, semi-stunned by a blow to the back of his head, nearly collapsed and had to be held up by his mates.

'Run,' shouted Holcroft. 'Not far now. That's the place, there.'

Indeed, Palmer's free school could be clearly seen. It was dark, seemingly uninhabited, not a candle or lantern alight anywhere near it. Holcroft could see the gap that led to the water of the Thames, the wet stone stairs and the wave-glint reflected from the choppy waters beyond. There was no one there. No craft. No wherry or boat. No one was attempting to make a swift escape by water.

Holcroft did not hesitate. He leapt at the front door with a flying kick, all his fifteen stones concentrated through the heel of his right boot, smashing the lock and bursting it open. 'Inside, everybody inside. Now.'

He pushed the fusiliers into the large classroom, spookily dark, empty and cold. He seized Miller by the shoulder as he passed through the smashed door.

'Take five men and stand guard here,' he said, breathlessly. 'Nobody to come in or out. You have permission to shoot, if you need to. There is a big double door to the stables outside to our left; it should be locked. These are the only entrances. Keep the stables sealed. And this door as well. And watch that opening in the fence yonder. It leads down by a set of stairs to the Thames. Narrey is here somewhere; I'll use the rest of the men to search. Keep any curious locals out of here. I'm going to find him.'

Holcroft took a pair of fusiliers with him, one of them the Dublin man – Corporal James 'Briny' Bryanston – who had spoken up in the Strand. He sent the rest of the men in groups of three to search the school, with orders to arrest anyone they met – man, woman or child – and bring them to the large classroom by the entrance, gagged and bound securely, and under watchful guard.

It didn't take Holcroft long to realise that Palmer's school and St Mary's Foundling Hospital were both deserted. They walked across the empty open-air courtyard, the whipping post painting a long black shadow in the moonlight. The soup cauldron was there on its stand, half filled with rainwater, the fire hole beneath filled with muddy black sludge. The classrooms were empty, broken chalks still in the groove at the bottom of the blackboards. Someone had removed the printing press and there was a large, square, lighter patch on the wooden floorboards where it had stood. The patch was lightly covered with grey dust. Dust, indeed, was everywhere.

Holcroft and his men searched cupboards and closets, they peered under desks and tables. They saw the other search parties from time to time, moving about with their pine torches held high. No one had been seen; no one was arrested. In the long dormitory of St Mary's, Holcroft poked at a mound of dust-covered soiled baby napkins in the corner of the room with the toe of his boot. The pungent aroma of faeces could still be detected. But only faintly. On a table at the side of the room, an abandoned bowl of cow's milk had dried to a curling rind of grimy cheese.

He could smell something else. A meaty, rotten smell. He went through the dormitory, through the doorway at the rear. There was a large table, covered in dust, a huge cracked porcelain bowl set upon it, a place where a baby might be washed. A sideboard with a jug and a dried-up napkin, and a pile of muslin cloths, an old grey linen towel. The rotten smell was stronger in here.

Holcroft told his men to stay where they were and followed his nose – and soon wished he had not. He found a door in the corridor outside the wash-room. It was firmly shut. But he knew something bad was inside. The door stuck at first, then he used his weight and his shoulder and suddenly it popped open. He blundered into a small dining room of some kind: a six-foot pine table was in the centre of the space, with a great china soup tureen in the middle, with the handle of a ladle poking from the top, and the lid lying on the tabletop beside it. Four bowls were set in front of four places. One bowl had been overturned amid a scatter of spoons and knives, side plates and shrunken, dried-hard crusts of rye bread.

It was the occupant of one of the chairs on the far side of the room that drew Holcroft's eyes. It was the figure of a middle-aged man in a once-black, stained and rotted cassock, with a metal crucifix around his neck. A priest. Father Palmer, he presumed. His flesh had melted away, leaving black, leather-like skin over skull and wisps of hair. The jaw hung loose, exposing good white teeth framing a black void. One hand rested on the table, poking out of a ragged sleeve, the meat long gone, dissolved away, leaving only the

brown bones of his fingers and arms, connected by yellowish carti-
lage and ligaments. He had been dead for some months.

There were three more desiccated bodies in the room, curled on
the floor in the positions of their final agonies, the chairs kicked to
the side of the room: a woman short of stature but by the scraps of
her decayed dress once someone of considerable girth – Maria Matthews, Holcroft supposed – and another two priests: the younger
was the man who had shown Holcroft around the school on his two
previous visits – Father Williams – and there was another priest
that he did not know.

This was Narrey's work – Holcroft knew it immediately. Poison.
These four had sat down to a humble dinner of soup. They would
have said grace, then begun eating at the same time. After the first
spoonfuls they had died within minutes. Holcroft recalled Aphra's
words to him three years ago: 'You know as well as I do, Holly, that
Narrey rarely allows anyone who can identify him to live.'

Holcroft backed out of the room and shut the door behind him.
He would deal with these long dead unfortunates when he had finished his search – they would not mind waiting a few more hours.
By this time it was clear to him that Narrey was not here. Nobody
had lived or worked here for months, nobody had nursed newborn
children or studied their letters, or printed seditious pamphlets.

Holcroft felt a great leaden weight in his stomach. He felt foolish, embarrassed. He had deliberately disobeyed orders and wasted
everyone's time.

Then came the sound of a loud crack – the sharp report of a flintlock musket. And a more distant rattle of arms. Pistols. He could
hear a roaring sound, the kind made by an angry crowd. A rioting
mob. And dislocated shouts. He realised that the mistake he had
made could end up being a great deal worse than wasting his men's
time. The sound of glass shattering could now be heard.

'Enough,' he said to his two men. 'He's not here. No one is alive
here. Briny – find the other searchers and tell everyone to get back
to the front. We're leaving.'

Back in the classroom by the smashed front door, Holcroft knew it was going to be bad. One of the fusiliers, moaning weakly, his belly sodden with blood, was lying on his back at the rear of the room. The row of large windows on the front wall had been smashed and the rest of Miller's five men, as well as the returning searchers, were kneeling among the shattered shards, sheltering below the lip of the three windows, or either side of the broken door, or taking cover behind overturned desks.

As Holcroft walked in the door somebody outside shouted, 'Fuck the Papist King!' and flung a burning branch into the room through the shattered window, and an earthenware pint pot followed it and crashed on the floor, breaking apart and spilling some dark liquid that looked and smelled like whale oil. The two missiles landed yards apart but the oil began to leak over the floor. A pistol cracked from the darkness outside and a ball punched into the wall by Holcroft's head. He could make out a mass of people in the street, adults, children, some hundreds of folk grinning and capering in the light of torches and lanterns, blood-red faces in the firelight, open mouths; they were shouting, roaring, howling. He could see weapons being waved, pikes, swords, carving knives, and a pistol or two. Some tuneless drunk was bawling an old nursery rhyme, the words only half-heard over the tumult: 'The Grand Old Duke of York'.

'Get your head down, sir,' shouted Miller. Holcroft fell to his knees and began to crawl towards the door. A green glass bottle was hurled through the window, shattered on the floor. A large lump of rock crashed after it.

'Right,' Sergeant Miller said, 'first section: up now, cock your pieces.' A handful of fusiliers, eight or nine men, rose from their places of cover beneath the window sill and aimed their flintlocks out into the darkness. There was an animal like roar from outside; pistol shots sounded, two very close together, the bullets flying high and ricocheting round the classroom. None of the fusiliers flinched. 'Take aim,' said Miller. 'Try not to kill the kiddies, lads. We ain't savages. Fire!'

The thin volley crashed out, a dozen spurts of flame stabbing into the dark street. There was a horrible girlish scream and a fit of loud cursing, a pistol fired back from outside, smashing into the ceiling and releasing a shower of snow-like plaster.

'. . . he had ten thousand men.' The drunk was still belting out his child's ditty.

'He marched them out to Salisbury Plain.'

'And he marched them back again . . .'

'First section: reload,' shouted Miller. 'Second section: up lads, on your feet.'

Holcroft was by the ruined door. He stooped, picked up the burning branch and hurled it spinning out of the window. 'Want to take over, sir?' whispered Miller.

'You are doing fine,' said Holcroft. 'Carry on, sergeant.'

'Second section: take aim. Pick your targets, lads, choose 'em well. Fire!'

The musket fire lashed the street outside. More shouts of pain and rage.

Holcroft poked his head out of the open door, a swift assessment. There were three or four bodies on the cobbles, a large pool of blood by the burning branch. And a sea of angry folk. They were, at least, keeping well back – the two volleys had done that much – the Savoyards were taking cover behind barrels, behind a large four-wheeled overturned hay cart, in the decrepit brick buildings on the other side of the street. By God, there were a lot of them. Three, four hundred. Men, women and children, watching, laughing, excited by the sport. Some leaning from windows in the houses, some clustered on the low roofs. And there were more coming on, hundreds, a tide of folk heading down the street from the Strand to join in the fun. His eye was caught by moving spot of red. The burning coal on the cord of a matchlock musket. A tall man in a rakish, broad-brimmed hat pinned up on one side, a rank-rider perhaps, was boldly standing at the side of the upturned cart, using it as a rest and pointing the matchlock at Holcroft, squinting down the barrel. He ducked inside as the musket fired and a burst of splinters exploded from the door frame.

'First section: on your feet. Cock your pieces . . .'

We're trapped, thought Holcroft. *If we leave here we will be torn apart. And someone, soon, will succeed in setting this building on fire and then we will roast.*

He pulled the Lorenzoni from his sash, cocked it, waited for the echoes of the fusiliers' volley to die away, and spun round the doorframe. He pointed the pistol at the tall man in the broad-brimmed hat, a dozen yards away, who was now concentrating on reloading his matchlock, pouring powder down the long barrel.

Holcroft shot him through the skull, knocking the man down in a spray of brains and blood. He dodged back through the door before the man's legs stopped jerking.

'This is no good. We're going to have to make a run for it, John.'

Miller looked up at Holcroft with sombre eyes. 'I think I'd rather go down fighting in here, captain, if it's all the same to you. There's hundreds of the bastards out there, armed and angry. I'd say our end is pretty much certain either way.'

'No, John, I think we can make it. If we run hard, some of us will get away . . .'

Miller raised an eyebrow. 'Whatever you think is best, sir.'

'Cease firing! You soldier-boys in there, stop your shooting!'

The voice was a bull bellow and coming from directly outside the school.

'Hold your fire, sergeant,' said Holcroft.

'Flag o' truce, you King's lickspittles. I'm showing the flag o' fucking truce!'

Holcroft darted his head around the doorframe. He could see a huge man, a flesh mountain with a vast shaven head, standing alone in the centre of the cobbled street holding what looked like a dirty linen bed sheet in one enormous hand.

'Show your white flag, soldier-boy,' the man bellowed at him, 'and we'll have us what they call a parlay. All nice and friendly. No need for anyone else to get hurt.'

Holcroft handed the Lorenzoni to Miller. He unwound the scarlet sash from his waist, took off sword belt and coat, stripped off his shirt. He flapped it out the door.

'I see it, soldier-boy. My, that's a nice clean one. Not sure I've ever seen a flag o' truce so lovely and white. Now step outside and we'll have a little chat.'

Holcroft put his coat back on his bare torso. The night air was freezing.

'I should go, sir,' said Miller. 'There's no trusting these folk.'

'No, John. You and the lads watch from the windows. Keep the muskets trained on him. If he makes the slightest wrong move, you can shoot him down like a dog.'

Holcroft stepped out of the doorway. The big man stood with his arms by his sides, the bed sheet trailing in the mud by his huge booted feet. Behind him the Savoyards were emerging from their bolt holes, more curious about this captain of King's men, that they had trapped here like a rat, than afeared of him.

Holcroft ignored the people who gathered on either side of the vast, bald man.

'You wanted to talk to me,' he said.

'Your name is Blood, yes? Holcroft Blood.'

Holcroft nodded. A woman in the crowd, a pretty, rake-thin type with a beak of a nose, gave a huge, gasping sob, and covered her head with her shawl.

'Don't mind her,' said the giant. 'She's just a little excited to be meeting you tonight. See, you killed her man Michael. He was my brother. Her husband, my brother, dead as a stone by your hand. I said she could have you when I'm done.'

Holcroft shrugged. 'I had no quarrel with him but he would have murdered me, if he could. You will be Patrick Maguire then, the so-called king in these parts?'

'Aye, that's me. You did for my other brother, Francis, too, in Mincing Lane.'

'So what? I defended my house, my wife and myself. I'd do the same again.'

'See that body lying there with the top off his head. That was my last living brother. His name was Seanie. Saw you pistol him just now, with my own eyes.'

'Is this all you wanted to talk about? Because, if that's it . . .'

'I want you to know why you must die tonight. It's personal. Vengeance, see?'

'Oh, I *must* die, must I?'

'Aye, you must.' The huge bald man was calm. He gave no hint of anger or any other emotion. He seemed mildly happy, content, even a little pleased.

'When you've recovered from all your grief and sorrow, you know where to find me.' Holcroft turned to go back into the school. He saw Miller standing at the doorway with a levelled flintlock. Half a dozen fusiliers were peering out of the shattered windows, pointing their pieces at Maguire and the mass of raggedy folk around him. Holcroft glanced once more at the crowd, which looked like a savage horde in the red firelight. Some of the Savoyards had blades, rusty swords, knives. One had a half-pike. A few had pistols of various sizes. A stout fellow had gathered up Seanie Maguire's matchlock and bandoleer of charges and was leaning on the grounded weapon with his ankles crossed, almost as if in a parody of a soldier at rest.

Holcroft was nearly at the door when he heard Maguire's bull rumble: 'I know you are not a coward, know that sure as I know anything. That's why I reckon you will fight me – man to man, toe to toe. It'll be a fair fight because I am a fair man. No guns, no knives, just our bare fambles.'

Holcroft turned around slowly. 'Why would I choose to fight you without weapons? You've ten stones on me, easily. Five inches in height. Longer reach, too.'

'And you're twenty years younger, son. But I'll tell you why you'll fight. For them poor sons o' Mars over there.' Maguire jerked his chin at the fusiliers at the shattered windows.

'I'm listening,' said Holcroft.

'If you beat me, fair and square, if you can knock me senseless, or punish me so bad I can't come up to scratch after a count of ten, or make me yield, or kill me even, I give you my word you can all walk away free as the birds. If I beat you, knock you cold, or kill you – your body is mine, or rather, it's Sally's over there' – he nodded at the thin weeping woman – 'but the rest of you can go free. Jacob Creech here will stand surety for me, if I'm unable to speak up for myself for whatever reason.'

Maguire reached behind him and seized the shoulder of a villainous-looking man with long greasy grey hair and a rust-blotched but still serviceable cutlass cradled in his arms. He pulled the man in front of him, showing him to Holcroft.

'Creech, you heard my words, yes? You'll make sure my wishes are followed.'

The man smiled and revealed a full set of surprisingly even white teeth.

Holcroft looked at Maguire, measuring him with his eye. He was enormous; tall as an apple tree and thick in chest and belly. His arms were a heavy as another man's thighs and lumped with muscle. His great hands and fingers were like bunches of sausages. But he *was* a good deal older than Holcroft, and carrying a quantity of extra weight, and he looked like he would move a little more slowly than he might.

'I know you are no coward,' Maguire said. 'But I'd like to make this crystal clear: if you won't fight me, for whatever reason, don't matter why, I will burn that fucking school to the ground with all of you inside it. And any man who lives through the inferno will wish that he had not when I pluck his body from the ashes.'

'I'll fight you, sure,' said Holcroft, nodding slowly at the big man. 'For my own vengeance and for my pride, and for the arrangement that you offer – the lives of my men – and for one more thing besides. A condition.'

'This is not a fucking negotiation.' Maguire seemed irritated for the first time. 'I'm no wheedling merchant. That is the arrangement. Nothing else. What I offered to you. The lives of your men – and yours, if you can beat me. Take it or leave it.'

'This *is* a negotiation, and I will tell you why. For one thing: I think you want to fight me. I think you want to pound me into red meat to avenge your stupid and incompetent brothers. I think you'd rather do that to me with your own hands than set fire the school. And I will give you the chance. There's another thing to consider: we are not defenceless, you could die in the battle over the burning school . . .'

John Miller, with impeccable timing, chose that moment to pull back the dog-head on his fusil to full cock. The metallic click seemed louder in the silence. Maguire glanced at the sergeant by the doorway with the levelled musket pointing at his head, then looked back at Holcroft without showing the slightest trace of fear.

'. . . and another thing to mention,' said Holcroft, 'is that you don't know what it is that I want from you. My condition. It might be something you are willing to give me. I'll tell you now: it is a question. You answer it honestly and I swear I'll fight you, just as you want me to, man to man, toe to toe, empty-handed.'

'What is your question?'

'I want to know where the Frenchman is. Your employer. I don't know what you called him – he calls himself Narrey – but his true name is Henri d'Erloncourt. He is a man who deserves death many times over. I thought to find him here. Where is he?'

'If I tell you all that I know about his whereabouts, you will fight me?'

'Yes, if you speak the truth.'

The big man smiled. 'I can tell you this, soldier-boy, the honest truth, with God as my witness . . . I have no notion where that creeping French sodomite is now.'

Maguire threw back his head and roared with laughter. The crowd around him giggled and snickered too.

'Tell me what you know,' grated Holcroft. 'He was here, was he not? Under your protection? Where is he now?' He felt the first stirrings of true anger. He was looking forward to punching the arrogance out of this big Irish sack of lard.

Maguire mastered himself. 'I sent him packing in the summer, end of June, I think – him and his hard man Guillaume. I'd had enough of their ways. I spread the word that nobody was to set foot in the school again. And since their baby enterprise had proved to be unnecessary, they went away quiet as mice. Ha, soldier-boy. You're here on a fool's errand. The Frenchman hasn't been in these parts for six months! So, now, enough chatter – we fight.'

'Wait! Narrey – the Frenchman – he came back a week or two ago. You did not see him? Or hear of him?'

'Not a word. If he came to London he did not set foot in the Liberty. I doubt that he came to Rum-ville at all – I'd have heard something from somebody. I have many good friends all over this wicked old town. Now, son, time for talking is done.'

'What do you mean their baby enterprise proved to be unnecessary?'

'Exactly that. They had some fancy design with the doxies in St Mary's in case they needed a baby, a baby boy, God knows why, and in the end there was no call for the child after all. Waste of time. Guillaume whispered this to his bum-boy, who told it to me. That's all I know. But enough of this: toe the line, soldier!'

Holcroft nodded. He went over to Miller and began to take off his blue coat, the frigid night air almost painful on his bare chest and back.

'What say you, sir?' whispered Miller. 'How about I just shoot the big bugger in his fat head and be done with it? Then we take our chances.'

Holcroft looked over at Maguire, who was stripping off his filthy rag of a shirt, surrounded by a gang of grinning, back-slapping Savoyards. 'I'll fight him. I gave the brute my word. And I told my brother Tom I'd deal with the bastard, too.' He handed the sergeant his big blue Ordnance coat, and hopped up and down on his toes a few times, swinging his bare arms in wide circles.

However, he was not concentrating on the coming fight. He was not planning how he might defeat this monster. His head was reeling at the thought of how neatly he had been played by Narrey. The letter from Aphra had been a fake. That was clear now. Narrey had written it and arranged for it to be delivered it to him to send him on this doomed quest into the heart of Maguire's territory. Narrey had tricked him into coming here. Manipulated him into putting his head into this trap.

He had been a damn fool. And now he was going to pay for his foolishness.

Chapter Thirty-seven

10 December 1688: Palace of Versailles

His Most Christian Majesty Louis XIV, by the grace of God, King of France and Navarre, watched the jet of the fountain soar thirty feet into the air like a foot-thick pillar of water. It was one of the simplest of the hundreds of elaborate fountains in the gardens of Versailles – a single, towering water-spout set in the centre of a perfect circle of blue water – but it was the one that he privately admired the most.

The Orangerie that surrounded the lone fountain and its circular pool was almost deserted that crisp December morning. Apart from the slim, beautifully dressed young man standing beside him, and a dozen servants following the royal promenade at a discreet distance, there was no one else that Louis could see, save for a lone gardener two hundred paces away, on his knees tending to the roots of one of the fragrant orange trees, which had recently been replanted in their large square wooden boxes for the winter as a protection against the cold weather.

'Barillon says he is finished,' said Louis. 'He says that James Stuart will never again rule his Three Kingdoms. He says I should wash my hands of him – give James a pension and somewhere to live and make my peace with the Prince of Orange.'

'With the greatest respect, Majesty, Barillon is an old man and he is a little jaded – he gives up too easily,' said Henri d'Erloncourt. 'Things have gone badly, yes. No question. The defection of the Army officers to William's side was a severe blow. But James has not lost the game. He has suffered a major setback. And it may be that he must quit England for a little while. But he is by no means finished. Nothing is yet settled in England. You might say that he has had to *reculer pour mieux sauter*.'

'Do you truly believe that, Monsieur le Comte? On your honour? You are not merely attempting to disguise your complete failure to achieve your mission?'

'My mission, Majesty, with which you honoured me three years ago, was to ensure a Catholic succession for the throne of England by whatever means necessary – if you will forgive me, sire, those were your exact words. I carefully made my dispositions to ensure a successful outcome. Yet, in the end, the mechanism I designed was not required. I was ready but, in the event, it was not necessary to make the substitution. James has a son, born in the ordinary way of his wife Mary; and the boy will be raised in the True Faith. Under my watchful eye a Catholic succession for the King of England has been assured. I would not say, therefore, that I had failed.'

'If you wish to split hairs, Monsieur, I could say to you that if James is expelled from his country, and thereby loses his throne, then his son, however correctly he is raised, will be the son of a nobody. The kingdom will fall to a Protestant; the next King of England will be a heretic. Can you still claim your mission a success?'

'You are right to chastise me, Majesty, all has not gone according to plan, but I do not believe the contest to be over. James may be forced to quit England. But if he is offered support from his friends, from a benevolent royal patron, perhaps in the form of men and arms, as well as money, he might attempt to regain his crown.'

'Are you asking me to fund a full-scale invasion of England to restore my cousin James to his throne? Can you be serious, Monsieur le Comte? The expense would be astronomical; we would need troops sufficient to conquer the entire country – and then hold it by force – two hundred thousand men, maybe more; and they would have to be supplied across the Channel, perhaps with the Royal Navy against us. It would be impossible. Every Englishman's sword would be raised in anger. I suspect, Monsieur, you are beginning to lose your grip on the actuality of the world.'

'No, no, Majesty, you mistake my intent. I do not recommend an invasion of England. Certainly not. It would be quite impossible, as you say. But James Stuart is the monarch of three lands. And one of these, although small in size, and more distant, is the most sympathetic to our cause. We would need only a modest number of troops, for the native population and their national army would surely rise up to support the Stuart cause – which is the cause of their own True Religion.'

'You speak of Ireland,' said Louis.

'I do, Majesty. And, furthermore, I do not advocate the total conquest of the British Isles. I speak only of fomenting a lasting civil war in the Three Kingdoms that will keep them occupied for a generation or more. If James Stuart were to land in Ireland with a sizeable – but not overwhelming – force of French troops, say, only a few thousand, five or six regiments and some light artillery, then they could provide enough of a threat to force the Prince of Orange to come over the Irish Sea with his armies and fight them. Equally matched, the war could grind on and on for years. We could be opening a second front in the back parlour of our greatest enemy in Europe. Opening a bleeding wound in his flank that might, with luck, never heal. Civil war in Ireland is good for France – and the longer it lasts the better.

'However, that is only the long game, Majesty, the far-seeing strategy. In the short term: with William's attention directed west to a Catholic rebellion in Ireland, and with his Dutch and English troops occupied against James's rebel forces, we would have a free hand in northern Europe. We could move against the fortified towns of the Low Countries, subdue them at last, make a concerted drive into the heart of the United Provinces, and with little or no interference. We could campaign further, against those heretical principalities of the Holy Roman Empire. All of this we could do with impunity since the bulk of the military resources of the Prince of Orange would be occupied hundreds of miles away in Ireland.'

The Sun King looked at his spymaster with fresh respect. He said nothing for a few minutes. He watched the fountain shooting up, and the water tumbling down eternally. He looked at the ripples in the perfect pool, ever expanding, ever radiating outwards in a continuous progression, serene and unstoppable, like the power and glory of France itself. It was a metaphor – no, it was a sign from God himself!

'I have misjudged you, my dear d'Erloncourt,' he said. 'I confess that I have recently become vexed by the situation in England and the humiliation of our poor cousin. But your words are a balm to my soul. My confidence in you is restored.'

'I am most deeply honoured, Majesty. You know that I live only to serve you, and through your person, to serve the glory of France itself.'

'Your counsel is good, Monsieur, and your wisdom much appreciated. But I wish you to take charge of this business yourself – personally. I want you to go to Ireland with our troops when the time is right and to direct their use and operations.'

'You wish me to go to Ireland? Sire, I am not a man made for battlefields, my weapons are quill and ink, a discreet pouch of silver, a quiet word in a man's ear . . .'

'Nevertheless, I wish you to go with James as my personal envoy. You are right, Ambassador Barillon is too old and set in his ways. He's a defeatist. You will act as the liaison between James, rightful King of Ireland, and the forces of France. You may take your man Guillaume du Clos with you. He will look after you on the field of battle. Indeed, it might be wise to give you a military title – nothing too grand, but of not inconsiderable rank, either. Colonel d'Erloncourt – how does that sound?'

'Sire, are you sure I could not serve you better if I were to remain in France and co-ordinate events from here? Your Majesty still has many enemies lurking in the shadows, even in Versailles, and I fear that in my prolonged absence . . .'

'You must deal with them before you leave, Colonel, or leave them until you return, because you *are* going to Ireland. Only you will be able to judge exactly the degree of military aid that James should receive from his gracious patron. Too much help and James will quickly vanquish William and send him back to Holland where he might interfere with my own plans. Too little and he will be easily defeated and William can once again forget Ireland and turn his attention to the Low Countries. It is a delicate balance and you're the only man I trust to find it. Achieve this and you will be doing inestimable service to me – and to France. Go to Ireland, my friend, and start a war. Set good Irish Catholics against the Protestant heretics – and God grant that this war will rage, to the benefit of France, for a hundred years or more.'

'As you command, Majesty,' said the Comte d'Erloncourt, and bowed.

Chapter Thirty-eight

10 December 1688: Liberty of the Savoy

The first punch to the head from Patrick Maguire nearly knocked Holcroft senseless. And he'd even partially deflected this looping, overhand strike of the Irishman's iron left fist with his forearm. After a pair of slow, almost ponderous feints from Maguire's right, the big left came unexpectedly quickly, and shockingly powerfully over the top of his defence, crashing past his forearm to skid over the top of his head.

Holcroft staggered back in surprise at the strength of the blow, dizzy, his ears ringing. He struck out almost at random with his left fist and connected with Maguire's huge, naked hair-matted chest. It was a poor blow but hard enough to check his opponent and give Holcroft time to gather his scattered senses.

Holcroft was no weakling, he was reckoned a strong man, but he found that was no match for the massive Irish criminal. Holcroft knew he had to stay away from his enemy. Another punch like that first strike, two at most, and he would be out like a snuffed candle. He had to stay away from that big left hand to have the slightest chance of surviving this bare-knuckle bout. Even then his chances of survival, he was coming to realise, were vanishingly small.

Patrick Maguire's style of fighting was strange to Holcroft, who was more used to the unstructured rough and tumble of a street brawl, where you pummelled your opponent, butted, grappled and bashed him with anything that came to hand until he fell to the ground, whereupon you kicked and stamped on him until he begged for mercy or stopped moving. The king of the Savoy, however, had clearly had some expert training. His lieutenant Creech had drawn a yard-long line in the mud of the street with his cut-lass and Maguire put his right foot on the scratch and his left foot shoulder-width apart and slightly behind the right, and had taken a stance with his body sloping backwards, both fists extended, the right further out than the left.

Holcroft, unused to this formality, had put his foot on the line and lifted his fists in front of his face. Maguire hit him in the ribs, a short hard right that drove the breath from his body. Holcroft stumbled a good two yards backward. He felt a firm shove in the small of his back, propelling him back to the centre of the circle of hundreds of Savoyards, who were chanting and cheering for their king.

'You must toe the line, solder boy, toe the line!' shouted Creech in his ear. And Holcroft found himself going forward and placing his foot gingerly back on the line in the mud. Maguire feinted with his right, and punched full strength with his left, and out of instinct, Holcroft ducked and the blow shot over the top of his head.

He fired a hard left that smashed into Maguire's cheekbone, split-ting the flesh, and felt the jolt of the impact all the way up his arm. It was like punching a boulder. And yet the big man hardly seemed to notice the blow. He pistoned out a right cross and caught Maguire's square chin full on, and the big man's head did indeed rock back a fraction. But that was all.

Those two blows would have felled a lesser man, thought Holcroft. *Might even have killed a smaller opponent.* Maguire jabbed with his right, jabbed with his left, and Holcroft ducked, dodged and fended the strikes off with his raised forearms. The Irishman repeated the move, right jab, then left; he feinted twice with his right, and clob-bered him with that stunning overhand left, which Holcroft only partially stopped. Once more he was sent reeling backwards – and that was when he realised he was going to lose this fight, that Patrick Maguire was going to kill him.

He peddled back wildly, trying to get clear of his enemy's big, smashing fists. And once more he was pushed forward towards

Maguire by the howling crowd – he felt a hard blow in his back, above his kidneys, from someone in the mob behind as he was propelled to the line. *Least it wasn't a knife*, he thought.

Holcroft concentrated on avoiding being hit. He dodged and danced and ducked, moved out of reach of Maguire's long arms, often switched which foot was touching the line, to Creech's howls of outrage. Maguire seemed reluctant to move, he planted his feet and swung his huge fists – which was the saving of Holcroft. From time to time he came in and delivered a solid blow to Maguire's body. He got in a good hard one on a spot on his opponent's left side below his short ribs; Maguire gasped, and immediately belted him across the cheekbone with a lightning right. Holcroft stumbled away on jellied legs, he could feel his cheekbone beginning to swell. His head was swimming but he held on tight to the memory of the sound of Maguire's gasp as his own blow had gone home.

Holcroft came up to scratch, and concentrated on dodging Maguire's barrage, firing off a low right whenever he was able and trying to hit the same spot on the ribs under the Irishman's left arm. Holcroft found his mark, and on the fourth time of striking there, he received an acknowledgement of his efforts in the form of a scream of outraged pain from Maguire and a massive left jab to the face that burst through his defence and sent lightning flashing around his brain.

By a combination of luck and skill, he managed to avoid Maguire's swinging blows, and when he couldn't, he took the brunt of them on his forearms – which were now purple and red, swollen twice their normal size, and shrieking with pain. Occasionally, he managed to plant a good hard facer on his opponent, but not as often as he wished, and each time he hit his foe, his own hands exploded in pain. He stepped back from an uppercut from Maguire's right, ducked a big left and popped another hard right into the big man's left side. Maguire bellowed. He charged forward, leaving the line in the mud, seeming to forget all his skill, arms swinging, one-two, one-two, like twin battering rams. Holcroft dodged beneath his left arm, and managed to get a left and a right, both as powerful as he was capable of and in quick succession on to his chosen target. With a pain-muted blast of joy, he heard the ribs crackle like kindling as his right fist smashed into the Irishman's left side.

Maguire howled with rage and pain and dropped to his knees.

'Toe the line, toe the line both of you,' shouted Creech.

Maguire looked at his long-haired lieutenant, sheer murder in his eyes. 'One more word out of you . . .' he grated. Creech went pale and clamped his mouth shut.

Maguire turned his gaze on Holcroft. 'I'm going to kill you now, you weaselly little shit.' The huge man's eyes were bloodshot. He seemed completely insane.

He charged Holcroft, trying to scoop him up in a bear-hug. Holcroft got below the arms, smashed another fist into Maguire's broken left side and was moving away, when the Irishman's flailing backhand caught him on the side of his head and knocked him flat. Maguire was on him like a tiger, stamping his heavy boot where Holcroft's head had been an instant before, Holcroft rolled fast, and rolled again, as Maguire chased after him, kicking, stomping, and screaming his rage. The crowd of Savoyards moved with the fight, the circle stretching, elongating when necessary but staying intact. Once, as he rolled and rolled, Holcroft caught an upside-down glimpse of the fusiliers standing at the window. Only Sergeant Miller had his musket up in the firing position. The other soldiers were too engrossed to remember that their own lives, too, could be at stake.

Maguire stopped – panting, puffing, spitting and blowing streams of phlegm from his gaping mouth. Holcroft rolled once more and climbed to his feet.

'All right – huh-huh-huh – you've had – huh-huh – your fun.' Maguire was labouring hard, like a spent cart-horse; his left hand was clutching his injured ribs but his face was hardly bruised at all.

'Come and fight me like a real man – back to the scratch – huh-huh-huh – or the deal's off.'

The Irishman seemed calmer. Holcroft approached him with caution but also with a glimmer of hope. Something was forming in his mind – a plan.

'We toe the line and start again. Or I'll tell my men to kill you all now.'

Holcroft nodded. He had always loved patterns. Sequences made him strangely happy. He loved it when the world displayed its underlying order. He could recall clearly every blow or combination of blows that Maguire had made against him in this bloody bout. And, in one shining moment, as he limped painfully up to the scratch line, he realised that this most dangerous of fighting men had a weakness. He had a pattern of behaviour. He was predictable. Not when he lost his temper, of course, then his savage rage was unleashed and the pattern became random. But when he came up to the line, and adopted the strange leaning-back stance, he almost always followed a sequence of punches, which he was probably unaware of. Right jab, left jab, right jab, left jab, slow right feint, another slow right feint, then the huge overarm knockout left. His favourite killing blow. Somebody had drilled this pattern into him at a young age. It was a good combination. It had nearly finished Holcroft in the first few moments of the fight. But it was predictable and that made it very dangerous – for Patrick Maguire. Whenever Holcroft hit him, whenever he was stung, Maguire instinctively went back to the safety of this simple combination. The plan was forming in Holcroft's mind.

Holcroft grinned at Maguire. 'Ready now?' he said. 'Got your breath back?'

They both put their feet on the line. Maguire feinted with his right. Holcroft barely moved. And suddenly he knew he had made a colossal mistake. The right was still coming. It was no feint. It smashed through his half up-held forearms, crunching into the

BLOOD'S REVOLUTION | 333

side of his head and hurling him backwards. He landed hard on his back in the muck of the street and, looking up, saw Maguire's huge grinning head hovering above him. He rolled fast but Maguire had not moved.

Holcroft got slowly to his feet. His head spinning, he felt sick, his legs seemed to be made of water – but it was his poor bruised forearms that hurt the most.

'Ready now,' said Maguire, who appeared the soul of cheerful good humour. 'Got your breath back, soldier-boy? Well then, toe the line.'

Holcroft put his foot on the cutlass scratch. He flashed out a fast left jab that smacked into Maguire's jaw. It was a good crunching blow. But Maguire shook his head, seemingly shaking away the pain. Then he saw the big man reset himself. Here it comes, he thought. He flinched as Maguire's right jab came screaming towards him, blocked it, blocked the left jab, dodged the right jab, blocked the left. The slow right feint followed as sure as day followed night, and then another feint and then, when the big left overarm came loop-ing in, he got right down beneath it and smashed the hardest right he had ever managed into Maguire's injured side, on the exact spot that he had hit so many times before.

His fist dug itself like a spade deep into the Irishman's flesh. He thought he heard a horrible liquid squelch. But the faint noise was drowned out by Maguire's echoing shriek of agony. The Irishman stumbled back, eyes screwed shut, stunned by the extraordinary pain of his crushed organs, and Holcroft quickly stepped in and smashed a straight left into the big man's nose. Followed by a sec-ond blow to the same spot. Then a crunching right to the big man's mouth. And another left. Another huge bruising right. Five mas-sive blows to the face in a matter of a few heartbeats. The big man crumpled to his knees, his face a mass of cuts and blood, but he was still clutching double-handed at his left side below his ribs, as if that pressure would heal the massive damage within. Holcroft took his time. The final right was a downward blow, with all his weight behind it, that smashed into the side of Maguire's chin, dislocating the jaw and knocking the king of the Savoy to the cobbles.

Holcroft stood panting, above the unconscious body of the man he had bested, and let all the sour energy of combat drain from his body. His knees felt like they might buckle at any moment, his forearms screamed as if they had been beaten with solid iron bars, his ribs ached, he was close to vomiting, his swollen face and poor crushed and pummelled head felt twice their normal size.

The ragged Savoyards in the circle around him were staring at him in disbelief. Some were drifting away. Some were hurrying away. The crowd of hundreds was melting before his eyes. He could sense no animosity nor danger from them. None at all. They were just people, London citizens now.

'Right!' he slurred. 'Let's go. Sergeant Miller! Where are you?' His battered, swollen eyes were closing fast; he knew that the darkness was coming for him.

He thought he could hear the sound of marching. Boots crashing on the cobbles. The cries of an Army sergeant. He peered to his left through fat and slitted eyes and saw a wall of red-coated men, advancing in an impeccable column down the street towards him. Pine torches ablaze, orange light glittering on shined buckles. Muskets at port. Yellow facings and belts. Shiny black shoes. And was that young Lieutenant Rupert Pittman marching out in front of his forty men – looking nervous as a colt yet trying to be as stern as God Almighty at the same time? It was.

He heard a roar behind him and, with the last of his strength, he whirled. And there was Patrick Maguire, rocking gently but on his own two feet once more. His face a bloody mess. His jaw was hanging loose at a strange angle and blood dripped in fat droplets from his smashed lips. Jacob Creech stood beside him, supporting his weight. Maguire reached down and snatched the cutlass from his lieutenant's unresisting hand, a long, curved blade. Rusty but serviceable. The big man snarled like a beast, hefted the cutlass above his head, took one hesitant step forward and began his lumbering charge . . .

Crack! There was a deafening discharge close to Holcroft's right ear. His Ordnance brain said: flintlock, three-quarter ounce ball, standard fusilier issue. He fancied he even saw the heavy lead ball strike, a large black hole suddenly appearing in the centre of Maguire's broad hairy chest, which an instant later filled with blood. The big man was jerked off his feet, punched up and back by the power of the musket ball in the midst of his mad, blood-flecked charge. His body thudded down. The cutlass clattered to the cobbles. The big man kicked out once, twice. He let out a long, angry, bubbling hiss. And was still.

He turned and saw Sergeant Miller with the long flintlock still at his shoulder, a trickle of black smoke emerging from the muzzle.

'Fine shot, John,' mumbled Holcroft.

'I was trying to put it between the bastard's eyes,' growled Miller.

Holcroft tried to smile. He was about to speak when his legs collapsed under him. He was aware of his body tumbling. Then the blackness rushed in.

Chapter Thirty-nine

11 December 1688: River Thames

The moonlight on the black water really is quite beautiful, James thought. And after the upsets and heartache of the past few weeks, the gentle lapping of the river waves against the side of the skiff was a sweet and soothing music for his soul. Ahead of him he could make out the stern of the ship that would take him to France, and into exile.

It was not the end, he told himself, it was a small setback. He would not give his enemies the satisfaction of holding his body in their prisons; he would not risk the fate that had befallen his father Charles or the traitor Monmouth. He would escape their heretical snares and be free to gather his strength – and his cousin Louis of France, that good and kindly monarch, would surely succour him.

Louis would give him men, and arms, and money, Ambassador Barillon had promised this to him many times – and many times he had refused French help, on the advice of his Protestant advisers. What a fool he had been! But no more. Once in France he would accept the Sun King's generous aid and plan his triumphant return to these shores, at the head of a powerful and loyal army. There would be a mighty reckoning. He would show all these Protestant jackals that he was God's anointed on Earth – that he was the true King of the Three Kingdoms. All their duplicity and weasel-words and their many foul and painful betrayals would be punished, when he returned in glory . . .

It was the personal betrayals that hurt him the most. He did not care that Parliament would not do his bidding, that ridiculous parcel of wheedling merchants and fox-hunting squires; nor was he concerned that the stubborn bishops of the Church of England had defied him – they were double-damned heretics to a man; it did not trouble him that the town corporations had made his life difficult, nor that the Justices of the Peace in the shires had resisted his calls for toleration for those of the true, Catholic faith. They were not his friends, he'd never trusted them, or rewarded them, or raised them up – he had never let *them* into his heart.

It was the perfidy of the English soldiers that bruised his soul. The officers, the friends and comrades from his younger military days, the men who had sworn a personal oath of loyalty and who, when the time came to fight for their King, had gone over to the other side, almost without a shot being fired. False friends they had turned out to be. Traitors. A revolution, he had heard they were calling it, a 'glorious' revolution. And yet how could such ingratitude and disloyalty, such base behaviour, be described as glorious? It was not even the officer corps that he blamed. If he peered into his secret heart, at the place of deepest hurt, there was one figure who loomed there: Lieutenant-General John, Lord Churchill.

Jack's betrayal was like a burning knife in his soul. His departure at Salisbury with his coterie of friends and with four hundred other discontented officers and men had wrecked any chance he had of fending off William's invading army. Jack's betrayal had hurt him more than the defection of his daughter Anne, a devout Protestant, who no doubt had been led astray by Churchill's bitch of a wife.

He recalled with bitterness the note that Churchill had left for him on that rainy night in Salisbury, when his dear old friend, his most trusted confidante at court, had abandoned him to join the ranks of his enemies.

'I am actuated by a higher principle,' Jack had written piously when he admitted at last that he was deserting his King, to whom he owed so much, indeed to whom he owed everything he possessed. Churchill went on to claim that his actions came from 'the inviolable dictates of my conscience and a necessary concern for my religion, which no good man can oppose . . .' What humbug! The double-dyed traitor had the effrontery to sign off that infamous letter with the words: 'Your Majesty's most dutiful and obliged subject and servant, Churchill.'

Dutiful be damned. There would be a great reckoning one day. Jack Churchill would pay for his crimes. And God would punish Churchill, even if James could not. God would damn Churchill to Hell. God would damn them all to Hell.

James fumbled at his feet in the bottom of the skiff and picked put a heavy cloth-wrapped bundle. The tall French frigate was only thirty yards away. A new chapter beckoned. Louis would set things right. His royal cousin of France would support him. And he would be back to claim his vengeance. But, for now, it was over. He hefted the cloth bundle in his right hand, feeling its weight, feeling its moment. Inside the folds lay the Great Seal of England, a circular metal mould that had been used since time immemorial to affix wax seals to all great documents of state. The Great Seal symbolised the approval of the Sovereign. Without the seal, no law could be passed, even if every man jack in both Houses of Parliament demanded it. The Great Seal was the symbol of law, of rightful authority under God Almighty.

It was the symbol of true kingship.

James held his right hand over the side of the skiff. He hesitated for a brief moment – and let the heavy cloth bundle fall from his fingers. The Great Seal hardly made a splash as it sank beneath the black surface of the Thames.

'God damn them *all* to Hell,' he whispered.

Chapter Forty

3 January 1689: Tower of London

When Holcroft awoke, for a long, uncomfortable moment he had no idea where he was. He was lying in a narrow cot with two thin blankets over him and he was cold. His breath plumed in the frozen air. Above him were smoke-blackened ancient oak beams. If he turned his head he could see a pool of weak sunlight on the stone-flagged floor in the centre of the room, and a simple wooden table and chair – both old and much battered – and a large empty fireplace with a basket of split logs and kindling beside it.

Holcroft recalled with a sinking sensation where he was. He was in the Tower of London, in the White Tower, in the cell that, long ago, had once housed his father, Colonel Thomas Blood. He had been in there for more than three weeks. Josiah Widdicombe, he suspected, had allocated that particular cell to him deliberately. As a joke, perhaps, or maybe as a taunt.

His face and body still hurt, even though it was now twenty-four days since the brutal bare-knuckle fight with Patrick Maguire, as did his hands and forearms. He pulled them from under the blankets and looked at them. The swelling had gone down, at last, but the skin was still dappled yellow, brown and green from elbow to wrist. The memories of the night of the fight, fragmented and jumbled, crowded his early morning mind. Lieutenant Pittman had taken command of the company and they had carried him, and the injured fusilier, on makeshift stretchers across London to the Tower, arriving a little before dawn. He remembered Pittman making his report to Major Glanville in the Inner Ward and the acting Constable of the Tower smiling cruelly while he pretended outrage at Holcroft's disobedience, then ordering the captain's incarceration in the White Tower until a suitable panel of senior officers could be convened for his court martial, which would most likely be held in January.

He had been vaguely aware of Christmas Day – Widdicombe, unbidden and unrewarded, had brought him a goose leg, a slice of plum pudding and a glass of brandy from the officers' mess and wished him the compliments of the season. But he could find little joy in his heart at the anniversary of Christ's birth: in less than a month he would most probably be dead. The court martial could not very well exonerate him. Perhaps, if he had caught Narrey, if he had returned to the Tower with a live French spy in chains, he might have been reprimanded or fined and his conduct on Salisbury Plain, and his escapade in the Savoy, might have been overlooked. But the fusilier who had been shot in the stomach in Palmer's classroom had died. He died because Holcroft disobeyed orders and deliberately took that man into danger.

He wished he had another blanket or a quilt or a heavy cloak to put over the bed. But wishing was useless. If he wanted to be warm, he would have to light the fire. Then he would summon Widdicombe by banging on the door and shouting, and send the little gaoler out for some hot food. In a few moments, he would do that, when he could find the strength to get out of the bed.

A strong memory came to him of visiting his father in this very cell – was it seventeen years ago? His father had believed that he was to be executed, just as Holcroft now did, and he had displayed a magnificent indifference to his fate. Holcroft hoped, when the time came, that he might emulate his insouciance. *What was it Father used to say? 'Keep the faith, son, and we'll come up smiling yet.'*

It seemed most unlikely that Holcroft would come up smiling from this ugly situation. He remembered the boy-thief Matthews, who had also occupied this same cell, and who had died here, poisoned by Narrey – or Henri d'Erloncourt as Holcroft supposed he must now think of him. No, he would always be Narrey in his mind – Henri d'Erloncourt would for ever be the foxy little fop he had known as a child. Narrey was the cold-blooded spy and poisoner who had escaped scot free and was now presumably back in France, safe and sound.

Holcroft did not want to think about his failure. But he could not help himself: Matthews had been the beginning of this sad road. If he had not been asked to investigate that debt-ridden Savoyard clerk, he would never have incurred the murderous wrath of Narrey; he would not have been attacked, twice by Maguire's men, nor felt the need to seek out his enemy in the Liberty of the Savoy. There was a symmetry to it that he found oddly comforting. It showed the underlying order in an apparently chaotic world. It had all begun when he came into this cell to interview Matthews, and it would end for Holcroft when they came to take him away to face his court martial and, shortly afterwards, his firing squad. All men must die. But somehow it seemed better for a man's life and his death to be part of a pattern, better anyway than to die randomly. There was a chance that his life and death might have some meaning – even if he could not understand what that meaning might be.

Aphra Behn had come to see him on the fourth day of his incarceration, when such was the state of his face that he had been almost unrecognisable to her. After some awkward pleasantries, he had had to admit that he had been lured into the Liberty by a false letter purporting to come from her – when, in fact, as was now plain, it had been written by Narrey in their private code. His intelligence about their relationship was apparently excellent.

'He is a first-class operator,' she had said, after he'd recited the contents of the false letter to her from memory. 'And we were far too lax in our security. We should have invented a proper cypher or not used one at all. But he is good, we must grant him that. Apart from the bit about you liking my plays, it was nearly faultless. A wholly credible blend of truth and fiction: you might like to know, Holly, that Benedict has indeed taken up the reins of Jupon's work, and has sworn he will avenge his master. Narrey was particularly clever to include that part.'

Holcroft thought he detected a glint of moisture in Aphra's eye.

'Are you weeping?' he said. 'Are you weeping for me?'

'No, of course not, you ninny-hammer. It's just so damnably cold and draughty in here. Besides, you have not been tried yet. I'm sure the court martial will see sense and let you off with a slap on the wrist or perhaps a small fine.'

'No, Aphra. Not this time. It will be a guilty verdict – and the firing squad.'

She poked at the corner of her eye with a grubby white kerchief then said: 'You may be comforted to know that, as of mid December, I have had confirmation from Benedict that Narrey is back at Versailles; he was seen meeting the Sun King. You and Elizabeth are safe from him, I believe. If we let sleeping dogs lie.'

Holcroft frowned at her. 'Sleeping dogs? Hmm, you're comparing Narrey to a fierce dog that is asleep, and suggesting that, if we leave him alone, do not take any action against him, he will leave Elizabeth and I unmolested. Is that it?'

'Well done, Holly! I'll make a poet of you yet. Furthermore, with King James gone, and William and Mary set to ascend the throne, I cannot imagine that Narrey or any other French agents will be welcome in England anytime soon.'

'So Dutch William will take the throne. Has it really been offered to him?'

'Not as such, the Lords are conferring. But he will be offered it, I'm told, and he will accept and will rule as joint monarch with Mary. There is some nonsense about a Bill of Rights that must be agreed first, a sort of Magna Carta for the modern age, that guarantees that Parliament is the supreme power in the land and no Catholic can ever sit on the throne of England again, blah, blah, blah.'

Lying in his freezing bed three weeks later, Holcroft still could not quite believe that the Protestant Dutchman and his English wife were to rule the land in James's stead. It had been so sudden. It was not as if the King were even dead.

That thought made him feel uneasy. If a monarch, appointed by God, could be removed by the actions of mortal men and replaced by another, where did that leave the sacred institution of kingship? Was a king in truth no better than the captain of a company, who might be transferred to another company of soldiers, or summarily dismissed, or court-martialled and executed? Thinking about it made his head hurt.

Half an hour later, the cold drove him out of the narrow cot, and with one of the blankets wrapped around his shoulders like a cloak he thumped on the door to summon Widdicombe. When he had given the old dwarf a few pennies and instructions to bring a quart of ale and a fresh game pie from the Red Lion, he dressed himself and bent down by the fireplace to get the blaze going.

While he waited for his food, he sat at the table and reread the letter that Elizabeth had sent him four days ago. It was cheery and light and full of gossip from her parents' household. Her sister Alice had a suitor, a handsome fur merchant who traded with the Muscovy Company and was believe to be very rich. If only Alice could bring this paragon of English manhood to the altar! She made a passing reference to his present incarceration and impending court martial – choosing to believe that it was all a silly mistake and no doubt it would all be sorted out satisfactorily in due course. She sent him her love and asked when they might be able to move back into the house in Mincing Lane as the Gray's Inn Lane house, although jolly to be in over Christmastide with her family, was rather crowded.

Holcroft stared at the bars of the small high window and thought about his wife. She was deeply irritating in many ways, sometimes too demanding, sometimes a little stupid. Always too loud. But he felt a glow in his heart when he pictured her. And, despite every-thing, he missed her – even her voice.

He pulled out pen, paper, quill and ink pot and began to write. He greeted her warmly, apologised for not writing sooner and invited her to return to the house in Mincing Lane as soon as she wished to. He gave her permission to hire another cook, an extra maid and a footman, too, to keep her company. He gave her the details of the London goldsmiths who held his money and promised to instruct them to release all his funds to her in the event of any unforeseen circumstances.

He informed Elizabeth that the danger from the Maguire family was past – but he refrained from mentioning that all the members of that criminal clan were dead at his hand – and he apologised for subjecting her to the slightest peril. He promised that it would never happen again, if he could prevent it, and urged her to move in immediately and make the house ready for his return, where they would be joyfully reunited once this small present difficulty had been overcome.

He hesitated, unsure how to sign off honestly. Then he looked into his heart and wrote: 'Your loving husband, Holcroft'.

He had barely taken a bite of his game pie, and drunk more than a sip of his quart of ale, when the door to the cell burst open.

There was little Widdicombe, and behind him loomed the figure of his enemy William Glanville and the mitred headgear of several fusiliers. The major, trying not to smirk, held a sheathed small-sword in his right hand. Holcroft could see that it was his own weapon, surrendered when he had been committed to the Tower.

'It is time,' said Major Glanville. 'The court is ready for you.'

Holcroft was escorted by four flintlock-bearing fusiliers, none of whom he knew well, down the stairs and out of into the Inner Ward. He was hustled over the cobbled courtyard to the office of the Master-General of the Ordnance and Constable of the Tower.

As Holcroft walked in the door he half-expected to see his friend and mentor Lord Dartmouth seated behind the familiar long desk, and then he remembered – Lord Dartmouth had been abruptly dismissed by the interregnum government, a group of peers of the realm, and General Frederick von Schomberg, the Prince of Orange's second-in-command, had been appointed to the office.

The new Master-General of the Ordnance was a square-faced elderly man with piercing blue eyes that shone from under the cascading curls of a magnificent chestnut periwig. He looked at Holcroft, a neutral expression on his florid, pouchy face, and said in a commanding voice: 'You are Captain Holcroft Blood, yes?'

Holcroft admitted he was. He saluted the half-German general briskly and snapped to attention two yards in front of the table, feet hard together, spine straight, shoulders back, his eyes fixed on a point a foot above the general's splendid wig.

He was aware that Major Glanville was drawing Holcroft's sword from its sheath and placing it on the front part of the long desk, parallel with the line of five senior officers who sat on the other side of the oak in judgment upon him. When these men had questioned him, and interviewed any witnesses that might be brought before them, when they had examined all the evidence, they would make their decision, and the position of the sword would be changed. If the verdict was innocent, the handle of the sword would be turned towards him, indicating that he was free to take back the weapon and resume his duties as a soldier. If the verdict was guilty, the point would be towards him, indicating that death was to be his fate.

'I shall be acting as Judge Advocate,' said General Schomberg, his English perfect, 'and my judgment and that of my colleagues comes with the full force of law. The verdict is final. Any sentence shall be carried out at dawn tomorrow.'

Holcroft said nothing. He looked discreetly at the four other judges, all of whom he knew. There was Sir Henry Sheres on Schomberg's right, summoned from his sick bed in Deptford for this tribunal. By the looks of his red-veined, half-closed eyes and blotched face he was already extremely drunk, although it was not yet ten of the clock. Beside him was Colonel Percy Kirke, who Holcroft had not seen since he had played cards with the man for pennies in that tent on Salisbury Plain. He remembered with an inward wince that his last words to Kirke had been to call him a disgrace to his family, his service and his country. On Schomberg's left sat another man that Holcroft had insulted in that same tent, another man who had deserted to William's side that night: Colonel Charles Godfrey. The last member of the panel had once been his closest friend, it was the man whose friendship he had rudely and angrily rejected at Salisbury – Lieutenant-General John, Lord Churchill.

Holcroft looked at Jack, whose expression was one of grim authority.

Major Glanville read the charges: 'Firstly, that Captain Holcroft Blood of His Majesty's Ordnance did abandon his post on the eve of combat on Salisbury Plain, leading his men and his guns away from the battlefield without any express orders from a superior officer and without the knowledge or desire of his own command-ing officer, the Comptroller of the Train, Sir Henry Sheres, here present—'

Sir Henry said loudly, 'Quite right! Damn right! Didn't consult me at all.'

There was a pause and Glanville continued '. . . in contravention of all the laws and customs of war; that the accused has in fact dis-played rank cowardice in the face of the enemy, a crime punishable by death.'

Glanville took a breath. 'Secondly,' he said, 'that Captain Blood disobeyed the lawful orders of his superior officer, the acting Master-General of the Ordnance, namely myself, given to him on the night of the ninth of December in the year past. He did wil-fully and deliberately lead the men of the eighth company Royal

Fusiliers under his command into grave danger in the Liberty of the Savoy, and that in pursuit of a private venture, he did cause the wounding and subsequent death of Private Jennings. For this grave crime, too, the punishment must be death.'

Glanville carried on for another monotonous five minutes, reading out several lesser charges, all of which according to him merited death. When he had finished speaking there was a long silence. Holcroft looked along the line of stern military faces. Jack, he thought, appeared sad and resigned. But he received a shock when he caught Colonel Percy Kirke's eye. The man appeared to wink at him. Holcroft frowned. He looked at Kirke again and there it was, a definite wink.

'D'you have anything to say to the first of these grave charges, Captain Blood?' said General Schomberg. 'Do you admit your guilt?'

Holcroft drew a breath. It crossed his mind to say that the Salisbury charge was utterly preposterous, three of the men sitting at this table had turned their coats at the same time that he had led the Train back to London. The hypocrisy of it sickened him to his stomach. He could see no point in arguing with them and shaming his judges.

'I did what I thought was right in the circumstances, sir,' he said.

'That is all you wish to say?' Schomberg seemed taken aback. 'You offer no defence for your actions?'

'No, sir. Only that I took what I believed to be the only honourable course.'

'Very well, then. Now concerning the second charge, disobeying orders, taking your men into the Savoy, how do you plead? Do you admit your guilt here as well?'

Holcroft could see that Major Glanville was grinning like a baboon. Perhaps he ought to make more of an effort to defend himself.

'I believed that there was a French spy, codenamed Narrey, hiding in the Liberty of the Savoy, at a Catholic-run school there.

I took my men into the Liberty, hoping to arrest the spy. It turned out that I had been tricked. I deeply regret the death of Private Jennings and I admit I made a grave mistake. If I could change the way things turned out, I would. But all I can do is say again that I did what I thought was right.'

'Very well, I believe we have heard enough. I do not think it necessary to bother with the rest of the charges. Gentlemen? Are we all agreed?'

Schomberg looked left and right at the other members of the panel. It occurred to Holcroft that these hidebound military men had already decided the outcome of this court martial long before he was marched in front of it. He was glad he had not begged and pleaded for their mercy. He would try to emulate his father's courage at dawn the next day. God give him the strength to die well. Sir Henry Shere's eyes were closed and he was snoring. Percy Kirke elbowed him in the ribs. Sir Henry came to abruptly. He sat up and said loudly, 'Guilty! Guilty as charged.'

General Schomberg leant over to him and whispered at length in his ear. He turned to his left and conferred briefly with Colonel Godfrey and Jack Churchill. Jack did something strange. He passed over a buff-coloured folder, stuffed with papers, which Schomberg took and dropped on the table in front of him.

'Right, I think we are all agreed, are we not gentlemen?' He looked right and left again and was met with nods from all sides.

Schomberg reached forward and touched the naked blade of the sword. He swivelled the blade around until the point was aimed at his own heart – and the worn hilt was pointed towards Captain Holcroft Blood.

'This court fully exonerates Captain Blood from all the charges presented today and rules that he is cleared of all wrongdoing in these matters.'

'What!' Major Glanville shouted the word. 'This must be a mistake. This is outrageous, sir. I appeal to you. This has been a gross miscarriage of justice.'

General Schomberg fixed the major with his piercing blue eyes. 'Outrageous, you say. A gross miscarriage of justice? Are you mad, sir?'

There was a sudden quiet in the room. Schomberg said: 'Captain Blood's behaviour on Salisbury Plain is not something that any man at this table has a right to criticise, and certainly not condemn him for. Even me, as I was on the opposing side of that field. He behaved, as far as I can see, perfectly honourably. Refusing to fight his guns because he wished there to be no unnecessary bloodshed, and yet also refusing to allow them to be captured by the enemy. There is no case to answer there. And when he took his men into the Liberty of the Savoy I believe that he was acting with the best intentions and intending to capture an agent of a foreign power. A spy. It is unfortunate that Private Jennings was killed, most regrettable, but he was a soldier on active service. Captain Blood, as far as I and my colleagues are concerned, behaved well, in very difficult circumstances.'

Major Glanville stared at him, his mouth working silently.

'I will admit that I discussed this case with my fellow judges yesterday and earlier this morning, and we all agreed that since a court martial had been convened we must then sit in judgment. We also agreed that the charges were ridiculous and that Captain Blood must be exonerated. Furthermore, we decided that since it is a difficult business to gather together five busy senior officers such as we, we should also endeavour not to waste public money and our own valuable time by dealing only with *this* trivial matter today. We decided that, since *you* are here, Major Glanville, and so is Captain Blood, we should take this opportunity to deal with a more vexing matter. I refer, of course, to the report written by Captain Blood last summer and delivered to my predecessor Lord Dartmouth. The title of the report is . . .' Schomberg looked down at the tabletop in front of him, at the paper-stuffed buff folder sitting there. '. . . *The Review of Various Corrupt and Immoral Practices in His Majesty's Ordnance.*'

William Glanville's smirk was gone; his skin was a dull grey and a bead of sweat had swelled at his forehead at the rim of his wig.

'How . . . how did you get hold of that review?' he stammered.

'Lord Churchill was kind enough to share his copy with the rest of us. Am I right in thinking Lord Dartmouth allowed you to make a copy of it from his original?' said Schomberg to Jack. 'The original that seems rather oddly to have gone missing.'

'Something like that,' said Jack.

'Well,' said Schomberg, 'I should like to say that this court is grateful to Lord Churchill for bringing this matter to our attention.'

There was a chorus of mumbled assent from the table.

'I have read this review,' Schomberg said, 'which has been ably compiled by Captain Blood and I must confess that it makes for shocking reading. As you must be aware, Major Glanville, you appear frequently in these pages and in a poor light. There are detailed examples of you and your friends keeping false musters, indulging in gross peculation, large-scale pilfering, falsifying accounts, fraud . . .'

'Lies, sir, they are all black lies invented by Blood solely to discredit me.'

Holcroft took a menacing step towards Glanville. 'I wrote that report, sir. I signed it and I attested on my honour that everything within its covers was the truth. If you say to me that it is all lies, then you are calling me a liar. Is that the case?'

'Yes it is. You are a liar, sir. A dishonest, gutter-born fabricator . . .'

'Very well,' said Holcroft, smiling for the first time that morning, and showing rather too many of his teeth. 'Then I shall demand satisfaction from you, Major Glanville, for those ugly words. Or an immediate grovelling apology, right now, and your admission that you are a thief, a cheat and a fraudster – that you are a dishonest and cowardly swine who is not fit to wear that uniform.'

Glanville goggled at him. But he said nothing.

'Excellent, yes, a duel to settle this,' said Schomberg, clapping his meaty hands. 'I despise corrupt quartermasters: the curse of every army in the world. And bringing you, Glanville, in front of a court martial would cause a rare stink. Scandal, disgrace, embarrassment, all that. I shall act as your second, Major, unless you would prefer another gentleman. Or unless you wish to admit your guilt and apologise to Captain Blood. No? I thought not. Right then. Tomorrow at dawn. Goodman's Fields. That's where the Ordnance gentlemen usually meet for these sort of things, is it not?'

'I will act as Captain Blood's second,' said Jack. 'That is, if he will have me.'

'I would be most honoured, my lord,' said Holcroft, and bowed stiffly.

Epilogue

4 January 1689: Goodman's Fields

Captain Holcroft Blood met Major William Glanville in the morning of the following day at a little after six of the clock. The encounter took place in an area of grassland outside the City dotted with grazing cattle, about half a mile northeast of the Tower of London.

The two combatants were accompanied by their seconds and the eminent London physician Arnold Whicker in his fine black carriage. Both combatants stripped off to their shirt-sleeves. They drew swords and faced each other in the freezing mist, their feet crunching the frosty grass. The seconds conferred, Major Glanville was asked a final time whether he wished to apologise to Captain Blood for his remarks.

He declined.

The two men faced off. Saluted. And began. Glanville rushed at Blood with a lightning-fast slashing attack, which had Holcroft on the defensive. His hands, still not fully recovered from the fight with Maguire, were clumsy on the sword hilt. Glanville lunged and lunged again, and Holcroft parried for his life. Glanville slashed for his eyes, but his opponent moved back in time.

Holcroft survived the onslaught. The fought, they fenced, probing each other for weakness. Glanville favouring attack after attack. Holcroft defended himself deftly. Until such time as he thought he had detected a pattern to the major's wild assaults. After a few more minutes of sparking steel and pluming breath, Holcroft was sure of it. When Glanville attacked again in the same wild, frenzied manner as before, Holcroft chose his moment, flicked his opponent's reaching sword point away, and neatly ran the corpulent Ordnance officer through the body with his small-sword.

Holcroft's blade went in above the major's navel and burst clean out the other side. He pulled the long blade clear and stepped back.

Major Glanville said only: 'Oh!' and looked down at the blood blooming red on his white linen shirt. He stared at Holcroft over his drooping sword, tried to speak, and collapsed on the white-rimmed grass. Fifteen minutes later, Arnold Whicker rose from kneeling by Glanville's side and pronounced the major dead.

As Jack and Holcroft were walking back towards the Tower, leaving a beaming General Frederick von Schomberg and the little doctor Whicker to load the limp body into the carriage, Holcroft said: 'Jack, I'd very much like to thank you.'

'For what?'

'For standing with me today as my second. For the court martial yesterday. For bringing the false muster review to General Schomberg's attention . . .'

'Say no more about it, Hol. It was the greatest of pleasures.'

'How *did* you get hold of the report? I thought it had been destroyed.'

'I stole it!' Jack could barely conceal his glee. 'After you mentioned it to me, I went to see Lord Dartmouth and asked him for a copy. He denied its existence, which was when I knew it must be very damaging. Dartmouth and I spoke of other things, and I happened to spot it on his desk under a pile of letters: *A Review of Various Corrupt and Immoral Practices in His Majesty's Ordnance* by Holcroft Blood. I waited till he was distracted by an Ordnance officer coming in, and slipped it among my own papers. I had my clerks make a faithful copy the same day, working them furiously, then I got your Sergeant Miller to replace it on the Master-General's desk the same evening. I don't think Dartmouth ever knew it was gone.'

'That was brisk work, Jack. I thank you for it again. You saved me.'

'I take it you forgive me, then? For all that business on Salisbury Plain . . .'

Holcroft walked in silence for a few more crunching steps. He could not find the right words for his friend.

Jack found the pressure intolerable. He said very quickly, indeed he almost blurted: 'I know you think that I betrayed the King to whom I owed everything, for my own personal gain. I know you think that of me, Holcroft. And it is true that I have not suffered from that most difficult of decisions – perhaps the most difficult I have ever had to make. But I will tell you, I *must* tell you, and I earnestly hope you will believe me: I did *not* do it solely for myself. I did it because I believed I was serving God, and my fellow countrymen best, by leaving James's side. I believe that I averted a long, bloody and cruel war by my actions. You may hate me for it, despise me, but I only did what I thought was right in the circumstances.'

Holcroft lifted his head. 'I think that is the only thing any of us can ever do,' he said. And, at last, he smiled at his old friend.

Historical note

My Holcroft Blood is a semi-fictional character. There was a man of that name and background and he did some of the things I have him do in this series of novels, but I've also taken a good many liberties with the historical man's life, career and personality. I have no evidence, for example, that Holcroft was, as we would describe it today, somewhere on the autism spectrum – although he was, apparently, rather withdrawn and mathematically inclined, indeed quite brilliant at all things numerical. However, whenever possible, I have adhered to the historical truth as we know it.

The real Holcroft Blood was the third son of the notorious out-law Colonel Thomas Blood and we know that he went to sea shortly after his father's attempt to steal the Crown Jewels from the Tower of London in 1671 (as told in my novel *Blood's Game*). The historical Holcroft served in the Royal Navy during the Third Anglo-Dutch War (1672–4). He then studied gunnery and engineering as a Cadet in the Royal Guard of Louis XIV, probably under the false name Leture, but unfortunately I haven't been able to discover very much about what he did while in French service.

Colonel Blood was reputed to have spied for Charles II in the later part of his career, and his son Holcroft was mysteriously granted a sinecure by the Merry Monarch in 1676; he was appointed as Clerk of the Crown and Peace in County Clare, Ireland, for unknown services to his King. Holcroft was well paid for, but never took up, this post (the work was done by a local deputy) and he is listed as being 'so absent by the King's command'. This is all the evidence I have that Holcroft may have worked as an espionage agent in France. It is flimsy, admittedly, but it makes sense to me. By its nature, spy work is kept secret long after the fact, so there is no reason we should know what Holcroft was up to when abroad for more than a decade.

The real Holcroft Blood was back in London around the time that James II came to the thrones of the Three Kingdoms in 1685, and we know he was employed by Lord Dartmouth, Master-General of the Ordnance. He married Elizabeth Fowler, daughter of the barrister Richard King, and widow of Captain Fowler of the Royal Navy, in 1686 – although I have moved the wedding date to a year later in this novel for dramatic purposes. Their relationship was stormy, to say the least, and contained a good deal of physical violence and infidelity. She shouted at him several times in public calling him a 'rogue' and a 'dog'. But I must admit that the volume at which Elizabeth normally speaks is an invention of mine – and probably a gross slur on the lady's memory. For that, apologies. Also, I have no evidence that Holcroft was at Sedgemoor in July 1685, although as the Train from the Tower was a powerful one, and it was further strengthened by a 'bye-train' coming up from Portsmouth, to bring the royal artillery up to twenty-six guns, it does not seem unlikely that as a junior Ordnance officer, well trained in France, he might have taken part in the battle.

The Royal Train of Artillery was commanded by its Comptroller Colonel Henry Sheres (later Sir Henry) and the guns were, as I have described, positioned to cover the main road to Bridgwater behind the Bussex Rhine. Colonel Sheres missed most of the battle as he was sleeping in Middlezoy, a hamlet two miles behind the lines, although I've no reason to believe that he was the sad drunk I've made him out to be.

Monmouth's army, hoping to surprise the royal force, made a long, looping night march and attacked from the north but, as in the novel, Monmouth's regiments mistook the glowing matches of Dumbarton's as the centre of the King's line, rather than its right flank. The guns of the Train were indeed all pointed in the wrong direction when they attacked and had to be quickly moved in the middle of the night after all the draught horses had bolted and the civilian drivers had fled in panic.

One of the most interesting characters to take part in the battle was Peter Mews, Bishop of Winchester, who had served with distinction as a Royalist captain in the civil wars against Parliament. At the age of sixty-six, he took his fine carriage down to Somerset to see the battle of Sedgemoor and, in the nick of time, he offered his horses to help move the stranded guns of the Train. He, rather than Holcroft, was the true hero of that night's work. However, Bishop Mews was not, as I have him, one of the Seven Bishops who resisted the King's order to have his Declaration of Indulgence read out in every pulpit in the land. He would almost certainly have been among their number, as a staunch defender of the Established Church, but he was ill at the time when the Seven Bishops (and the Archbishop of Canterbury) were making their stand against the King's declaration. Having come across Bishop Mews when I was researching the fight at Sedgemoor, and rather admiring him, I wanted to involve the piratical old prelate even more in my story, and so I invented his part in later events.

Louis Duras, Earl of Feversham, did indeed sleep through much of the battle of Sedgemoor, and was teased for it long afterwards. However, it may not have been his fault. His skull was damaged by a falling timber in 1679, indeed nearly smashed in, but he was trepanned and eventually recovered. But this injury meant that he slept unnaturally deeply and could not be easily roused, even in an emergency. He did take command near dawn, ordering the cavalry attacks on the routed Monmouth regiments and overseeing the hunting down of the fleeing rebels. However, it was clearly Lord Churchill's victory. His swift and decisive actions when the enemy attacked out of the mist in the darkest hours saved the royal army and led to the failure of the rebellion.

The Duke of Monmouth's execution was indeed botched by Jack Ketch, who took between five and eight strokes of his short-handled axe to partially sever Monmouth's neck. The final strand was cut through by a knife. The London crowd, many of whom were supporters of the Protestant Duke, were incensed by his gross ineptitude and the hapless executioner had to be escorted away from Tower Hill to safety by soldiers, otherwise he would have been torn apart by the near-rioting mob.

My dastardly French spymaster Narrey, who witnesses the Monmouth execution, is an entirely fictional creation, as are Patrick Maguire and his three brothers, but the Liberty of the Savoy was a real place, under the jurisdiction for complicated historical reasons of the Duchy of Lancaster, and it was notorious even into the nineteenth century for its squalor and lawlessness. A colony of Jesuits was established in the Savoy at the beginning of James II's reign (1685) under one Father Palmer, who set up a free school for local children. Some four hundred pupils were educated there each year, half Protestant, half Catholic, and were taught Greek, Latin, poetry and rhetoric for no more than the cost of quills, ink and paper. The school, which was abruptly closed after the Glorious Revolution, also had a printing press.

The Warming-Pan Plot, which I have co-opted into this novel, was real, or rather it was believed to be real at the time. After the birth of James's son and heir (who later became known as the Old Pretender and was the focus of future Jacobite rebellions), a rumour spread throughout the Three Kingdoms that the child was not born to Mary of Modena but was introduced into the birthing chamber in a warming pan, a long-handled brass container normally filled with live coals used to heat up chilly or damp beds. It is untrue, of course, but many people, including Princess Anne, then second in line to the throne after her sister Mary of Orange, believed that the baby was, in the parlance of the day, 'supposititious', i.e. substituted with the intent to deceive.

It was the birth of a male heir, who would presumably be raised as a Catholic, that was the trigger for the Glorious Revolution. Until then (10 June 1688) many Britons would have been content to allow the deeply unpopular but sonless James to continue to rule, believing that the next monarch would be Protestant Mary. The birth of James Francis Edward Stuart changed all that: the Three Kingdoms were now facing the prospect of a Catholic dynasty and potentially a return to the bad old days of Bloody Mary, Protestant martyrs and the forced reintroduction of the Romish faith.

When I began researching *Blood's Revolution*, I was struck by how unjustly James II was treated by his subjects – particularly by Jack Churchill, whom he had favoured all his life, and who, indeed, owed him his whole career. Churchill's betrayal of his master deeply wounded James. But his desertion, along with the other plotters from the English army, undoubtedly prevented a good deal of unnecessary bloodshed. I genuinely think that Churchill was doing what he thought was best for the country – but he also happened to be doing what was best for the Churchills.

The change of regime was not entirely without violence – there were some small skirmishes and rioting across the country that claimed several lives, and certainly a great deal of blood was spilt later in Ireland (to be told in the next book in this series) – but it could have been a great deal worse. Without the defection of a large part of James's officer corps, a bloody war between William's troops and James's army might have raged across England and perhaps elsewhere for months, maybe even years.

James was, without a doubt, a difficult man to deal with, autocratic and tactless, who believed that as King it was his right to rule as he pleased. But the civil wars that destroyed his father, the first King Charles, had changed that model of governance for ever in Great Britain. The rule of autocratic kings who governed by their Divine Right could no longer be tolerated. For the British people, Parliament was now sovereign. And the laws of the land were made by this gathering of (wealthy and Protestant) representatives of the folk who were to be governed. We in the twenty-first-century West sometimes take this form of government for granted but, in the late seventeenth century, it was very far from the established norm.

Across the Channel, Louis XIV had taken his country on another path. In contrast to Charles I, the Sun King had *won* his civil wars (a prolonged series of conflicts known as the Fronde) and was moving away from what we might very loosely call 'democracy' and was determined to concentrate all power in his own hands. Louis was a dictator, appointed by a Catholic God to rule France as he saw fit, and most people in Great Britain did not wish to be governed in this way. Catholicism, for many British Protestants, meant rule by a brutal tyrant.

The irony is that James was not trying to become another Sun King, he did not seek absolute power, he was merely trying to introduce more tolerance in Anglican Britain for Catholics – and other dissenting groups such as Quakers and Baptists, etc.

Today we prize tolerance very highly. But it was an attempt to foster tolerance in the Three Kingdoms that brought about James's downfall in the Glorious Revolution.

Acknowledgements

I'm a writer of fiction, a storyteller, and not a professional historian. But I do lean heavily on those brilliant men and women who provide the background information, the real history, from which I draw the inspiration for my novels. David Chandler's fascinating book *Sedgemoor 1685: From Monmouth's Invasion to the Bloody Assizes* was my guide in writing the early part of this book, and I would recommend anyone interested in the Monmouth rebellion and its terrible aftermath to read it. Richard Holmes's biography *Marlborough* is also an excellent source on the part that Jack Churchill played in the momentous events of the day. John Childs's brilliant book *The Army, James II and the Glorious Revolution* was also of immense help, as was the erudite *James II* (part of the Yale English Monarchs series) by John Miller.

I would also like to thank Roger Emmerson of, among other organisations, the wonderful re-enactment group Colonel Holcroft Blood's Ordnance, http://www.holcroftbloods.co.uk, for allowing me to watch him firing his seventeenth-century cannon and for being so patient in answering my technical enquiries and for checking the battle scenes for accuracy; and also (Colonel) Barry Upton of the First Regiment of Foot Guards, a fine body of seventeenth-century re-enactors, who brought the Battle of Sedgemoor so colourfully and noisily to life for me in Bridgwater in July 2016.

Lastly, I'd like to thank my hardworking agent Ian Drury, of Sheil Land Associates, for his always-excellent advice and constant support for my literary efforts, and my talented editors Katherine Armstrong and Martin Fletcher and the rest of the team at Bonnier Zaffre for their enthusiastic help in bringing this book into the light of day.

Angus Donald
Tonbridge, 1 March 2018

Want to read
NEW BOOKS
before anyone else?

Like getting
FREE BOOKS?

Enjoy sharing your
OPINIONS?

Discover

READERS FIRST

Read. Love. Share.

Sign up today to win your first free book:
readersfirst.co.uk